THE ACCIDENTAL AGENT

THE ACCIDENTAL AGENT

By

Mack Mangham

ISBN 1-58721-271-4

1stBooks – rev. 03/03/00

ABOUT THE BOOK

An intelligent action-adventure novel, written with the tense plotting of John Grisham and the vibrant characters and dialog of William Goldmen, *The Accidental Agent* will seize you with its first sentence and thrust you unrelentingly through to its final unexpected climax. Like Agatha Christie's *The Witness for the Prosecution*, it ends, then ends again, then again – and once more. With each resolution, you relax slightly, only to find on the next page another climactic reversal. Like N. Night Shyamalan's *The Sixth Sense*, when you reach the end, you will sit stunned, asking yourself, "How did he do that?" "How could I not see that coming?"

Mangham mixes characters from Tennessee Williams and Truman Capote with those of Toni Morrison and Charles Frazier. He blends action and tight plot lines like John La Carre's and Tom Clancy's with those of David Guterson and E. L. Doctorow. His style is uniquely his own, however, as when he describes the sailor's myth of the "sun setting twice" in tender and wistful poetic phrases evoking a haunting beauty bordering on the ethereal.

A tale of intrigue, suspense, murder and mystery, *The Accidental Agent* is alive with characters that make you laugh, cry; depressed and exalted. Some you will detest, and some you will retain forever as symbols of hope and courage. From Blackie, the retarded deckhand to Beth the seductress; From Stewart the sociopathic hit-man to Ann Madison the millionairess set on revenge; From Agular the international drug baron to Andropolus the Greek who walks away from a fortune to find peace of mind; from Cherokee the captain of greed to Brian and Susannah the couple who unwittingly and accidentally become the center of a revolving gyroscope of action and fear; These characters will sweep you along a winding path, deeper and deeper into a seemingly bottomless pit of unsolvable riddles.

Clear your calendar for the next three days before ever reading the first line.

ACKNOWLEDGMENTS

This novel has a few debts to pay.

First of all, it could not be possible without the help of Pat Warthan of Atlanta and Bobby LaBrant of St. Petersburg. Without the two of them, Ken Carter, then of Goddard Collage, and I would not have been able to get together to lay the foundation. Ken had a six-hour layover in Atlanta, and I was in Balsam NC. Neither of us had a car at our disposal, so Pat and Bobby got Ken and me together in Commerce, Georgia, for the two hours that started it all.

Next, this novel could not have been possible without the grant from Goddard Collage in Plainfield, Vermont. If Brian Withers had known about Goddard, he would have gone there.

The people at Mountain Projects Inc. in Waynesville, North Carolina, made it possible for this novel to get on computer at a time when I couldn't afford one of my own. Jacque Haney Sherrill, Patsy Dowling, Wanda Brooks, Brenda Stiles and Mary Phillips all generously offered their computers down in the dungeon, and administrator Bob Leatherwood gave permission for me to be there at all hours of the night typing. I never left the building unlocked, and none of the computers were ever left running. Thanks to Mary Lou Blackstock of Florida A&M University.

The encouragement of many creative people has much to do with the completion of this novel. Thanks is due to Harry Belefonte, Carol Channing, Harrison Ford and Anthony Hopkins. Also, years ago, there was tutorage from some greats I was lucky enough to know and work with; Philip Wylie, Louis Bromfield, Robb White, Ferrol Sams and Michael Shaara. Jeff Shaara, Mike's son, has also been extremely helpful.

Jean Detre at MCA certainly needs to be thanked. Carolyn Krupp at Julian Bach Literary Agency was also very helpful. Peter Israel at Putnam's was one of the kindest people I have ever worked with. Perry Knowlton from Scribner's and Curtis-Brown offered great encouragement for many years, and I hope he's not dismayed that I think of him as my own personal Maxwell Perkins, although I am certainly no Thomas Wolfe.

Creative encouragement is absolutely useless without technical assistance in the cyber age. Thanks is due to Gordon Pike from Haywood Community College and Tim Hyatt of Computerized Business Solutions, both of Waynesville NC. Appreciation also goes to Sue Levere of the Computer Center at Western Carolina University in Cullowhee NC. They make magic out of cyberspace. A special thanks is due to Rich Hovey of REA Consulting Engineers for both technical and creative support.

And remember---

If you're not very rich,
very intelligent
or very good-looking,
then you need to smile a lot
and be very kind.

Who said that?
I did. And it's copyrighted.

To Isabelle Blakey,

My cohort, mentor, companion

And Muse,

Who keeps the love and laughter

Going and going.

The world needs more Isabelles.

Today I'll pretend you're still alive.

Some days, that's the only way I can make it.

I wake up in the mornings and even before I open my eyes, I can feel the pain. The absence. The emptiness.

And then some self-preservation part of me kicks in, and says, "Let's pretend he's still alive today."

If I pretend hard enough ... sometimes ... I can fool myself ... and begin to feel that it's really so. Except then ... when reality comes back ... it's as if you had just died all over again.

I've always heard there's no loss like losing your own child. I didn't believe it. Not after losing Arthur. There couldn't be anything worse. I thought.

A lesson there. Don't ever think things are so bad they can't get worse. They can. They do.

When you died ... were killed ... I ...

There really is no pain like losing your son.

Your parents are supposed to go before you. And your husband.

But when your son is killed ... murdered ... there's an emptiness that aches ... I suppose ... for the rest of your life.

Even revenge doesn't take it away.

But planning the revenge does. Getting the revenge helps. But when the revenge is over ... the ache comes backs.

It's always there.

From the diary of Anne Madison
(Four months after Michael's death)

Multi-colored sails of Hobie-cats moved in a colorful ballet far out across the bay. Beyond them just the vaguest suggestion of the barrier island, six miles away, separated the bay from the Gulf of Mexico beyond. A cloud moved in slowly from the west, darkening the water. Brian gazed at the drifting colors through the water-spotted window of an old, unpainted dock-front restaurant. On the oilcloth table in front of him were a newspaper and a small note pad. The newspaper was opened to the "Help Wanted" section where some classifieds were circled. The note pad had a neat printed heading: "From the desk of Brian Withers, Department of Social Sciences, Gulf Coast Community College."

Brian turned his gaze from the Hobie-cats, sipped his coffee, and returned to the classifieds and the pad. Four phone numbers were written on the pad, three scratched through, the last one waiting to be called and then scratched through or circled, depending on the outcome of the call. More likely scratched through, thought Brian.

God picked on Brian from time to time, most often in the winter on grey overcast days. Seasonal affective disorder, or SAD, one of his buddies in the psychology department called it. But Brian knew it was just God, playing with his head, picking on him to keep from being bored.

He took his pad, stood up, and turned toward the pay phone in a secluded corner of the almost empty room. The small, disheveled waitress almost bumped into him as he turned.

"Would you like your coffee warmed up?" The grating voice expressed boredom.

"Yes. Please. And maybe a fresh cup and saucer? And some more ice water?"

She managed to look *really* annoyed, as if he was keeping her from some pressing social engagement -- which didn't require combed hair.

"I know I'm imposing." Brian apologized hurriedly. "I'll make it worth your while."

He moved toward the phone, *her* phone, he thought, but he would use it anyway.

He punched in the first three digits of the last number on his list, had a quick change of mind, held down the receiver for a moment, replaced the quarter and dialed home. A Susannah attack. He needed a shot of Susannah. An hour without Susannah is like a day without sunshine -- especially when you have an acute case of seasonal affective disorder -- S.A.D.

2

"Hello." Her voice WAS -- really WAS -- like sunshine. No! Simile was too weak here. Her voice WAS sunshine. Not "like," – "was." Sunshine and Florida orange juice.

"Hello," she said again, smiles curling up around the syllables.

His sun came out, and God left to pick on someone else for a while.

"Zannah -- it's me -- just checking in."

"You think I don't know that voice?" She smiled. God, what a smile, he thought. He could actually hear her smile.

"Hi," he said, soft and safe.

"Any good news? Any news at all?" Her voice and smile always lifted him, took away cares, and made his own smile come to life.

"I'm always either too late, too stationary, or too over-qualified."

"Those are pretty much my complaints, too. Is there anything you can learn from this?"

"Yeah. Come earlier. Quit the teaching job. And become slightly dumber?"

"No. I think I like the present options better. What's the game plan for the rest of the day? You home for supper before leaving for your night class?"

"Not really enough time. I'll grab a sandwich and be home around eleven. Provided Mrs. Simpson doesn't want to impress me with her own private research into the Mesopotamian culture."

"Tell Mrs. Simpson you have a jealous wife at home -- waiting to be loved. One who kills to keep her man. Or better yet, charge Mrs. Simpson for your time after class. There's your second job. She's loaded, and would love to pay for a handsome, young Western Civ. teacher to give her private lessons."

"I wish. She's also loaded with the most powerful -- and probably jealous -- husband in Panama City. Besides, I'm not into women in their fifties. I miss you."

"Poor baby."

3

"Why do people have to take second jobs anyway? I don't want to have to stay away from you twice as much."

"Because while it is one of the great lies of humanity that two can live as cheaply as one, even society admits that three definitely cannot live as cheaply as two. Remember? We're going to be three instead of two. And I have to quit my job at the bank."

"Oh, yeah. I keep forgetting why I'm out here being miserable-- away from you."

"Only because you love me -- us -- the two of me."

A late-night January sea-fog drifted along the waterfront, leaving moisture on everything it touched. Foghorns sounded lonesomely through the night, and the distant bell buoy clanged sadly. Waves washed in past the pilings which extended far out beyond the end of the pier, showing how much longer the pier had been before some wayward hurricane had taken away much of the decking. Only the first four or five of the ghostly pilings could be seen in the vague reflection of the blinking neon lights farther down the water's edge. Through openings in the fog, the signs flashed out the words, "BAR," "FO D," "BEER & WINE," "M TEL," but in the thick fog they only caused an undulating glow, sort of a visible presence, close, touchable.

An old man sat on the end of the pier, a fishing pole held out into the receding darkness. He was so motionless he could hardly be seen. From his mouth hung a cigarette that he never moved from his lips between inhalings. Every so often the cigarette glowed brighter for a few seconds as he drew through it. On the dock beside him were two carpenter's toolboxes, obviously intended to be used as tackle boxes.

Somewhere far out in the blackness, offshore, away from the coast and lights, a low hum, barely audible, grew slowly, haltingly, steadily but only barely closer. At first it was a hum, then -- a moan -- then the muted purr of a small outboard. As it grew from a hum to a purr, it also moved cautiously back and forth through the blackness, obviously looking for, seeking, trying to find -- something.

A place to land?   A piling to be avoided?   Some recognizable landmark?

Louder -- but not loud. Soft. Careful. Searching. Closer. To the right. Closer. To the left. The scrape of a small skiff against a piling.

The man moved to light another cigarette. He let the lighter burn for a long time after the cigarette was lit. Much longer than needed.

The motor stopped. The boat scraped against the pilings as it moved closer.

"Need any help?" asked the man on the pier.

That was what he was supposed to say.

"I wish your lighter was brighter," came the answer.

That was what he was supposed to say.

"Sorry. One size lighter. One size light."

CONTACT.

The small boat became dimly visible, now a few feet from the end of the pier, moving closer, more defined.   Five feet. Three feet. Two. One. THUD. The gunwale of the boat was a few inches below the edge of the pier. The lone man in the boat reached out and took the two toolboxes from the pier. Then he put two fish creels onto the pier, placing them close to the man who was fishing. In a matter of seconds, with a quick push away from the pier, the boat was gone. The sound of the soft, careful, paddling moved away in the dark, farther, farther, softer. The motor started, muffled by the fog, moved off into the dark, and slowly into silence.

The old fisherman flicked his cigarette into the fog. Psst. He stood, picked up the two creels, propped his pole over his shoulder, and started toward the shore.   He moved slowly through the blackness, feeling for the sides of the pier as he went.   The closer he came to the shore, the darker the pier became; unlit buildings along the shore jutted out and blocked off the distant neon lights that dimly reached the end of the pier. The sound of a distant jukebox began to thud in his ears, not

5

enough to hear the melody or words, just the thumping, beating of the accented bass. Twice the man faltered, stumbling in the dark. When he reached the shore, he felt his way carefully to the sandy path leading through the sandspurs and sea oats up to the shell-covered road where the old truck was parked.

The climb up the sandy hill made his breath come heavy. He reached the old truck in a blackness that impeded even motion. Placing the pole and the creels in the bed of the truck so gently that no sound was made, he quietly opened the door to the cab. Only one small squeak sounded from the bottom hinge. His pants sliding onto the seat made more noise than the closing door.

He reached down to feel for the key he had left in the ignition. It was not there. His mind raced rapidly. Had he put it in his pocket? Had it dropped on the floor?

Then he heard the breathing. Not heavy. Almost restrained. On the seat beside him. He reached quickly for the gun in his belt, but he never got to touch it. He felt the first stab of the long knife. It seemed to go into him forever, always moving, continuously, deeper and deeper, never reaching an end. He felt nothing more after that. The quick rush of movement faded in the dark, and the last thing he heard was the vague suggestion of a soft laugh.

Cherokee stood on the dock, shading his eyes against the sun, at the same time trying to hold his pea-coat closed against the raw January wind. He watched Blackie tying the *Miss Betty* to the dock. Then he turned and motioned for the dock boy to get some flat dollies out to the commercial fishing boat. On deck, the Swede opened the storage doors, getting ready to bring out the huge wire baskets of red snapper, grouper and scamp.

Most commercial fishing boats are comparable to the work trucks; looks and the body are not important as long as they get the job done. What is important is the engine, the pump, the steering, the toilet, the sleeping quarters. There is never enough time to take care of the looks of the hull as long as it floats and keeps the rest above water. Commercial boats are mostly streaked with the color of rust.

Right next to the galley is the bunkroom, compact and efficient, often the largest enclosed area on the ship. Six to eight bunks are there, often partitioned off into pairs with separating walls. Many commercial boats are equipped to stay out for as long as four weeks.

The best fishing is done on what the men call "the middle ground," a misnomer since it was thought to be about mid-way between the North Florida coast and the Cancun Peninsula of Mexico. Actually the middle ground is only about a hundred miles off shore.

Most of the commercial fishermen are often drifters and better educated than they appear or want known. Some are hiding -- from the law -- from families ---from society. Some are looking for adventure and romance -- the open sea -- the Errol Flynn Complex. They spend their days "on the hill" sitting in bars, reading, watching TV, taking care of the ship's pet (which is never allowed to go out to sea with them). An unseemly gentleness surrounds them, especially where their pets are concerned. When they are out on the water they work hard, read a lot, and for the most part eat extremely well.

Cherokee was an escapee from the state penitentiary in Canon City, Oklahoma, where he had been serving fifty years for murder. Also he had not one drop of Indian blood. He just happened to be dark skinned and looked vaguely Indian.

The Swede had been three years at Texas A&M, but the pressure of studies in law brought on what some call a "nervous breakdown." The Swede preferred to call it "an extended blue funk." He was fishing just to drop out a while. He told no one in the town or on the boat that he was at Texas A&M: he didn't know why; he just didn't want anyone to know. But Cherokee had already made it his business to find out about The Swede's past. Like Cherokee, there was nothing Swedish about him except his light blond hair and his Nordic looks.

Blackie was handsome. His good looks, his honest and trusting eyes, belied the fact that he was mentally retarded, and

7

his mental slowness belied the fact that he was from a family worth millions. Every October a chauffeur-driven Lincoln limousine brought Blackie to the docks of Carrabelle. His father found a captain he could trust and paid him to watch after Blackie. Then in May the Lincoln limousine returned to get Blackie, this time taking him up to Six Flags over Georgia where he worked for the summer. That was the way Blackie liked it. The only time he got into trouble was because of his good looks. And usually a woman was involved.

Travis, the owner of the fish house, leaned out of the upstairs window, inspecting the catch. Money is the driving force in Travis' life, and since fish equals money, the boat's catch is of supreme interest to him.

"How'd you do?" Travis called down to Cherokee.

"Great," yelled Cherokee. "Probably 6,000 pounds. The best ever." He sort of danced around, having trouble containing his own excitement. An almost childlike quality filled his movement and his eye in spite of his harsh, angular, and slightly wrinkled features.

"You were lucky with the weather," Travis called back. He was as excited as Cherokee, but his mental cash register was too busy calculating for him to show much pleasure.

As with most fish houses, the owner also owned most of the boats that fished out of his docks. For Travis, the *Miss Betty* was one of a fleet of four. Drifters passing through the small town would come by looking for a job fishing -- the life on the open sea, the romantic life. Travis would put them on one of his boats on a trial basis. The amount of money made depended on the catch. Sometimes a boat might stay out three weeks and the captain might make only three or four hundred dollars. Sometimes a spell of bad weather would drive them back after only three days on the water, and the crew would have spent their time in their bunks reading, earning nothing. Then -- every once in a while -- like now, a boat would strike it lucky, coming back with a bonanza, finding the mother lode they all sought. Then even the newest crew member might make as much as five hundred a week.

Weighing in the fish was always a matter of much interest to everybody concerned. Travis would be glad to try to lower the record of the catch a few hundred pounds when dividing up the shares. Cherokee and the crew would be equally willing to up the catch if they alone weighed it in. As Henry, the dock, man placed one wire basket of fish after another on the scales, Cherokee and Travis added up the weight together to insure accuracy -- and keep track of one another.

Unloading and cleaning the boat after docking took a little over three hours.

Cherokee had been close in his estimate. 6,372 pounds. It was *his* personal best. When he walked into Travis' office to sign the receipts and verification of the weights, lights were coming on along the waterfront as day faded. Travis offered him a drink when this particular ritual was performed, and Cherokee always accepted. Travis did keep a good quality of liquor in his bottom desk drawer.

"Wouldn't it be great if all the trips were like this one?" Cherokee still had trouble being calm, he was so excited about the size of the catch. He sat down across from Travis, still smiling.

"I could live with that." Travis was able to smile slightly now.

"What's this?" asked Cherokee, picking up a sheet of typed paper with a man's photograph attached to the top left corner. "Brian Clayton Withers. Who's he?"

"That's a resume some college teacher dropped off here the other day. He's looking for a second job and I had put an ad in the paper."

"What for? You don't need no more help here."

"Henry's leaving in a few days. Got a job over in Apalach. So -- we'll need a new dock man."

"This guy any good?" Cherokee held up the resume. "Will he work?"

"Oh, no. That's not even possible. The guy's hours at the college don't fit. Besides, how long do you think a college professor would stick with a job like dock man? Seemed like a nice enough fellow. Needs another job 'cause his wife's expecting their first baby in about six months. But this one is your classic text-book case of somebody being overqualified."

Cherokee chuckled. "That would be funny, wouldn't it? A college professor filling in for Henry?"

As he put the resume back on Travis' desk, his calculating mind had fully processed all the necessary information: Brian Clayton Withers, 1207 Ave. B, Carrabelle Florida (904) 555-5534, age 32, married; profession, teacher. Cherokee particularly focused in on, "Type of work seeking: Anything will be considered."

Beth stepped out of the shower, dripping water on the mats that tried unsuccessfully to protect the wall-to-wall bathroom carpet. She was not one to worry about whatever mess she made. There was always someone, somewhere who would clean up behind her, usually someone paid for with her father's money. She dried off hurriedly, went to the walk-in closet nude, pushing the "playback" button on her answering machine as she passed it. Her attention was divided between what to wear and the messages she listened to as she rummaged through her clothes.

"Hi, Beth. This is Anne. I was wondering if you could help me study for that algebra test tonight. I'll take you to dinner if you can. Your choice of restaurants. Talk to you later." "Tuesday; 1:13 PM."

"Beth. This is Joan down at Kinko's. We've finished typing your biology paper. You can pick it up anytime. We got it done ahead of time. Bye." "Tuesday; 1:56 PM."

"Hi." A sultry male voice. "I miss you. I haven't seen you in about seven hours now. "'Seven hours without you is like seven years. Seven hours with you is like seven minutes.' Corny lines from corny old movies.

"I'm sitting here in this office wondering why you can't make the simple, obviously correct decision to quit college like any normal American girl and come work for me where we can

10

be together all the time. You could be making the magnificent sum of $5.85 an hour, which surely is the dream of every American girl. And then I wouldn't be having to call to see if you could gave dinner at the country club tonight.

"I seem to remember you have a class tonight, right? One of those 6:30 to 9:15 jobs. What about 9:30 ish or -- whatever. You say." "Tuesday, 2:23 PM."

Click. Whirrr. Bzzzz. Rewind. Hummmm. Click.

Wow! Biiig decision here!!! Dinner and studying algebra with Anne. Or dinner at the country club with Steve. And no algebra. Gosh. That's a hard one. If I really work on this and weigh all the possibilities, I should be able to come up with a decision in about three seconds. I think I'll choose -- Oh, God, this is such a strain on my brain. Yes. I'll do the *right* thing. I'll go with Steve.

I'm sure that's what daddy would want me to do.

Beth was down to the shoes now. She had put on some flats, but after making that momentous decision about dinner, she quickly ditched the flats for heels. And in view of the voice Steve was using today, the highest heels she had.

Dressed, made-up, and ready, Beth hurried through the all-white apartment. White rugs, white furniture, white armoires, white mosaics on the white walls -- definitely an easy place for an albino to get lost. She stopped at the etagere close to the front door, opened it, looked inside for a pair of earrings that matched her dress. But since everything in the etagere was white and the shelves were white, finding the earrings was not quickly done. Digging through one of the jewelry boxes there, she settled for another pair, equally as white, equally attractive, but just a tad smaller than the pair she would had wanted.

She looked in the last mirror she would pass before leaving the apartment, never completely displeased with what she saw, but at the same time never completely satisfied. Tonight she was about an "eight" on *her* scale -- and easy "ten" on anyone else's. Steve would not be unhappy. But her father would. Steve's construction company was her father's biggest rival. Until Steve had come to town, her father had the largest

11

construction company in northwest Florida. Now Steve's company got most of the bids that her father lost. Oh, well!! Daddy didn't know and probably wouldn't find out. And Steve wasn't about to tell anybody, even if he did keep saying his wife didn't understand him, and he was laying the groundwork for a divorce. Beth had seen enough bad movies and TV mini-series to know how much that line was worth, -- which wasn't half-bad for a twenty-seven-year-old college junior.

She opened the door to leave, took two steps out, then remembered her textbooks. Hurrying back to the bedroom, strewn with clothes and towels that would be picked up tomorrow, she rummaged through the books and notebooks above the computer. *Analyzing Informal Fallacies*, the green grammar book, and the green spiral. Color-coded classes, no less. Not only was she intelligent, good-looking, wealthy, and hornier than average -- she was color-coded. It just doesn't get any better than this.

Down in the parking lot, she still had enough daylight to find the keys to the Corvette. Throwing the books on the seat beside her, she drove confidently from the lot to the road facing the Back Bay, then turned right and headed toward the lights of the Hathaway Bridge in the distance.

"I've got a handout for you tonight," Brian told the class, in his relaxed, smiling manner. "And when I pass them out to you, I want you to keep them face down. O.K.? Until I tell you to turn them over. Think you can do that? What about you, Edna? Is that hard for you to understand?"

He liked to tease the students who made the straight A's, as long as they didn't mind. It brought about some smiles, and kept some of the others from falling asleep. Also when a topic got really boring, he occasionally gave all the facts backward or in reverse order, or deliberately wrong just to jar the class enough to start them arguing with him. Just to make sure they would stay awake.

"We all have two biological parents, right?" He walked across the front of the room, handing out the papers to be passed back along the rows. "I know this isn't a biology class, but we're going to talk a little biology here for a few minutes, O.K.? How many parents do you have, Mrs. Simpson?"

Mrs. Simpson was flattered. A 'C' student, but flattered. Brian knew she would be -- and there was hardly a chance she wouldn't know the answer.

"Why, two," smiled Mrs. Simpson. "Just like everyone else."

"You're sure?" asked Brian, knitting his brows like a prosecuting attorney, cynicism in his voice.

"I'm really sure," she smiled back, this time with more confidence.

"And Cheryl? How many grandparents do you suppose Mrs. Simpson has?"

He chose Cheryl on purpose, since she seemed to be maybe thinking more about her date for the weekend than the matter of propagation. It wouldn't embarrass her, and he made it a point to call her by name before asking so she wouldn't have to admit that she wasn't quite with the rest of the class.

"Four, I suppose," smiled Cheryl.

"You suppose? Is there any possibility that she might have only three?"

"No." Cheryl began laughing. "I'm sure she has four."

"O.K., now. Are we all paying attention here? We're going to get into a little geometry. It's coming up. I know you thought this was a class in Western Civilization. But remember what I told you. All of the disciplines are interrelated. Don't forget these things, folks. There will be quizzes from time to time."

Giggles and nervous laughter came from the class. A few more people who had been on the verge of dozing had decided to come along with the rest of the gang.

"O.K. now. Bobby, take a guess at how many great-grandparents Mrs. Simpson had. I have faith in you. I believe you can do this."

"Eight," answered Bobby, jokingly counting on his fingers.

"Ah, ha," pointed Brian. "Eight! Is there anyone here who has reason to disagree with Bobby? Anyone think maybe Bobby is stupid? Or stayed out too late last night? -- No? -- Well --- I guess -- we can all see something emerging here, can't we?" He counted very pointedly on his fingers now. "Two parents. Four grandparents. Eight great-grandparents. We can see this is progressing geometrically rather than arithmetically. Eight -- sixteen -- thirty-two -- sixty-four -- a hundred-twenty-eight. Just think of that! Six generations back, and a hundred and twenty-eight predecessors. And how many years do you think might make up a generation? Uh -- Deborah?"

"Why'd you call on me?" laughed Deborah. "You know I can't do math."

"Aw, come on, Deborah. Let's just take your own family for example. How old were your parents when you were born?"

"Gosh, I don't know. Twenty-two. Twenty-three."

"All right. So Deborah is twenty-three years apart from the generation before her. Anybody else?"

"Twenty-five."

"Thirty-one."

"Twenty-one."

"Seventeen."

"Seventeen?" Brian looked surprised. "Your mother was a child bride."

"Not at the time," came an answer. The class laughed.

"You know," said Brian, smiling and looking around at the class, "at different times in history, generations were separated by even fewer years than they are now. During the time of *Romeo and Juliet* most people were married and had children even at fourteen and fifteen. At times, during the Dark Ages, the average life span was only in the forties. People were grandparents, even great-grandparents, in their forties. But you knew that, didn't you?" He looked around, a vague smile.

"Well, for the sake of simplicity let's just say that a generation is twenty-five years. It's really more like twenty on the average, but for you doubters, we'll say twenty-five. O.K.?

14

"Now -- if we go with twenty-five, that will give us four generations every century. Right?" Many nods. Some frowns from the ones who were still counting.

"Eight generations in two centuries. Sixteen in four centuries." More frowns. "Am I going too fast here?"

He went to the board and quickly drew diagrams, figures, and numbers to illustrate. "Remember now. We are progressing arithmetically here and not geometrically as we did with the grandparent thing. See? The grandparents doubled each generation, multiplying by two. This time we're *adding* four generations each century. See? Get it? If not, don't worry about it. It'll come to you at 3:00 in the morning, and you'll jump out of bed screaming, 'I got it. I got it.' Insight is great. It makes us all feel so smart."

"O.K." Back to the board. "Working this way, we have thirty-two generations in 800 years. Take my word for it. And 800 years ago would put us right around 1200 a.d. Right?" He worked it out on the board rapidly, and heads began to nod.

"O.K. Now I want to ask for some guessing. Remember I asked you not to turn over the handouts? But I know you! You're eager. You're craving education and starved for knowledge. Right? How many of you have already looked at the handouts? Come on. 'Fess up. You won't get expelled. I just want the guessing from those of you who don't know for sure. Come on. Who's looked?"

Six hands went up. All of them were 'A' students. He knew they would do it. They were always eager.

"Get out," he smiled, pointing toward the door, joking with them. "I lied." Then to the rest of the class, "Remind me never to get those people for character witnesses if I ever get arrested."

He went back to the board, pointing. "All right. I want some guessing here. No right or wrong answers. O.K.? Carla? How many grandparents do you think you had thirty-two generations ago? In 1200 a.d.? In round numbers. Just a quick guess. Now! Now!!" He moved toward her quickly, snapping his fingers, smiling, teasing.

"Uh, uh. Four thousand."

"Four thousand. Good guess, Carla. Any others? Higher? Lower?"

Twenty thousand."

"Ten thousand."

"Naw. What are you'al talking about? It's more like five or six hundred."

The class was now talking among themselves, some adding and multiplying on the back of the handouts.

Mallie got out his calculator. "Hey, he yelled. "It's over a million."

The class got quiet and turned to look at Mallie.

"It's over a million in generation twenty," he said. "I didn't get any farther. Over a million!"

Shocked, the class became quiet, looking at one another, some looking at Brian as if waiting for him to correct Mallie. Some were still doing more math of their own.

"Surprising, isn't it?" asked Brian. "In just a second, when you turn the hand-out over, you'll see a computer calculation taking you back thirty-two generations. To the year 1200 a.d. You'll see that -- at that level *you have* over four billion grandparents. Don't believe me? Turn it over now. Look at it. Think about it... and what the ramifications are."

He waited as his audience turned over the printout and saw the computer calculations. A rumble of whisperings and surprised voices moved through the room. Some talked with their neighbors; some showed clear signs of obstinate disbelief.

"There are a few points that need to be made here, however," said Brian. "The most important -- and the reason I wanted you to be exposed to this piece of genealogical geometry -- is --- is --- *that* -- are we paying attention here, people? --- Considering the huge amount of forefathers you had in the year 1200 a.d. --- there is not a single person you will be reading about in this Western Civilization class -- from Hammarabi and Ramses to Charlemagne, Caesar, and William the Conqueror --- that you probably are not related to!" Strong pause. Eyes moving quickly and teasingly from one side of the room to the other. A suggestion of a smile.

"This is not a 'boring,' or 'stupid,' history class we have here. This is the study of your forefathers, your family, your family tree. All of these people we study about -- and people make history and civilization -- are really probably related to you -- directly, indirectly, obliquely, or distantly." Again a quick survey of the room.

"The second point that we have to consider is --- and I'm going to let you decipher this one for yourself -- or discuss it with your biology prof -- is -- there were not four billion people on the earth in 1200 a.d.!" Pause. "How'd that happen? How'd they do that? Well, we're going to get on with the Hammarabi Code and the Babylonian Empire tonight. You're going to have to figure that paradox out for yourself -- on your own time -- or pay me overtime after class. Onward and upward to ziggurats and cuneiform -- and things *civil*, hence civilization"

Three hours later, Brian was still talking about the Tigris, Euphrates, Mesopotamia, and the Fertile Crescent. Some students started pointing to their watches.

He had already kept them twenty minutes past dismissal time. With apologies he let the class leave and was immediately surrounded with about one-fourth of the class -- the usual after-class coterie wanting to discuss some point or other that caught their interest.

Ten minutes later the group had thinned out, but Mrs. Simpson -- the ever-present Mrs. Simpson -- was still waiting heavily to expound on something, when an attractive blond appeared at the door. She looked carefully over the group, spied the person she was seeking and moved into the room.

Just then Mrs. Simpson had her chance. "Professor Withers, I wonder ..."

"Brian," he corrected her. He disliked the feeling of being set apart from his students by formality.

"Brian," she smiled, continuing. "Should we still consider the Code of Hammurabi to be something civil considering the amount of barbarism in it?

"We have to consider the amount of barbarism there was before the code. Even the Decalogue -- the Ten Commandments -- in their brevity would have ---"

"Excuse me," the attractive blond interrupted. "I'm sorry to interrupt -- but it is important." She smiled almost seductively.

"Quite all right," smiled Brian. Suddenly a small part of him felt very unmarried.

"Beth!" said Mrs. Simpson, turning to the blond.

"Mother, I hate to bother you like this, but I left my wallet and credit cards at my apartment. Can I borrow some money -- or one of your cards?"

"Beth, darling," Mrs. Simpson smiled. "This is Brian Withers, my Western Civ. professor. Brian, this is my daughter Beth. She goes to school here, too."

"Nice to meet you, Beth." God! Killer eyes.

"Mother talks about you frequently. Nice to meet you." Is there a ring? I can't see his left hand yet for that pile of papers he's holding. "I'm taking Western Civ. during the summer semester. I'll be sure to get you." She winked while the other eye did double duty, taking him in more completely.

"Looking forward to it," answered Brian.

Mother and daughter did a quick financial transfer, and Beth was moving away toward the door. She turned to face them just before leaving. "Lunch sometime soon?"

"Sure, dear," answered Mrs. Simpson. "Any time you say."

"Not you, silly," smiled Beth. "Brian. If I'm going to take his class, I've got to start sucking up."

Brian smiled a little awkwardly. "Sure. I guess so. Why not?" Why not, indeed?

After all the students left -- almost an hour after dismissal -- Brian gathered his paper, books, and briefcase. Locking the classroom door behind him and heading for the main front door, he never saw the figure watching him, concealed in the shadows under the stairs.

The Panama City *News-Herald* had only a short article about the dead man found in his truck out on the bay road in Carrabelle. All identification had been taken from the body and the truck, but by tracing the truck identification number, the sheriff's office had been able to identify the body. The man had lived in the area over twenty years, and worked on one of the commercial fishing boats. There was no immediate family. No apparent reason could be found for the killing.

Susannah moved about the kitchen happily, cleaning up after baking the cake, preparing a snack for Brian when he got home from his night class. The CD player was separating the sounds of Eric Clapton's "Tears in Heaven." On the kitchen table was a letter she had been writing to her mother and father in North Carolina. In the letter she had not mentioned that Brian was looking for another job. Neither had she mentioned that she was going to have to give up her job at the bank in another few weeks. The doctor had strongly advised it since the miscarriage on the first pregnancy. Susannah would never let her parents know there was soon to be a financial bind; they would insist on helping. She and Brian were still young enough to know they could take care of all their own problems.

When Susannah heard the car pull in the driveway -- well after 11:00 -- she hurried about the living room, picking up. She liked to have the house neat when he came home. The car door closed as she was putting away the morning paper.

Brian opened the front door, dropped his brief case and books on the floor noisily. "Honey, I'm home." It was their satire on the stereotype of a 60's sitcom. The corniness was intentional.

"Oh, sweetheart, I've missed you. It's been so long." She knew the script too.

He held his arms out to receive her. "How 'bout a kiss for your man."

"You big lug, you." (Barbara Stanwyck!) She rushed into his arms, and the theatrical satirical kiss soon -- very soon -- evolved into a kiss of sincerity and intensity.

She pulled away first, almost laughing. "Are we Ali and Ryan, or what?"

"I was thinking more of Liz and Richard, myself."

"Nah. We're way too cute for them. This is a *Love Story* moment if I ever saw one." She kissed him again without the playing, and they moved toward the couch. "What would you like first, sex or food?"

"Hard choice."

She poked him in the ribs with her elbow. "Your whole future depends on your answer, you know. You could spend the rest of your life on this couch."

"But would there be food?"

"Oh, you're incorrigible. Food, food, food. You're turning my *Love Story* into *The Alien That Ate Chicago*."

"No. I don't really need all of Chicago right now. Just some of that chocolate cake I smell."

"No you don't. That's for Janie's shower tomorrow. I've got a ham sandwich for you."

He let his mouth turn into a pouting shape, and the corners of his lips twitched. He wiped an imaginary tear from his eye.

"You're not going to get any. I can't go to the shower with a cake with a huge slice cut out of it."

"You could if you really loved me." Still petulant.

She led him to the kitchen, took a ham sandwich from the refrigerator, put it in front of him. He swung his leg over the chair, sitting. He looked up at her defeated, then took a bite out of the sandwich.

"Oh, well," he said. "I guess this is a good second."

She poured him a glass of milk, and while he was busy enjoying the sandwich, she slipped a rather good-sized individual chocolate cake in front of him. He looked up with a broad smile.

"You're right," he said. "This really is *Love Story*. Me Ryan. You Ali."

She leaned down to kiss him, but was stopped by the ringing of the phone.

"Damn," she said. "That never would happen in *Love Story*." She left to answer the phone.

"Hello," she said into the phone, from the other room. Pause. "No. This is the home of Brian and Susannah Withers."

Pause. "Are you the man who called earlier?" Wait. "Maybe the number is similar to ours. I'm sorry. I can't help you." Pause. "No problem. Good luck."

"Wrong number?" Brian asked from the kitchen.

"Yeah. That's about the fourth time in two days. Someone must have a new number close to ours."

"Nobody's got our number, baby. Not the romantic Bri and Zannah."

Eric Stewart sat at his desk facing a window that looked out over North Peachtree. In the distance he could see the afternoon backup on I-75 and I-285. He wanted to get home early because of his son's sixth birthday, but the call had just come in about the body found on the bay road. That left him with some work he hadn't planned on. Now he wasn't even going to get home at all. He had already called to tell Audrey not to wait on him. He hadn't told her yet that he wasn't even going to get home for a few days. Damn. This was the sixth birthday party he missed. Zero for Six. Great dad!

On the wall before him was a map of the southeastern United States. On the map were colored pins, some green, some yellow, -- some black, some red. Most of the colored dots were along the Gulf Coast. A few inland in Georgia, Alabama, Mississippi and Louisiana. One place in particular had more dots than any other place on the map: the north Florida coast from Panama City to the east about a hundred miles. Along the stretch of small fishing villages; Apalachicola, Eastpoint, Carrabelle, St George Island, St. James, Alligator Point, Panacea. Around and over the small villages and hamlets was a collection of green and yellow pins. Two black pins were among the others. As he turned back to the map from his mini-vacation traveling up I-75, he placed another black pin on the map, this one just to the west of Carrabelle, right on the edge of the water line which showed the Apalachicola Bay.

Eric Stewart went over to his coffee maker and poured another cup. Again he stared out of the window toward I-75 ---

and Chattanooga. The sky looked as if it might snow tonight. He would miss that, too. He always enjoyed playing with Simon in the snow.

He had already called for a reservation on flight 372 out of Hartsfield at 6:34. Oh, well. That's the breaks. At least the pay's good. Better than a teacher, which he had worked at for four years. The bureaucracy and hypocrisy had defeated him. The Peter Principle ran rampant. The whole system was second only to the military in putting rules over reason. And closing the gap fast.

Two other jobs and he came to this concrete palace high above the streets of Atlanta, where he could sit apart from the bureaucracy and hypocrisy. It was a job, in a sense, removed from reality. He had been reminded, when he began this job, of the medieval Star Chamber, James I's group in the mid-1600's who took the law into their own hands to bring retribution to those who escaped their just due by loopholes in the law. The members of the Star Chamber hunted down -- and annihilated -- those who went free from punishment for crimes they committed. The Star Chamber righted the wrongs of a blind justice.

He looked at his watch. Four-fifteen. Not much time before take-off, and so much to do. He went to the cabinet across from his desk, opened the second drawer, and looked through the files there. A neat, organized man, whose time was so valuable that organization was a necessity. "Carrabelle." Behind the heading were seven other sub files. He pulled out one. "Kannon, William." Studying the file he glanced at the photo of the rugged face, angular, hard. The picture was made without the subject's knowledge, and the head was turned, looking over his shoulder, making the photo seem somewhat posed, studied, affected.

"Rucker, William, 44, DOB; 3-14-50. Born: Lexington KY. Mother: Denise Kannon, nee Abernathy, occupation, waitress, presently retired. Father: Robert George Rucker, occupation construction worker, presently retired. See files for Denise and Robert in 'dependents.'

"Rucker (aka Cherokee, Slasher, Slugger) presently working as commercial fisherman in Carrabelle, FL. Known to have met with agents of Agular on at least four occasions to date.

"Killed John Parrish on 6/23/84 in Denver, Colorado after finding Parrish in bed with Rucker's own wife Helen. Convicted of second-degree murder and sentenced to forty-to-fifty in Canon City, Oklahoma Prison. Escaped 10/21/88 after stabbing and killing a prison guard, and severely injuring another one."

Stewart scanned the remaining fifty-three pages hurriedly. He had to absorb as much as possible in only fifteen minutes. His eyes paused briefly on the phrase, "strong sociopathic tendencies; dangerous; may be responsible for at least three more deaths. Details on p. 42."

One more cup of coffee later, Stewart closed the folder, looked at his watch, put on his suit coat, overcoat, checked his gun, picked up his pre-packed overnight bag, and left the office. He wanted to call his son to say, "Happy Birthday," but was afraid of the feelings the conversation might bring about in him.

At Hartsfield International he boarded flight 372 for Orlando under his own name. In Orlando he would board another flight to Tallahassee under the name of Wayne Henderson. A rental car was already waiting in Tallahassee for Wayne Henderson.

Susannah, beautiful and vibrant, clipped the leash onto Dempsey's collar. The ginger and white mostly-Cocker Spaniel was a gift to her and Brian from the Dempsey Dumpster outside of town almost a year ago. He was emaciated, shivering in the cold, and still managing to be lovable. They had taken him home with firm intent on taking him to the animal shelter the next day. So much for firm intentions!

Locking the door behind her, Susannah and the well-fed, happy Dempsey headed for the two-car port and the used Triumph TR-6 with the top already down. Dempsey had trouble controlling his tail as he jumped around, anticipating the ride -- especially in the car with no top. He loved that one the most.

Susannah's long, brown, glossy hair flowed in the wind as she moved onto the street and headed for the small shopping center where she would drop off Dempsey at the vet's for a shot and do some shopping while Dempsey endured the indignities of the vet's examination. There was a sale on winter coats that Susannah wanted to check out, even though she knew they couldn't afford any. Not with the baby coming, and her having to leave her bank job soon. But looking was cheap and fun: it was the wanting that hurt.

When she turned onto U.S. 98 along the water, she realized she had rushed the season by putting the top down. The pleasant warmth back at their tree-protected house that was out of the wind had given way to a chilling breeze as she moved along the edge of the Gulf. The water white-capped across the bay, throwing a bright reflection on her, but the wind stung with a coldness that would soon turn uncomfortable. Youth and vanity prevailed however. There are few emotions more exhilarating than driving a convertible, knowing your hair looks great being whipped by the wind, and certain that you're attracting the gazes of most, and the envy of many. Discomfort can always take a back seat to vanity -- especially if you're under thirty. The cold wind was affecting even Dempsey. He left his post hanging over the passenger door with his ears standing out in the wind like wings. He was now settled down more comfortably -- and more importantly, warmly -- in the bucket seat beside Susannah.

She pushed a tape into the player, and Aretha Franklin's "The First Time" poured out around the speeding Triumph. Perfection, she thought. The sun, the water, the music, the movement, the distant coasts of Dog Island and St. George. It doesn't get any better than this. The only thing that could make it perfect -- besides a little warmth and Brian beside her -- would be a rum and diet Dr. Pepper. Except that she couldn't drink with the baby coming, and also it was frowned on by the Florida Highway Patrol. And the City of Carrabelle Police Department -- all two members of the city police. Not that she and Bri hadn't done it before. But together they could take turns riding shotgun and watching for the law.

Closer into town, she slowed down as traffic became more congested. On the water side now fish, shrimp and crab houses began to block the view of the bay with the unmistakable smells of fresh sea-life becoming heavier in the air. This, too, was part of the perfection; the various smells of the sea, as numerous and distinct as the many sounds of a symphony orchestra. All of this was certainly worth the trade-offs they had weighed before coming here. Bri could have gone with either the University of Missouri or Western Carolina University, both certainly more prestigious, regarded as more scholarly, and -- hardest of all to give up -- both offering more money. It was doubtful as to whether or not the same decision would be made now.

When money is low is when it is most important.

To dispel all of these unwanted thoughts, Susannah looked out at the water, the sun, and the passing fish houses. And just as suddenly she knew with certainty that if the decision had to be made again, she and Brian would make the same choice again. The place was too beautiful, too friendly, too fine, too perfect to give up. Missouri and Western Carolina couldn't compare. Yes. They would make the same choice again. Dempsey sat up and sniffed the salt-water smells, affirming that the right choice had been made.

At one of the docks, some commercial boats were being loaded, others unloaded, some coming in from weeks on the Gulf, others preparing for weeks where their neighbors had just been. The men working on the boat and docks were for the most part a happy, joking group. They were glad to be going out, to spend their time on the water fishing, reading, engaging in fellowship with their shipmates. They were glad to be coming in, to be going to bars, spending time with women, taking lots of showers, going to Panama City for expensive evenings. Easy come, easy go. Most of them had nothing or no one to save for; the future was uncertain and alien. The present was the important time. "Take the cash, and let the credit go."

Some of the men on the boats looked out to the highway and saw the beautiful woman in the small convertible speeding along U.S. 98. Whistles and cat-calls sounded joyfully through the air, none of which Susannah heard because of the wind and John Bayless' "Time to Say Goodbye." But out of the corner of her eye, she could see some of the waving and gesturing.

She smiled but did not turn her head. Oh, sure, guys. That's really what turns a woman on. A lot of waving, jumping up and down, whistling and screaming. How romantic! First-rate foreplay. Then for some reason which even *she* didn't know, she suddenly turned toward them, smiled broadly, and waved a generous, all-encompassing wave. There you go, boys. I'll make your day. You couldn't catch me in this car anyway. She imagined them telling themselves, "She wants me. She *really* wants me."

After leaving Dempsey at the vet's, she browsed through the clothing store with that excellent sale on winter clothing. Some great buys for next year -- providing the fashions didn't change -- and if you could afford them. She tried on three cold-weather dresses, two that really interested her, one that she wouldn't take at any price, a really tacky mixture of day-glo lime, yellow, and coral -- with sequins yet. She was trying that on just for laughs and got plenty which she kept under her breath. While the sales-girl watched her, Susannah posed and pranced in front of the three-sided mirror, studying the monstrosity as if it were a great prize. She laughed to herself again, wondering what the help was thinking about her. She could see two sales-girls off to the side eyeing her with suspicion. It really was one of the ugliest dresses she had ever seen. After looking at it in the mirror a few minutes, she asked if she could go outside to see how the colors looked in natural light. Once outside she could feel heads turning from all over the shopping center -- and probably laughing. When she handed the dresses back to the saleslady, Susannah remarked on how much she admired the monster. She would be back, she said, when her husband could come with her to see it -- if it wasn't sold. The saleslady smiled understandingly. Don't worry, honey. It'll still be here.

Before she went in to get the grocery shopping done, she stopped at a pay phone to call Brian, to see if he wanted anything special for dinner that night. The call to Panama City was long-distance but minimal with the pre-paid card. After four rings, Bri's answering service came on.

"Oh, damn," she said to his machine. "I've just punched enough digits to equal fifty light years, and you're not there. You have no classes this morning, and not enough money to be doing anything interesting or exciting, so you must be having an affair. Probably with Mrs. Simpson. The buxom Mrs. Simpson. I called to see what you wanted for dinner tonight. I'm at the store getting ready to shop. Dempsey is at the vet's getting his annual humiliation. Now that I know you're out having a fling with that wealthy Simpson babe, I'm going to get hot dogs for you and steak for me. Sorry I missed you. Oh, I forgot. Love you."

Shopping done, a short stop by the drugstore. Pick up a dog treat for Dempsey, and -- why not? A dark chocolate Milky Way as a treat for herself. Back to the vet's for Dempsey. Along the waterfront by the unloading boats and the waving, whistling men. "She's coming back I told you she really wanted me."

At home she let Dempsey out and struggled to get the three bags into the house in one trip. After a few ungraceful maneuvers -- and twice dropping two separate bags -- she gave up, left one bag on the ground and took the other two in. Then she was back to get the other bag, this time without the sunglasses.

An exceptionally good shot through the zoom lens. Clear, straight on. Tight. The best shot of all. Better than the drive along U.S. 98, the wave at the fishermen, on the steps at the vet's. Better than the picture of her at the pay-phone, in the grocery store, the drugstore, and better, but only barely, than the picture of her in the lime, yellow and coral sequined dress. Click. Click.

Brian sat at one of the outdoor tables, facing the Miracle Strip, The World's Most Beautiful Beach. The sun and its reflection off the water made sunglasses a must, but the January air also made a heavy jacket just as necessary. Brian had ordered a rum and diet Dr. Pepper to sip on while he waited. He had some essay assignments to grade during the wait. He read the papers begrudgingly. Most pretty sophomoric ... but after all, they were written by sophomores.

As the lunch hour approached, the other tables began to fill up. The outdoor speaker system was playing some bearable dentist-office music. "Because You Love Me" was being played by some generic orchestra with lots of strings and French horns. Something he certainly didn't feel compelled to pay much attention to, and definitely good for conversation and grading papers.

" ...it was during the Babylonian expansion and prejudice that the empire reached its Golden Age." Not quite sure what that means. No signs of great writing at all, and a definite hint that the writer had gotten some help from somewhere -- like copying from two separate encyclopedia sources and not being able to blend them gracefully. "It was at this time that the Babylonian Empire swooped down on Israel, bringing about their Diaspora, or "scattering" of the Jews to the four corners of the seven seas."

Brian smiled. The facts were vaguely correct -- more or less .. but the writer would never win any prizes -- unless there was one for mixed metaphors. "After the Diaspora, the Jews had not had a homeland until after World War II with the establishment of Israel. Victims of the Diaspora were to be ..." A shadow fell across the page. Brian looked up to a tall, rugged-featured man holding a beer.

"Mind if I sat with you for a few minutes?" the man asked. "All the other tables are filled. I noticed you were alone."

"I'm expecting someone in a few minutes." Brian looked at his watch. "About twelve o'clock to be exact."

"I'm meeting someone too. I won't stay long."

"Sure," said Brian. He motioned toward the opposite chair. "But your time is limited," he smiled. "I'm waiting for a good-looking blond. Definitely more my type."

"I understand completely," smiled the man. "Mine's a redhead. Not natural, I'm pretty sure." Deep thought, but with a smile. "In fact I know for sure, come to think of it. If you know what I mean." The smile became boyishly evil.

"You're a teacher, it looks like." The man nodded toward the papers in front of Brian.

"Yep." Brian smiled at him. "You can always tell by the teacher's badge -- a load of papers to be graded. Not papers that have *been* graded, mind you. Papers that have to *be* graded."

"What do you teach?" asked the man. He obviously spent a lot of time outdoors. Very dark. Sun wrinkled.

"Western Civilization," Brian answered. He could tell immediately he needed to clarify. "It's like world history .. only without the east; China, Japan, and the African countries."

"I admire that. I do. I really think learning is a great thing. I never had much myself. Quit school in the eighth grade. But I have great respect for learning. Both sides of it. Those who teach, and those who learn. It's great."

The man had suddenly touched that secret spot deep in Brian. A bridge reached out from Brian and lights lit up along the bridge in ascending order. Brian had noticed for years that education was valued most by those who had the least of it. A certain breed of man there is with great intelligence and sensitivity --- and little education --- who condemns himself as stupid because of a meager education ... the breed who cannot tell the difference between education and intelligence. Brian had met some quite a few such men who were recognizably intelligent but had convinced themselves of their own lack of self-worth because they did not know the right words, phrases, equations, or systems. A beauty of simplicity emanated from them that Brian found irresistible. He wanted to reach out and say to them with absolution, "You are more educated than you know, certainly more educated than many who claim to be. Your own modesty and envy attest to that. It is not a matter of a piece of paper, my friend, not a condition granted to you by the state, but rather a condition of self, a frame of mind, an attitude. You already have what you covet. See yourself as equal to ---

even better than --- the man you envy. You are more enviable in what you understand and he does not. Be proud that you have your selfless, unegotistical intelligence."

But Brian didn't say all that.

"That's admirable," Brian said. "But don't confuse education and intelligence."

"Oh, I don't have any trouble there," said the man, taking a swallow of his beer. "I just don't think I got too much of either one."

"Not," said Brian. "You may not have gone to school as long as you would have liked, but you're an intelligent man. I can tell."

"Oh, no. Not me," smiled the man. But then his curiosity overcame him. "What makes you say that?"

"I can tell," Brian said. The man looked confused. "I just can." Brian held his drink up as if in a toast. "I've had thousands of students over the years. You get to know when you talk to a person for a few minutes ... without even analyzing .. or trying. And you can tell. You just know. And you're an intelligent man."

The man smiled, suddenly embarrassed, then quickly changed the subject. "Where do you -- uh where do you teach?"

"At Gulf Coast." The man looked confused. "The community college. You passed it on the way to the beach. If you came from the east."

"Oh, I came from the east all right. About eighty-five miles. A little town called Carrabelle."

Brian started to say that was where he lived, that he commuted every day. But something stopped him, a small alarm.

"Oh, yes," he said instead. "I know where that is. Some good places to eat over that way."

"I fish on one of the commercial boats there. The *Miss Betty*. You know anything about commercial fishing?"

"No." Brian caught the waiter's eye and motioned for two more drinks. "I've fished for my own enjoyment some, but not even much of that."

"There's a guy on our boat studying law at Texas A&M. Just took some time off. Sort of dropped out a while. Commercial fishing's good for that. People who just want to get away for a while. I was on a two-week trip once with a doctor. The kind of doctor that takes care of sick people, not the teaching kind."

"That's interesting," said Brian. "Maybe that's what I need. To drop out a while."

"It works," said the man. "I've seen it work wonders for people in knots. The clear sky, the feel of the ocean, no worries. A lot of thinking goes on out there. A lot of things get solved. It's just you and space. And you and yourself .. or you and God."

Suddenly it sounded less romantic to Brian; now it sounded lonely. "Yes. That's something we can all use," he said, feeling a little hypocritical.

The waiter came to the table with Brian's drink and the man's beer. The man reached into his pocket, taking out a large roll of bills.

"No, no," said Brian. "Let me."

"No," smiled the man. "Let me. I insist."

Brian looked at the roll of bills and decided that he was in the wrong business. Commercial fishing suddenly didn't seem so lonely. The romance was coming back.

"Thanks," said Brian. "Thanks very much." He extended his arm in a handshake. "Brian Withers," he introduced himself.

"William Rucker," said the man. "But people just call me Cherokee."

They shook, and the man's hand was firm, solid, and rough from many hours of hard labor.

Brian held up his glass in a toast. "To your health, Cherokee. Thanks for the drink."

Cherokee toasted back. "<u>Salud</u>. Thanks for being my friend for a while."

Again Brian was moved by the man's sincerity and simplicity. His openness. Strange that being a man's friend for a while could be one of the small moments in life that would become a memory. But suddenly a memory was made.

Just then an attractive blonde came out onto the terrace and headed toward their table. Brian stood up to greet her as did Cherokee.

"Hi," smiled Beth. "Sorry I'm late. I have no excuse except that I'm just disorganized and slow. I'm late. What can I say? I'm always late. It's one of those tragic character flaws"

Brian and Cherokee looked at her, smiling.

"Is it our turn now?" asked Brian.

"You're on!!" said Beth.

"We've missed you," said Brian. "Beth, this is Cherokee. Cherokee, Beth."

"Hi, Cherokee. Nice to meet you." She extended her hand to greet him.

He shook her hand, a little awkwardly, vaguely embarrassed. "Same here," he said.

Beth and Brian sat, but Cherokee remained standing.

"Well," he said, still awkwardly. "I guess I'll leave now." He nodded toward Beth. "Nice to meet you." Then to Brian. "Nice talking to you. I enjoyed it."

"Oh, don't leave," said Beth, looking at him pleadingly. It was part of her charm. She managed to make everyone around her feel as if he were the center of her attention. "I just got here. I just met you."

"Thanks," said Cherokee. "I'm meeting someone soon. I'll go wait at the bar inside."

"If she doesn't show up, come back and eat with us," said Beth. Brian couldn't conceal his enjoyment at watching her work her charms on a perfect stranger. She had an almost professional quality about it. An industrial-strength charmer.

"Thanks. I will," said Cherokee, easing himself away.

"Well 'Hi,' again," said Beth, turning her attention and charm to Brian now that the other man in her life was gone. "Tell me about your day. What have you been doing? Besides grading paper?" She nodded at the papers in front of him.

It's fun, lady, but I'm not falling for it. Just lunch, ma'am. Just lunch.

As they talked and later ate, from the fourth floor of the hotel next to the restaurant, the camera caught all of the charm and glitter of her smile -- just as it had caught the handshake between Brian and Cherokee, and before that, Brian alone, grading papers -- and before that a few good shots of Brian's face straight-on when he first walked onto the terrace to look for a table. The camera suddenly became enamored with Beth's smile, hair, and luminescent skin. But the important shots were the many of Brian and Cherokee together, especially the one of the handshake. Click, click. Click, click.

The Florida Marine Patrol officer backed his trailer and boat down the ramp at the mouth of the Carrabelle River. Getting out of his car to slide the boat into the water, he could see the bay and the islands off to the south. The wide river hugged the village of Carrabelle to the north. Back across the street behind him, a small waterfront bar indicated it was open at 9:00 in the morning, by a flickering neon light and three trucks parked in front. Oystermen's trucks, the officer could tell by the looks of them, old, beaten from use, spattered with mud and salt water, rusting from exposure to salt air, and more especially the left-over oyster shells in the truck beds.

Early to be drinking --- but not for an oysterman. Of all the lives to live, it is one of the hardest, requiring a strong back, complete dependence on the weather, and a willingness to be up and out on the bay by five or six o'clock each morning. Glare from the sun and reflection from the water bring on early skin cancer and cataracts. Winter storms and extreme cold limit the number of already limited days allotted by the state in order to allow the oyster population to regenerate. The oystermen have a saying that seems more true than humorous; "You scratch a poor man's ass when you depend on the weather for a living."

The marine patrol officer could picture the men inside the bar, drinking beer, talking very little. He knew some of the defeat they were feeling. He had oystered for two years way back there, before he had set some goals and decided he had to have more for his family.

The morning sun still cast coral and pink glows on the billowing white clouds off to the west, not storm clouds but puffy cumulus mountains. A chilling wind came down the river from the north, but the officer seemed not to notice; he was so busy tethering the boat, pulling the car and trailer out of the loading ramp.

The boat started up with a push of a button, a comfortable soft purr of a well-tended engine. With a calculated flick of the finger, the officer turned the boat into the wind and headed up river. Along the banks of the village, friends waved at him as he passed the cafe, the loading docks, the marinas, the grocery store. He waved back at them, unable to distinguish who they were. He wondered as he watched the passing village, how many little towns in the world were lucky enough to have their whole main street run along beside a wide river and look out to the huge bay with islands in the distance. People could actually sit in Jimmy's Restaurant, drinking morning coffee, eating breakfast, and look out to a view that others would pay hundreds a day for. And the irony was that the people eating in Jimmy's Restaurant .. and most of the people in the little town for that matter .. never really "saw" the beauty that surrounded them. But he himself was also guilty of not seeing that same beauty. Only once in a while .. like today .. did he take the time to look at what he overlooked on most days.

He moved on past the last marina on the right, and Mary Jo's Restaurant on the left, where the main street became a high soaring bridge that turned south and sailed up and across the river. The boat suddenly, almost magically, moved into a setting that was so different it should have taken hours to reach. All signs of the town and any civilization were gone, immediately after moving under the soaring bridge. Now on both sides of the river, savannas spread out from the river's edges, and the little town seemed hundreds of miles away. Only by looking back under the bridge could he confirm that any civilization was near.

The river slowly, imperceptibly, over the course of three miles, narrowed, and the savannas moved closer to the boat as it made its way up river. The boat's wake lapped through the marsh grass and reeds along the banks, rolled softly again on the soggy shores where sand crabs and egrets moved along the water's edge, searching constantly for something to eat. A small alligator, startled by the boat, rushed into the water and became hidden in the dark, cypress-stained river. Two more wide turns, and suddenly the shores moved away, opening onto a broad basin where the river diverged, the New River to the north, the Crooked River to the east. The large basin was the point where the two rivers met to form the Carrabelle River, the point called Three Rivers.

The boat angled to the right where the savannas gave way to a swamp crowded with tall cypress trees, twisted banyans, interweaving, entwining water vines and saw-grass lining the shore. The boat moved into semi-darkness, a dismal place where the tall cypresses blocked out most of the morning light, and swamp birds screamed out from hidden places. Alligators appeared more frequently, and now and then water snakes slithered across the path of the boat. Every once in a while an egret or crane would rush up from nowhere and flap noisily through the cypresses which now became even more numerous.

The boat traveled slowly now, barely five miles an hour, disturbing the swamp and its population as little as possible. The motor whirred softly, but the swamp knew it was being invaded. The officer watched the passing dreariness, again wondering how often he failed to see the beauty around him. As dark and as dismal as the place was, there was still beauty in it.

Suddenly the banks of the Crooked River moved up from underneath the water, not very high, only a few inches or more, and the sides or the river were now more defined. Now there was land for possum, raccoon, and an occasional deer. The land was low, close to the water, but the suggestion of a swamp was still there. The river widened slightly, letting in a little more light. Up ahead was a small basin where he would turn around and head back.

36

When he reached the basin and started the turn, he paused. Something in his law-enforcement training stirred in him. Something was different. Something was wrong. He came here once a week on his rounds covering the rivers, and something ... something was not the same. He stopped the motor and suddenly the sounds of the forest rushed in around him. He looked slowly, carefully along the water's edge, through the dense forest. A strange smell that he had not known here before rose up to meet him.

One of the thick bushes on the edge of the basin was broken and leaning out over the bank, part of its leaves down in the water. He drifted toward the broken bush and saw something floating back under branches, held in place by the drooping branches, locked from the flow of the river. He held back some of the branches and picked up the fishing creel. It looked almost new .. and was empty. Pulling the boat to the bank, he stepped onto the low land, looking about even more carefully. Then he saw the plastic bags scattered about the ground. He didn't have to smell the fine white powder inside the Ziplok bags to know what it was.

Moving cautiously, he studied the landing. Off farther, behind a large cypress, he saw another creel. He opened it with his handkerchief, careful not to smear any fingerprints. The bags in the creel were filled with the same fine white powder, and again he did not need to smell or taste it to know what it was. He did anyway. Opening one bag, he let his finger touch the powder and then touched his finger to his tongue. It was.

Then he saw what he had smelled all along. The body was starting to decompose. The driver's license in the wallet was for Joe Sterling, seventeen years old. There were some papers in his pocket that surely had to be homework assignments... "p. 312-316 Yeats. Answer questions. p. 317. Not essay form, just questions .... p. 179 .. odd numbered problems on volume of sphere and cylinder..." The face on the body had a beginning beard, not an intentional one, just not clean-shaven.

An old car was parked on the road that stopped about fifty feet back from the basin. One door was open. The key was turned so the radio could stay on, but sometime during the days past, the battery had run down. On the front seat was a sheathed knife. When the officer took it out, again careful not to disturb any fingerprints, he saw the dried, days-old blood on the blade --- lots of it.

Brian overslept. It was the day of his first test in his Tuesday-Thursday class. On a hunch that he might oversleep, Susannah tried calling from the bank where she worked. She wanted to call at 9:00, when the alarm was supposed to go off, but at that time a conference was taking place, and she was busy getting it arranged, meeting the people, introducing them. Two men in the conference took up two of the outgoing lines for an annoyingly long time, trying to get information which Susannah could tell should have been obtained before the meeting started. When she finally got to a phone it was 9:45. Brian answered the phone with a voice that clearly revealed he had been sound asleep.

"Hello," he rasped.

"I was afraid of this," she said. "I just knew you'd answer the phone."

"Why shouldn't I? It was ringing."

"But you're not supposed to be there."

"Hey, lady! I live here." He nuzzled into the phone, trying to get closer to her.

"Not for long. If you don't get to work and make the money to pay the rent."

"What's the bottom line of this conversation?"

"It's 9:45 is the bottom line."

"Oh, damn." His voice was suddenly wide-awake, tinged with a slight bit of panic. "Talk to you later." He hung up and started running.

Two cups of coffee, gulped rather than tasted, and a four-minute shower later, he was dressing, with only a few spots of water dotting his shirt from his hurried drying. Don Imus was on MSNBC, giving somebody hell. Dempsey thought all the rushing was part of some game for his sake and kept getting in the way, tugging at socks, running ahead between the kitchen and the bathroom.

The bed was left unmade, the wet towels on the bathroom floor, the coffee-pot left on, and when he grabbed a cheese Danish from the refrigerator, he absently left his coffee cup on the shelf in the refrigerator. After looking a few minutes for his cup of coffee, he gave up and poured another. Dempsey was still running in and out of Brian's fast-moving feet. It was a good game.

Hair wet, shirt damp, briefcase clutched, and Dempsey underfoot, he headed for the door where he had to maneuver past Dempsey to keep him from getting out. It was 10:10. He had an hour and fifty minutes to get ninety miles, which wouldn't be bad if the last fifteen miles weren't along 15th Street -- which was laughingly called the business by-pass, but like every other by-pass in the country, had become busier than the business route.

He backed his Z-car, an '85 Nissan 300-ZX, to the street slammed on brakes to avoid hitting the maroon Dodge Dart that seemed to materialize from nowhere. Mumbling some not-too-mild obscenities, he waited until the Dart was clear, then slammed into forward, burned rubber to the street, and headed toward U.S. 98.

Turning right, he stayed slightly above the speed limit through Carrabelle, then along the edge of the Gulf to Eastpoint, over the causeway and bridge spanning the Apalachicola River. At that point in his trip, he became aware for the thousandth time, of the beauty of the ride. Each time he started up the soaring bridge spanning the Apalachicola River, he felt as if he were flying up and over the river, the bay, the gulf, the town. He looked down on St George Island six miles to the left, and St. Vincent's Island west of that. The river, wide and stirring, flowed from the right, winding down from the north, Chattahoochee and Georgia. And the town of Apalachicola lay hidden before him under a blanket of trees, showing only the courthouse, the restored River Inn, two microwave towers, and a distant water tower. He could imagine he was soaring in a glider above the layer of tall oaks that hid the old ante-bellum and Cape Cod houses looking out across the bay with their widow's walks standing guard.

Alanis Morissette was singing, "Thank U" to him on the tape player.

Always at this point, he glanced quickly to the rear view mirror to see Eastpoint moving away six miles behind him, becoming lost in salt spray and mist. This time he also saw a maroon Dodge Dart not too far behind, moving onto the rise of the bridge.

Through Apalachicola he took the bay road, not particularly smart since it was residential, but he thought he might be able to pick up some needed time. Not so. In fact he lost some. As he turned back toward U.S. 98, he could see the maroon Dart two blocks behind him.

Ninety-eight moves away from the water between Apalach and Port. St Joe, and because of not following the coastline, here it stays much straighter. It was here that he moved the Z up to 70 and 75. In the rear-view mirror he could see the maroon Dart still back there.

St. Joe slowed him down with its stoplights, and then Highland Park, where 98 is no more than twenty feet from the water's edge, still kept him at a slower pace. The long crescent turn of the shore, right on the edge of the Gulf gave him the feeling that he was maneuvering his catamaran in a wide bank against the wind. He could feel the pressure of the wind off the water, pressing against the car as he turned into it. At the end of the long crescent, he could see the maroon Dart closing in from behind like another Hobie-cat creeping up in a race, closer, closer, surely about to overtake him. But never quite getting too close. Always dropping back just when it was right to take the lead.

Mexico Beach slowed him down again. With Cape San Blas off to the left, jutting out into the Gulf, he turned from it and along the strip of deserted houses and condos that looked out across blinding white sand and lucid, clear aqua water. In mid-

January the long magnificent beach was like a ghost town on the water's edge, little to remind anyone of what it would be like in June, July and August. And the maroon Dart was always back there.

Mexico Beach ends very abruptly. Its stores, houses, bars and restaurants stop immediately where U.S. 98 moves onto the government land where Tyndall Air Force Base begins. The highway crosses a short bridge spanning a small inlet, and suddenly the village of Mexico Beach gives way to a forest completely populated by nothing but trees and underbrush. The long stretch of forested land girds both side of the road for many miles before the hangers, barracks, officer's quarters, and landing strips emerge -- a long, barren straight stretch of road broken only by signs warning travelers not to stop on this government property: "People stopping on this restricted highway will be interrogated."

Brian looked back and saw the Dodge Dart. He thought of the consequences of stopping -- on this forbidden land. Would the Dart pass him or not? Would an Air Force Patrol really appear from lord-knows-where and take him in for questioning? Would they question the driver of the Dart? And how much sense would it really make if he actually told them why he had stopped? O.K., dummy. There's your answer. He looked at his watch. Good time so far. He hoped 15th Street wouldn't be its usual hazard.

After the Air Base, another soaring bridge led up and over a bay to Parker. He couldn't help himself. He sped down the bridge to the first red light, turned right and immediately became lost in some of the back roads that wound around East Bay. The move had been so sudden there was no way anyone could have followed him. He cruised along the canopy roads where the trees now and then opened up to the two-story condos of this affluent neighborhood. He glanced in the rear view mirror before each turn. No one there.

One sudden turn took him to a dead-end where the street became a boat ramp into the bay. At the expense of a few needed minutes getting to his class on time, he stopped and waited, alternately looking behind him and out across the bay, the engine purring softly. Back at Mexico Beach he had crossed into the central time zone, so looking at it one way he had come eighty miles in twenty minutes.

He watched the morning sun sparkle on the dark January water. After a few seconds, he backed the Z-car to the corner, turned quickly and headed back toward U.S. 98. Hitting the by-pass in south Calloway, he turned right on the six-lane that made the two-mile arc to become 15th Street with its row of continuous stop lights, one after the other. When he reached Transmitter Road he suddenly swung north to get to 23rd Street where there were fewer stop lights and more lanes. Just getting there was a mess, because he had to weave around some back streets to reach it. On 23rd he wove in and out of traffic like someone in a skating rink, rushing to get through yellow lights before they became red. Just after he passed Highway 77 and the sprawling mall, moving up onto Harrison Ave., he crossed in front of a blue station wagon, moved over one more lane, and looked into the rear view mirror to see if he could cut back.

Damn! How could it be? About half a block back the maroon Dart moved in and out of traffic behind him. Still there. He must have moved on up the by-pass and waited. Whatever the guy in the Dart had done, it worked.

When Brian came up to Florida State University on the north and Gulf Coast Community College on the south, the Dart was still in sight. He turned into the faculty parking lot, backed into his reserved space, locked the car and hurried toward his classroom in the Social Studies Building. At the top of the steps leading up to the entrance, he turned and looked back to see the maroon Dart moving slowly through the faculty parking lot. No more than a hundred feet away, looking right at him, Brian could see the driver was wearing glasses. They looked in one another's direction for a few seconds, eyes locked. You had to give him this. The guys had balls. This is not being followed; this is being stalked.

The high-school student's death and overdose was reported in the back pages of the Tallahassee *Democrat* and the Panama City *News-Herald*, but it was front-page big in the Carrabelle and Apalachicola *Times*. The boy had been a junior at Carrabelle High School, was active in sports, and died of an overdose of undiluted coke. No foul play was suspected in his death, but the large amounts of cocaine and marijuana found with the body, along with the bloodied knife, indicated some connection with a drug ring, possibly some connection with the death of the fisherman whose body was found in his truck on the beach about a week before.

In his office high above Atlanta, Stewart (aka Henderson) placed another black pin where the village of Carrabelle touched the blue waters of the Gulf of Mexico.

Susannah sat watching TV with Dempsey, waiting for Brian to get home. Dinner was ready, the table set, even with candles tonight, and the fire crackled romantically. On the couch, reading the latest John Grisham novel, she heard the TV announcer mention the "landing of the Crooked River outside Carrabelle." Her attention caught now, she turned and looked to the screen.

"The youth apparently died from an overdose of uncut cocaine. Authorities do not suspect any foul play connected with the death, but are not ruling out some possible connections with an organized drug-smuggling ring. Also there may be a connection between this death and that of a fisherman found on the beach a week ago." Then the announcer went on to another story. Susannah heard the Z-Car turn into the driveway. Dempsey jumped up, barking, his official greeting to any member of the household. He also liked to show off the fact that he could recognize the sounds of cars that belonged to him.

"Hi, hon," Brian said, coming through the door.

"'Home is the sailor, home from the sea, and the hunter home from the hill.'" She kissed him . "And just in time for a rum and Dr. Pepper. I was about to start on my Shirley Temple without you."

"Wordsworth," he said. Yes. A rum."

"Wrong," she answered. "Henley. Stick to your own field, professor. Lemon tonight?" she asked from the kitchen.

"Yes, please. And I'll bet you. Wordsworth. It's almost my field."

"Never. What do you want to bet? Cube or crushed?"

"Cube. A night of wild love-making."

"Strong or weak? What kind of bet is that? We both win."

"Medium. That's the idea. No losers."

"Look in my English poetry book up there, on the right, Mr. Smartass. You're about to lose a good night's sleep. Here."

He took the drink from her, held it up in a toast, and they touched glasses. She was drinking plain Dr. Pepper. No alcohol for her. She didn't want to get junior, drunk, addicted, deformed or retarded.

"I feel like a heel, drinking when you can't. But I really need it tonight. It's been a helluva day."

"Tell me about it! We must have had half the people in the county in the bank today. Loans, mortgages, wills, attorneys, the beginnings of two different suits. The world is turning litigious."

"That means it turns red in acid and blue in alkali, right? Or is it the other way around?"

"No. That's the EPT. Plus for pregers, minus for good luck."

"I thought that was one if by land and two if by sea."

She kissed him. "I'll stop this right now, before we get lost in an infinity of misplaced adages and garbled metaphors. Get the book. You're not getting off that easily."

He got the book, sat on the couch beside her, facing the fire and thumbed through the index on lines, finding what he wanted. "O.K.! You ready for this? You're about to eat crow -- or humble pie. You can have your choice."

"Lay it on me, big boy," she smiled.

He turned to the page, then raised his eyebrows and laughed with a mixture of embarrassment and disbelief.

"What does that mean?" she asked. "Who gets the night of romance?"

"Neither of us. We're both wrong. It's Stevenson, as in Robert Louis."

The *Treasure Island*_guy? No way." She took the book from him. "I don't believe you. You never give up."

She looked at the page he held open. "I don't believe this. You did something to my book. This is a misprint."

"Yeah, sure. At least it's not so bad for me to miss it. As you pointed out, it's not my field. But you!" he smiled teasingly, pointing at her. "Who's got the master's in English Lit.? Whose field is it?"

"Oh, you." She hit him gently with the book. "I always did get Henley and Stevenson mixed up."

"No excuse. Give back your masters."

"Well, I do."

"Yeah, and I always tell my students that Charlemagne ruled the Roman Empire. I always get the Roman Empire and the Holy Roman Empire mixed up. Just a minor technicality -- and about five hundred years apart. But it's not much of a mistake."

"Oh, shut up." She pushed him playfully. "Stevenson was never one of my strong points. In fact, that one line of his is the only thing worth remembering. I have that on good authority from two of my major profs at Western Carolina. Not important at all. What about your day?" She changed the subject rapidly, still smiling.

"Well, you won't believe it. Strange, strange day," he said. "I was followed this morning. Or more like stalked. A maroon Dodge Dart was on the street -- here -- when I left this morning. And it followed me all the way to the college. Right into the faculty parking lot. Like he didn't even care about being seen."

"One of your students. Probably one of your female students who's fallen in lust with you. I'll scratch her eyes out."

"No. It was a man. In his thirties. Wearing glasses. He drove right by me at the steps of the Social Studies Building. No more than a hundred feet from me. I half-way expected him to toot the horn and wave at me."

"Some male student who's fallen in lust with you. I'll scratch HIS eyes out."

"Not."

"Could you see his face clearly?"

"Not really. The car had that slightly tinted glass. I could only see enough to know he was wearing glasses."

"Did you tell the police?"

"No. I would have felt stupid. I didn't even think to get his tag number."

"Like being on one of those quiz shows, isn't it?" she smiled, trying to ease his tension. "Everybody at home and in the audience knows the answer, but when you're in the hot seat, it ain't so easy."

"Exactly," he said. "I feel so stupid that I didn't get the tag number. I even watched him drive away, out of the parking lot." He took a sip of his rum and diet Dr. Pepper. "Curses. Foiled again."

"The only thing to do is drink, eat, be merry, and make love until you get a grasp on it. Thinking about it -- worrying about it -- won't solve a thing."

"You're right," he said. pulling her to him on the couch. "You're absolutely right. Come here and help me forget." He kissed her, and together they slid into a horizontal position. Dempsey looked over from where he lay in front of the fire, but looked away, back to the fire when he was satisfied this wasn't going to be a fight.

"What a fine way to spend a cold January night," Brian said. "A fire, good food waiting, a good drink, and Zannah -- my Zannah. 'A loaf of bread, a jug of wine, and thou beside me in the wilderness.'"

She sang softly an old song she remembered, "You'd Be So Nice To Come Home To." Brian joined in with her, and together them sang it to the end.

"How could you have an autumn moon with winter stars?" he asked.

"We're so cute we should be on the Oprah Show," she said.

"I'm not so sure Oprah would want ---"

She quieted him with a kiss that lasted --- and lasted --- and lasted.

Down the street, in the cold darkness, a man wearing glasses sat in a maroon Dodge Dart. The man could not really see much from where he sat, only the reflections of the firelight coming through the window.

Saturday morning Brian took the cars down to the do-it-yourself car-wash, the Triumph first, then the Z-car. Both times Dempsey insisted on coming along, mostly to get in the way. Brian knew Dempsey wanted to be squirted with the hose, but it was too cold. Dempsey just didn't realize how cold it was.

After he finished washing the second car, Brian pulled it over to the side to dry it off. Two other cars were waiting to pull into the washing bay.

The sun felt warm on Brian's back and arms as he moved the chamois cloth back and forth over the shiny body, massaging the white metal with the same tenderness reserved for Zannah's smooth body. He knew he should be doing this in the shade rather than the sun, but two reasons stopped him: he was enjoying the feel of the sun after the past two cold months and -- there wasn't any shade anyway. When the car-wash was not so busy he would stay parked inside the bay to do the drying.

He stopped for a few seconds to wipe his forehead on the sleeve of his shirt. He was starting to sweat slightly. Opening the door, he took a sip of his diet Dr. Pepper -- out of the bottle. He and Zannah both preferred bottles to cans.

The music from the cassette player came out louder. Rachmaninoff's *Rhapsody on a Theme by Paganini*. He felt a little classical today. The Renaissance man, he liked to think of himself. Especially on weekends when he could more freely indulge his fantasy. The cassette tape was just coming up on "The Eighteenth Variation."

He stopped work and with his Dr. Pepper in his hand, looked out across the bay to Dog Island beach. Multicolored Hobie-cats were moving back and forth across the water. The music swelled behind him, and he floated off on dreams and fantasies. There were two old movies he had seen somewhere in his past with "The Eighteenth Variation" as their themes. He seemed to remember a dancer named Moira Shearer in one of them.

And then there was Howard -- way back there in graduate school.

Howard, a beer-drinking buddy of his, had majored in music. Instead of writing a master's thesis, music majors who majored in an instrument, had to perform with the university symphony orchestra. Howard played the piano in a way that would cause Liszt envy.

Everything came easy for Howard. He was preparing for a career in concertizing. He imagined himself playing in all the capitals of the world. And he <u>was</u> a good pianist, not because Brian and his friends thought so, but because he had been praised by his professors, lauded by such instructors as Carlyle Floyd, Ernst von Donyani, and Leonard Bernstien. Howard was destined to go places.

He gave many recitals, most in Opperman Music Hall which seated about four hundred people. He played with quartets, quintets, duo pianos, always great, always called back for many encores. And he was so pleasant about playing encores for his audiences. He loved it. So it wasn't work for him. His professors had a hard time getting Howard to understand that part of show business -- even classical show-business -- was to always leave the audience wanting more.

"The Eighteenth Variation." -- beginning to swell on the recapitulation from the inside of the little car.

For his master's opus, Howard chose Rachmaninoff's *Rhapsody on a Theme by Paganini*. Friends would drop by and stand outside his apartment in the dark to hear him practice. Fellow students would hang around the halls of the Music Building to listen to him in the odd-shaped practice rooms. Brian and the girl he was dating then would slip into the back of

Wescott Auditorium to hear him practice with the full orchestra. He was great! He was magnificent! Brian and date had to refrain from jumping up, clapping and screaming each time Howard would come to the climactic ending. They weren't supposed to be there, hidden in the balcony of the darkened 2000-seat auditorium. Neither were any of the other hundred or more trespassing admirers who hardly breathed to keep from being discovered in the dark balcony.

"The Eighteenth Variation," swelling more on the car's stereo -- power, beauty, assertion.

The night of the concert more than 3000 people showed up. Students, faculty, towns-people, promoters and agents from New York, and friends, friends, friends. People were backed up in the halls upstairs and down, lined up along the back of the auditorium and balcony, along both sides of the outer aisles, sitting on the carpet on the inner aisles, some in evening dress, some in blue jeans. The program played "build-up" with the thousands; Howard was saved until last. A romantic program. Some Tchaikovsky, Gliere, Prokofiev, Ravel -- then the *finale* -- Rachmaninoff.

Howard walked on stage, white tie and tails, to thunderous applause. He knew he had a lot of friends, but this was overwhelming. He smiled his big, friendly, open smile, and held out his arms in appreciation. He sat at the piano, waited for silence, maybe said a brief, silent prayer. He looked to the conductor and nodded. The strings, pizzicato. The faint woodwinds. Then enter the piano.

About four bars into the piano entrance, Howard stopped, looked up, back at the keyboard, then standing, whispered something to the conductor. He sat down again. Waited. Nodded once more, and the strings plucked on the violins announced a new beginning. When the piano entered, this time he played only two bars. No one in the audience could hear anything wrong with what was being played. Whatever was going on was known only to Howard. He wrung his hands, took out a handkerchief and wiped his forehead. There was desperation on his face -- dread -- fear -- horror.

He nodded once more. The violins were plucked. Then the piano -- but only about twenty notes. The stop this time was punctuated by the frustration of a fist pounding on top on the piano. This time the conductor came over to Howard. A short conversation during which Howard never took his eyes from the keyboard. He nodded. His lips moved. He nodded again. The conductor returned to the podium, raised his baton, brought it down to the accompaniment of the plucked violins. This time the piano never entered at all. Howard got up and rushed from the stage. He passed his girlfriend standing in the wings, rushed down the stairs, out the stage door, and no one at FSU ever heard from him again. He could not be reached. He had vanished completely. Callers to his home in Tampa were told only that he was traveling -- somewhere in Mexico, sometimes out west, sometimes in Europe. No one ever completely believed it, but what could anyone do? Parents don't lie. Do they?

"The Eighteenth Variation." The last booming, pounding chords vibrated in the speakers, rocking the Z-car slightly. Brian, flooded with memories, looked out across the sun-reflecting waters. The Hobie-cats seemed to move to the music with the distant white sand beaches of Dog Island as a backdrop.

Then suddenly "The Nineteenth Variation" began.

"Rachmaninoff," a vaguely familiar voice said from behind Brian.

He turned to see the man who had bought him a drink at the beach-side cafe in Panama City. The man with the great envy of education. The man who had sat with him until Beth came.

"Cherokee," the tall man reminded him. "The fisherman who lives here in Carrabelle."

"Yes. Right," said Brian. "I remember. How are you? It's good to see you."

"Brian, isn't it? Brian Withers?" The man smiled, holding a beer can up as if offering a toast. "I have a good memory for names."

"Yes," smiled Brian. "You certainly do." He was incredulous. It was not uncanny that they might eventually

50

bump into one another in a town so small. But that the man --
Cherokee -- would remember his name -- after so brief an
encounter.

"Washing your car, I see. Can I help you?" Such openness,
such eagerness.

"No. No, thank you. I mean I'm almost through. Thanks
anyway, though." This is no way for a Renaissance man to
behave. What was there about this man that made him lose his
composure?

"What are you doing today?" asked Brian. "You have the
advantage over me, since you can see what I'm doing. Or have
been doing."

"I've been shopping. Buying groceries for the boat." He
pointed to the grocery store in the shopping center behind him,
then to the bags of groceries leaning against the side of the car
wash. Dempsey had been busy investigating both the man and
the shopping bags.

"Dempsey," called Brian. "No. No." Dempsey moved away
from the bags.

"Oh, he can't hurt anything," said the man -- Cherokee. "It's
mostly cans and boxed goods. I've got to go back for the meats
and produce later. We've got a trip coming up Monday. Out to
the Middle Grounds. Or maybe off the coast of the Yucatan.
We hear they're biting good down there."

"Do the Mexicans mind? When we fish down there, I
mean? Off their coast?"

"It's international waters. They can't do much about it -- as
long as we stay ten miles off-shore. But they don't mind. At
least they don't seem to. Not as much as our guys do when they
come up this way."

"They do that? Come up here?"

"Sure. As long as they stay ten miles off-shore, there's
nothing we can do about it. Once in a while they might have
some engine trouble, or something like that, and they have to
come in for help. They have to call in and get permission first.
They aren't treated very good here. Especially if they need
repairs that will take a long time and have to unload their catch.

51

The fish-houses give them only about twenty - twenty-five per cent of the going rate. Pitiful." The man seemed to understand fairness and humanity.

Just then Susannah pulled up in her Triumph, the top down in order to get more sun. "Hi, babe," she smiled. "I'm going to run up to Tallahassee for a while. You want anything?"

"Yeah," smiled Brian. "I want to go with you. How 'bout that?"

"No dice, babe," she smiled. "I'm meeting Natalie at Governor's Square. It's a girl thing. You wouldn't like it. Trust me. In fact you'd hate it."

"Well, what am I supposed to do? Me and Dempsey?"

"You're creative. I know you'll find something to keep you busy. Beside. That's not my problem today." She looked over toward Cherokee. "Hi! How are you?"

"Fine, ma'am." He touched the rim of his cap.

"I'm sorry," said Brian. "Honey, this is Cherokee. Cherokee, this is my wife Susannah .. who you can tell has no consideration for my feelings on my day off."

"Poor baby." Susannah feigned sympathy for him. "Nice to meet you," she said to Cherokee.

"Nice to meet you, ma'am," said Cherokee, touching his cap again.

"I'll be back around five, honey. You and I have a dinner date, remember?"

"Been looking forward to it for the past month." He walked to the car and kissed her.

She kissed him on the lips, an affectionate kiss. "We only made that date this morning. But I love it when you talk like that."

"One morning without you is like one month," he paraphrased from another of their old favorite black and white movies.

"And one month with you is like one morning," she completed the paraphrase, and then drove off, turning onto U.S. 98, waving back to them.

52

Cherokee remembered that vision. He had seen it before, from the boat. He turned to Brian, smiling. "Beautiful woman. You're a lucky man."

"Thanks," said Brian. "I am. I know it. Many times each day."

No hint of anything about the beach cafe, the drinks, the blonde. The Blonde. THE BLONDE. No raised eyebrows. No wicked smile. The man had class.

"Would you like to come down and see the boat? She's all clean and -- shipshape. A little pun there. You could have a cup of coffee. Or a beer. You ever been on a commercial fishing boat before?"

"No," answered Brian. "That sounds good. I'm wifeless for the afternoon anyway. Put your gear in the back seat. And we'll go pick up your other packages so you won't have to come back."

At the dock, Brian helped Cherokee get the groceries on board, Dempsey running back and forth along the boarding ramp. Cherokee stopped in the middle of the ramp, embarrassed, looking as if he needed to say something and not sure how to say it. They were standing side by side on the ramp, sort of dead-locked.

"What is it?" asked Brian. "What's the matter?"

"It's just -- just that there's an old shipboard superstition." He clearly hated to say what he was about to say. "About animals on the ship. It's supposed to be bad luck." He cleared his throat unnecessarily, nervously.

"No problem," said Brian. "I feel that way about him in the house sometimes -- especially when he has an accident." He sat the groceries on the dock and started toward the car, taking Dempsey with him. "He can stay in the car. As cold as it is, maybe nobody'll turn me in to the SPCA. C'mon, Dempsey. Here, boy."

Dempsey was just as happy in the car as he was on the dock. He was a happy dog. So happy under any circumstances, that Brian was sure at times that he was simple -- maybe even retarded. Well, as long as you're not living in a dumpster, anyplace is good. You can afford to be happy.

Dempsey wagged his tail from the front seat of the Z-car. Brian lowered the windows, not because it was needed but because he was afraid that if he didn't, someone would pass by and start worrying about that "dog locked in that car." Hell, the temperature is in the low 40's. I'm a wuss, he thought. I'm worried about what some passer-by will think. Somebody who's erroneous, and doesn't even know me.

He started back toward the boat where Cherokee was waiting, still embarrassed.

"He'll be fine in there," said Brian, trying to ease Cherokee's pain.

A man called out from the dock in front of the fish house. "How's the loading coming, Cherokee?" The man started moving toward them, obviously curious about the new man.

"Going fine, Travis," smiled Cherokee. "You know I love to spend your money, boss."

The man was closer now. Brian had talked with him a few weeks ago, about the job in the classifieds. Brian could see that the man did not recognize him -- yet.

"Brian, this is Travis, the owner of the boat and the dock," said Cherokee. "And doing very well at it, as you can see. He's buying his fifth boat, and he's only thirty-two. Pretty good, huh? Travis -- a friend of mine, Brian."

"Nice to meet you, Travis." Brian shook his hand. A very limp handshake.. Almost like a phantom handshake, thought Brian.

"Same here," said Travis, then looking at Cherokee. "You know you're not supposed to have beer on the boat, Cherokee." He looked at the six-packs in the top of one of the bags.

"Yeah, I know," said Cherokee. "Good rule, too. That's not beer though, Travis. That's coke. They just put it in beer cans." He smiled his broad winning smile. "You know I'm your best captain, Travis. I wouldn't break one of your rules. Not a captain as good and dependable as me."

A strange underplay of gamesmanship was going on here, Brian could see Cherokee was winning. Travis looked for a way to change the subject.

"It's not too good to lock your dog in the car like that," he said to Brian, nodding toward the car. "Could get over-heated, you know."

Brian had wondered who would be the first. "I'm only going to stay a few minutes," he said. "It's pretty cool today." Dempsey was actually curling around, trying to get warmer. Stereotypes, thought Brian. Life is easier if you can live by stereotyping. So much easier. And stupider.

"I got to get back," said Travis. "Paper work to do."

"So long, boss," said Cherokee, smiling. He was in control. He might not be the boss, but he was definitely in control. "Stop down and have some coffee later if you want to."

Travis did not answer, disappearing into the fish house.

"Seems a little unhappy about something," said Brian. They were carrying the groceries on board again.

"Oh, he's easy to get along with -- as long as he doesn't like you. It's when he starts liking you that he's a pain."

In the galley, Brian was surprised at the efficient use of space. Cherokee introduced him to two other men who were there, Blackie and The Swede. Cherokee opened beers all around -- or rather the coke that was in beer cans. Blackie and The Swede sat on the edge of their bunks, Brian and Cherokee sitting at the table -- which had a raised edge around it he found out later to keep the dishes from sliding off in rough weather.

The Swede was open and friendly, intelligent and humble, somewhere in his late 20's, but with eyes that seemed to have seen far more than most his age. He liked to ask questions, but didn't like to answer them. His hair was blond from the sun, and his skin dark from exposure, but he did not have the wrinkles around his eyes that Cherokee had.

Blackie was the one who got most if Brian's attention. He was one of the most handsome -- no, beautiful -- men Brian had ever seen. He didn't talk much, but his cobalt blue eyes seemed to be fascinated by everything that happened or was said around

55

him -- fascinated but totally uncomprehending. His black hair was well-trimmed and shined with a natural lustre. He spoke, for the most part, only when asked a direct question, and his voice was soft, deep, compassionate. He seemed to smile most of the time, even when a smile was inappropriate. But the eyes were constantly moving, constantly twinkling as if he were getting ready to say something exceptionally clever. Brian was ashamed of his own thought when he saw a great similarity between the eager-to-please Blackie and the equally eager-to-please Dempsey. But he couldn't help it.

Cherokee showed him around the boat, explaining what was unfamiliar, pleased to have company in what he obviously thought of as his home. Blackie and The Swede were equally as proud to have a visitor on board. Later they sat back in the galley and bunk room, Brian mostly listening to Cherokee and The Swede talk about the coming trip, planning the menus, the itinerary. They were both interested in making sure they had plenty of books to read. Brian could tell from the sound of the conversation that it would be a disaster to run out of reading material.

Most stores in the little village, from grocery store to barber shop, had a large supply of used paperbacks that they sold cheaply, or exchanged. The fishermen along the docks had brought so many books into the town that some stores looked like small libraries. But it was a way to get the fishermen to come in and, maybe, spend some money while they were looking through books.

Brian was impressed and interested in what he was learning. A new world was opening up to him. He, the Renaissance Man, was coming to a part of the world he hadn't known existed. That so many men with so little education should read so much -- and be so intelligent. He had long ago given up equating education with intelligence, but he had not known that the relationship might be of inverse proportions.

And Blackie. Something endearing came from such innocent openness. He would do anything for anyone to get word of approval. Shine shoes, bring the newspaper, clean the house -- fetch. It was clear that Blackie's capacity for recognizing good and evil might easily lie in the company he kept. He had been brought up well with a sense of right and wrong. That showed. His first response, when pressed for one, was always the moral one. But when the others teased him, he was easily swayed in search for approval. Brian thought, how many of us do give up conviction for approval, a pat on the back, or even just a smile. God, we're a lonely species, even when surrounded by what we call our peers.

Brian briefly fantasized a scene in which Blackie, in the right clothes, walked into Brian's class. All of the co-eds turned to gawk, whispering in curiosity, and then vying for his attention. Hair like midnight, the smile of a tooth-paste ad, and those cobalt blue eyes that let someone see right into a his soul, at the same time looking right into other people's eyes with more understanding and compassion than they had ever experienced before. The girls would flock around him -- and poor Blackie would not know how to deal with it all -- the adulation -- the lust.

The ancients used to honor their Blackies. Each village cared for, loved, and even revered what later was to become called the "village idiot." The ancients knew that the Blackies of the world served two purposes for God. First, the people were judged, in their afterlives, by the way they treated their Blackies; and second, God himself, from time to time, inhabited the bodies of the Blackies to see how those around him were behaving. So a person could never know for sure, when he looked into the trusting, open, and penetrating eyes of a Blackie, that he was not looking into the eyes of God.

After his second beer, Brian said he had to leave, shook hands all around, looked once more into Blackie's God-eyes. He was accompanied to the boarding ramp by Cherokee who invited him to come again. Clouds had moved in from the west while Brian was down in the galley, and as he got into the very cold car he wondered what kind of thoughtless, inhumane person he was to shut Dempsey in a car where he could have suffered from heat exhaustion. Dempsey quickly moved in front of the heater to try and get warmer.

During the parting there were a few moments when Brian and Cherokee stood together on the ramp, shaking hands again, Cherokee with his left hand on Brian's shoulder. They presented a good, clear picture of cohesive camaraderie, two men involved in a mission, a purpose. Two separate cameras, blocks apart, operated by two men unknown to each other, caught that pose, that handshake, that camaraderie. One camera was operated by Eric Stewart about a block to the west. He knew now that Cherokee would be going out on a trip Monday. There were things he could do now, before Cherokee left, but he had made the judgment call to wait. What he had to do must be done, but there was no urgency. He had decided that by waiting he might make his mission have even more meaning, especially after buying a beer the night before for a very drunk Cherokee.

They had talked for a while, never exchanging names, two people in a bar trying to impress each other. Stewart called it playing "plane." There are people who, on a plane trip, talking to the person next to them, whom they'll never see again, seize this opportunity of a life time. They can for a few hours, be anything they want to be, a movie star, a brain surgeon, Barbra Streisand's manicurist, or maybe just an elephant trainer. Last night Stewart had been a real estate investor, passing through on his way to Kingston, Jamaica, to meet a friend, a Broadway actress, and they would, after a few days on the beach, fly to London where she was opening in a revival of *Same Time Next Year*. All lies, obviously. Cherokee had chosen to own a fleet of fishing boats here and in Panama City. He was going out Monday, undercover on one of his own boats, trying to see if it were true, as he had been told by reliable sources, that some of his boats were being used to smuggle in drugs. He was working with the knowledge of the DEA and the FBI, and would be in contact with them at times while on the trip. But *they* would not let it be known that they were working together. Lies too, obviously. Well mostly -- or quite a bit -- or *some* of it.

The all-white apartment glowed warmly from the indirect and track lighting and numerous candles. Well-dressed, beautiful people wandered through the rooms, eating, drinking, talking and listening to the background piano being played from the corner of the large dining room. Very much like something out of an old 40's black and white movie. Except that the clothes and hair styles were not quite so severe. And the piano music was not Gershwin -- for which everyone gave unconscious thanks. The piano was -- "funky" could be an appropriate word -- playing quietly hip renditions of tunes by the Beatles, Simon and Garfunkel, Sting and Eric Clapton -- oh, and Randy Newman -- all with inappropriate but interesting touches of Rachmaninoff and Debussy.

The hum of party chatter drowned out the music frequently, but no one really noticed, least of all the piano player. Beth moved about the rooms, visiting briefly with couples and quartets, asking if they had everything they needed.

"There's plenty of food and lots of liquor," she'd smile as she moved past the guests. "Don't be shy. He who holds back stays hungry -- and sober." Dressed in solid white herself, she managed, through her vivacity, not to blend into the background. Not at all. Steve, the boyfriend, stood off to the side, chatting with a complete stranger, not really listening to what the stranger was saying as he watched Beth move through the crowd.

Brian and Susannah smiled and talked to complete strangers of their own, looking, they would have been pleased to know, much like Ali and Ryan, right out of *Love Story*. Occasionally Susannah's infectious laugh could be heard above the drone and buzz, that wonderful hearty laugh of sincere attention that caused some to turn their heads and smile, perhaps even laugh along with her contagious laughter.

When Susannah and Beth first met, each knew how the other felt about Brian -- but there was no indication that either knew anything. Susannah was sure of her hold; Beth was sure of her power to win. Neither thought of the other as a threat. Brian, knew what they both knew and decided the smartest thing to say is something else.

Early in the evening, Beth had introduced Brian and Susannah to Steve Briggs. Beth was playing her "dippy blonde" role, which was essentially a lie, since she was capable of keeping up with anybody intellectually. She had found out long ago that she could go farther by pretending to be "not too smart" rather than by letting anyone know she was capable of a completed thought.

"Brian. Susannah. I'd like you to meet my friend Steve. Steve, this is my Western Civ. professor-to-be. And his wife." A small afterthought there, Susannah noticed.

Steve shook Brian's hand, smiling his sun-tanned smile. "Brian. Susannah. Delighted to meet you."

Susannah immediately caught the significance of the white, untanned skin around the base of his left-hand ring finger.

"What do you teach, Brian?" asked Steve. He oozed rich, beach-boy charm.

"Western Civilization," smiled Brian. "When people stay awake."

"I'm sure they do," answered Steve. "I've heard a lot about you from Beth. And what about you, Susannah?" His charm shifted to her. "What do you do?"

"I work in a bank. They call me an assistant manager, but I'm really just a glorified coffee-getter. What do you do, Steve?"

"I have a construction company. Sort of in competition with Beth's father." He smiled at Beth as if there might be a private joke there. "He wouldn't really approve of Beth dating his competition."

Two thoughts flashed through Susannah's mind immediately: 1) Beth's father probably wouldn't approve of her dating a married man, and 2) "wouldn't approve" implied that her father didn't know about this arrangement. Probably for very good reason. During all this great detective work Susannah still maintained her beautiful smile, and that occasional infectious laugh.

Steve managed to break away from Susannah's magnetism and look back to Brian. "You've already become quite a legend on campus. The Renaissance man, they call you."

"Oh, why did you have to bring that up?" smiled Susannah. "You have no idea how hard it is to live with someone so perfect, so completely well-rounded. Intellectually, that is."

"I'm sure the title is well-deserved," said Steve.

"Modestly forbids me to comment," smiled Brian.

"Modesty may forbid comment," teased Susannah, "but you love every minute of it. And you know it." She turned to Steve and Beth. "No one's brought it up in the last two or three days. You may just have saved an ego from being dashed."

"A catholic mind I think is the phrase," smiled Steve. Brian was truly impressed. And flattered.

"You don't know the half of it," smiled Susannah. "He's not only envious of every person on the cover of *Time* magazine; he wants to *be* every person on the cover of *Time*. From scientist to athlete to explorer."

"Not a petty ambition," smiled Steve.

Stewart, or Henderson, watched the movements of the four from his position close to the piano. He was not dressed for the occasion. He had not known he would be at this party. He had followed Brian and Susannah over from Carrabelle, came into the apartment building behind them. When he walked down the hall by Beth's apartment, some of the partyers in the hall started moving back into the apartment. Assuming that Stewart was coming to the party, they ushered him in. Once inside he was less noticeable than he had been in the hall. He knew the one person at the party from his past would never be able to recognize him because of the plastic surgery done on his face after the land mine in Colombia. At one point Beth passed him and urged him to have more to eat and drink. She patted him on the shoulder as she pointed to the bar and buffet.

On the trip over, Stewart realized he was not the only one following Brian and Susannah. The maroon Dodge Dart made the same trip. Stewart became aware of the man in the Dart a few days before. He made it his business to find out who the man was and why he was involved in the triangle developing between Brian, Beth and Cherokee -- or the quartet, if he added Susannah.

Stewart was not a person to relax or let his guard down. Even with a drink in hand and one under his belt, he was aware, vigilant, ready. He could not allow himself ever to become vulnerable. Being vulnerable could cost him his life. It was therefore necessary that he really like his job -- since he was never away from it. Not in his office in Atlanta, not at home with his wife, not when he slept, or even when he was playing with his son Simon.

Watching all the beautiful people, Stewart was as inconspicuous as Beth's white furniture against her white walls. There was really no reason for him to hide from anyone in the room -- except one. He made it a point to stay unseen by the man called Brian Withers -- the Renaissance man.

Looking out across the mass of laughing, talking partyers, Stewart was not surprised to see the man from the maroon Dodge Dart come into the room, much in the same manner as he, Stewart, had done, surrounded by people who had drifted out into the hall. Stewart watched to see how long it would be before the perfect hostess would show the man to the bar and buffet.

Less than five minutes. She seemed to have a knack for spotting people without a drink or a buffet plate. She stood beside the man, smiling, pointing toward the bar and food in the dining room. Stewart watched as the man made his way to the refreshments, glancing now and then toward Brian and Susannah whom he spotted within seconds after entering the room. The man from the maroon Dart was even more inappropriately dressed than Stewart, but then Stewart could excuse that. The man made far less than he did. Stewart had already made it his business to find out that the man was good, but no match for him.

The man was not aware of Stewart, involvement, of that Stewart was sure. Wouldn't it be ironic if they were to wind up talking to one another? Casual party banter. Stewart thought he would make it a point to try and work it out.

Stewart looked about the room, at Beth, at Brian, at Susannah, at the man -- at Steve, the man Beth was dating at the time. The circle was getting tighter, certainly closer. The only one lacking in this immediate circle was the common denominator -- Cherokee. But chances were they would all never be together. Even the chances of this many of them being together were very slim. One of them, two of them would always have to be absent. If they were all together at one time, it might be like two parallel universes meeting, cancelling one another and leaving -- nothing.

Stewart smiled at what he knew. The man across the room, from the maroon Dart, could not know it all. Completely unaware of any of it were Brian, Susannah, and Beth. And from the time Stewart became aware of the man from the maroon Dart, and his purpose, Stewart decided to delay his own purpose, just to see how the game was going to play. He had it within his power to stop the whole plan at any given moment. *He* could choose. But just knowing as much as he did, sitting back and watching was about as close as he would ever come to having a vacation. He was enjoying the show that was taking place before him. But still he had to stop it at some time. It was mandatory. It was his purpose. He was being paid handsomely to do just that. Stop it.

Stewart could not keep from smiling, probably for the first time in years, as he watched the main characters move about the room right before his eyes. Never would he have imagined this turn of events. His smile became a light chuckle.

Later as he and the man from the maroon Dart exchanged idle banter by the piano, Stewart thought of the song, "Send in the Clowns." from *A Little Night Music*. The clowns were all here.

The boat rolled up and down with the giant swells that moved across the wide and threatening Gulf of Mexico. The

Middle Ground is not only noted for its copious numbers of grouper and red snapper (though fast dwindling). It is also less turbulent and rough than the surrounding waters, because it is shallower. If the waves were this big here on the Middle Ground, Cherokee wondered what it must be like on the waters off the Middle Ground.

He took six fish off the line he just brought in, baited the eight hooks again and dropped the line back in the water. He had been going from one line to another since daylight. Now he was beginning to tire. He took a sip of the black coffee he had in a plastic bottle wedged in some tight ropes to keep it from rolling overboard. He looked in a 360-degree turn, studying the horizon. No land. No birds. Only swelling waters and the boat -- which seemed to become smaller every day. Off to the west, dark thunderheads moved toward the boat, an ominous indication of an on-coming cold front, even if he hadn't listened to the NOAA Weather Forecast, which he had been doing. Also from the dock Travis had kept him posted by marine band radio of the on-coming bad weather.

After two days of rain that the clouds contained, the temperature would drop harshly as the cold front moved over them. Old fishermen always think they can tell how cold the following front will be by the darkness of the clouds bringing in the cold front. It made good conversation and entertained the tourists so much that even most of the fishermen never stopped to realize that it wasn't so. The few who did kept on telling the story anyway.

Like their entertaining story of being able to watch the sun set twice in the same evening. They thought that was a good omen for catching fish. "I've seen the sun set twice." "I saw the sun set twice last night; good fishing today."

An optical illusion to be sure, and one for which no one ever stopped to explain the physical reasons. It was much more exciting to think that some temporary abrogation of the laws of the universe had taken place.

For the sun to "set twice" takes a special combination of meteorological conditions, none miraculous -- but rare. The late afternoon has to be calm and the water completely smooth. The sky to the west usually has a faint suggestion of a mixture of mauve and coral. The reflection of the fading mauve sky is matched exactly by the mirror-smooth water. Where the sky and the water meet normally forming a horizon, on an evening such as this, the two are so perfectly matched that there seems to be no horizon. The sky and water flow together so seamlessly that their meeting cannot be seen. The meeting place, the vanishing point, has become invisible, been erased.

A long thin horizontal cloud has to be just close to the horizon, but above the horizon, not touching it. The long cloud also reflects the same vague mauve that is in the sky and water, so that it, too, becomes invisible. The sun, easily seen with the naked eye on these mauve and coral evenings, a deep orange, not at all blinding to the eye, moves slowly down, "setting" behind the perfectly unseen horizontal cloud. Because the sky, cloud and sea are all the exact same mauve, even to the most educated eye, the sun is surely setting. But strangely enough -- or naturally enough, depending on one's acceptance of the laws of the universe -- a few minutes later the sun emerges below the invisible cloud and gets to sink again below the actual horizon.

The fisherman who has seen this event is sure he has have seen the sun "set twice." He also feels he has become related to the cosmos as never before. But most important of all, he gets to experience for a few minutes, something that becomes an indelible part of him -- a world without a vanishing point.

The vanishing point is so taken for granted that no one ever really notices its importance -- until it's gone -- which it never can really be -- and in no other place does it occur accept on the water on an evening such as this. In a world without a vanishing point, a man feels impending descent, falling off the edge of the world. He feels the dizziness and giddiness of the last few seconds of time and stability, and suddenly he hopes to God there is a God -- because he's there -- on the precipice at the edge of the world.

Cherokee took his plastic bottle of coffee and grappled his way along the rising and falling gunwales of the rolling boat.

Now there was less sun as the western bank of storm clouds moved closer. He took a long look into the wind before going below.

"Getting rough," said The Swede.

"Yeah," said Cherokee, "not even good enough for going back to the hill in."

"I was thinking the same thing. Ride it out. Hell, we've fished in the rain before."

Cherokee looked around the bunk room. "Where's Blackie?"

"He's still on deck. You didn't see him?"

"Naw. I guess I was too busy looking at the clouds."

Then he thought he had better check. He stuck his head up out of the galley. Blackie was working some lines in the left stern, earphones on, tuned surely to some country music station, preferably one with lots of Garth Brooks and Clint Black. Blackie happened to turn his head just as Cherokee looked out at him. A broad smile broke across his face, and he waved, not just a hand but a whole arm, so generous was his greeting. Cherokee waved back through the spray that was starting to blow across the deck, then turned back to the galley and bunk room.

"Happy as a kid," he said to The Swede. "Want some?" He held up the coffee pot after pouring himself some.

"Sure. Thanks." The Swede passed over his large enamel cup, closed his copy of *Zen and the Art of Motorcycle Maintenance*.

Cherokee half-filled the enamel cup, passed it back and then sat on the edge of his own bunk.

"What do you think about him?" he asked.

"It could work."

They both knew they were not talking about Blackie. There was no confusion here.

"He's got a killer of a wife."

"An expected baby."

"And a need for more money."

"That's always a good sign."

They were quiet for a few moments, their eyes locked on each other.

"The teacher thing is sweet." The Swede said. "Nobody would expect."

"Least of all, himself," smiled Cherokee

"He's no dummy."

"Yeah, but there are ways of disguising things."

"I don't get you."

"I'm still working on it. But it can be done. I'll tell you about it when it gels."

"Well," smiled The Swede, "if anybody can get it done, you can." He reached over and playfully slapped Cherokee on the cheek.

Cherokee slapped him back lightly, smiling. "It's a 'me' thing. You had to be there."

The Swede lay bank on his bunk. opened his book. "Well, like I said. My money's on you. You ain't done bad by me so far."

"You're safe in the hands of Cherokee," he smiled.

"You really think he'll do it?" asked The Swede.

"Trust me."

Out over the snow sparkling in the morning sun, the private dock pointed across the cold lake. The distant skyline of a cold Chicago rose silhouetted above the surrounding smaller buildings, reaching for a heaven that was not there for her.

Anne Madison sat at the dining room table, staring out through the huge glass wall that framed a picture of most of the grounds on this side of the Madison Estate. Trimmed and manicured to beyond-perfection, even now, covered under fourteen inches of white coldness, the lawn still showed the perfect lines of a perfectly planned palace in an imperfect world.

Anne Madison, even on warm sun-massaging summer days, could feel the coldness of an empty place inside her. Like a swallowed-whole ice-cube, it lay in the pit of her stomach, refusing to melt, even after seven months of freezing pain and ache. It lay cold as the ice on the lake in front of her beyond the frame of two hundred square feet of thermal insulated glass that proved a poor insulation against her emptiness.

Only a woman who has lost a child to the inexorably slammed door of mortality could know that hard and terrible emptiness. It had been a death made even worse by accident rather than a disease, leaving the mother lost in a maze of wondering what if she had done something differently that day. Maybe she should not made him go to school, not have been so hard on him about his geometry grade, or maybe she should have given him the Porsche he had wanted for his sixteenth birthday instead of the TransAm. She found herself wondering why there was no defining name for a woman who has lost a child as there is for a child who has lost his parents, a woman who has lost her husband, a man who has lost his wife. They were all left with the awful but defining terms of orphan, widow, widower. But the ever-grieving childless mother was left to be -- nothing -- no name -- nothing but a person with a part of her own life ripped from her, placing her in a category too horrible to be graced with a name.

She spent much of her time always aware that her child was a part of her in a way no man could ever know. Not even the whole woman could imagine. A human being had lived inside of her for so long that the bond was never recognized to its fullest until it is suddenly and Godlessly broken. She stared out across the snow and frozen lake to the distant and cold silhouettes of such unfeeling things as towering buildings. The cold chrome shinings from the distant moving cars were so far away that only their reflections came across the cold and empty space.

"More coffee, Mrs. Madison?" asked the petite lady in the blue and white uniform.

Silence. No response. Unmoving. The continual stare.

"Mrs. Madison?"

"Yes? What?" She turned calmly as if nothing more would ever be able to startle or touch her again.

"More coffee, ma'am?"

68

"Yes. Please"

She turned back to the snow and ice. The uniformed lady picked up the cup and saucer, filled the cup, and then placed them back on the table.

"Thank you." No emotion. Passionless,

"Yes, ma'am." The maid felt as if she were intruding on some very private moment. She turned and left quietly through the swinging door.

Somewhere off in a distant room, a vacuum cleaner came alive. A few minutes later came the sound of the front door closing, three rooms away. The footsteps were not heard on the thick carpeting or above the distant vacuum cleaner. The man in the black suit and bow tie moved silently across the room carrying a small silver tray containing four letters and a postcard.

"The mail, Mrs. Madison," he said softly.

No response. The motionless stare out through ice and snow.

The man placed the silver tray on the table beside her coffee and then left, going back to some work somewhere in the carpeted, draped, and dustless mansion.

A phone rang somewhere in another room. Only once.

In the snow far off to her right, a man shoveled snow from a bricked walk that led to the glass-covered, heated garden house.

Anne Madison took a sip of the hot, black coffee. She looked at the tray of mail as if it had materialized from nowhere. The corner of a postcard under one of the letters showed a beach-and-water scene. She stared at it, thinking for a moment. White beaches. Warm water. Maybe the Riviera. Would it help at all? Would it be more than superficial?

She took another sip of the coffee. It was hot, steaming, but it did nothing to the ice-cube in the pit of her stomach.

She opened the letter on top. It was a well-concealed bill for fuel oil. Slightly over twelve hundred. Should have gone to her accountant.

She pressed a button hidden under the edge of the table. In less than a minute, the lady in the blue and white uniform came through the swinging door.

"Yes, ma'am?" she asked.

"Ask Mrs. Knight to step in here a moment, please."

"Yes, ma'am," Same two words. Different inflection. This time a statement instead of a question.

The blue-and-white uniform left the room.

A few minutes later a neat, orderly-looking woman in a well-fitting dress-suit came in from another door.

"You wanted me, Mrs. Madison?"

"Yes, Mrs. Knight." She handed the woman the bill, almost as if it were distasteful to her. "Would you see that this bill gets to the accountant. And call the company and see that they know where to send it in future."

"Yes, ma'am." Pause. "Will that be all?"

"Yes. Thank you, Mrs. Knight."

"Thank you, Mrs. Madison."

Mrs. Knight left the room, and Anne Madison picked up the post card, looking at the stock picture of attractive young people walking and playing on a generic beach, all smiling generic smiles. The same picture was used for any one of thousands of coastal towns anywhere in the country. She turned the card over.

"Having a wonderful time. Wish you were here. Ran into a friend of yours here. Will be seeing him again soon. H."

She knew that would be Henderson. Or Stewart. Or one of the many other aliases she had discovered he used. At any rate, they were all the same man. The one who would fix things. And make her life a little more bearable. A small part of her suddenly felt a little less lonely, slightly avenged.

The green pine-covered hills flowed by at eighty miles an hour as Brian and Susannah sped along Interstate Seventy-Five. The towering loblolly pines spread out on both sides, stretching miles before them as they crested a high point on the six-lane heading north. Winding like a great concrete river filled with speeding traffic, the mega-road reached out before them in midday sun, rolling gently over the hill country.

The Interstate had been built out in the country to avoid the congestion of towns and cities, and commerce had flocked to it to form the congestion it sought to avoid. It was now a megacity half a mile wide and two thousand miles long.

Susannah slept on the passenger side, her head on the favorite pillow she took everywhere they went. Brian steered the Z-Car in and out of traffic, always taking pains to stay behind two or three cars that were traveling as fast as he. Once in a while a car or semi passed the little convoy, and he was tempted to take up behind it, but remembered the old adage about safety in numbers. As he drove, his head and left hand moved to the rhythm of Diana Krall's "Peel My a Grape."

He enjoyed speeding along the mega-road, weaving in and out of slower cars, listening to good music while Susannah slept beside him. He felt like her protector, her transporter; Holden Caulfield standing sentinel on the edge of the precipice, keeping the children in the rye from falling over the cliff as they played; Brian Withers, the Catcher in the Rye; G.S. Garp protecting his children from the UnderToad.

Susannah stirred. She was waking. He never felt so protective when she was awake -- but then he had her sunny company.

"Where are we?" she mumbled.

"On a relatively small, but egotistical planet, hurtling through space on a slowly expanding universe."

"In little less existential terms, please."

"Moving up on Exit 66 and Fuel City."

"I need to make a pit stop." Her mouth was still partly in the pillow. "I can last two -- maybe three exits. After that, look for a place to buy oars."

"I was aiming for the buffet at McDonnough."

"Never make it."

"Prepare for landing then. Exit 66 just ahead. Darn. I hate to lose this four-car cover."

"Trust me. It's better this way."

Don McLean's "Vincent" was playing now. Brian envisioned the Van Gogh paintings on the music video. He showed it for his classes when they were studying the impressionists.

The exit came up fast, and the car slowed rapidly. Wheels down. Flaps down. The wide right turn to Fuel City, a small village in itself. Flaps lower. Banking turn. Coming in for a smooth four-point landing.

"We've touched down," he said.

"Bitchin'," she answered, coming upright. "I'll catch you in the restaurant in a few minutes." She opened the door and headed swiftly toward the building, holding her jacket closed against the cold wind. He smiled, watching her imperative gait. God, I love you Zannah.

He filled the tank, then pulled the car away from the pumps before checking the oil, cleaning the windshield, checking the skis on the rack above the car, tightening one of the bunji cords. Then he came inside and handed the man at the control counter his Discover card. After signing the receipt, he went to the men's room, and returned to the food counter. Zannah was sitting on a stool, looking at a menu.

"I thought you'd like some great country ham and fried chicken at McDonnough," he said.

She smiled. "I think I know who really wants the country ham and fried chicken."

"Am I that transparent?"

"Plastic wrap. But some happenin' dude."

"If there is anything I've always wanted, to fulfill my dreams,

got to be some happnin' dude."

"You've achieved your goal." She nudged him playfully with her elbow. Even with her hair not quite its perfect self, she was still beautiful. She started laughing at him, and the contagion of her Dyan Cannon laugh caught him, surrounded him, and he began laughing with her. When they came back to the cold outside, they broke into a run for the car, a run that instantly turned into a playful race.

"Beat you," he said, laughing as she closed the door.

"You parked with your side closer." Smiling. "Cheater."

When the radio came back on, Michael Bolton's "Georgia on my Mind" rushed out of the speakers.

"Music for the occasion," he said. "In the heart of Georgia, what else would you expect?" Then he saw the maroon Dodge Dart in one of the stations across the way. He knew he would not let Zannah know.

The Dart was never far behind them, all the way around I-285, through the snow-covered hills of North Georgia, over the almost impassable road through Balsam Gap at 3600' altitude. The last time Brian saw the Dart was when they pulled into their hotel in Maggie Valley, near the bottom of the slopes.

By Sunday afternoon, after two days and one night of non-stop skiing on the Cattaloochee trails, both Brian and Zannah were ready to leave for a rest at home on Monday morning. He left her to shower and get ready for dinner as he took the car to be filled and check the oil, water, tires and windshield fluid. Just as he was putting the finishing touches on drying the windshield, he looked at the station across the six-lane and saw the maroon Dart. He wasn't surprised. What really had surprised him was that he hadn't seen it in the past forty-eight hours. The driver of the Dart was preparing his car for the long trip back to Carrabelle, just as Brian was doing. For the first time, Brian could see the man clearly. The lights from the overhang highlighted the man with the glasses.

He looked to be around 35 - 40, a little bit stocky, light brown hair, a pleasant face, not at all sinister as Brian had suspected. Most of the times before, the man wore a hat, but now, when it was cold enough to warrant one, he was without it. Once the man looked over, then quickly away as he saw Brian watching him.

After paying for his gas, Brian pulled onto the six-lane, drove two blocks and parked at an intimate little lounge he and Zannah liked. Inside he went to the bar and ordered a run and diet Coke. (These places never had diet Dr. Pepper. He and Zannah learned to curb their strange preference in public. But once in a while he forgot.)

"Sorry," the bartender said. "Sunday. All we can serve is beer. Or wine."

Brian smiled. "Lowenbrau Dry."

On his second sip of beer, the man from the maroon Dart sat at the stool beside him.

"Can we talk?" the man asked.

"I don't see why not," said Brian. "We've been living together the past two weeks."

When the bartender came, the man pointed toward Brian's beer. "The same," he said.

The two men remained quiet until the bartender brought the second beer and the man with the glasses paid for it.

"Could we sit over in one of those booths?" The man nodded toward the side wall.

"Sure," said Brian, getting up and walking to one of the booths in the quiet room.

Only four other people were in the lounge. The soft music in the background was letting Aretha Franklin sing, "The First Time Ever I Saw Your Face." No symbolism, thought Brian.

The two men sat facing one another for a moment. The silence seemed so long that Brian wondered if he was supposed to speak first. He studied the man's face and saw it slowly change from confidence and determination to confusion and slight desperation.

"Speak," said Brian. "You've come 500 miles for this. Go for it."

"God. I thought this would be easier," said the man. "I wish we could start over."

"Too late," said Brian. "Simon says no steps backwards."

"Name's Fordham. Henry Fordham." The man extended his hand. Brian always aware of civilities, shook the man's hand.

"Withers, Brian Withers." He smiled. "But of course you already know that."

"Yeah." Fordham nodded.

"You should," Brian chuckled. "You've been following me for over a week now." Another slight chuckle. "You're awfully persistent. And a little more than obvious."

"I was trying to be a little obvious."

"I hope you're not gay. You've wasted a lot of time if you are."

"I'm not. And the time hasn't been wasted."

"Then what *are* you doing?"

"I'm with the FBI, " said the man, looking as if the words were alien even to him.

"Sure," said Brian. "And I'm an Alaskan bullfighter. You can do better than that."

"But I am." The man seemed to gain back a little confidence, nodding his head in emphasis, blinking his eyes quickly, like a kid begging to be believed. One baby step forward.

"And I do brain surgery in my spare time," said Brian. Go back two giant steps.

"Here, look." The man pulled out his wallet, showing official looking cards. "See? I got the I.D."

"You can get this stuff a hundred places," said Brian, flipping though the I.D.'s. "Most of them advertise in *Soldier of Fortune*."

"I am really. Look at the I.D.'s." The man was slightly agitated. "What would it take to get you to take me seriously?"

"Kill somebody." Brian took a sip of his beer.

"What?" Shock. Surprise.

No sense of humor here, thought Brian.

"Well, at least let me see your piece," smiled Brian. He was beginning to enjoy this now.

"I can't do that. Besides, nobody calls it a 'piece' anymore."

"Weeelll. I don't know ---" Brian was shaking his head pityingly. Suddenly his expression changed, his eyes wide, maybe even -- fear? "What's that?" he asked. He had heard the slight clicks before he felt the piercing points of pain on his shins.

"Razor sharp daggers," said the man. "Concealed in the soles of my shoes. Capable of slicing an artery with only the slightest pressure. Do I have your attention now?"

"Complete and undivided," said Brian. He sat up straight, remembering the daggers concealed in Lotte Lenya's shoes in that James Bond movie. Wicked. "I didn't really know such a thing existed. This is like a bad B movie."

"Now. Really look at those I.D.'s," said the man. "They don't get shown to many people. Most just see this one." A car salesman card. "Or this one." An insurance man's card.

"OK! OK!" Brian studied the I.D.'s, wondering now if he were sitting across from a psycho.

"What do you want with me?" I haven't done anything."

"It's not what you've done or haven't done. It's what we want you to do."

This really IS a bad movie, thought Brian. I've seen some Vincent Price flicks that are more believable than this.

The sharp points of pain were gone now. He had heard another slight click before they left.

"Me? Do what?" He sat straight up, not moving. The beer hadn't been touched since the sharp pain.

"That's what we need to talk about. But you have to believe."

Now Brian felt as if he were at a healing being performed by a minister ordained by mail. He could see the man placing his hands on Brian's head. Heal! Heal! Heal!

"Well, I don't have much choice right now. Do I?"

"God. I was really hoping this was going to be easier." The man shook his head. "I don't want your patronization. I want your cooperation."

Now the man became slightly more believable.

"What could I possibly do for you?"

"You're in a position to be very -- no, extremely helpful -- to the agency right now."

"Explanation, please."

"You'll get to know everything. Later on. If you decide to cooperate."

"Cooperate? You make it sound so -- underhanded."

"All right. 'Help us.' Is that better? But you're close anyway. In my line of work, just about everybody I deal with is underhanded."

He sounded more credible now -- now that Brian was in a position to pay more attention.

"Are you -- your agency -- underhanded?

"Sometimes we have to be. To catch the bad guys. To save lives."

"The ends justifies the means. Is that it?"

"Sometimes." A vague smile, the first. The smile revealed a soft, friendly face.

"Does your wife know about me?" Fordham asked.

"No. But you have been pretty obvious. I had to work at keeping her from knowing you were behind us all the way up here."

"I'll be doing the same going back."

"Why? You know where we're going"

"To see if someone else tries to contact you." He motioned to the bartender for two more beers.

"Contact me for what?"

"Right now, we'd rather you didn't know. Until it becomes necessary."

"But if I don't know, how am I supposed to know if whatever I don't know happens?"

"It may not become necessary. Right now I just needed to meet you. I knew you were aware of me. And I wanted you to know that I knew. I also wanted you to have a vague idea of what was going on."

"Well, you're losing on that point."

The bartender brought over the beers. Fordham paid fast, before Brian could get his money out. There was silence while the bartender took the money and the empty bottles, replacing the used glasses with fresh frosted ones.

77

"I don't have the vaguest idea of what's going on," continued Brian after the bartender left. "I'm clueless. You haven't told me anything I didn't already know. Right?"

"Wrong." smiled Fordham. "Now you know -- " He counted on his fingers for Brian's enlightenment. "(1) I'm not trying to pick you up." He smiled broadly at this revelation. Amused. "(2) Who I am, (3) who I work for, -- if you can bring yourself to believe it, (4) that I not concerned that you know I'm following you, (5) that -- for right now -- it's best your wife Susannah doesn't know -- if indeed she doesn't already, (6) that I -- we -- may ask for your help sometime soon, (7) that there is a purpose to all this -- even if you don't know it right now. Sometimes things that are expected to happen just don't."

Brian was now impressed at the organization of the man's mind. So impressed that he had to say so.

"I'm impressed," said Brian, a sly smile creeping up the corner of his lips. "I'm not sure I believe everything you say, but you say it so confidently that I have to be impressed. You have the makings of a great con man, Fordham."

"And you have the makings of a great Renaissance man, Withers." Fordham smiled. "That's what might make you the perfect man for what we have in mind for you -- what we might have to ask you to do. You like rock music, but also classical. And then, by counterpoint, you like sports, both spectator and participatory. Point: You're interested in Western Civilization and English and American literature. Counterpoint: You work on your own cars and are contemplating a motorcycle. Point: You write erudite articles for scholarly publications that pay only in prestige. Counterpoint: You sail, ski and listen to tapes of sci-fi on your Walkman when you jog. Point: You need more income now that your family is going to become larger in six months. Counterpoint: You contemplate earning extra money be working at -- of all things -- weighing fish at a fish house."

Brian's mouth fell open slightly, a look for which he chided his students. A slack jaw and an open mouth, he told his class, can make you look so stupid that it's almost irresistible not to call on you.

"How do you know all that?" he asked. "Not that it's an insult to be called a Renaissance man. But that stuff about the baby? What I listen to when I'm jogging? The job on the dock?"

"Now, you can be truly impressed. The Renaissance man out-foxed by the con-man." He smiled. Score one for the FBI.

"Awesome," smiled Brian. "You know too much."

"It's my job," smiled Fordham

Maybe it is, thought Brian. Maybe it really is.

The darkness of the night, the loss of electricity, enhanced the crackling glow of the strobing lightening -- followed by rolling, rumbling, ominous and long-lasting thunder. The only sound more ominous than December thunder is January thunder. Both have a longevity and loudness that can't be equaled in summer storms. Or maybe just the irony of the out-of-season sound makes it seem so. Thunder and lightening do not belong in the winter. They are as spring and summer as flowers, nesting birds and long hot days. The anachronism of thunder in winter can be frightening by its mere unexpectancy, like God going into Hell -- Orpheus descending.

The flashes of lightening out across the Gulf lit up the Earth from above and below. From the twelfth floor condo, looking through the sliding glass doors and glass walls opened onto the balcony. The lightening was ubiquitous, coming from all directions at once, out of the sky, up from the water, a gigantic flashbulb aimed at the naked bodies across the bed. It flashed on the mating of two magnificent, beautiful bodies entwined in the consummate moment of uncontrolled passion, the coming together of a man and a woman that attempted to emulate the ecstasy of the rolling winter thunder.

The moment reached and held as long as possible, the moment passed, the moment remembered, Beth looked up at the almost constant lightening above her, so constant she could watch the movement of the low, swirling, twisting clouds. Simultaneously Steve looked down to the tossing turbulent water crashing onto the beach, lit by flash after flash, accompanied by constant roaring thunder. Truly a night created for the enjoyment of the strong, the unafraid, no night for the weak.

The two lay in one anther's arms, silently, looking out at the majestic show before them. Finally, after propping on his elbows as long as he could, Steve dropped his head onto the pillow, moaning slightly.

"That was fantastic," he said, his neck and shoulders aching slightly from arching his back so long to watch the thunderstorm.

"I kind of thought so, too," said Beth. "All the visual effects probably had a lot to do with it."

"You're marvelous, you know that?" His voice was raspy from physical exhaustion.

"Well, I know. But it's still nice to hear somebody say it once in a while." He could see her teasing smile in the lightening.

He snuggled his nose and mouth into her neck, kissing her gently. She rubbed his back and felt the rise of enjoyment from his lips and tongue along her neck. The pleasures of the night were stirring again, and the pulse of passion was slowly rising to another crescendo. But unromantically enough Beth suddenly developed a muscle cramp in the right calf.

"Oh, damn." She rose quickly, throwing Steve off to the side, causing him almost to fall onto the floor. "Damn! Damn!" she said, jumping to the floor and massaging her right calf. "Oooo," she moaned.

Steve rolled into the pillow again, knowing to leave her alone. Many times before in the midst of their love-making, Beth exhibited her low level of potassium in the throws of turbulent passion.

"This needs to go into the text-book of Unique Positions in Sex," he laughed. "The Whooping Crane Position."

"The Hopping Crane," she said, still jumping around on her right leg, still rubbing the force of the cramp away.

"Or maybe the Screaming Stork," he said. "The Cursing Crane."

"I'm not so sure I like that stork reference, considering what storks are most associated with."

"Certainly nowhere near the Missionary Position," he said.

She was quiet for a moment, wishing the pain away.

"Is it any better?" Steve asked. "Can I do anything?"

He asked out of politeness only. She always had to rub it out herself. Couldn't stand anyone else's touch when it happened. Had to be left alone until it went away.

"No. Thanks," she answered. "It's almost gone."

She continued to massage the calf, moaning just audibly. As the pain subsided she sat on the edge of the bed, still rubbing the calf. He placed his hand on her bare hip and rubbed it tenderly.

"You ready for something to eat?" she asked. "Want me to start dinner?

"Can't," he answered. "No electricity, remember?"

"Oh, yeah. Right." Then. "Are you hungry? We could go out."

"Not really," he answered. "You?"

"I guess not. I would like a little something though. Maybe a glass of milk."

"Here. Take the flashlight." He reached in the night table beside the bed and handed her a large camping flashlight.

Taking it from him, she turned it on. Blinding light flooded the room.

"Out, out, damn spot," he said. "Out I say."

She turned the light off immediately. "'Fie, my lord,'" she quoted. "'A soldier and afeared?' You want anything?"

"I'd really like a glass of water," he said. "Since you asked. In fact much water. That was a workout."

"Coming up," she said. "Can you tell how far up the beach the electricity is out?"

"At least to Captain Anderson's. Maybe even to the bridge. You can see the reflection of lights from downtown though."

"Too far to drive for a tuna melt," she said from the hall. "Six miles is too far for a lot of things."

81

"Peanut butter and jelly in the cabinet," he said from the bed. "Oh, there's some luncheon meat in the fridge. And mayo. You'll find something. I have faith in you."

"I really would like a good steak. Sex always makes me hungry. And a baked potato -- and some sautéed mushrooms."

"You like baked potatoes and mushrooms with your sex?" he asked, still watching the lightening display from the bed. "Really kinky. Show me that one sometime. Sounds more interesting than the Screaming Crane."

"I found something to eat," she said, back at the bedroom door, shining the flashlight briefly toward Steve, then quickly up to the ceiling. "A pre-made Hoagie all wrapped and ready. Looks like something you got for lunch and didn't get around to eating. Want some?" she asked. "I'll split it with you."

"No, thanks," he answered. "You go ahead. That's from about a month ago."

"Uugh." She spit out what was in her mouth onto the plate. "What do you do that for? You could kill somebody."

"That's what it's for. If anyone breaks in, they're bound to eat it. Paybacks are hell."

"Also detrimental to the health of your main squeeze. Oh, well. Back to the drawing board." The light moved off down the hall.

"What time is it?" he called from the bed, still surrounded by lightening and thunder.

"The clock on the sink say five o'clock. You take it from there."

"Somehow I have the feeling it's electric. The one on the dining room wall in battery. I think."

"How's 9:52 sound to you?"

"A little more realistic. I'll go with that one." He rolled over on his stomach and picked up the binoculars from the floor beside the bed.

The horizon was hard to find tonight -- so dark -- little difference in color between the sky and the water. When his eyes became able to distinguish the breaking point, he scanned across the finely shaded line. One shrimp boat far, far out was moving eastward, weathering the storm. In the flashes of lightening, the boat appeared stark white, strobed into a flat line drawing, unreal, but perceptibly moving. Another one closer in was moving westward, being tossed more than the other, fighting its way into the wind. Still a third, almost directly in front of him, farther out than the others, appeared to be headed straight in. The port and starboard lights let him know which way it was moving.

Just then the phone rang.

"Don't answer that," he called to the kitchen.

"What do you think? I'm dumb or something? I know better."

"Smart girl," he said. "An 'A' for the day."

He reached over and picked up the phone on the night table. "Hello."

"What are you doing out there in the dark?" A smiling woman's voice. "You can't be working, with no electricity."

"As a matter of fact I am," he answered. "We've got those hurricane lamps out here. Remember?

"Yes. But I detect the distant sound of sleep in your voice."

"Hoisted on my own petard," he chuckled. You've caught me. But I don't think I was sleeping long. What time is it?"

"Five 'til ten," she answered.

"Oh, well. I haven't been asleep more than ten minutes or so. How are the kids?"

"Fine. We ate supper without you."

"Smart move. Any calls?"

"A & L Electrical Company. But they're going to call your office tomorrow. About the bid on the job in Dothan."

"I'll be home in about half an hour. Or however long traffic holds me up."

"O.K. See you."

"Love you."

"You too."

Click.

"She sends you her love," he called out to Beth.

"Yeah. Right. Give her mine also."

"Hey?" he called out to her.

"What?" she answered.

"Would you bring -- oh, never mind. I can get it."

"What? I can handle it. Trust me."

He was already in the kitchen beside her, reaching under the sink. He pulled out a hurricane lamps and lit it with matches from one of the drawers.

"There," he said, standing beside her with a towel wrapped around him. "Isn't that better?"

"Much," she smiled. I'm making sandwiches out of something that looks like olive loaf. Is it safe?"

"Olive loaf?" he wondered out loud. "Oh, yeah. Only a week old. Should stay down." He picked up the flashlight and left the kitchen.

"What are you going to do? With the flashlight, I mean?"

"Take a shower," he called back.

"I don't think so," she answered.

"What's the problem?"

"No water. Pumps aren't working. Or I would have brought that water you wanted."

"I wonder what a Pepsi spitz bath would be like?"

"Pretty sticky, I imagine. But it would taste good to lick off of you later on."

Back in the bedroom, he looked again out to the boat that was heading toward shore. Again it took a while to get his eyes adjusted to the dark horizon and the dim lights. There they were; port and starboard lights. Or really starboard and port, if you read from left to right. Coming in. Just as his eyes found the boat, a strong beam of light shot out from it, hazy through the driving rain, Then it went off. Then on again twice. Then blackness.

Steve looked at his wrist where his watch would be if he could see. With the right index finger he pushed a button on the Indiglo watch. The dial lit up well, illuminating the digital figures. Ten o'clock.

He took the powerful flashlight, put it directly against the glass so there would be no reflection in the room. Then he pressed the button. On. A few seconds. Off. On. Off. On, off. Stillness. As he watched the lightening and water through the binoculars, the in-coming boat turned on its light again. For about three seconds. Then off again. Steve, the light still pressed against the window, turned it on three times. On, off. On, off. On, off.

"What are you doing, goofy?" laughed Beth suddenly, from the bedroom door, balancing a plate of sandwiches in one hand, the hurricane lamp in the other.

"Just playing," Steve answered, turning to her smiling. "Sending secret signals to an off-shore ship."

"You fool," she laughed again. "Here have some sandwiches."

"Ummm. Looks good." He took two sandwich halves and bit into one. "Great cook."

"You should see what I can do with a loaf of rye." She sat on the edge of the bed, eating, looking out at the storm.

He placed his hand on her back tenderly, rubbing her. Then he turned to the phone on his side of the bed, picked it up, and punched in a number. Beth continued to eat slowly, staring out at the rain and lightening over the water. The thunder still rolled across the sky and sea, a little softer now.

Steve listened to the phone and heard three rings. Then the other end was picked up. A radio in the background was playing country music.

"O.K.?" a voice asked.

"O.K.," answered Steve and hung up.

"What is that all about?" asked Beth. "'O.K.?' That's what you say when somebody answers the phone?"

"Nobody answered the phone, babe," he said, tugging at her sheet playfully. "It was a machine. I didn't feel like leaving a message, so I just hung up on it. O.K.?"

"O.K.," smiled Beth. "You told off that machine."

"Hurry up and finish eating," he said, swallowing his last bite of sandwich. "And then turn the light out. This is the greatest night in the world for lying in the dark -- and watching the storm."

"And I do like the way you like to watch a storm." She blew into the chimney of the hurricane lamp, and the room went dark.

Surrounded by glass that let in the light of the storm, they stared out at the rain and Gulf a few minutes. High above the surf, the view from the twelfth floor gave them the view of eagles. The rain blew past them in sheets, driven by wind that howled around the corners of the building, sweeping across the balconies with a cacophony of moans and sighs. Far out on the dark horizon, three boats moved in the treacherous waters, one headed toward the shore, a shore that had no docks or fish houses, a shore lined with high-rise hotels and condos, all darkened by the power outage. The night truly was not one for the meek.

He knew he would be late for the meeting. But they would wait. And it would be worth it.

Eric Stewart sat in his office looking out over the north of Atlanta, I-285 and I-85 in the distance. The warm office with the northern exposure did not deceive him into believing the weather outside was anything but bitterly cold. The bare trees in the distance, blowing in the early February sun gave a hint of the biting chill. Cold mid-winter days always look cold, even when the sun is bright, the ground is bare of snow, and you're sitting in a warm room looking out at the sunny day. There's a feeling that filters through the warmth to let you know the looks are deceptive. Cold has a look about it that can't be hidden, even when it's bright and sunny.

Stewart looked through the pictures on his desk, many, many pictures, some covering broad expanses, some zoomed in so tight that it seemed the camera was within two feet of the face it had frozen in time. The pictures were divided into categories, sorted by some design known only to Stewart.

He picked up one of the pictures, studied it carefully, even looked at it through a magnifying glass. He placed it back in the same stack, then turned to another stack, took the third picture from the top, examined it carefully through the magnifying glass and replaced it in the same stack, but now it was the fifth picture down.

He looked up from the photos, stared out the window a moment, watching the traffic on I-285, then turned to the framed picture on the shelf across the room. He was in the picture, smiling, handsome, sedate. Next to him was Audrey, beautiful, beguiling, showing the charm that had attracted him to her fourteen years ago, his senior year at Northwestern. Next to her was Simon, not quite six, even though they called it "Simon's sixth birthday picture." It was taken two weeks before his sixth birthday party, the party Eric had to miss -- because he had to fly to Tallahassee that afternoon.

Simon was going to be as handsome as his father, as charming and comforting as his mother. It showed in his face -- the happy face of a child who was loved. The trusting, smiling eyes looked out at Eric across the room.

He picked up the phone, punched in his home phone number and listened to five rings on the other end.

"Hello." The voice of a child. Unafraid. Certain.

"Hi, Simon." Eric's voice was softer than when he spoke to anyone else -- except Audrey.

"Dad!" Happiness. Joy. Excitement. Love. "Where are you?"

"I'm at the office. Where are you?"

The boy giggled. "I'm home. You called here." Another laugh.

"You are? What are you doing?"

"Playing."

"Playing? Outside?"

"No." Simon laughed. "It's freezing outside."

"You play outside when it's snowing. It's colder then than now."

"Yeah, but it's more fun in the snow."

"What are you playing?" Eric's voice sounded like love vocalized.

"Nintendo."

They talked about three minutes of things interesting to only a child. Eric made him laugh, and he laughed himself from the glee in the child's voice.

"You coming home soon?" asked Simon.

"In a few hours."

"Will you be here in time for supper?"

"Sure. Will you be there?"

Simon giggled. "Of course."

"Well, good. Then we'll have supper together. O.K.?"

"O.K." Pause. "You want to talk to mom?"

"No."

"You sure?"

"No. Just you. I just called to talk to you."

"O.K. But I got to go now. Billy's waiting on me."

"Well. I guess that's important too. See you at supper. O.K.?"

"O.K. 'Bye, dad."

"'Bye, Simon."

"Oh. Dad. Dad."

"Yes?"

"I love you too. 'Bye."

"Well, I'm glad. 'Bye, Simon." Simon didn't hear what his dad had said. He hung up after his last sentence.

Eric hung up the phone and kept his hand on it as he stared out the window toward Buckhead. If he kept his hand on the phone he could hold on to the connection, the tie, the bond between himself and Simon. But then he had to break the connection and get back to work.

Looking once more briefly at the picture across the room, "Simon's Sixth Birthday Picture," he released his son and turned back to the pictures on his desk. One stack contained pictures of Cherokee, easily the largest stack. The next two stacks were about even in height, one of the Swede, one of Steve Briggs. Off to the side were smaller stacks of Brian, Beth, Susannah. One stack with only six shots in it were pictures of a man Eric had seen Cherokee talking to in Panama City. On three different occasions.

After studying the pictures a few more minutes, he selected the top picture from each stack and tacked them to a bulletin board in a very neat, straight order. Then he wrote in neat, precise printing on the bottom of each picture: Cherokee (William Rucker), The Swede, Steve Briggs, Brian Withers, Beth Simpson, Susannah Withers, and under the last picture of the man with the handsome white beard, "????????"

He stepped back from the pictures and looked at them. A smile slowly crossed his face. He could have been finished with this job long before now if it hadn't been for his curiosity and sense of humor -- or, his *curious* sense of humor, he thought. He was ready to close it when two things had happened. The FBI man showed up. And Cherokee got in touch with Brian Withers.

Brian Withers. The Renaissance man. The man who liked Rachmaninoff. *Rhapsody on a Theme by Paganini.* "The Eighteenth Variation." He didn't belong in this *menage.* He was apart from the rest. Of that Stewart was sure.

Now the operation was like a game to Stewart, a big board game where the pieces moved on their own without any help from him or anyone else. Now, when things were slow in the office or on other assignments, he would fly down for a few days to see how the game was progressing, following the characters back and forth between Carrabelle and Panama City. He had even started on another new case just to let this particular one ferment, age and develop a better vintage. Besides, if he had closed it out when he first had the chance, he wouldn't have known about the two new ones, the un-named man and Brian Withers.

The dark knight in armor of mail came riding alone up the dusty road leading to the castle. His horse had a shield of mail down its nose, along each side on the head and covering both sides of its body. Judging from the amount of flowers and greenery in the background and in the sides of the dusty road, the mail had to be unbearably hot.

The knight pulled back on the reins, bringing the steed to a halt in a whirlwind of dust. Looking cautiously, studiously at the castle, the knight removed his helmet. He was sweating profusely in the hot sun-baked coat of armor. He looked from one side of the castle to the other, seeing no signs of life. Deserted. His cold, pale blue eyes turned to look carefully through the woods on either side. Anyone had hidden there? Waiting in ambush?

Holding the helmet under his arm, he approached the moat. As he came closer he saw that the drawbridge was down, leaving the castle open to intruders, bare, the bridge spanning the moat in a silent welcome. His eyes narrowed in suspicion, and his movements became quicker, more alert. Still no signs of life.

He hoisted his banner, the pennant proclaiming the House of Hohenzollern. The Hohenzollerns and the de' Medici's were friendly, close, allies in this section of Austria at this time. And a de' Medici castle, deserted, was an incredible sight. The de' Medici's did not lose battles here. Certainly not in their own castle. Oddly, the de' Medici banners waved in the silence, high above the turrets, ragged, untended.

How could this be? A gothic castle this size -- unoccupied? Unmanned? Open for any intruder, any stray beggar or witch who wondered by. Any peasant family in the area could enter and take away the valuables, tapestries, jewels, foods, windows. If they hadn't already.

Now he saw that the houses and sheds of the burgers huddled around the outside of the high stone walls of the castle were also deserted. There were no merchants in the shops built in the shadows of the castle walls. Some buildings even used the castle wall as their own back wall.

The carnage must have been great. He had never seen such a large castle and its supporting burgers so completely deserted, much less one belonging to the House of de' Medici.

"Ho," he called into the vacuum from the entrance. "Sir Albrich from the House of Hohenzollern approaches."

Silence greeted him, sounding even more quiet after his call.

"In the name of King Otto, I beg entrance and refuge."

The castle was so quiet and void of life that his voice left a small, vibrating echo. Not even dogs barked at his greeting.

"Is anyone here?"

He placed his helmet back on his head and began a slow, cautious entrance across the still, reflecting moat. The horse's steps clattered out on the wooden drawbridge, breaking the still, soft silence.

"We'll have to stop here," said Brian, turning off the VCR. "But one thing we want to make sure of. We don't want to think of the Dark Ages as a time of ignorance and stupidity. The Medieval Period is often referred to as the Dark Ages -- and of course -- as we noted earlier -- the names we give to periods and eras are given in retrospect. No one living in that time referred to the period as Medieval or The Dark Ages. It couldn't be 'Medieval,' because to them, it wasn't in the middle of anything; it was their 'present,' their 'now.' And no one is going to call his own time the 'Dark Ages' with all the connotations of evil and ignorance.

"But it was not a period of evil, ignorance, and stupidity -- especially by its own standards. And remember, we want to avoid ethnocentrism.

"We refer to it as 'The Medieval Period' only because it is in a space between two periods of great learning and knowledge, the Greek and Roman Empires before it, and the Renaissance after it. We refer to it as "The Dark Ages' only because by comparison it was not as bright with knowledge and learning as the Greek and Roman Empires and the time of the Renaissance. Before and after the Dark Ages were two such outstanding periods of knowledge, thought, and discovery, that it is considered 'Dark' only by comparison, not by fact.

"The Greek and Roman Empires." He held his left hand out as if holding them in awe and respect. "And the Renaissance." His right hand now held the period of the rebirth of knowledge.

"We think of ourselves as very intelligent and learned. But suppose --- in a hundred -- two hundred years, there is a burst of discoveries, new insights, new findings, space explorations undreamed of now. Then -- a thousand years from now, people

91

will be sitting in Western Civilization classes referring to the 'Fountain Age' of the 22nd century burst of knowledge, and to the time we live in as the 'Second Dark Age,' or 'The Age of Stupidity.' But we don't want to have them think of us as stupid and ignorant. And indeed, we are not. But they will be referring to us as this 'Second Dark Age' between the Renaissance and the 'Fountain Age.'"

He surveyed the room quickly. "Were people of the Dark Age stupid and ignorant?"

Most heads shook, 'no.' A few "No's" were vocalized.

"Good, he said. "We certainly don't want to stereotype all the people living between 475 and 1400 -- the Quatrocento , Do we? That's almost a millennium -- a lot of stupid people over the dam. And don't forget --- we're all descendants of most of them. Remember?"

His voice changed abruptly as he saw it was 9:25.

"Sorry we ran over. I'll make it up to you next week by keeping you only five minutes overtime.

"Read -- and think about -- the next two chapters. I don't know the numbers. On the rise of the feudal system and the manorial estates -- and the chapter on the rise of Charlemagne and the Holy Roman Empire. You'll find murder, greed, suicide, treachery and incest -- everything we hold dear in a good movie -- or that afternoon soap opera. Have fun with it. Enjoy it. Make fun of them. Find something to laugh at. Now, get out of here. Go, go, go."

He ended many of his classes with the same last few sentences concerning greed and incest, having fun with it. The class had come to feel they weren't actually dismissed until that part came. The good part. Like Liberace closing with, "I'll be Seeing You," or Bob Hope with, "Thanks for the Memory."

The class was moving toward the doors -- except for the few who always stayed to ask questions or to add to the topics covered. Brian had been able to add many pieces of interesting trivia to his lectures by stories he got from students -- after he verified them of course. And he noticed that good trivia kept many students interested in the main events, like a good spice on a piece of bland meat. Among the lingerers always was Mrs. Simpson. She usually had at least two questions, and always missed at least two names in her notes on the lecture. But now he viewed her differently since he had come to know her dynamite-eyed daughter.

During the last five minutes of overtime, Brian noticed Beth sitting in the back of the class. He didn't see her enter, but she was coming to the endings of his night classes more frequently. Now she was moving forward through the outward- moving crowd.

"What was the other name of the banking family -- besides the de' Medici's?" someone asked.

"Don't make me say that again," said Brian, smiling. "The Fuggers. You just wanted to hear that said in a classroom again, didn't you?"

"Any editorial comment on that?" asked another man.

"Only that the name is appropriate for most bankers, right?"

"Who did you say was the French king on the King's Crusade with Richard the Lionhearted?"

"Philip II. And it's Richard the Lionheart, if you want to be really proper. Not 'Lionhearted.'"

"And they were lovers, didn't you say?"

"I'm not one to gossip about the private affairs of others, but that's what James Goldman tells us in *The Lion in Winter*. I didn't start that rumor."

"And who was the Muslim who worked with Richard to bring about the treaty making Jerusalem an open city?"

"Saladin," Brian answered.

"Did he and Richard have something going?" asked a young woman.

Brian smiled devilishly. "I'm not going to say anything about that. It's not mentioned in anything I've read." His smile broadened. "But it sure had been something unthinkable until the two of them met -- considering the amount of carnage both had caused. But remember what was the accepted lifestyle among the Janissaries -- the Turkish army. O.K., guys. Get out of here. I've got a wife waiting at home for me who hasn't seem me since yesterday morning."

"That's what you get for being such a good teacher," said Beth, next to him now. The other students were beginning to leave with the exception of Beth's mother.

"Were you looking for me, dear?" Mrs. Simpson asked Beth.

"Actually I was going to try and talk Brian into going for a drink -- but then he started on that pitiful wife routine," she smiled.

"And it's true," smiled Brian. "The woman's going to leave me if I don't start spending more time with her."

"That's all right," teased Beth. "I'll take her place in a minute. You won't go wanting. I promise."

"Why, Beth," laughed her mother. "Don't be so forward. Men like the shy, demure type more. Especially the married ones."

"I wish I'd met this man ten years ago," smiled Beth. "Before he ever met that pretty wench at F.S.U."

"You mean when you were twelve and I was twenty-one?" laughed Brian. "I'm sure your mother would have enjoyed watching that match. Besides," smiled Brian, "I'm not so sure that I would have been too interested in a twelve-year-old -- even considering how well she turned out."

"I think you've been turned down, dear," said Mrs. Simpson.

"No chance of a drink then?" asked Beth.

"Zannah's waiting. True and wonderful wife whom I love."

"Then I guess sex is definitely out of the question?" smiled Beth.

When Brian started toward his car through the cold and dark parking lot, he could tell from a distance that someone was leaning on one of his front fenders. As he got closer, he could see the figure moving from one side to another, shifting his weight. Oh, well, thought Brian. If it's a mugger, he'll be surprised. Fordham is around here somewhere. At least Brian

94

could rest securely about anything that happened to him. After all, he had his own private bodyguard.

Then the thought suddenly hit him for the first time; suppose Fordham was not free to interfere. Suppose that mission -- whatever it was -- was so important -- and surely it would have to be to involve the FBI -- that Fordham couldn't jeopardize his position by interfering. For the first time since talking with Fordham a week ago, Brian realized that Fordham's presence in his life guaranteed him nothing. There had been no arrangement, no deal. Brian still didn't even know what was going on around him -- only that he wasn't supposed to talk about it -- to anyone -- whatever it was.

As he continued to approach the car, holding his overcoat around himself tighter to block out the cold wind, the figure appeared more menacing in the dark parking lot. Maybe it was a student who wanted to get something he missed in the lecture. Or maybe it was one of those students who kills his professor over a bad grade. Brian smiled at himself.

The man was a large, tall person. Extremely tall. Now he was almost motionless. Brian's gait slowed. He turned to see if he could spot Fordham anywhere around. He could not. Still he knew Fordham was somewhere close-by, watching. Right now that didn't seem to help much.

Brian coughed an unnecessary cough. He wanted the man to know he was coming. Didn't want to surprise him. You sneak up on these types, no telling how they might react.

The vague silhouette of the head changed. The man was looking toward Brian now.

"Hi." It was a friendly voice. Vaguely familiar.

"Hi," said Brian. The wind was colder now, a freeze coming.

"It's me. Cherokee," the dark specter said.

"Oh." Brian's muscles relaxed. "I was wondering who it was. You had me a little concerned."

"No. It's not a mugger. Or a serial killer," said Cherokee. "Just your friendly neighborhood fisherman."

"Actually, you did have me more than a little concerned." Brian was unlocking the car now, putting his briefcase and books in the back seat. "It's good to see you. What are you doing here?"

"I was wondering if I could bum a ride back to Carrabelle with you. Either now or later. I could make myself scarce until later, if you got other things you need to do before going back."

Even though the words weren't said, Brian could tell that Cherokee was thinking about Beth. Brian could imagine the man thinking that Brian had this great thing going in Panama City -- and still a great thing going in Carrabelle. Captain's paradise.

For a moment Brian thought about saying he did have something to do. But he really did want to get home to Zannah. They hadn't spent more than half-an-hour together since day before yesterday. He hated to burst such a beautiful bubble as Cherokee had in mind but --

"No. Nothing to do," said Brian. "Be glad to have your company. Hop in." He unlocked the passenger door, and Cherokee was in fast. An even colder wind gusted across the parking lot.

"I really appreciate it," said Cherokee. The vague smell of fish was clinging to the man, even though you could tell he was clean and wearing Davidoff's *Cool Water*. A fisherman's occupational hazard -- the ever-present smell of fish, no matter how much you wash and scrub and rub with lemon juice -- like formaldehyde on an undertaker, mineral spirits on the painter, grease smell in the clothing of the chef. And just when the smell of fish finally does wear away, it's time to go out fishing again. But it was a clean smell. The smell of honest labor, Brian was not offended by it.

"My pleasure," said Brian. "It's a long ride. I get tired of myself sometimes."

"Well, anytime you want company, just let me know. I have to come over this way a lot."

Brian started the engine and moved out of the parking lot. The inside of the car was still very cold, really cold.

"You do seem to be over here a lot," said Brian. Why don't you just work out of one of the fish houses over here? I'm sure with your experience and knowledge, you could get a job easily."

"I've thought about it. It's just that now I have friends in Carrabelle, and everybody knows me there. And you can walk down the street barefooted and without a shirt if you want to just run up town for a coke or something. You can't do that in a big city. There's just something about a small town. You know what I mean?"

"Yeah. We feel the same way. You're right. You can't beat a small town for being yourself."

Cherokee was also thinking about the fact that in small waterfront towns and unpopulated counties the law didn't look on the drifter and maverick as suspiciously as the law in larger towns. Or even small inland towns. The fishing and seafood industry depends on the migrants, the vagrants, the homeless. A small commercial fishing village is a good place to hide, if you're running from the law. You mind your own business, keep your nose clean, maybe even become a little part of the community in an oblique way, and you'll get along fine. It's not that the law's dumb; it's just that there are so few lawmen, and they have other things to do beside bother the quiet, peaceable fishermen.

The car was on U.S. 98 now, heading east on the "by-pass." The heater was just beginning to put out a vague bit of warmth. Cherokee was rubbing his hands together in front of one of the vents.

"Man, it's cold out there," he said. "Going down to 24 tonight, I hear."

"Really? I knew it was going to freeze, but I didn't know how cold. Can you keep warm on the boat when it's that cold?"

"Oh, yeah," smiled Cherokee. "Most boats are really tight. We can get that place steaming with just one of those little ceramic heaters. You know the kind I mean?"

"Yeah. We use those too. Really good. But what about when you're out on the water? With no AC?"

"Then we use kerosene. Works just as well. Better even. We have to turn it off after about half an hour. That's the only problem with it. Turning it off and on you get those fumes. Not like you used to years ago though. If you didn't have to turn them off and on, you wouldn't get those fumes at all with the new ones. But we do. Have to turn it off and on all the time. Because it gets so hot from it."

Brian felt nervousness, anticipation, coming from Cherokee. The man was talking more than necessary.

They were passing a doughnut stand just before the bridge crossing the inlet to Tyndall Air Force Base. It was a favorite of all the people on the base, as well as people from Mexico Beach and St. Joe. A really popular stopping spot for people headed back east late at night. No place to sit down and drink your coffee. Not even a room to go into. You just stand outside and place your order at the window. The various kinds of doughnuts, twists and cruellers are lined up in show windows on each side of the ordering window.

"I always stop here to get some coffee and doughnuts to take with me. And something to take home to Zannah. You don't mind, do you?"

"Sounds good to me. My treat, too. Even for your wife."

"No. You don't have to do that." Brian knew that the fishermen didn't make much money. They might hit a good catch once in a while, but then they blew it all drinking and partying. Although it did seem that Cherokee, The Swede and Blackie were a little different than the average waterfront men. They didn't drink as much as the others; they were a lot quieter than most. And then there was that large roll of bills Cherokee had that day at the restaurant on the beach.

Brian pulled in at the dough-nut stand. Six cars were already parked there, some with people having doughnuts and coffee in them, some waiting for drivers who were standing in line to order. Three people were standing at the window, waiting.

"I hope this place isn't slow tonight. As cold as it is," said Brian, opening his door.

"Right. I hope so too," said Cherokee, getting out and pulling his meager sweater around him. He was dressed poorly for such a cold night. His shivering body showed it.

When they got to the window, Brian ordered his usual medium-sized coffee, two glazed doughnuts, and four chocolate glazed to take home for Zannah and himself later. Cherokee ordered a large coffee and three cinnamon twists. Brian had his wallet out and was ready to pay when the woman told them how much it was.

"Here. Let me get this," said Cherokee. "I insist."

He pulled a roll of bills out of his pocket, another large roll and thumbed through at least twenty-five or thirty hundred dollar bills, before he got to the fifties, the twenties, and then the tens he was looking for. He placed a ten on the counter and the woman gave him his change.

Back in the car Brian sat his coffee in the car caddie, got out a doughnut, and turned east again on 98, heading for the soaring bridge that crossed the bay to Tyndall.

"These are great," said Cherokee, his mouth half full. "I should have gotten some for Blackie and The Swede."

They had come only about a block on the six-lane. Brian turned left quickly, darting into a closed filling station, pulled back out to the right.

"No problem," said Brian. They were opposite the doughnut stand again, waiting for a gap in the on-coming traffic.

"You didn't have to do that," said Cherokee

"I know. That's why I didn't ask. You would have said, 'no.'"

"You're a piece of work, man."

The Z-Car darted across a small break in the traffic flow, and came back to the same parking place they had a few minutes before. Cherokee hopped out, shivered his way hurriedly to the window, and came back within two minutes carrying a large bag of pastries. He had hurried and didn't have time to put the roll of bills in his packet, holding it in his left hand.

"Thanks, guy," he said. "That was noble of you. The guys on the boat owe you."

"No time wasted," said Brian. "Just time made use of."

Again they were headed toward the rising bridge. Cherokee was trying to get the money in his pocket.

"You want the dome light on?" asked Brian.

"Nah. I can make it." He was trying to eat and drink coffee too.

"That's a lot of money to be carrying around," said Brian. "Don't you think it would be better in a bank?"

"You know the old story. 'Easy come, easy go,'" smiled Cherokee. "This'll be gone in two weeks. Besides -- you make such an impression on people when you pull out a wad of three -- four thousand."

"I'm impressed."

"See? It works."

"I didn't know fishermen made that kind of money."

"Oh, they don't. This isn't all from fishing. Hell, it would take me four months to make that much fishing. Man, these are the best cinnamon twists I ever had."

"That's a good place to get pastries all right."

"No. This money isn't all fish money," said Cherokee.

One of those kinds of conversations, Brian thought. We're going to carry on two at one time. The food and the money.

"Part of it's from a inheritance," said Cherokee.

Yeah, right. thought Brian. I'll believe that when your mother becomes a virgin again. Look at you, man. You're a nice guy, but you're a drifter. You're from a family of drifters, and it shows. Nobody in your family ever had a thousands bucks at one time in his life -- much less three thousand. Don't insult my intelligence.

Instead of saying all that -- or any of that -- Brian said, "Really? That's interesting."

"And then I got some of it from another job. I got a part-timer that pays off good now and then."

That's more like it, thought Brian. Now, that one, I believe. And it's probably something illegal too. You just have that shady look about you, Cherokee. I hate to stereotype you, but I can't help it.

100

"But still," said Brian, "you need a checking account, man. You could lose a lot of money carrying that much around with you. Or get yourself robbed flashing around a wad like that."

"Man, these are great cinnamon twists," said Cherokee.

Brian wondered if that was 1) changing the subject, 2) another part of their two-part conversation, 3) a lapse in the man's brain waves, or 4) all of the above.

"I stop there just about every time I come home," said Brian. "That's why I have to jog all the time. Or play baseball or tag football."

"You do that stuff?" asked Cherokee. "Baseball and football and stuff like that?"

"Yeah. It's good for you when you have a job as sedentary as mine -- when you don't move around a lot."

"I was wondering how you stayed in such good shape," said Cherokee, starting on his last cinnamon twist. "Nah. I don't believe in banks. They make too many mistakes."

O.K., though Brian. A quick reverse to the left and a fake to down-field. The rules haven't changed; the game just got faster.

"My father lost all his money in an S & L scandal," said Cherokee.

All right!!! Yes!!!

"And nobody's going to try and rob the old Indian man."

Brian was reasonably sure that, from a psychological point of view, people who referred to themselves in the third person had an ego or authority problem and were trying to make themselves appear more important; the mother telling her child, "Now listen to what mother tells you."

Cherokee pulled a long, lethal-looking knife out of his pants leg. "And I don't think anybody that tries to mess with the old Indian is going to get too far."

I believe that, thought Brian.

"Well," said Brian, "that would certainly discourage me from messing with you."

"Man, I can keep anybody from messing with my money."

"Still, it doesn't seem wise to carry so much."

"There's always more where that came from."

They were now leaving the main part of the base, coming to the long deserted stretch of pine forest that lies between the base and Mexico Beach.

"Travis told me you were looking for a part-time job," said Cherokee. "Is that right?"

"Yes, I am." This felt a little uneasy. He knew Fordham was one of the three sets of headlights behind him, but it still felt very strange to be talking about looking for a job with a man like Cherokee.

"Zannah's expecting in about six months," said Brian. "She'll have to give up her job working at the bank soon, and then we'll be having more expense coming up. A part-time job would help a lot."

"I might be able to help you out there, pal."

I'm not even going to ask. Just let this one unfold by itself.

"It really wouldn't involve much," said Cherokee. "Mostly just going back and forth between Carrabelle and Panama City. And you do that all the time anyway."

"Who would I be working for? And what does it pay?"

"Oh, the pay's good. Real good. I can tell you that," smiled Cherokee, patting his pants pocket where the money wad was resting.

"That's a lot of money, Cherokee." He started to ask if it was legal, but didn't. He didn't want to put himself in jeopardy, and he suddenly realized that it might be Cherokee that Fordham was waiting to contact him. He was 99% sure that whatever Cherokee had in mind was nowhere near legal. You don't look as rough as Cherokee and walk around with three thousand dollars in your pocket from selling Avon.

"Damn right, it's a lot," said Cherokee. "You could be making some of it too. Easy."

"Who would I be working for?"

"This guy I know. You probably wouldn't get to meet him. He stays out of the country a lot."

Yeah. I'll bet. Way Out. "Well who would I get my instructions from? And what would I have to do? How would I

102

get paid?" He knew he was sounding almost just a little <u>too</u> naive, but Cherokee was not one to catch subtleties.

"I guess from me," said Cherokee, now a little embarrassed at himself. The idea of him telling a college professor what to do -- and getting away with it -- suddenly seemed incongruous to him, beyond his league. "Yeah. Me, I guess. The man over me wouldn't ever be around to do it, so I guess it would have to be me. If that wouldn't bother you."

"That wouldn't bother me." Again Brian was impressed with the man's modestly. "But what would I be doing? Is it something I can do? Would it interfere with my main job?"

"All you'd be doing is carrying stuff back and forth between Carrabelle and P.C. Fish mostly."

"Fish?" Brian was genuinely surprised.

"Not like a truck load, or nothing like that," Cherokee hurried to correct any misunderstanding. "Just a small package. Four or five. Maybe six. And they'd be wrapped good. Wouldn't smell up your car or anything like that."

"And just take them to somebody in Panama?"

"That's right. And you go over every day anyway. Right?"

How do you know that? Last semester I went only on Monday's, Wednesday's and Friday's. It was just this semester, thanks to Dean Warren, that I got stuck with a Tuesday and Thursday class. Only because Dean Warren had a nephew with a masters who wanted to teach at Gulf Coast and didn't want any Tuesday's and Thursday's.

Cherokee had his own thoughts going. You'd be the perfect cover, the perfect front. Nobody would ever suspect a college professor. You wouldn't -- couldn't -- get mixed up with anything like this. You might even be worth more than anyone who's ever done it before. And you sure got a lot more sense.

"Yeah. I go over every day. That's right." Brian, for the very first time, wished he could talk to Fordham. But he couldn't. That was made clear in their second meeting. Even though he saw Fordham every day, sometimes as many as ten and twelve times, Brian was never to make an effort to start a meeting between them. He was to wait for Fordham to contact him first.

"What about the pay?" continued Brian. "How much is it?"

Cherokee's mind was racing. Too little might let him get away. Too much might scare him away. Make him suspicious. And Cherokee really wanted him. He would be good at it. The best so far. There was plenty to offer, but how much was too much, how much too little?

"Hey?" Brian asked.

Cherokee pretended he hadn't heard. "Huh? What? What did you say? I was listening to that song on the radio. I love that song." George Michael was singing, "Father Figure."

"How much is the pay?"

Can't wait any longer. It's time. "A hundred a trip."

Brian held the wheel tighter to keep from showing his surprise. Then he said casually, "Maybe I could live with that. I don't know." He was being facetious. A hundred dollars more a week, just for carrying a small load of fish to Panama City!! Of course he could live with it. And of course it had to be illegal.

"Two hundred," said Cherokee hurriedly. Brian's attempt at humor had been taken seriously.

"I'm sure I could live with *that*," said Brian. He had two conflicting emotions going on; A) It would be wonderful to make that kind of money so easily, and B) it would also be illegal to make that kind of money so easily.

Cherokee broke Brian's conflicting reveries. "It wouldn't be all the time. Only about three times a week. Once in a while five."

My God!!! Brian's mind was reeling again, and he was trying to keep from showing his shock. I thought only once a week. We're talking a thousand a week here. He swallowed hard and tried to think of something to say.

He pushed the 'seek' button on the radio. There was nothing wrong with the station that was there. He just needed to do something. He didn't know what to say, how to say it, when to say it.

"What do you say?" asked Cherokee.

"It's hard to turn down something like that."

"Really wouldn't make much sense, would it?"

"I guess not."

"But maybe you shouldn't say anything about it. Even to you wife."

"I don't suppose so."

"People always think there's something crooked going on when there's that much money around."

"Yeah. It's the first thing that comes to mind." And I'm still tied up with that first thing.

"So -- you think you'd like to do it?" asked Cherokee.

"I know you won't be offended if I said I'd like to think about it a while. Would you?"

"'Course not. You always know where to reach me when you decide."

And you always know where to reach me too, thought Brian. God, I'd give anything to talk to Fordham right now.

The cold shimmering reflection of the Panama City Beach skyline slipped by on the cold Gulf waters as the slow-moving *Panama Queen* headed for the dry-dock in Destin. There is not much charter-boat deep-sea-fishing in February, so that was the logical time to have her keel scraped and painted.

There were plenty of dry-docks in Panama City, but Captain Andy had an uncle in Destin who needed the business. He called his uncle by his whole name, Aristotle, even though the uncle had shortened it to 'Totty' when he came to America. It was one of the few Greek names that Americans didn't have too much trouble with, but he had wanted it shorter. Aristotle had a big house that he lived in alone since his wife had died, so he would put up the three men on the boat while they stayed there, working on the hull. He enjoyed having the crew around, someone to visit, the voices of younger people in the house.

The *Panama Queen* bobbed up and down jarringly on the cold, choppy Gulf. The man at the wheel was steering directly into the oncoming wind and white-caps. Both were coming out of the west which, rough though it was, was easier than if they had been coming at an angle. An angle wind and wave would rock the boat even more.

"This is a bad wind," said the young blonde from the rear of the cabin.

"Aye. 'Tis," answered the white-bearded man from behind the wheel. "I would have put this trip off, but Aristotle has the dock rented right after we get off. And lord knows, he needs the money."

"I'm looking forward to some of his fantastic Greek salad," said the brunette deck-hand from the charting table. "We should have gone over there yesterday when it was calmer. One more day of the old man's great Greek cooking."

"I thought about that." said the bearded man. "But it being Sunday, I figured you boys were out with your beautiful girlfriends -- or sitting in your favorite bars, complaining about the life of a charter-boat fisherman." He smiled at the two young men, and his handsome Grecian features became young again in spite of his white beard and wrinkled eyes.   "Hell, Captain Andy," said the brunette. "We were just sitting around hoping you'd call and say we were going over."

"Besides," said the blonde, "it was too cold yesterday to do anything. Unless your main squeeze had the day off."

"You boys should have let me know," said Captain Andy. "I sure wasn't doing anything either. Reading the paper. Sitting next to the stove." His whole name was Andropolus, but he had done a little Americanization himself. "You boys have a life," smiled Captain Andy. "I got a stove instead."

"Oh, hell," said the blond. "Andy, you got more going for you than a stove. You handsome devil. Compared to you, Hugh Hefner is a dweeb -- a freakazoid. You got it all, Andy."

The other deck hand said something, but Captain Andy had zoned out. He was staring at the beach hotels and condos on the north shore of the Gulf, remembering the days when the beach was long and pure, a small town beach that had just started calling itself "the World's Most Beautiful Beach." And it had been. Lord, was it ever a pretty place. A place made for young lovers.

Andy, young and handsome, strong and muscular, a copy of Michelangelo's *David*, strolled bare-foot through the sand, his trousers rolled up, his shoes and socks in his hands. He had no way of knowing that twenty years later right where he was walking would be standing the Shoreham, flanked on both sides by hotels even taller and newer.

He topped a sand dune bordered with sea oats and saw her standing on the wooden walkway in front of the old beach house just two houses away. She waved at him, smiling, and called out something that the sea wind blew away before it reached him.

He waved back to her and started moving faster. Along the way he broke off some sea-oats to bring her a bouquet. Back then it wasn't illegal to pick sea-oats, but back then no one knew that the beach was being blown and washed away. Back then a lot of things were simpler, sweeter, kinder, softer. Back then the world was still safe and a place where a young man and a young woman could be in love, and the world made things easier for them instead of harder as it does now. Back then a man like Andy and a woman like Stephanie could meet on the beach, kiss with passion, and then go into her uncle's house and lie together the night, and nothing could happen that couldn't be taken care of with penicillin. Back then, people didn't have to play the games, get to the bottom line, lay the cards on the table. Back then love could be taken at face value. Things didn't have to be analyzed, studied, and looked at from every angle before a commitment. There was no commitment then; there was love instead. There was no meaningful relationships, no contracts, no agreements, no arrangements, because back then there was love.

Oh, Stephanie, Stephanie. God, if there were only still Stephanie.

By the time he reached her, he had a handful of sea oats. She held out both arms, open to him, and as he went to hand her the bouquet, she moved past it to his arms, his face, his body, his mouth. He picked her up and swung her around, kissing her at the same time. Whenever he was with her, there was no other

107

time for him, no other place. Only the here and now. Time can stand still for young lovers. All space and time come together and the universe becomes finite in the implosion of days and years and the outer reaches of space.

Back then -- back then -- Stephanie -- Stephanie --

"Captain Andy."

"Captain Andy."

Captain Andy finally heard the voice, blinked his eyes, and turned to face the blond.

"What is it, son?" he asked.

"You want me to take the wheel a while?"

"I guess." His smile was infectious. "Yes. I could use a rest."

The blond took the wheel and Captain Andy went to the charting table where the brunette was drinking a cup of coffee. The young man motioned to the coffee.

"Yeah, I would like some," said the captain.

The young man got up and went to the galley to pour a cup for Captain Andy. He had to grab the side of the cabin one time when the boat was thrown sharply to the left by an especially large wave. When he came back he placed the coffee in front of Captain Andy. There was regard and respect in the motion.

"Thank you," said Captain Andy, smiling the smile that made him *David*.

Stephanie -- Stephanie -- back then -- back then.

Sometimes February in North Florida can be as raw and bitter as the Februarys on the Great Lakes. Comes a wind as chilling and biting as the winds off the waters of Lake Michigan, and the temperature, while not much lower than thirty degrees, is laced with a humidity that makes the bones ache with cold. Like ice in the center of your arms, legs and shoulders is the chill of a North Florida February cold.

Plain grey and flat are the clouds, no rolling bulges, no tossing billows, only monotone grey from horizon to horizon, so unbroken that you can't tell whether it's even moving or not.

The day allows no shadows, only an undetermined source of light coming from no direction in particular, and a spray of salt water covers everything from car tops to yellow slickers even ten and twelve blocks away from the bay. Occasionally a sea mist will come floating off the Gulf and obscure anything more than twenty feet away. And the whole town on the edge of the water is erased into a blur of grey on grey.

Brian walked into the little cafe that hung out over the edge of the water, carrying his textbook and a note pad. Taking a seat by the window, facing the river, he ordered coffee. Then he opened his book and pad and began to write notes for the next two weeks. He had mounds of notes from teaching the course, but this text was new to him, and he would find parts in it that had not been in the others. He had to brush up his notes every time the college changed texts -- which seemed to be frequently -- and probably more for the advantage of the book store and publishing companies than for the students, he suspected.

Occasionally he would come across a section or a name that required more study, more encyclopedia work, research into biographies, autobiographies and other textbooks. The more he could discover about every aspect of the lesson, the more interesting the lesson would become, to him and to the students.
The spice to go on the gruel, his old college professor had called it, the things of soap operas and bad 'B' movies. Make the gruel palatable, said old Marganthau, and they will eat it, want it and be eager for it.

He wrote some notes of embellishment on Charles Martel -- "The Hammer" -- The first of the Carolingian rulers. He took a sip of coffee and looked out at the greyness covering the river. He could see nothing past the dark water lapping at the dock below. The lessons he was preparing were for two of the "off-semester" courses he was teaching. Three of the classes he was teaching were Western Civ. II covering the Renaissance to the present. Two of the classes, including the Thursday night one, were Western Civ I, covering the time from the beginning of civilization to the Renaissance. These were the "off semester" courses, because they would normally be taken during the first semester, not the second, or spring, semester. ("Give me a break," the students laughed. "Spring, hell. It's freezing.")

Brian liked the off-semester courses. They seemed to attract the people who didn't get hung up on rules and sequences. And then there were the really devil-may-care students who even took the second semester first. They were the ones completely unconfined by convention.

He began writing again when something caught his eye, something moving vaguely out in the mist over the water, a quick, undefined movement. He looked out of the window, straining his vision, and while he stared, it moved again. Strangely, he was looking directly at it when it moved, but he could not make out anything about its size, its shape, its color. It was only movement. And movement in a strange place. Whatever it was, it was above the water, supported by -- what? He held his gaze intently, watching the space in the fog. It happened again. But this time he caught it.

The movement was not in the mist outside, but a reflection of movement inside, a reflection in the window. Relaxing and turning to a table across from him, he saw Fordham three tables down, pretending to look at a menu. When their eyes met, Fordham gave a slight jerk of his head toward the door, then closed the menu, got up, left a dollar at the table for his coffee and left the cafe. Brian did the same and followed at a distance.

Outside he got in his car and started down U.S. 98. He didn't know what Fordham was driving today; he had recently taken to going to Tallahassee every few days and exchanging rentals. The last time Brian had seen him, Fordham was driving a Dynasty.

Over the arching bridge that spanned the Carrabelle River, Brian stayed on 98 until he reached a section directly on the edge of the water. Lighthouse Point it is called. Just opposite the lighthouse was a spit of land, covered with brush oak, reached by a small dirt road, branching off now and then with smaller roads going to both sides of the spit. Brian pulled off the second road to the left and stopped after about thirty feet. The road ended abruptly on a small ledge some ten feet above

110

the water. There was just enough room on his left for another car.

The spit was barren, the day too cold for anyone to be out here -- off Lighthouse Point, in the fog and mist, no warmer than thirty-five degrees, and with a sharp wind blowing chill and cold in from the Gulf. Anyone who was unfortunate enough to have to be out here today would be too busy trying to get home to pay attention to the car parked on the edge of the spit.

The Dynasty pulled in beside him. Brian didn't know what he was supposed to do. Go get in the Dynasty? Wait for Fordham to come to him? Get out and walk around?

Fordham got out of his car and walked to the ledge, looking down at the water, unable to see much in the mist. Brian guessed he was supposed to do the same thing. He got out, walked to the ledge about five feet from Fordham.

"You from around here?" asked Fordham.

God, this is silly. They don't even make movies this bad anymore.

"Yeah. Some of the time." He knew Fordham wouldn't knew what to make of that statement, but what the hey, some times absurdity just needed a little more absurdity.

Fordham looked at him strangely. "Some of the time?"

"Well, like, not all of the time."

Fordham looked around the scrub oaks to see if anyone might be listening. Furtive looks. Brian had to work to keep from smiling. The wind and the water splashing on the rocks directly below them effectively prevented anyone more than five feet away from hearing them. Brian, upwind from Fordham, could hardly hear Fordham himself.

"Is the fishing good around here?" asked Fordham.

"Not today," answered Brian. The man was definitely into overkill.

"Is it all right?" asked Fordham.

"Are we changing subjects here?"

"It pays to be on the safe side."

111

"Right now it would pay to be on the warm side. Can we get into one of these cars?" Brian pulled his coat tightly around his neck and chest.

"No. No." Fordham looked stunned. "We can't be seen in a car together."

"Hell, Fordham. Give me a break. Anything to get warm."

"No," said Fordham. No laughter in this man. He was dressed for the day better than Brian. He knew ahead of time they would be meeting in the cold.

"O.K.," said Brian. "But can we hurry? I'm freezing."

"Did he offer you anything?"

"Who?"

"Rucker."

"Rucker? Who's Rucker?"

"The fisherman. You gave him a ride back last night."

"Oh! Cherokee."

"Cherokee? You have pet names? Spare me."

"That's his name. His a.k.a. you'al would call it. Yes. He did."

"What doing?"

"Carrying some fish to Panama City a few times a week."

"He said it was fish?"

"Am I stuttering?"

"Fish?"

"He didn't know me well enough to trust me with drugs. So he's going to start me off with fish."

"Who said anything about drugs?" Fordham couldn't have looked more surprised.

"Nobody. But I'm not your average Ph.D. I figure when somebody offers me $200.00 a trip to carry fish to a fishing city, there's probably something illegal going on. And this coast is noted for its isolation and probable drug landings."

"It's drugs," said Fordham. Brian was pleased that Fordham had finally had enough balls to come clean with him. "And more," continued Fordham.

"More? How much more."

112

"Later. But for now we'd like you to do it. Work with him. Can you do it?"

"More? I want to know what more."

"We can talk about that later. It's really not important right now. But you could do your country a favor by helping with this."

"Spare me. Do the words, 'Just say "no,"' ring a bell?"

"Why not?" Fordham seemed unable to believe Brian wouldn't jump on this.

"What about 'I'm scared,' for one?"

"You'll be covered at all times. Safer than you would be shingling your roof."

"That's another thing I plan never to do, too."

"You had to know all this was leading to something."

"Read my lips, Fordham. No. N.O. No. I've got a wife. And a kid coming. I'm not about to start playing Douglas Fairbanks, Jr. at this point in my life."

Fordham seemed stunned, incredulous. "Why didn't you say all of this when we first talked? Up at the ski place?"

"You never asked me to do anything 'at the ski place.' You just told me you were waiting for someone to contact me. You didn't tell me much, actually, Fordham. You know, I'm freezing here."

"I don't know what to say." Fordham looked like a man with a punctured dream.

"How 'bout, 'Let's go someplace warm.' That would be a good start."

"Does that mean there's a chance? That you might change your mind?"

"No promises. It mainly means I'm freezing."

Fordham looked out through the fog. "Do many people in Apalach know you?"

"Some. A few."

Fordham looked dejected again.

"All right," said Brian. "Almost none. Does that make you happier?"

"How about the River Inn?"

"Fine with me. It's bound to be warmer than here."

"Twenty minutes?"

"I'll save a table for us."

"Not in the dining room." Fordham shook his head. "Room 212."

"Order something to eat. Something hot."

Twenty minutes turned into forty because of the fog. At times it was so thick that they could move only ten miles an hour. When they finally got to the River Inn, Brian was far more interested in getting something warm to eat than he was in listening to what Fordham had to say.

"Call room service. Get something to eat. And lots of hot coffee. Lots."

Fordham picked up the phone and waited.

"Kitchen -- then Room Service -- Oh, O.K." He turned to Brian. "The kitchen doesn't open until 5:00. And there is no room service. There are only two floors, after all."

"Aaaww, Henry. This is not going well at all."

"The bar is open. You want a drink?"

"Why not? Nothing else is working."

Fordham started toward the door. "What do you want?"

"Rum and diet Dr. Pepper. Don't say anything." He held up his hand to quiet the objection he could see coming from Fordham. "There's a Junior Food across the street. They always have diet Dr. Pepper. Get one from there, and a shot of rum from the bar -- with a glass of ice on the side. I'll mix my own."

Fordham left the room, still in the overcoat he had worn all day. Brian studied the empty room where Fordham was staying -- this week -- this day -- maybe only this hour. Although it wasn't really his nature, Brian found himself pulling open drawers, looking in the closet, in general being what he hated -- a spy.

Nothing in the room revealed any information about Fordham, nothing personal, no reading material, not even a toilet kit. No spy would ever be able to tell whether Fordham shaved with a blade or an electric, used tartar control toothpaste or a

114

brightener, read mysteries or biographies. The only thing a good spy could discern about Fordham was that he was tall and had a 34" waist (from the three pair of pants in the closet) and favored oxford dress shirts. The man either kept all his personal things in his rental car or grew no beard, and produced no body fluids that required masking. The room had the vague scent of Liz Claiborne's *Curve* which Brian had decided was not left by the cleaning lady.

When Fordham returned, Brian was standing next to the refurbished steam-heat radiators, rubbing his hands together, trying to become as much a part of the radiator as the existing laws of physics would allow.

Fordham handed him the rum, diet Dr. Pepper and glass of ice, placed a paper sack on the wooden seat of a straight-back chair, and then cordially held out his own drink in motion of a toast.

Brian returned the gesture, then drank about half the drink he had quickly mixed. The rum burned going down. And after. Good! Heat!

"You make a good drink," said Brian.

"Thanks," said Fordham. "Now can we talk?"

"Sure. I've already said all I have to say."

"Why won't you do this?" Fordham seemed sincerely confused.

"Why would I?"

"What's wrong with $600.00 a week -- just for driving some fish over to Panama City?"

"Never thought of myself as a fish chauffeur. You mean I'd get to keep the money?"

"Why not? It's better to pay you out of their budget instead of ours."

Brian thought for a moment, then took a sip of his drink.

"I know you're not telling me everything you know about all this."

"True," Fordham nodded.

"I know it has something to do with drugs -- and more."

"Right."

"That means somewhere around all of this, someone -- some people -- maybe many people -- are carrying guns, possibly someone already killed."

"Right again."

"Where's the safety factor for me here? And is $600.00 really that great when you think of standing at the bottom of the bay in cement shoes?"

"You'll be under protection all the time."

"Un-huh."

"You want more money? Is that it?"

"Well, I'm not really thrilled about all this, Hank. Not yet."

"What if we pitched in another -- say, thousand a week?"

Brian looked at him slack-jawed. "Now I'm getting more interested. It's starting to sound like my kind of work."

"You'll do it then?"

"I need to think on this a little bit, Hank."

"Tomorrow? Can you tell me then?"

Brian knotted his brows, thinking. "Yeah. I can do that."

Fordham relaxed slightly. He moved to one of the upholstered chairs in front of the closed-up fireplace.

"I need to be going," said Brian. "Zannah's worked up a good Indian dinner. I'd ask you over, but I know you wouldn't come."

"That's true. Here. Take this with you." He handed Brian the paper bag he had brought back to the room earlier.

"What's this?" asked Brian, looking at the sack.

"Some more Dr. Pepper. And a bottle of rum."

Brian smiled. "You're a good man, Hank."

"I'll catch you tomorrow. In the meantime, do me a favor."

"You name it."

"Don't call me 'Hank.'"

"You got it."

"See you tomorrow."

"O.K., Hank."

Susannah stared into the flames over the top of her wineglass -- half filled with Evian, with a twist of lemon. She sat on the floor, leaning back against the seat of the chair,

116

Brian's legs straddling her, her arms resting on his thighs and knees. The corduroy trousers felt warm and secure to her over his hard muscles.

The lights were out, and they watched the fire as intently as if it were a murder mystery on TV.

"A millions bucks for your thoughts," she said, not turning to face him.

"What happened to a penny?"

"Inflation. Besides, that sounds so corny. If you're going to be corny, you might as well be extravagantly corny."

"Well, you've stumbled onto a man with absolutely no principles. I'll do anything for a million."

"Would you really?" She turned to him smiling.

"Even sleep with Demi Moore," he answered.

"No. You've got that backwards. You're the one who would have to pay. She's the one who would do anything for a million."

"I really kind of like it better my way."

"Of course you would." She turned back to the fire. "You're a chauvinist."

"That, my dear, is one of the smoothest *non sequiturs* you've uttered this evening."

"My *non sequiturs* are all smooth. If nothing else."

A long silence followed, finally broken by Brian.

"Zannah ---." His courage wavered.

She waited.

"I think I'm about to get involved in something that may be over my head."

"Please don't tell me we're going to buy another boat."

Pause.

"What made you say that?" he asked.

"I know you've been hanging around that fishing boat a lot lately. Something's going on."

"No. It's not that. I'm perfectly happy with our little Hobie-Cat."

"I am too. That's a relief."

Another long silence followed.

117

"Well?" she asked softly.

Suddenly he blurted it all out. He overflowed. He told her about the car that followed him for two weeks, even followed them to the Maggie Valley in Carolina. He told her about the conversation with Fordham in the bar, the 'chance' meeting with Cherokee in Panama City. (But he left out that he was there to meet Beth.) About the meeting with Cherokee at the car-wash, on the boat, then the ride back with Cherokee last night. Then he told her about the meeting with Fordham that afternoon.

"All of *this* has been going on around me?" she asked. "And I haven't even noticed? Well, make me feel dumb, will you? I may have to turn in my wife's spying license."

Another pause. Shorter this time.

"I think I'm going to do it," he said.

"The pay's good," she nodded. "For a part-time job."

"The hours aren't bad,"

"You could be doing something for your country," she nodded.

"It would be an interesting little diversion," he answered.

"You could be shot," she nodded again.

"The hours aren't bad," he answered.

"You could get killed."

"The pay's good."

She turned to face him, turning away from the glow of the fire. "What are we talking about here? I would like to have my baby's father around to help me raise her -- him -- whatever,"

"Fordham doesn't see it as dangerous. He'll be trailing me most of the time."

"Does that mean he'd be the first to discover the body when you get -- wasted, or whatever they call it now." She turned her face back to the fire.

"That does seem to follow, I guess. Yes. I suppose he'd be the first to find the body."

"Oh, you dolt." She turned around again half playfully and started pummeling his chest with her fists. "You are so stupid sometimes. Can't you see that I'd rather have you poor than dead?"

He held her fists, smiling at her. "But you're going to have me either way. There are no options. The multiple-choice portion of the conversation is over. You're going to have me vibrantly alive, <u>and</u> far better off than we are now financially. I promise you."

"How can you promise that? You know this is a risk."

"No more than getting out on U.S. 98 during rush hour. And we both do that every day."

She looked at his face with the fire flickering on it. They looked into each other's eyes with searching and meaning. She was looking at daring, risky, and handsome; he was looking at beautiful and sunny.

A slow smile moved on her lips like a thought. "You know you wouldn't even be thinking about this if it were summertime. You wouldn't even give it a second thought. You'd be too busy doing all your outdoor things, sailing, etc."

He smiled. "You're probably right."

He nodded. She nodded. And together they smiled.

"Seasonal affective disorder," she said. "SAD. SAD. SAD."

When Anne Madison backed the Mercedes out of the six-car garage, she carelessly backed into a snow bank on the far side of the clean, radiant-heated driveway. She didn't even bother looking back, put the car in 'forward' and drove out the long, curving driveway to the gate which she opened with the remote, almost too late. She seemed oblivious to things going on around her. Once on the street, she turned and headed toward Lakeside Drive. Snow banks straddled both sides of the street which was lined with high walls of other estates, well landscaped and manicured between the sand colored brick walls and the few feet of snow-covered lawn to the never-used sidewalks. No other cars were on the cold, deserted street, which was well plowed and maintained beyond its use.

Just as she reached Lakeside Drive, a light snow began. She absently turned on the wipers and lights, pulled out into a break in the traffic and headed toward the distant skyline, distinguished by the Wrigley Building and the Sears Tower. After coming to a stoplight at 158th Street, she turned right and headed for the shopping center four blocks back from Lakeside. Once there she parked in the almost empty parking lot, got out and walked absently through the light snow that was not yet sticking to the asphalt or sidewalks. At the Secret Garden Florist, she turned in, going directly to the counter by the front window.

"Mrs. Madison," smiled the clerk. "Nice to see you."

Anne smiled briefly, nodding, not speaking.

"We have your arrangement ready," said the clerk. "I'll get it for you."

Again Anne smiled, not answering.

"We could have delivered it for you," said the clerk, returning with a large arrangement of multi-colored flowers. "You didn't have to come out on such a bad day."

For the first time Anne Madison spoke. "I wanted to take it myself today. Thank you anyway."

She took the arrangement and headed toward the door.

"Have a nice day," said the clerk, rushing to hold the door -- too late.

Anne smiled back again and chose not to answer.

Back at the Mercedes, she placed the arrangement on the floor in the back seat, then drove through the light snow back to Lakeside Drive. The digital clock on the dashboard read '11:23AM, Feb. 20.

At the cemetery she parked in front of the largest headstone. The old arrangement -- from last week -- was covered with snow piled high from accumulation. Even the writing on the headstone was obscured by snow drifts almost four feet high.

She got out of the Mercedes, walked in her high designer boots through the snow banks in the falling snow, carrying the new arrangement to the grave. Picking up the old arrangement, she automatically made a hole in the snow for the new one. The flowers and sprays gave out an incongruous burst of colors against the cold, bleak surroundings of snow and graves; bright reds, yellows and violets which seemed to be made even more vivid by the solid whiteness.

She reached out and gently brushed away the snow from the headstone, slowly revealing more and more of the etched writing. Dates, name, that slowly moved into light from behind a heap of snow, illuminated to be read by all who would take the time and trouble to be enlightened.

DAVID MICHAEL MADISON
April 10, 1981-December 20, 1997

To An Athlete Dying Young
To-day, the road all runners come,
Shoulder-high we bring you home
And set you at your threshold down,
Townsman of a stiller town.

A. E. Housman

Beth lay on the bed in her all-white bedroom which matched her all-white living room, which matched both her all-white dining room and her all-white bath room, not to mention her all-white kitchen and her all-white guest room and bath. The guest room itself was almost totally unnecessary since almost all of the guests who stayed over stayed mainly in order to sleep in Beth's personal all-white bedroom.

She lay on her back on the bed, draped in her all-white gown and negligee, looking up at the two pictures she held at arms' length. Outside the February wind whipped around the corners of the balcony, but the thinness of the white clothes she wore indicated how warm and comfortable it was in her self-contained haven -- retreat -- place of security.

Patty Larkin's "Good Thing" came from the CD player in the living room, piped into all the rooms with perfectly balanced equalizers to impeccably mounted and hidden Bose speakers. The sound was soft yet compelling, just the right music for her calmly agitated, restrainedly romantic, but indecisive mood.

In her left hand she held an eight-by-twelve black-and-white shot of Steve Briggs, unposed, probably even unknown to him. His head was turned over his shoulder. He was smiling, showing his perfectly photogenic teeth. The picture, the pose, was one of a successful, thirthysomething, upward-mobility-moving professional. This ultimate example of success exuded confidence and the self-poised certainness of a born winner.

God, what a smile, thought Beth. God, what a hunk. In his thirties, and almost as much money as my father. That would make for an easy transition; moving from daddy's money to Steve's.

He's married, but that presents no problem. I've overcome that handicap before with ease and agility.

In her right hand was a picture of Brian Withers, another eight-by-ten black-and-white, this one posed, from the Commodore, the college yearbook faculty section. He wasn't looking over his shoulder but straight into the camera -- and pulling it off extremely well. His smile was not as broad as Steve's, invoking the look of an intelligent, learned man, the sure winner, the man of charisma, the handsome epitome of the Renaissance man, the man of certainty and knowledge.

God, what a brain, she thought. And what a hunk. Great buns. In his thirties -- maybe even late twenties. Up and going. On the move. Engrossed in academia. Which happens to be a sure path to non-wealth. And also married. But again, that matters little. No wife yet made was ever a match for me. And if anybody could ever be swayed to wander into a strange bedroom, it surely would be the Renaissance man, the man in constant search of the new experience. There has to be a little bit of the Don Juan Complex in every Renaissance man.

Besides, she thought, it's time to move away from Steve. This stuff he's messed up with is going to come to a head soon. He thinks I don't know what's going on. But I do. Those buddies of his dress too well and wear too much gold to be making it all in the construction business. And that little game with the flashlight out over the water. Just playing? Give me a break!!

122

She reached over, propped both pictures on her dresser facing the bed, stretched out on her stomach and looked across to both men. It was not so much a matter of choice or option. In her world it was easy to have them both. Right now, since that decision had already been reached, it was just a matter of priority.

The three men worked amid dust and debris, scraping the bottom of the boat with such vigor that they had worked up a sweat in spite of the cold temperature. The blonde and the brunette had both taken off their jackets and were now working in their shirtsleeves. Captain Andy was still wearing his jacket but was sweating only slightly. His age did not keep him from working any slower than the two younger men under the boat with him. But he *was* working slower today. His age was not what was making him work slower; it was his memories.

Captain Andy did not hear the radio turned to the rock station, which played "Breakfast in Bed" by UB-40. He did not hear the two deck hands singing along with the radio, stopping now and then to chat about idle nothingness.

"What do you think we need to do with that bad spot by the propeller?" asked the brunette.

"I'm hired from the neck down," smiled the blonde. "I don't get paid to think."

Captain Andy heard none of this. As he worked at scraping the last of the barnacles from his section of the hull, what he heard was something from forty years ago and seven thousand miles away.

"Andy --- Andy," the soft melodious voice called from the rocky coast of the Aegean Sea. "Come look at this."

Stephanie waded in the rocky water, looking for shells, a thin calf-length dress, a broad-brimmed bonnet making her silhouette even more appealing against the bright Greek sky. He walked to her slowly, watching for jagged rocks as he went.

"What is it?" he asked when he reached her. God, she was beautiful.

"A starfish. See?" she pointed. "Wrapped around an oyster."

"The starfish is sucking on the oyster for food," said Andy. "The oyster will die."

"That's horrible." She looked pained.

"Everything's got to eat something," smiled Andy. "Some oystermen break starfish in half, thinking they're killing them. But half a starfish will regenerate into a whole one again. Two for one."

She leaned against him in the calf-deep water. "I'm glad I have you." She looked at him lovingly. "I'm glad we're spending our honeymoon here in Greece. Where our roots are."

"Even if we can't speak a word of Greek?" he laughed. "And none of our families are left here to help us with the language?"

"It's still perfect." As she leaned against him in the water, her waist-length hair blew around his bare chest, wrapping him like a vest of love. "It's the most perfect honeymoon I'll ever have."

"Well, I hope so," he chided.

"The most perfect in the world."

They had come a long way since that perfect honeymoon. Years filled with love and respect -- and tradition. Four children. All loving. Honorable. Raised with 'old world' values.

Captain Andy turned from the hull, walked to the side of the dry-docked boat, and started climbing the ladder that rested against the deck.

"Giving up?" asked the blonde deck-hand.

"Just a little paperwork I forgot," said Captain Andy.

Captain Andy climbed the ladder to the cabin above them. The two deck hands looked at each other.

"He's getting too old for this kind of work," said the blonde.

"No," said the brunette. "It's her. His wife. He's worrying about her again."

"That must be costing him a fortune."

"More than he's got. That's for sure."

In the cabin, Captain Andy pulled a box from under his bunk. The box contained letters, bills, private papers. Thumbing through the top of the pile, he found the bill from Oakcrest Retreat, Mobile, Alabama. Inside was a bill that needed to be paid before the first of the month. He pulled out his checkbook, took the bill, and sat at the table in the galley. He began writing the check; Feb. 21, 1998, *Pay to The Order of* "Oak Crest Retreat." He skipped the amounts and went down to <u>For</u>; March for Stephanie Andropolous, Acct. # 17524. Then he signed; "Anthony Andropolous" and went back to the amount. Saving the amount until last was like holding onto the money a little longer. He wrote slowly; "Four Thousand, Six Hundred and Seventy-Eight & 29/100 --" Dollars. Then he wrote the number in numerical form. When he had finished, he sighed heavily. There was a slight pain in his chest. He pulled out the return envelope, placed the return stub and the check in it, and wrote his return address on the envelope.

Stephanie was worth it. If anyone in the world would ever be worth that much each month, it would be his Stephanie. She was as beautiful to him now as she had been that day on the Aegean Sea, some forty-odd years ago. She was ever-kind, ever-loving, ever-caring. To her the world was a thing to be celebrated, 'a thing of beauty --- a joy forever.' The world would be a better place for having Stephanie in it, a kinder, gentler place.

Stephanie....

Stephanie....

"Stephanie," he said aloud, softly.

Brian raised the trunk of his car and placed the package inside, gently, resting it on the clean, unspoiled carpet that covered the bottom of the trunk. Then he went to the back seat of the car, got out a piece of clear plastic, and placed it under the package. He stood back slightly and looked down at the package for a long time. He was stepping over the threshold. Into a new world. A world of double-think and new-speak, where words meant only what you wanted them to mean in retrospect, a world of constant revisionism.

When had he crossed the line?

When he said 'Yes' to Fordham? When he said 'Yes' to Cherokee? When he just now, a few minutes ago, took the first package to be delivered? Or would it be later? When he handed the package to the man in Panama City? Or when Cherokee would give him the two-hundred dollars tomorrow? When 'Hank' gave him the thousand on Saturday?

God!! How do you know the exact moment you go bad? Turn corrupt? How do you know the exact moment of any occurrence? Maybe there is never an exact moment --- an exact moment for anything. Maybe it's all a gradual state of 'becoming.' Maybe there never is one exact time that can be separated by the two phrases, 'I am,' 'I am not.'

Maybe there never is. -- No. There has to be. If you draw a line and step over it, there is one, and only one, precise moment when your center of gravity, your physical center of mass, passes over that line. There is a moment. It's not a gradual becoming. It is precise, marked by a particular nanosecond, a moment so central to the becoming that the act of the moment is the becoming.

There is a time when you become committed, committed to something, to someone, an idea, a principle. But what takes places in the molecules and atoms of the brain to cause that commitment? When you're riding along the freeway and you miss Exit 72, you're committed. You're committed at least to Exit 73. There is always a moment of commitment. But what makes it? How can you tell when that exact moment is?

This musing is not accomplishing much, he thought. Probably not anything. There are more acts and deeds to be stacked on top of this one, which itself was already placed on others -- and others before that. See the world change before your eyes at your own doing. "But I have promises to keep. And miles to go before I sleep. And miles to go before I sleep..."

126

He reached to the side of the trunk where he kept some plastic trash bags and placed the neatly wrapped package of about six 'grouper' inside one of the bags. Double safety. Don't trust just that plastic sheet beneath it. Just in case there might really be some fish inside the package. Big chance! No sense in ruining the lining of his trunk --- just in case.

He closed the trunk, got in the Car and started off on U.S. 98 toward Panama City. Back there somewhere, he knew Fordham was watching everything, following. They would both soon meet another link in the chain, the man who was to receive the package in the trunk.

The watched and the watcher traveled west in the morning sun which threw a glare from the cold Gulf waters on the left. Both were secure in the knowledge that there was at least safety in numbers, both completely ignorant of the fact that they were being followed and carefully watched by the third man. Back there somewhere, shielding his eyes from the glare of the sun and the water, fully aware that things had changed dramatically in the last three weeks, was Stewart.

Brian left long before necessary in order to get to his class. He had some new work to do on the docks before going to the college. After all, he was moonlighting now, a two-income man.

Four times on the trip he saw Fordham behind him. Twice at stop lights their eyes met briefly. There was never a hint of recognition when it happened. Both looked away immediately. Fordham was now driving a metallic brown Grand Marquis. His agency must have increased his travel pay, thought Brian.

A mile behind them, Stewart, in his blue Buick LaSabre, watched every move they made. He knew that Brian was drinking coffee which was probably cold by now, and eating some doughnuts from the IGA deli in Apalach. He knew that Fordham was drinking a Mountain Dew and chewing some Big Red cinnamon gum. He also knew that in the trunk of Brian's Z-Car was a package, rolled in newspaper, wrapped almost too neatly, placed carefully inside a plastic trash bag, sitting on top of another piece of clear plastic.

At the city dock in Panama City, Brian walked slowly, searchingly along the wooden planks. He carefully read the boats' names as he passed them; *Miss Anne*, *Weak-end Retreat*, *Yellow Brick Road*, *Running Third*, *Hook, Line & Sinker*, some too cute, many named after some woman left back on 'the hill.'

He carried the package under his arm, still in the plastic bag to keep the contents from spoiling his blue and white crew neck sweater which was proving to be not quite enough cover against the cold wind off the river. Sixty feet behind him walked Fordham, dressed more appropriately in a black sweater, worn blue jeans, and a black knit cap, looking far more like a commercial fisherman than Brian. But Brian hadn't planned this delivery that carefully. It was all newer to him than it was to Fordham. Also he knew he had to stand in front of a class and lecture later in the morning. He did think to take off his tie before coming to the dock, even though it would not have shown under the high crew-neck sweater.

Fifty feet behind Fordham, Stewart kept up with the two men. He was dressed much like Fordham, except his careful planning had made him look even more authentic; his black sweater had some impressive looking holes in it, as did the brown Greek fishing cap. Both looked to be very old, either bought at some flea market or off someone on the dock. He also had an appropriately unshaven face, not the neat kind from *Miami Vice*, but a rough, scroungy growth that came down onto the neck. He looked very much the part of a wino looking for his next touch. The only thing that was out of character for a wino was his fast gait. No wino ever walked that steadily, that straight or that fast.

Brian came to the end on the dock. He did not find the name he was looking for. He had been told not to ask, to find it on his own. He turned and started back toward the other end of the dock which was at least three blocks in the other direction. He appreciated going back; the wind was behind him now, not biting into his face and ears, not blowing salt water from the pilings into his eyes.

128

As he passed Fordham, Fordham turned to prop against one of the pilings, looking as if he were about to board the boat docked there. Stewart did even better; when he saw Brian reverse, he stepped onto one of the unoccupied boats and sat on a keg, busily working on some rope as Brian passed above him on the dock. He remained occupied with the rope until Fordham passed him also. When Fordham was about fifty feet past, Stewart swung onto the dock and resumed following them.

Brian again searched the names on the sterns as he retraced his steps, just in case he had missed it the first time. When he reached the place where he had started, he moved more slowly as he began the three-block trek of new boats, new names; *Hide-a-way*, *T.G.I.F.*, *The Bounding Mane*, (obviously owned by a beautician), *The Office*, *Somewhere Else*.

After going about a block, he stopped suddenly. The two men behind him stopped just as suddenly, each looking busy at something other than the man ahead of him. Fordham and Stewart both could see Brian talking to a man on one of the boats. The conversation took longer than it should have, unless Brian was asking for information. The man on the boat pointed off down the dock, in the direction of the two men. Brian turned and looked in that direction briefly. Then there was more conversation. After a few minutes, Brian stepped onto the boat and went inside the cabin. The deck-hand stayed outside painting the deck.

Fordham moved up to the boat, followed by Stewart. A small bait-and-tackle shop was just across the dock from the boat. Inside, Fordham found a short-order food counter, ordered a hamburger he didn't want, another Mountain Dew which he did. When his order came, he paid and went to a booth by the front window to watch the boat that contained Brian and the package. A few minutes later, Stewart drank coffee and read a magazine just a few booths behind Fordham. Stewart could not see the boat from where he sat, but he could see Fordham, and Fordham was as much a barometer as he needed. As long as he kept up with Fordham, he knew he was keeping up with Brian. In a sense, he felt that Fordham was doing his work for him. It was like driving behind a guy who really knows the road on a rainy, foggy night, and you have never been on that road before. All you have to do is just follow the taillights, sit back and relax. He did see, as he knew Fordham had, the name of the charter boat before coming in the bait and tackle shop; The *Panama Queen*.

On board the *Queen*, Brian nervously looked about the cabin, waiting for Captain Andy to return. The blonde deck-hand painting on the rear deck had said the captain would be back in ten minutes. The radio was making a strange transition from Clint Black's "Put Yourself in My Shoes," to Chicago's "Just U-N Me" with it's many key modulations lending a strange out-of-body feeling to Brian.

On the chart deck surrounding the steering wheel was a frame which contained four pictures of what was obviously the same beautiful woman at four different times in her life. In the top left she was in her twenties, smiling at the camera, as if she were looking directly into your eyes, her long shining brown hair hanging over her shoulder. In the picture on the bottom right, she must have been in her mid-sixties, but the same smile, the same eyes, were there still. Her hair was white and much shorter, curled slightly, but still a youthfulness came through the wrinkles and grey.

Beside the montage was another picture, a family portrait, very posed, very proper, like one taken in a twenties' daguerreotype parlor. The handsome father sat in a Victorian chair with the handsome wife standing behind him to the right, her hand on his shoulder. Behind him on the left stood a beautiful daughter, her arm resting on the back of the chair, a poised young lady in her twenties. A handsome son in his late teens knelt on one knee to the left of the father, one hand resting on his own raised knee. Sitting on the floor in front, with one arm resting on her father's knee , was another daughter in her mid-teens. Another handsome son knelt to the right of the father. All of the handsome family had classic Greek features, strong, angular. All had toothpaste-ad smiles and Visine-ad eyes.

Brian was going deeper into a world he never suspected he would see firsthand. But what was even stranger than his being here was the fact that it did not really seem alien to him. It was not a world of guys in black hats against guys in white hats. The bad guys didn't seem all that bad. In fact the ones he had met so far were kind, gentle, smiling, hard-working and compassionate -- everything a mother would want in a son-in-law. So far.

The man coming on board now had to be Captain Andy. He fit the description Cherokee had given, only better. The elderly man in the captain's cap, with the white beard, looked like someone advertising a newly-released movie. 'Hemingwayesque,' was the word that came to mind. His soft eyes smiling, he spoke quietly to the blonde painting the deck. Brian could not hear the conversation above Enya's "Sail away, sail away, sail away," but from the expressions on their faces, Brian could tell there was a strong bond between the two. The deck hand pointed toward the cabin, and Captain Andy looked in to see Brian. The gentle captain waved at Brian through the window and started toward the cabin.

Coming into the cabin, the captain smiled and held out his hand.

"Hello," he said. "I'm Captain Andy. I'm sorry I kept you waiting. I understood you were to be here around two this afternoon." They were shaking hands as he spoke.

"No problem," smiled Brian. "It was only a few minutes. No harm done."

"Yes," said the captain, "but your time is valuable -- and you're on a tight schedule. You teach at Gulf Coast, I understand."

"That's right," said Brian. "Western Civilization."

"Aaah," smiled the captain. "I hope you give the Greek Empire its proper due. Show up those Romans as the copy-cats they were."

"It would be hard to play down the influence of the Greeks," said Brian. "Not only were they first in philosophy, medicine and theatre, just a few flukes of fate kept them from being the first civilization." Brian recognized the nationalism in the man immediately and patronized it.

"Those Mesopotamians and Babylonians did get in the way, didn't they?" returned the captain.

"Maybe we could just think of them as stepping stones. Laying the groundwork. Getting things ready for the Greeks."

The captain laughed heartily. "I like your style, lad. You know how to appease an old Sophist, don't you? Good man." Then just as suddenly his mood changed. "I don't want to be keeping you, Brian. It is Brian, isn't it?"

"Yes, sir. Brian Withers. I'm sorry. I forgot to introduce myself."

"How could you?" asked the captain. "I was talking so much. You have something for me, I believe."

"Yes, sir." Brian took the package from under his arm, handing it toward the man. "Here. Just as I received it."

"I'm sure it is." The captain took the package without ever taking his eyes from Brian's eyes. Brian could not remember anyone ever having such eye control. The man was hypnotic in his stare and smile. Brian also wondered how much the package he was passing on was worth. The figures spun through his brain.

"I have something for you to take back," said the captain, turning to a cabinet on the side of the cabin.

"Oh?" Brian was caught off guard. He hadn't known about this.

"Rucker didn't tell you?" the captain asked.

Brian shook his head. "No. He didn't."

"I'm sorry," smiled the captain. "Would it be an imposition on you?"

He was holding an expensive attaché case that he had taken from the cabinet. Brian looked at it, surprised. It certainly wouldn't be any problem. It was not that large or that heavy. There was no obvious reason to object.

"No problem," Brian heard himself say again. He hated clichés, and he had used the same one twice in the last five minutes.

Why am I becoming cliché-ridden, he wondered, and suddenly he had to hold on to the back of a deck chair; his world was slowly turning into a carousel -- and he was moving backward on it. Some of the other yachts tied to the dock began floating by him. He shook his head and fixed his eyes on the door just beyond Captain Andy's head.

"You all right?" asked the captain.

"Yes," answered Brian in a voice that sounded completely alien to him. "Fine. Thank you. Just not used to life on the high seas," he joked.

"Can I get you anything?"

"No. I'm fine. Really," smiled Brian. "But I do have to be going."

"Oh course," smiled Captain Andy. "It's been nice meeting you. I look forward to seeing you again."

How many times will I be doing this? Brian wondered, smiling to cover his thoughts.

The captain continued. "Maybe sometime -- soon -- we can sit over a glass of uzo and talk about the relative merits of Socrates, Plato, and Aristotle. Huh? It's not often one meets a fellow traveller who can talk about the great philosophers and the classics."

"That would be enjoyable," said Brian. "I look forward to it."

He was headed toward the cabin door.

"Until the next time," said the captain, holding out his hand cordially.

"The next time," smiled Brian, shaking the man's hand. Unreality was all around him.

He stepped through the door, nodded at the deckhand, and stepped very carefully up to the dock, holding the attaché case more tightly than necessary. With some small amount of difficulty, he walked off down the dock, dragging unreality along with him.

What had happened to his world, he wondered. What, two day before had seemed like a ruse, a mere joke, now seemed to be an earnest plot to engulf him and carry him into an undertow where he was having trouble breathing. Now his path -- his life -- had become entwined with another paradoxical character. The captain was not what he seemed to be. Or more precisely, he was someone who was hidden under the facade of a fine, enjoyable, handsome man.

Brian suddenly found himself disliking the fact that he liked the captain so much. Damn!! He's such a fine, educated man. But he's one of the bad guys. I can't like him. It's not in the game to like him. Is this what it's like to grow up? If so, I think I'll pass. I don't think I like this growing-up thing.

A dockside cafe caught his eye. There were some tables under umbrellas, but the cold wind off the Gulf made the outside a little raw. Beside, he never had been much of an *al fresco* man unless he was with someone special -- like Zannah.

He went inside, took a table by the window, and ordered coffee and a doughnut. Maybe if he sat down for a few minutes and got something in his stomach he would get rid of the dizziness.

As he sat sipping the coffee, still holding onto the attaché case unconsciously, he saw Fordham coming along the dock and smiled at the way he was dressed. Fordham moved more slowly as he neared the cafe, as if looking for some way to kill time while he waited for Brian to come out. Brian thought he could make it easier on Fordham by hurrying, but just then he didn't feel like hurrying. He suddenly felt that he was being pulled in many directions, trying to please many different people; it was time he pleased himself a little, even if only in such a small way as sitting and enjoying a cup of coffee. Hell!! Let Fordham fend for himself. *He* was the one who had gotten Brian into this strange point in his life anyway.

Fordham entered the cafe and went to a seat at the counter. The two never let their eyes meet.

Some of the deck hands and workers from along the dock began to drift into the cafe, some for an early lunch, some just for coffee. One disreputable looking, unshaven wino with a Greek fishing cap came in and sat next to Fordham at the counter. Brian looked at him briefly and felt sorry for Fordham.

The wino looked as if he reeked of dirty clothes and stale, spilt wine.

Brian looked out the window and back to the dock, the yachts, the river, and the Gulf out past the mouth of the river. What have I gotten myself into? he wondered again. Just three weeks ago his life was calm and uncomplicated. Less affluent, but uncomplicated. He had a good job, a great wife, and a dog that was a little too hyper and maybe retarded, but his life had been a peaceful one. Now he was carrying packages back and forth for somebody he hadn't met, didn't know, doing something strange, illegal, but still with the blessings of the FBI. What started out at a short-lived venture, now was turning into a lifetime project. -- like the Myth of Sisyphus. Push the boulder up the hill. It rolls down. Push the boulder up the hill again. It rolls down again. Push the boulder up the ---

My *is* is different than my own *is* now. I've lost my *is* --- and don't know whose *is* I have. Be still, world. At least slow down.

Brian watched as Fordham examined the briefcase. Fordham wore gloves against the cold, so no fingerprints were left on the case, not that that was a major consideration when you're on the side on the law. But the operation might be more sophisticated than most people gave it credit for, as Fordham pointed out at least twice since Brian started working with him. Maybe they could be, thought Brian. Maybe they did fingerprint things such as this briefcase. I know there's more involved here than I've been told. Fordham has said as much.

"I can't get in this," said Fordham. "Nothing I've got here works on these locks. And I don't want it to be obvious that someone's been tampering."

"What can I say?" Brian was less than a little confused about his role at the moment.

"You go on to your class," said Fordham. "I'll take this to the branch office here in town. Maybe they can help. If not, maybe an X-ray will shed some light."

"Whatever you say," said Brian. "But don't mess around with it so much that I wind up getting shot."

"Don't worry," laughed Fordham. "You're too important to us now."

"That would almost sound encouraging," said Brian. "If it didn't also sound scary."

"Don't worry. You're in good hands."

"Am I working for Allstate too?"

Fordham smiled as he put the briefcase in the rental-car trunk. "No. What you're working with is even more secure."

"As witness Sacco and Vanzetti. And Ethel and Julius Rosenburg."

"You seem to have a lapse of faith here."

"Just your plain first-job jitters. Remember, this is all new to me."

"We'll be gentle," said Fordham.

"How will I get it back?" Brian nodded toward the trunk where the briefcase was now secured.

"Have you ever had trouble finding me in the past three weeks?"

"You've always been there for me."

"Your protection in time of need."

"Can I go home and watch *Ally McBeal* now?

"Get outta here."

"I'm gone."

At 2:30, after his 1:00 class, Brian was interrupted in his office by the ever-charming, ever-gracious, ever-coming-on-to-you Beth.

"Hi," she smiled from the open door. "I haven't seen you in almost a week. That can put a girl in the dumps."

"I don't think a girl like you could ever stay in the dumps long. Besides, every time I see you walking across campus, a small squadron of guys seems to be following you."

"Every one but the right one, sugar."

136

"Don't pull that 'Sugar' charm on me," he smiled. "I'm a happily married man."

"That can be remedied."

"If it ain't broke, don't fix it."

"But I can fix it if I break it."

"You're a piece of work, Simpsom."

"Not bad yourself, Withers. What about a drink?"

He looked playfully shocked, holding out his watch. "It's only 2:30. Civilized people don't drink that early."

"Call me barbarian, but I do like an early afternoon sip."

"You're serious?"

"We <u>are</u> constantly civilized, aren't we? Well, let's make it a coke then. Or a cup of coffee."

"Civilization is what keeps us slightly above the animals."

"Not really. The main difference between us and animals is that we aren't afraid of vacuum cleaners."

He laughed. "Is that a *non sequitur*, or am I having auditory hallucinations?"

He got up from his chair, started toward the door, and together they walked down the hall. Other students and faculty hurried past them in both directions.

"What would you do if I took you up on your offer?" he asked, smiling.

"It's not an offer, darling. It's a cheap trick. And I'd show you the time of your life. But this is good. The question indicates that all is not lost."

He nodded at some students who spoke to him. "I may already be having the time of my life," he smiled.

"Have you compared it to anyone else -- lately?" she smiled backed at him, "to know for sure?"

"Lady, you don't stop, do you?"

"Only when I'm dead. And I'm not really a lady, in case you haven't noticed. More of a tramp."

At the snack bar on the first floor, he started to turn in, but she guided him by the arm, pulling him away. "Come on over to the lounge across the street. That way we can both get what we want. The place caters to both civilized and uncivilized people."

"No," he smiled, but moved on with her. "One of us is never going to get what he-stroke-she wants."

"Are you a betting man?"

"Not with duplicitous young ladies -- or beautiful tramps."

"I'm not that educated yet. English, please."

"Cunning -- deceptive -- double-dealing."

"Lordy. If you have a good education, can't you sound really elegant when you're insulting someone? Give a girl a chance, will you?"

"You start out with a two-mile advantage."

"I've had a lot of practice."

At the intersection, he asked, "Are you bragging or complaining?"

"Depends on who I'm talking to. In your case, it's just an explanation."

They were crossing the street now, U.S. 98, 15th St., and the cold wind was blowing out of the bay behind them.

"No explanations necessary," he said. "Nothing is going to be bought or traded here."

"Don't be so difficult. Humor me. I'm just a kid." A teasing smile from a luscious babe. How long are you going to be able to resist this, Withers? he thought. This is a good time to turn and run. Get away before it's too late.

In the bar she ordered a scotch and soda, he a plain diet Dr. Pepper. Every bar he and Susannah frequented stocked it for them because of their favorite drink -- rum and diet Dr. Pepper. When the drinks came, he started to pay, but she put her hand on his wallet and gave the waiter a five-dollar-bill which seemed to appear from nowhere as easily as if done by David Copperfield.

"Let me get this," she said, smiling. "You're living on a teacher's salary. I'm living on daddy's. One of the wealthiest daddies in north Florida. We'll let daddy pay. O.K.?"

"Tell daddy 'Thanks.'"

"What daddy doesn't know won't hurt him. I'll let him think it's for a flat tire or something. I'm afraid daddy is about as prudish as you are about drinking before five."

"Only on Tuesdays am I prudish. Wednesday, I'm petulant."

"And what is Thursday's child?" she asked.

"None of them can compete with Briggs Construction Co. -- a fair competitor of your daddy's, I imagine."

"Oooh," she smiled. "We've been doing a little behind-the-scene detective work, haven't we?"

"Not really. A lot of students <u>do</u> envy you. And envy talks, you know. Besides, Zannah and I met him at your party, remember? That little "I'm-having-a-few-friends-over spiel of yours that fed and watered about two hundred people."

"Oh, yes. I forgot you met him there. That was a pretty nice party wasn't it? You know, I don't know who half of those people were."

"You do know how to give a party, lady."

"You can do a lot of things when you have money."

"You know," he smiled, "I don't think I ever met anyone who's so consciously aware of being wealthy as you. And still so completely comfortable with it."

"You know what they say, sugar. If you got it, flaunt it. The best revenge is living well."

"You do get your revenge then, don't you?"

"I love it. I guess I've been around money so much, I'm just naturally comfortable with it. I *know* I sure would be *uncomfortable* without it. Besides, it's always on other people's minds anyway. So I just go ahead and answer their unasked questions."

"That's considerate of you," he smiled.

She looked at him for a moment, her smile frozen as she tried to determine if his statement was in jest or sarcasm. He was not completely sure himself. Somewhere in this conversation something with a tinge of annoyance had touched him.

"I try to be," she said, not taking her eyes from him. "Considerate, that is."

"And you are. Almost to a fault."

139

"You know." Complete eye-lock. "If you ever feel like having an affair, I'm available. And would love to accommodate you."

"You move too fast for me, lady."

"I'll slow down if you're thinking about jumping on board."

"It looks like a crowded train from where I sit. Briggs Construction Co. is taking up all the seats it seems."

"That can be taken care of at the next stop, if you're interested in the ride."

"Thanks anyway, but I'm already on a life-time long-distance commute." He looked down at his Dr. Pepper, breaking the eye-lock. Her eyes remained fixed.

"You can always just whistle

The reference to the Bogey/Bacall scene in *The Petrified Forest* was not lost on him. He looked at her instantly, smiling but still in a slight shock. The feeling of *déjà vu* made him feel as if he were lost in an installment of *The Twilight Zone*. Da, da, da, da. Da, da, da, da. This was the second time in three weeks he had heard the old Lauren Bacall quote. Zannah had just used it on the way home from Beth's party.

"What?" she asked, aware that she had touched a new nerve. God, she thought, he looks like he's going through a time warp - - *A Wrinkle in Time*. "What? Tell me."

"No." He smiled broader. "You had to be there."

"Oh. An inside joke? Something only you would understand?"

"Believe me," he assured her. "You really had to be there."

"That makes me feel left out." She smiled teasingly, rising to the challenge. "The more you resist me, the more attractive you become."

"You might want to try that yourself once in a while. A little reserve goes a long way."

"Not my style. But I have something that's hard to resist. Money always goes a longer way than anything else. Even love."

"Are you thinking about buying me now? Like Redford did with Demi in *Indecent Proposal*?"

"That's funny you should say that. I was just thinking exactly the same thing. See how alike we are?"

"That's really scary. Do you have as much money as he had?"

"Could you be bought cheaper?"

"I sort of fancy myself worth more."

"I sort of fancy myself as being attractive enough to get you for less."

"That you are, ma'am. Attractive enough, that is. It's just that I'm a one-woman man."

"Money can buy anything. Redford proved it."

"Iiiii ... don't think so."

"You're going to regret this," she smiled. "When you do decide to concede, out of nothing more than weakness of the flesh. And I won't have to pay a cent."

"If that happens, Lady Beth -- or Lady MacBeth -- I'll at least be in control of my own actions."

"Giving in to lust is not being in control of one's own actions. Or so I'm taught to believe in Psychology 101."

"Touché."

"You know, I almost got my daddy to buy me a McDonald's franchise one time. Just so I could be a MacBeth." She locked eyes with him again. "And it will probably happen -- eventually."

They both knew she wasn't talking about McDonald's.

Four o'clock in the afternoon. Cold February day. Almost sunset at this time of year in Mexico Beach, right where the central time zone starts. The sun low on the horizon, shining now and then in the outside mirrors, reflecting into his eyes. Brian warm in the speeding car. Luther Vandross singing on the radio. A Styrofoam cup of French Vanilla Cappuccino steaming in the car-caddie. Something vies for Brian's attention, be he doesn't know what it is. Just a feeling.

Something's happening. But what? It happens again. But no *déjà vu* this time. Just confusion. The world moving along as ordered and planned. Then a bump in space. An atom out of place. The parameters are askew. For a moment only. Then order and scheme again. Steaming coffee. Sting singing "Fields of Gold." The dark waters of the Gulf. The warmth from the car heater. Then -- zing -- wow-ee. The parameters go askew again. This time staying askew. Something is out of whack.

Then he got it. The driver behind him was blinking his lights, again and again. It was hard to see because of the glare from the setting sun. He couldn't tell what kind of car it was, but it had to be Fordham. Just had to be.

Brian looked for a place to pull over, or a deserted road to turn into. He found an oyster-shell road to the left, turned on to it, and drove away from the Gulf, driving slowly up a sea-oat hill to a row of deserted summer houses sitting on a high hill looking out over the highway and the Gulf. Not many things seem more deserted than summer houses in the winter. Empty house staring in loneliness at the cold Gulf, their porches holding a line of unused chairs.

For Brian at that moment the world seemed to be filled with empty house and unused chairs. He wanted to hear Susannah's voice. He needed her sunshine, her smile. Something about the empty houses and unused chairs made him overcome with cosmic loneliness. (How many chairs per person are there on Earth anyway, do you suppose? Counting classroom seats, theater seats, and stadium seats, and lecture hall seats, and restaurant seats, and living room chairs, and porch chairs, and dining room chairs, and kitchen chairs, and bus, train, and plane seats, and car seats? Twenty? A hundred? A thousand?)

Fordham pulled up beside him on the deserted oyster-shell road in the Blue Mazda XL -- Fordham's car *du jour*. Brian got out and met Fordham at the Mazda trunk where they stood over the briefcase.

"Any luck?" asked Brian.

"Only bad," answered Fordham. "Couldn't get any keys to fit it. And whatever's in there is wrapped in something like a thin lead-filled cloth. Or something that keeps an X-ray from going through it. No picture. No nothing."

"It's days like this that make you glad to be on the force. Right?"

"Not. I'd rather be home with my wife and children. Sitting in front of a fireplace, waiting for her to call me to supper."

"I'll bet you don't even *have* a fireplace."

"How'd you know that?"

Brian tapped his head. "It's part of my business. The American Dream is not the American Reality."

Fordham wiped the attaché case carefully, removing any remaining fingerprints, and then indicated for Brian to take it. Brian got it and started toward his car.

"See you on the way home," he called back.

"Yeah. Sure," said Fordham. "Whatever."

Down on the cold highway close to the edge of the Gulf some of the cars had already turned on their headlights. Summer resorts really suck in the winter.

Back on the highway, Brian stopped at the first pay phone he could find, got out and watched Fordham stop, far behind, surely puzzled. Brian dialed home.

"Hello." The sun came out. The world was less lonely. Susannah was back in his world again.

"Tell me everything's all right," he said.

"Not only is everything peachy. You've got meatloaf waiting for you when you get home. Now tell me I'm not the greatest thing that ever happened to you."

"You're the greatest." Meatloaf really *was* his favorite -- after maybe prime rib, lobster, and T-bone, which were all reserved for something special.

"I know that," she said. "But you can say it all you like."

"You're the greatest."

"How long before you get here?"

"An hour-fifteen."

"Can't make it faster?"

"My magic shoes are out being shined."

"I'll just have to wait then."

"I'm on my way."

"Go for it."

143

Click. Dial tone.

Fordham watched as Brian got in his car and pulled out on the highway. Stewart, farther back down the cold February road, watched Fordham watching Withers. As Fordham pulled out to follow Brian, Stewart pulled out and fell in line. There really was no reason for Brian to feel lonely; he was leading a small parade.

Captain Andy looked out at the cold, dark February night through the Plexiglas windows of the cabin of his boat. The dock was deserted in both directions. The security lights, in a straight, evenly spaced line along the waterside of the dock, like a row of well-trained soldiers, shone out to the edge of the darkness just beyond the stores and shops facing the water. Even the dock looked cold. A chilling wind stirred through the cold, dark air.

Even though no one was there to see him. Captain Andy pulled the curtains at the windows around the cabin -- even the ones facing the bow which looked out across the river to another dock separated by two hundred feet of water. No one walked along the cold dock across the river either. But Captain Andy needed his privacy.

He checked the door again to ensure it was locked. It was. He turned up the heat on the Toyosun kerosene heater that would already have heated the cabin well if there had been insulation in the roof. He had bought the boat years ago from someone in the Florida Keys. The roof was built to keep off the hot sun, not to keep out thirty-five degree temperatures. He turned off the radio's soft music -- the better to hear anyone approaching -- and went below to the refrigerator.

He took out the package of fish Brian had brought him two nights before and placed them on the cutting board he had brought in from the fishing deck out back. Opening the package, he folded back the newspaper and butcher paper to reveal six large grouper already cleaned. Unusually large grouper, almost two feet long, even after being cleaned. And fat -- very fat.

Opening the first large grouper, he took out three Ziploc bags of fine white powder. He placed the bags in a plastic milk carton on his right, and then quickly diced the beautiful well-dressed grouper into small bits which he swept aside into a large galvanized tub on his left. He systematically repeated the same motions with the other five grouper, taking from them a total of fifteen more bags of the soft snow-white powder.

When all six fish had been dispatched and diced, he took the galvanized tub out to the back of the boat and emptied the diced fish over the side into the dark river water. The water hose from the dock was within reach and he turned it on, cleaning the tub expertly, before sliding it upside down under the outside cleaning table. Then he brought out the large chopping board, washed it well and placed it on top of the cleaning table. Bringing out the plastic milk carton, he sprayed it well with the hose, thoroughly washing the eighteen sealed Ziploc bags. Turning off the hose, he took a plastic bottle of lemon Dawn and squeezed some over the Ziploc bags. Turning the hose back on, he took out one bag at a time and washed it thoroughly under the running water, scrubbing away the detergent and most of the fish odor, placing each clean bag over to his left on the stern storage-bin lids.

When all eighteen bags were cleaned, he turned off the water and placed the bags back into the now cleaned milk carton. By now his hands were aching from the cold. He carried the carton back into the warm cabin, welcoming the friendlier temperature. He sat in a La-Z-Boy recliner, which he kept there for himself in the slow winter months. In the spring, summer and fall the boat was too busy with charters to afford having the recliner on board, taking up needed space. He took a handsome attaché case from beside the recliner, opened it on his lap, revealing its handsome, clean empty interior, almost new. Drying each bag completely with a towel, he placed it carefully into the attaché case, arranging and re-arranging as he went. When he was completed and tried to close the lid, it would not close. He took out a few bags and moved others around inside the case, then replaced the ones he had removed. The lid still would not close.

He looked at his watch. Eight fifty-two. He shook his head in disbelief.

Once more he began the job of unpacking and repacking. This time he went completely down to the bottom row and began pushing the contents of each bag out to the edges. The bags slowly became thinner as the contents were distributed more evenly over the bottom. This would do it. He placed the second layer back in and went through the same process with each bag. It was going to work.

A quick look at the watch again. Nine-oh-four.

The last layer went faster, out of necessity. This time the lid closed, with difficulty, but at least it closed.

He placed the attaché on the floor beside the La-Z-Boy, went outside and made the rounds, releasing the four lines which secured the boat in its slip, came back inside, opened the cabin curtains all around, and pushed the button that began the soft purr of the motor. Always a pleasing, comforting sound to him.

He looked at his watch: nine-eighteen.

Moving gracefully out of the slip, the *Panama Queen* headed toward the mouth of the river, moved into the bay, crossed it to the Gulf and turned west, gliding past the distant tinsel lights of the sparkling skyline on the right. All of this had taken thirty minutes. Now his watch read nine-forty-eight. Another ten minutes to the Miracle Mile Condominium.

Once there the *Panama Queen*, from a mile off-shore, turned due north, heading directly toward the beach which contained no piers or docks large enough for a boat as big as this one.

Captain Andy reached over and turned on his searchlight -- for about two seconds. Off again. The skyline before him looked like something out of the world's largest theme park.

Then from the center of the twenty-story high-rise came a strong spotlight. Two times.

Captain Andy turned on his searchlight again. This time twice.

The light from the high-rise came back. Three times. Then only the brightness of the glittering skyline.

He turned west again. Then he reach over and turned off the pilot lights, then the cabin lights. He was running in total darkness now.

The cellular phone rang. He found it in the darkness.

"O.K.?" was all he said into it.

"O.K." he heard back.

Then he clicked off.

Ten minutes later the *Panama Queen* turned north again, headed toward an inlet where the lights of a small marina shown across the water. In the marina there was no more activity than there had been on the dock back in town.

The boat headed for a slip with the name "The Panama Queen" written across the top of the wall. Captain Andy pulled in, bow first, expertly coming to a smooth stop before touching any part of the slip. He was quickly on deck, securing the four tie-lines. Getting the attaché case, he swung onto the floating dock that separated the neighboring slip and walked to the main dock, turned toward the closed office, and moved into the parking lot. There he got into an almost new black Mazda truck with a sign proclaiming "A & L Electrical Contractor, 555-0550" on each door.

His watch again. Ten thirty-two.

He drove onto Thomas Drive, turned east, and went two blocks to a Waffle House which, despite all its lights proclaiming it to be open all night, was completely empty of customers. Only a chef behind the counter and two waitresses showed any signs of life.

Captain Andy entered, carrying his attaché, and sat at a booth in a corner surrounded on two sides by high plate-glass windows, ceiling to floor

When the waitress came, she smile. "Same as usual, Mr. Anders?"

"Yes. Please." He smiled back.

"Pretty cold out there tonight." She made the obligatory small talk. Always advisable for a good tip.

"It really is," he answered back.

"Mr. Briggs joining you again?"

"Should be here any minute."

She returned in less than a minute with his coffee.

"We have a special on pecan waffles this week, if you'd like that instead."

"No, thanks," he smiled. "Just plain ones are fine."

"I knew you'd say that," she said. "I just have to let you know."

"Thanks, anyway."

She left again, just as Steve Briggs came in the door. Captain Andy had seen his "Briggs Construction Co." truck pull into the parking space while the waitress was talking.

"Steve," Captain Andy rose and shook his hand. "Good to see you again. Always a pleasure to work with you."

"Thanks, Anders," Briggs responded, smiling, shaking the extended hand. "Always the gentleman. Saying just the right thing. Always a pleasure working with you, too."

He was carrying an identical attaché case.

As he sat down, he unrolled a set of blueprints on the table, and they both began studying the blueprints and talking about the electrical plan, its highlights and shortcomings, how it could be improved. The waitress came to the corner booth frequently, bringing their orders, refilling coffee cups, clearing away used dishes, asking if they needed anything else.

No other customers came in the diner the entire time the two were there. Fordham and Stewart, unknown to each other, still sat back at the city dock, befuddled at their ineptness in not being boy-scoutish enough to "be prepared." Neither had expected this new arm of the operation. Neither one knew about A & L Electrical Co. and its connection with Briggs Construction Co. Neither was aware that Captain Andy was the missing link they had been looking for all along, the link that implicated Steve Briggs who had been suspected, but not in connection with this particular operation. Nor would they be aware on this cold late February night as they sat in their separate, isolated cars wondering how long to wait before getting back to some place warm and friendly.

At the Waffle house, Briggs and Anders were getting ready to leave. The blueprints were being rolled up; the men were standing. The waitress came over with the check which Steve took before Captain Andy could.

"Thanks for letting us work here," said Steve to the waitress. "If it ever becomes an inconvenience, please let us know."

"Like we're so busy," the waitress smiled.

"Thank your boss, also," Steve continued.

"On nights like this, anything's appreciated," she said.

Steve left a five on the table. She tried really hard, but could not help looking at it before going back to the sink behind the counter.

As Steve and Captain Andy picked up their identical attaché cases, they were extremely careful not to pick up the ones they had brought in. The old switch-a-roo.

At the airport an hour later, Steve sat in the lounge having a drink he really did not want. The piped-in music was playing Peter Cetera's "You're the Inspiration." A man a few seats away wanted to start a conversation, but Steve let the man know he was waiting for someone who would arrive shortly. To keep it from happening again he moved to a deserted corner. Actually the entire lounge was pretty much deserted. Steve felt a little sorry for the man he had left at the bar; he seemed very lonely; but Steve didn't have time to give to lonely people.

The speakers announced the arrival of flight 278 from St. Kitts, Kingston, and Miami. Steve got up, picked up his attaché case and went to the deserted row of phones outside the lounge.

Very few people were on the concourse. Steve dialed a number, waited a few minutes and then began talking softly as the passengers came down the incline from the in-coming flight. The attaché case was close to his LA Gears as he spoke, alternately watching the attaché and the in-coming passengers.

149

A man in a double-breasted business suit, carrying an expensive overcoat, came to the phone next to Steve. Separated only by the protruding barrier, the two men talked, unheard to each other. As the man in the double-breasted suit talked, he held onto his attaché case which was the same make, model, and color as the one on the floor by Steve's new joggers.

The speakers announced the departure of flight 315 to Atlanta and Chicago. Five minutes. The double-breasted suit placed his attaché on the terrazzo floor next to Steve's.

The double-breasted suit spoke a minute longer, hung up, reached down and picked up the attaché closest to Steve and left to board flight 315. The Ziploc bags, which two days before, Brian had carried from Cherokee to Captain Andy, were now on their way to Atlanta --- or Chicago.

Steve talked only a few seconds longer into the phone on which a recording was telling him over and over again, "If you would like to make a call, please hang up and dial again.... If you would like to make a call please hang up and ....."

Steve said goodbye into the talking phone, smiled, said he would be home in a few minutes. He picked up the attaché at his feet and started down the concourse toward the parking lot. Outside a strange thing had happened to the cold February night. The wind was coming out of the south now, and the temperature had warmed noticeably, much more than it had been half and hour ago. Also noticeably there was more moisture in the air.

The Bermuda high had moved far enough to the east to start bringing in the winds off the Gulf, the warm, wet winds that would bring the kind of weather Florida was famous for in the winter. The Sunshine State -- "Where summer spends the winter--" Sometimes.

Brian came into his office from his 2:00 Western Civ. I class as the phone started ringing. Without sitting down first, he answered it. Fordham was on the other end.

"Come down to Captain Jack's restaurant right away. Use the side door when you get here. I'll be at the bar by the water."

"Who is this?" teased Brian.

"Don't fool around. This is important."

"Not even a, 'Please,' or, 'Could you possibly?'" asked Brian, smiling.

"Could you *please*? And hurry. *Please*."

At the bar, Fordham was drinking a Pepsi One and pretending to read a magazine in his most professional undercover agent manner,

"What's happnin,' Capt'n?" asked Brian, taking the seat beside him.

"I wanted you to see somebody. It maybe be your only chance."

"Like spotting a red-breasted something-or-other, right?"

"See the man at the last table by the water – in the dining room?"

Brian looked through the arched entrance to the dining room and the table far down at the end.

"Got him,," said Brian. "Now many points is he worth?"

"The most of all. He's the operative from the other agency – or another drug cartel. He's been following you for weeks now."

"That doesn't make me feel really warm and comfy, Hank."

As Brian stared at the man from this distance, he could make out only a few distinguishing features. He had the unsettling feeling of *déjà vu*. Something was familiar about the man eating Snow Crab legs at the farthest table. Brian had the feeling, I've been here before. In this time. In this room. With that man. But he knew it not so.

"Why do I need to knew this?" asked Brian, looking at Fordham.

"Don't take your eyes off him," said Fordham, looking into Brian's face. "Study him while we talk. Memorize his face. It may save your life."

"Oh, Hank, I don't like the sound of that," said Brian, his eyes fixed on the far man. "I just came along for the money, remember? To the best of my knowledge, I have total recall, and distinctly remember thing unsaid as well as things said."

"Well O.K.," said Fordham. "Maybe I exaggerated a bit. But we need to find out as much as possible about him; Who he is. What his game is. Where he lives. His real name."

"Hank, I already have a full-time job," smiled Brian. "This was just part-time, remember?" "But it does pay well," reminded Fordham. "This one and the one with Agular."

"Touché," said Brian.

"His present names are Stewart and Henderson. There are several other aliases. If you ever get the chance, find out as much as you can about him."

"Isn't that your job?"

"Two of us can cut the time in half. You get out sooner."

"You really are full of good answers today, Hank."

"Follow him. Go through his things. Anything. And stop calling me 'Hank.'"

"They never taught us stuff like that in Western Civ. School. Maybe one of the days I missed – Hank."

"We think he works out of Chicago or Atlanta. He goes to both frequently."

"He's getting ready to leave."

"Then I am, too. Trail him if possible. But he's elusive." Fordham stood up. "Don't forget. Learn everything you can about him. Follow him, if you have to. It'll be over faster."

"Don't you do *anything*?" smiled Brian." I do and do and do, and all I –"

"Oh, shut up, and take all that money. More than I ever made." Fordham was off trailing the man Stewart or Henderson or whatever.

Brian turned and stared out across the Gulf. The new man and *déjà vu* came back to settle on him again. He floated between to worlds, the real and the 'before this time.'

The exotic sounds of Rimsky-Korsakoff's *Capriccio Espanol* built to an exciting crescendo that kept growing louder, more intoxicating, then finally the clashing cymbals of the final chords as the audience sprang to its feet applauding, screaming, "bravo"-ing through the concert hall. The intermission house-lights came up slowly as the applause continued. Finally some of the audience began drifting to the lobby and rest rooms.

Most of Brian's students made an effort to speak to him as he as Susannah worked their way up the aisle to the foyer. The girls commented on how handsome he looked in his tux and black tie. His obligatory loose strand of hair draping down across his forehead lent a casual air of informality in spite of the tux. But as handsome as he was, he was put in the shade by Susannah in her black strapless full-length gown with the trumpet flare at the knees -- enhanced by her above-the-elbow black gloves and a necklace of rhinestones. With her long hair and constant smile, she was a twentieth-century version of the *Mona Lisa*.

"Some orange juice?" asked Brian, aware that most of the people in the lobby were looking at them. He couldn't help feeling proud of Zannah.

"Rather have water," she smiled.

"You got it," he said, leaving for the juice bar -- a good hundred people away.

From the juice bar, as he waited for the two waters, he could see the competition coming out from the auditorium through the opposite doors. Steve Briggs was dressed in the male mold of the evening, tux, and black tie, and Beth wore the same identical dress as Susannah -- only -- naturally -- white. There was no doubt that her thin sparkling necklace was made up of something totally unrelated to rhinestones -- and a lot more expensive than Zirconium.

Beth spied Brian immediately, then looked around for Susannah, found her, and, pulling Steve by the hand, headed toward Susannah who was talking to some of Brian's students. The talk was the usual small talk of concert intermissions; Wasn't the orchestra great? Didn't you like that arrangement of "Afternoon of a Faun?" -- or "Apres-Midi du Faun," depending on how affected you wanted to sound.

"Far better than I would have expected," said Susannah. "Outstanding for just a community college." She saw Beth and

Steve headed for her through the crowd. Thank God. Real People. Hurry up and get here.

"Zannah," smiled Beth. "Love your dress."

"And I yours," said Susannah. "There must be a red one around here somewhere"

"Don't you guys stand too close to each other," said Steve. "You're already creating a strobing effect."

"So, what's wrong with a strobing effect at a concert?" asked Beth.

Brian returned. "Is this the place where the parallel universes meet?"

"This is the place where good taste meets," smiled Zannah, taking her water.

"The two of you, side by side like that, look like something out of an early 40's black and white movie," said Brian.

"Something?" smiled Beth. "That deserves an explanation."

"How about 'you two exquisite looking ladies?'"

"Good explanation," said Beth.

"'Shut up, she explained,'" smiled Zannah, knowing only Brian would catch the quote from Benchley.

"How's the Renaissance Man?" smiled Steve, turning to Brian.

"Please," said Brian. "A flattering nickname, but it's becoming embarrassing"

"But you're so deserving," said Steve. He flashed his charming smiled which matched Beth's for ambiguous sincerity. "Besides. You know you *have* to be flattered by it."

"Thanks," said Brian. "Your charm is exceeded only by your recognition of intelligence." He wasn't sure he liked Steve Briggs. But he was secretly pleased with the title, Renaissance Man.

"Drinks after the concert?" asked Beth. "My apartment or the Top of the Gulf Lounge. Your choice."

Zannah looked at Brian.

"Thanks," he said. "But we've got that long drive back to Carrabelle."

"Besides," said Zannah, patting her stomach, "can't give the kid any alcohol. Gives him hiccups."

The lights dimmed three times and people began moving back into the auditorium.

"Well. Sometime soon," said Beth.

"Not within six months for me," smiled Susannah. "But I'll take you up on a milkshake anytime."

"I hear that's the 'in' thing after concerts now," smiled Beth.

"See you'al later," said Brian as they began moving apart.

"Enjoy the Copland," called Beth, pointing to her program. "He always makes me want to dance." They disappeared into the opposite doors.

Inside, the orchestra was tuning up -- that random trill of runs, arpeggios, and repeated notes, while the conductor talked to the concert master. The house-lights dimmed slowly, people still searching for their seats. The conductor stepped to the podium, immediate silence, a raised baton, suddenly brought down, and the recognizable melody of *Appalachian Spring* filled the room.

The lights in the car behind him blinked three times. Brian ignored the blinking as he sped along U.S. 98 on his way home. The moon threw a path of light across the waters of the Gulf, and the path of light moved with him as he turned and twisted along the coast road, moving through darkness, restrained only by the lines along the sides of the road. He felt as if, in the moonlight and its path, he was doing a marvelously fast dance along the road, a tarantula, a gallop, a spinning waltz to the music of George Michael and Queen's "Somebody to Love" which thundered out of his rear speakers. He was dancing along the highway as he sped in his little Z-Car --- dancing with the moon.

He thought of the Crow Indian Saying in one one of his reference books. He inserted it in one of his handouts, because it highlighted individuality and being one's own self, regardless of the flow of the tides around you; "Act like a crazy dog. Wear scarves and other fine clothing and dance along the road singing crazy dog songs after everyone else has gone to bed."

He was dancing along the road, singing crazy dog songs, dancing with the moon as he turned in and out around the bays and bayous, speeding along the winding, moonlit road, the path of moonlight on the water his partner.

"Somebody, somebody, somebody, somebody to love." The jazz waltz ended and segued to Dave Grusin's "Highland Fling" from *On Golden Pond*. The piano arpeggio flowed up and down the keys, and Brian and the moon-path raced to get home to watch David Letterman with Zannah, unless she was watching a video of *Oprah* from this afternoon. He was dancing all the way and singing the crazy dog songs, and the car a mile back blinked its lights again. Why won't Oprah ever go on Letterman's show? There's no answer. Blinking lights.

Reality check! Reality check! Brian was forced back to the world by the blinking lights. He had gone through this scene before, played this role before, and forgotten his part so soon. He had forgotten, as he did frequently, that he was now a pawn in a much bigger game than he had ever played before. Castles and knights, and queens and kings were moving and dancing all around him, dancing along the sides of their own roads, singing their own crazy dog songs.

Brian's own crazy dog song was one that praised the present moment. He often forgot his new role when he listened to good jazz or classical music, when he jogged along the beach listening to recorded books of his Walkman. He forgot it when he played sand-lot baseball or flag football, or when he was immersed in grease, working on the cars, or when he was talking to his classes about the Byzantine Empire and the Catholic Church both being the keepers of the past during the Dark Ages.

He realized as he looked for a place to pull off the road in the darkness, that he really spent very little time being aware of the new game he was playing, the new dance with the new crazy dog song. He always got too involved in the present moment. The present moment was always the one to live, the one to sing about, the one to dance to, the good present moments, and even the bad ones -- the S.A.D. ones affected by his seasonal affective disorder. Even they were to be danced to and sung to, because they were there. When they were there, they were the present. And besides, he always knew how to take the little mini-vacations he had learned from one of Dr. Dyer's books, the escapism that helped him through the S.A.D. ones.

He found the road he was seeking, off to the left, away from the water. He turned and went into the darkness about half a mile on the oyster-shell road. Fordham him moved up beside him in the new Lincoln Town Car.

"Nice set of wheels, Fordham," said Brian.

"I wish I'd had it when we went skiing in Carolina." Fordham was carrying a fairly large set of keys in his gloved hands.

"We?" Brian chuckled. "We're becoming a family now?"

"I'm with you'al more than I'm with my own family."

"Something just occurred to me tonight," said Brian. "In this game of chess that we're all playing here, compared to me, would you be a castle or a knight?"

"Say what?"

"In the chess game, Fordham. I know I'm a pawn. What are you? A castle or a knight?"

"I'm a pawn too. Definitely a pawn."

"Why do I have trouble believing that, Fordham?" Rhetorical question. No answer required.

"Let's look at that attaché again. Or should I say, one of those attachés. I've got a new set of keys here."

Brian opened the trunk. Fordham had a flashlight in anticipation of the trunk light not working, which it didn't. After all, this was the third time they had done this particular dance now.

"Here. Hold this," said Fordham, handing the flashlight to Brian who also had to hold the trunk lid up.

Brian held the light focused on the locks of the attaché. The night was a temperate one, not as cold as the week before. As Fordham, wearing gloves, worked with one key after another, Brian was still humming Dave Gruson's "Highland Fling." The

157

sixth key brought about a slight click. Brian stopped humming. The two men looked at one another.

"Do I dare say, 'Bingo?'" asked Brian.

"Please don't," said Fordham.

Fordham pushed the latches. They slid back. He laid the attaché down on the trunk carpet and slowly raised the lid. There was a heavy cloth, obviously lead-lined, covering the contents. Fordham lifted the lead-cloth revealing stacks, piles, -- no -- heaps of one-hundred dollar bills, neatly arranged in banded stacks.

"Now can I say, 'Bingo?'" asked Brian.

"Not yet," said Fordham.

"How about a long whistle?"

"Even worse," said Fordham.

"We really *are* in a bad movie, aren't we, Fordham? A long episode of *Candid Camera?*"

"Sorry, 'Fraid not." Neither Fordham nor Brian had taken their eyes off the money.

"How much is that?" asked Brian.

"At least two hundred thousand. Maybe three."

There was a heavy silence for a few moments as Brian let this sink in.

"What's it for? I mean why? Where's it going? I don't know what I mean. Just answer any one of those questions."

"My first guess would be that it's going out of the country to be laundered."

"What's your second?"

"It's payment for what's coming in."

Brian was quiet for a moment, still staring at the money.

"And my third might be that it's both. A and B."

"Can we just stand here and look at it for a few hours?"

"Sorry. You've got work to do. And I've got some of that real exciting sitting-in-the-car-and-watching to do."

Fordham carefully replaced the lead-cloth, closed the attaché and clicked the latches. He even closed the trunk lid before removing his gloves.

"On your way," said Fordham. "See you later. Or tomorrow. Whichever comes first."

"What should I do?" asked Brian.

"What you normally do -- if you didn't know."

"I would go home. To watch David Letterman. Or Oprah. Whichever comes first. And give this to Cherokee tomorrow."

"Then do it."

"But now I feel like I shouldn't keep it with me. That's a lot of money."

"But you don't know that. You don't know what's in the attaché. Remember?"

"Just think of the times I've let that sit in the car all night."

"Just keep on doing it then."

"I'll never be able to sleep."

"I don't believe that. I've seen how fast you can drift away from anything. Like trying to stop you tonight."

"Well -- I didn't know I was carrying half of Fort Knox."

"Just go on back to Carrabelle," said Fordham, "and see what feels natural to you when you get there."

Brian moved around to his door.

"I'm not so sure I'm happy that you came into my life, Fordham."

"I'd rather be home watching Letterman myself."

The azure waters of the Atlantic, the powdery-fine sand beaches, the trade winds that keep the temperature at a glorious seventy-four degrees in the day and a comfortable seventy at night. The soft tropical rains that come only between midnight and dawn -- all of these features used to mix together to make up the Camelot of the Atlantic -- Montserrat -- about as close to paradise as you could ever get without dying first. The slums were well hidden and easily avoided. Even the menacing-looking cloud rising from the volcano Soufriere only added to the exotic atmosphere.

The thin man in the white Dockers and the white Ralph Lauren polo shirt walked along the sidewalk of the cobblestone

159

street. He was in exile from his beloved Monserrat, thirty-two miles across the Caribbean. He could see the towering smoke funnel belching from the volcano Soufriere -- over there on Montserrat, his home. His move to Charlestown on the island of Nevis, he first hoped was a temporary one, but as the volcanic ash kept piling higher over the entire island of Monteserat, the move looked less and less temporary. He looked out at the tourists swimming, sailing, playing in the water along the sands of Nevis and regretted they would never do the same on what had been the world's perfect beach -- a beach -- an island -- that he had thought of as his.

He carried a totally unnecessary, richly ornate walking cane which he obviously enjoyed toying with as he walked, leaning on it when he paused, carrying it on his shoulders at times, using it to keep rhythm when he hummed, twirling it like a drum major every once in a while. He was having such fun, amusing himself almost like a little boy that his actions, smile, and sparkling eyes were in conflict with his handsome grey hair and the wrinkles around his eyes.

The little finger of the left hand was missing, a small imperfection, niggling some might say, but an imperfection nevertheless. The finger had gone some twenty years before, in his younger and wilder days, in a wager after he had read Rould Dahl's "The Man from the South," certainly a turning point in his life.

He, like the man in Dahl's story, had bet his little finger against a Cadillac that his lighter would light ten times in a row without missing. Since he was in financial straits at the time, he had wagered "something of little significance," his left pinky. His opponent had found the offer amusing and, to <u>his</u> mind, original, since he wasn't a reader and had never heard of Roald Dahl.

Obviously the man in the white casuals -- with the rich cane -- had lost the bet. But the next wager was one that put him on the road to where he was now -- extremely wealthy -- and somewhat infamous. He had asked for a rematch -- double or nothing, so to speak. The next two fingers against the Cadillac--and a hundred thousand -- dollars, that is.

His opponent, being a man of great wealth in search of amusement, couldn't find the will-power to pass up such a wager. So amused was he that he added to the pot another hundred thousand -- provided the same lighter be used. Our man in white could not find the will power to pass up such a generous offer. Truth be known, our man in white was hustling the wealthy man; he knew what his lighter would do; the first bet, he had failed on the eighth flick -- on purpose. That does say a lot about the determination and drive of our man with the unnecessary cane -- to deliberately give up a part of his anatomy, albeit "insignificant," to come to infamy so fast, with one chop of the cleaver, so to speak.

Needless to say, he knew whereof he spoke; no more appendages were lost, and he came away a far wealthier man, one on the way up, as his opponent smiled, wished him well, and left, carrying the little finger, well-wrapped, in his left pants pocket.

A black limousine followed the man in white, about a hundred feet behind. The driver watched the man's every move, trying to anticipate his random turns up side streets, down back alleys, watching for a signal that the man had found something he wanted to put in the car. Or a signal that he had tired of this particular recreation and wanted to be driven home. He could have easily stopped at one of the many pay phones along the way and, for a quarter, have the limo fetch him within a matter of minutes. But then he would not have been under the guard of the two men sitting in the back of the limo, well-dressed and well-armed, suited and tied, small armories unto themselves.

To watch the man in white stroll, carefree and aimlessly, along the beaches and by-ways of the isle of Nevis, one would get the feeling of a Sunday morning. But then all mornings on Nevis are Sunday mornings, just as all afternoons are Sunday afternoons. Every day is almost as good as Sunday on Montserrat.

The name "Tony" he did keep constant. His last name was the one that was changed, frequently at times, depending on which country was hosting him. Sometimes it was Montgomery, then Mountbatten, now Hernandez, now Agular. In the states -- when it was safe to be there -- it was Price. In Colombia, he was mostly Hernandez, even though there was nothing vaguely hispanic about him. On Nevis, he was Agular.

Today -- this month -- he was Agular.

Agular stopped at a high point on the cobblestone street, looked out over the beach with its tourists playing, and suddenly he tired of this particular Sunday morning. Maybe tomorrow's Sunday morning would be more exciting. The lilt and boyish glee were gone suddenly. He turned and signaled for the limo to come to him. The astute driver was by his side in seconds. The two guards never moved from their seats as Agular entered the car and sat behind them, far at the back of the extensive limo.

"Where to, sir?" the driver asked.

"Home. I suppose." The child was there again. Just the mood of the child had changed.

The limo circled the block, headed for the main road back toward the south end of the island.

"No, no, no," said a petulant voice. "Go along the little beach road. You know I like the little beach road the best."

The two guards did not move. No eyes even moved.

"Yes, sir," said the driver. "I forgot."

This was not entirely true. Just a few days before, Agular had declared that the main road was his favorite.

Nothing else was said by anyone for the remainder on the short trip back to the coral-walled estate, surrounded by acres of green, manicured lawns, and, yes, a eighteen-hole golf course of its own.

A guard opened the gates without question when the limo approached. Once inside, the road wound and turned past the golf course, a large man-made mountain of rock and trees which hosted a thirty-foot water-fall, a lake that had to be copied from some picture of mid-Ireland. An airfield, lined tastefully with royal palms and banyans, was almost secluded from sight on the other side of the road.

Nearing the house, the limo passed four tennis courts on the right, a large free-form shaped swimming pool on the left and then, just before reaching the six-car garage, a riding trail. The time spent riding in the car after coming through the gate was slightly longer than the trip on the cobblestone street outside the gate.

From the fourth floor tower sitting-room of the coral castle, Agular sat in a recliner and looked out of the doors to the balcony and the glistening Atlantic beyond. All of the doors and windows were framed with sheer curtains that floated gracefully in a sea breeze. Neither screens nor glass blocked the view through any of the doors or windows. There was no need for either. Never too cold, too hot, too humid, too buggy. Just Sunday-perfect.

Agular had a glass of orange juice in one hand which dangled loosely over the side of the recliner. A man in a suit came in and took the seat across from Agular.

"Charles says you tired of your walk this morning."

"Yes. That's true."

"A game of tennis? A swim?"

"It's one of those days, Jensen. A cosmic loneliness day. I seem to have tired of all my toys today, Jensen. Can you cure cosmic loneliness? I'm sure not. So you may as well go on about your own business -- whatever that is today. What is your business today. Jensen?"

"I was looking over the north Florida connection. Perhaps you'd like to look at it with me?"

"I think not. I need new worlds, Jensen. New worlds to conquer. New places to subdue."

"There's a new man working in the north Florida connection. I think you might find him interesting. He's a college professor. Western Civilization."

"How civil." Agular came back to the world around him. "You've piqued my curiosity."

"Have I?"

"Yes. Very. Tell me more."

"He's married. Expecting a child in five months. Tulane. F.S.U. Very learned."

"A family is good for a man. I like a family man. I was one three times. Or was it four? Do you remember, Jensen?"

"Three."

"Ah, ha." Agular laughed a hearty laugh. "It's good to have someone around to keep score. To tally up the mistakes. I think I have some children, don't I, Jensen?"

"Two. One boy. One girl. Both married."

"Very good, Jensen."

Agular is not confused or out of touch with reality. He knows all of this very well. And the people surrounding him know that he is very much alive and well. He just likes to play the fool, the eccentric. Never in his life has he asked a question to which he did not already know the answer. He likes to play with people's mind. And with his own.

"Tell me more about the college professor. That's a good gig. It might lead somewhere."

"A very good man. Very helpful."

"How did he come to be with us?"

"Through Cherokee -- Rucker. William Rucker."

"The fisherman. Ah, yes. An interesting man. Could be somewhat of a fool, I imagine. In the wrong circumstances. -- This professor. Does he know what he's doing? What he's into?"

"Cherokee thinks not. But others disagree. The man's not a fool. He has an A.B. from F.S.U., and M.A. from Goddard, and a Ph.D. from Tulane. Additional study at Nebraska, Oklahoma, Arkansas, Missouri, Ohio U., Florida A & M, and the University of Florida. That's not a record which lends itself to naivete."

"True. Also not a record which lends itself to us. I'm curious. Any pictures?"

"Right here. I thought you might want to see them."

"I do. I do."

Jensen passed over some photos. Agular studied them with the scrutiny of one who might be able to divine from hidden auras.

"A handsome couple. Extremely."

"Yes. Aren't they?"

"She could be a model -- and he an actor. They're almost too pretty. Too idyllic. Anything in their backgrounds questionable? To us, I mean?"

"Nothing. A slightly interesting touch. Beth Simpson, the girl involved with Steve Briggs, is very interested in Withers, the professor. She's making a strong move on him."

"Nothing like loyalty. A company girl. Staying within the family. That is interesting. Could be like watching a game of chess -- only with live players. But also a little questionable. Does she know anything?"

"No. Not a thinker. Wouldn't recognize anything if it were spelled out for her. You've met her. The gorgeous blonde -- who acts like the stereotype of the gorgeous blonde."

"Does Briggs know? And what about Withers' wife? Does she know? What's her name, by the way?"

Agular's mind instantly absorbed and categorized all data fed to him. Everything told to him, everything Jensen said, was immediately filed and capable of instant and total recall.

"Susannah. Susannah and Brian. She's a sharp woman. A master's of her own from Tulane -- where they met. Not much gets past her. She probably knows about Beth's move on her husband, but isn't going to let anyone know that she knows. Briggs has no idea. He seems to be genuinely fond of the girl Beth, even though he loves his wife and children. But he's too busy to see what's coming. Working with his construction company -- with us -- and keeping two households."

"You're right. A busy man. One household at a time proved to be too much for me."

"Also, ironically, but as it should be from our point of view, because of the woman Beth, Briggs and Withers have come to know each other, meet socially, and still have no knowledge of the other's connection with the network. They each think of the other as just someone they met through Beth."

"That *is* very interesting. Perhaps a credit to the operation of our network. Surely they will come to know about one another someday. Probably soon. Who is the link in their chain?"

"The captain. Andropopous."

"Ah. A nice man. His wife is in the nursing home, right?"

"Yes."

"Alzheimer's, I believe."

"Yes."

"A shame, isn't it, Jensen? A lot of the people in our pyramid are driven to us by misfortune. Andropolous -- and his wife. Withers -- and the coming baby. Cherokee -- and his mother. It would be a lot easier on the conscience if they were all driven by just plain old-fashioned greed -- like Briggs."

"Quite a few of our people do come to us out of need rather than greed. You're right."

Agular was still studying the photographs.

"I think I'd like to meet these two," he smiled. "Some intellectually stimulating conversation for a change. Oh, not that you're not stimulating, Jensen. Quite the contrary. But your mind goes to -- accounting sort of things. Not what I'm inclined to enjoy greatly."

"Yes. You're right. No offense taken, sir. I <u>am</u> a rather black-ink/red-ink sort of man."

"And a very good one too, Jensen. If you weren't, I'd drop you in a minute."

"I'll stay on my toes, sir."

"Let's get these young people down here for a visit. Surely, they'd love to come to Nevis in mid-winter. At least I think it's mid winter in the states now. They'd enjoy at least a long week-end."

"I'll get to work on it right away."

Jensen left the room, leaving Agular to sip his orange juice, stare out of the doors and windows, where the gently flowing sheer curtains framed the glistening Atlantic. He turned back to the photographs now and then. A beautiful woman. Extremely beautiful. It would be enjoyable to gaze at such beauty up close and in person.

"'A thing of beauty is a joy forever,'" he quoted aloud.

And then quickly, before anyone else could buzz in, he asked, "What is <u>Endymion</u>, by Keats?"

"Correct," said Alex Trebeck. "And that ends the catagory on 'Romantic Poets,' and Jeopardy. We'll be right back with Double Jeopardy after these words from our sponsors."

The night was the kind that brings most of Canada to north Florida for the winter, balmy, pleasant, in the mid-fifties. Stars and moon were shining in a moderate February sky. Fifteen hundred miles north, the same moon and stars were shining on three feet of snow along the U.S.-Canadian border.

Brian parked the Z-Car at Travis' dock -- plenty of parking space since it was after twelve -- and carried the attaché case through the arcade of the fish house to the dock and the ramp leading up to the *Miss Betty*.

Blackie was sitting on the ramp, listening to his earphones, sipping a beer. He was startled when Brian's shadow fell across his view of the water.

"Oh, hi, Brian." He looked up. The eyes of God looked into Brian's soul. "You scared me. I was just watching the water. And listening to some music."

"Hi, Blackie." Brian's voice always got softer when he spoke to Blackie. "Sorry I frightened you. No. Don't move. I can get by."

"Cherokee's not here," Blackie said. "He's at the bar."

"Sammy's or the Ebbtide?"

"The Ebbtide, I think. That's his favorite. I'm pretty sure. Yeah."

"I'll find him," said Brian. "I'm going to leave this attaché case here on deck, Blackie. You'll watch it for me won't you?"

"Sure, Brian. I can do that."

"Good man." Brian patted him on the shoulder as he passed again on his way back to the dock. "The Ebbtide, you say?"

"That's right. I'm pretty sure."

"Thanks," said Brian, leaving Blackie to listen to his Walkman and stand guard over two hundred thousand dollars.

Brian had come to enjoy going into the local bars and mixing with the fishermen and tourists. He had lived in Carrabelle three years and had never gone into a local bar until he started working with Cherokee. The small intimate, neighborhood bars rekindled a facet of his nature that had been dormant since he had started teaching -- visiting with two of his favorite types of people -- strangers and hard-working laborers. He found them both challenging and sometimes more edifying than the fields of academia.

"This seat taken?" he asked as he sat down at the bar next to Cherokee.

"Yeah. I'm saving it for a teacher/friend of mine."

"Well, I'll try to sound intelligent until he gets here."

"No. Just friendly and kind will do."

Brian was flattered at the unconscious viewpoint which the slightly intoxicated Cherokee had let slip.

"Well, that I can do. And it puts a lot less wear and tear on the brain." Brian motioned for a beer and placed a five of the bar.

"When was the last time you spent a few days on the beaches of a Caribbean Island?" asked Cherokee.

"Not in this lifetime," smiled Brian.

"Then you've won the jack-pot. Agular wants to meet you. And your wife."

"Whoa, hoss. We're going down this bumpy road too fast. First of all, who's Agular?"

"The man that signs the checks, man. The head honcho."

"I don't understand. Things have been moving pretty fast for me the past few weeks."

"Well, of course they have. But the money's been coming in pretty fast too, hasn't it?"

"Yes, but --," He had to agree with that. It had been two hundred a trip from the start, but he hadn't known that the attaché cases coming back were going to be counted as a separate trip. And at six and eight "trips" a week he was bringing home twelve and sixteen hundred a week. He really <u>had</u> fallen into a pile of it -- and come up smelling like Calvin Klien's *One*, especially with the other thou from the FBI -- and the certainty that he wasn't going to get slapped into the pen for the rest of his life for all of these lucrative but underhanded dealings.

"'Yes, but -- hell," smiled Cherokee. "When the man who signs the checks says, 'Jump,' you say,'How high?' Right?"

"Right," said Brian. He *was* right, thought Brian. When the man who signs the check says anything, you don't say, "no." Especially when the pay is this good.

"He knows your position," said Cherokee. "So he's leaving it up to you. Whenever you can get away. A weekend will satisfy. But could you make it a long week-end? Possibly four days? If not, three will do. It's something you and your wife will love. It's like being a part of the jet set for seventy-two hours. I wish he'd ask me back down there again."

"Three days is the best I can do right now." Brian was still staring into space with a look of stunned dismay.

"And Susannah?"

"Susannah?" Now he was even more stunned. He really wanted to keep her out of all this.

"Sure. You don't go on vacations without your wife. Have I got to teach you everything?"

"Susannah. Yeah. Sure. She -- she can make it." Boy, this new turn of events was really throwing him for a loop. He and Zannah had both talked about the advisability of keeping her as far from all of this business as possible. She already knew everything. While she had many concerns, certainly more than Brian, she couldn't help appreciate the money -- and the excitement. Now they were no longer Ryan and Ali in *Love Story*, they had suddenly become *Bonnie and Clyde*.

"And the best part is," Cherokee smiled, "Get this. You're on the clock the whole time."

"Well, that is a perk," said Brian. God, don't act too surprised. Don't blow this by acting like you didn't expect it. Rockets were going off in his mind. And bombs bursting in air.

"Just how much is my time worth, do you suppose? When I'm on the clock?" he asked after pushing back a few smiles and a really hard-to-suppress "Yaah-hooo."

"A hundred an hour, I'm sure. That's what it comes to now."

"Not bad for a second job, huh?" Brian smiled at Cherokee. His good friend Cherokee.

The purple/orange/pink/lime sail of the Hobie-Cat, filled with wind, blew out above the boat like a half-balloon, a semi-lighter-than-air balloon, taking up half the sky above them as they listened to the water hiss under the bow of the swift-moving craft. The mixture of sounds; the wind around their ears, the flapping of the jib, and the hiss of gliding through calm waters, all blended together to make a combination of sounds to make any heart swell. Peaceful, yet exciting; calm, yet invigorating; soft, yet turbulent. It is one of the best of times; it doesn't get any better than this.

"Get ready to come about," yelled Brian.

Zannah braced herself for the dive under the mainsail, the dive to the other side of the canvas deck.

The rudder turned; the bow turned; the deck was upright and horizontal for only a moment. Then, as the wind caught the sail from the other side, a violent jerk sped the boat ahead as it tilted precariously at an angle close to turning over.

Brian held the rope in tighter now and steered almost directly crosswind. The boat picked up so high on the windward side that both Brian and Susannah were hanging far out over the edge for ballast, their feet tucked under the wide nylon strap which held them in the boat.

"Yeeeooo," screamed Susannah, smiling, the wind from her back blowing her hair across her face and chest.

"Yeeessss," yelled Brian, lying out in space beside her. "Yes, yes, YES!"

They hung out over the side of the boat, almost horizontal in space, like flying bow-maidens suspended over water from five feet up, the boat soaring along on one hull, on one corner of the speeding triangle.

"Eeeee-haaawww," Brian let out a loud Texas cow-call.

"Eeeee-aaahh," screamed Zannah to match him.

For twenty minutes they rode the air of the afternoon sun, surrounded by blue water, blue sky and coral and pink clouds on all horizons. Then as they were about five minutes from the dock, the wind suddenly died to a gentle breeze, barely moving them toward the distant gas station, their landmark for the dock.

"That was great," said Zannah. "We haven't ridden the sky in a long time -- since last summer."

"We've got to do this more often. We haven't been sailing enough this winter. And it's been great sailing weather, too. What have we been doing?"

"Does they word, 'work,' ring a bell?"

"Is that what it is? I've been too busy to notice."

"Yeah. But aren't you glad you live in a time when you can use a word like 'disabuse' in public and not have to laugh?" said Susannah.

"One of the signs of the end of civilization as we know it," smiled Brian.

"Could you disabuse me of the view that you don't give a damn?"

"Frankly, my dear, I've long since given up trying to disabuse you of anything."

"As God is my witness," she said, holding a fist up toward the sky, "I'll never go hungry again."

"Worry about that tomorrow, Scarlet. Right now we need to ready for tying up."

He expertly steered the Cat into their slip, and together they hurried through all the steps of securing the boat, lowering the sails, folding them, and unloading their gear onto the dock. After finishing their work, they sat in some captain's chair on the dock. Zannah pulled out of the cooler two Dr. Peppers in plastic bottles, one showing signs of having been opened earlier for the insertion of some Conch Republic Rum. She handed Brian the loaded one. They unscrewed the tops simultaneously, touched their plastic bottles in a toast, and together offered the verbal toast, "Up yours."

"To the best of times," she said.

"And the worst of times."

"It is a far, far better thing I do..."

"Than I have ever done before."

Together. "Up yours. Up theirs. Up ours."

They drank, he savoring the unique blend of rum and diet Dr. Pepper, she just plain Doctor.

"Are we getting in too deep?" she asked, staring out at the water.

He knew that the subject had been changed, and he also knew what she was talking about. "I don't think so. We can always get out. Just stop."

"Are you sure?"

"Why not?"

"Maybe they're too big. To just walk away from."

"Zannah, darling. Have you ever seen anything so big that I couldn't walk away from it?"

"But this is different."

"It just pays more."

"No. I don't think so. I worry."

"Trust me. I can turn it off. Or run from it. I'm good at both. You should know that."

From the upstairs bedroom, no snow or ice intervened in the view of the wintry estate and the distant skyline, accented by the Sears Tower and the Wrigley Building. But even without the snow and ice, the coldness outside was still obvious in the barren trees and shrubs being whipped by the wind coming off

172

the lake. Anne Madison sat in the chaise lounge trying to read William Goldman's *Boys and Girls Together*, but her mind would not stay with it. She had read two pages before she realized she had no idea of what was on the pages, what the words had said. Always an avid Goldman fan (she had even known him slightly in high school), she read everything he wrote, and usually came back to *Boys and Girls Together* again every three or four years.

She respected his gift for natural dialogue, finding it always fresh and sparkling, even when she knew what was going to happen next. She was just as fond of his brother James who happened to be not quite so prolific and slightly more erudite, which somehow excluded him from the light escapism she found in William.

Softly, from hidden speakers throughout the room, came the bolero rhythm of Bocelli and Brightman singing, "Time to Say Goodbye."

William and James Goldman. William and Henry James. An Analogy? A comparison? More like a fragment from a wondering mind. *The Turn of the Screw*, Pragmatism, *The Lion in Winter*, Dustin Hoffman in *Marathon Man*, Henry II, *Butch Cassady and the Sundance Kid*, *The Ambassadors*, How pragmatic is pragmatism? The Plan*ta*genets, the <u>Plan</u>tege*nays*, Eleanor of Aquitaine, Richard the Lionheart and Philip II, Scylla and Janeway.

What am I doing? Anne Madison wondered. This is a waste of time. Idle indulgences.

She pulled her attention back to the pages in front of her. But suddenly the words, the characters, especially Rudy, made her feel lonesome, heightened her sense of lose. She briefly thought of -- and quickly ran from the memory of -- Arthur, Arthur Madison, who after a loving and wonderful marriage of twenty-five years, abandoned her in an instant by falling face down dead into his dinner plate in front of her and eighteen invited dinner quests who had come to help celebrate the beginning of their twenty-sixth year together.

Out. Out, damn spot.

The memory left on command, but was instantly replaced by the sight of David Michael, playing flag football on the lawn with some of his tenth grade classmates. Dissolve to: David Michael on the bedroom floor -- not breathing, and Anne's own hands in front of her, reaching for the handsome boy, trying to pump his heart, not really knowing what she was doing, hearing in the background, a woman screaming, crying out, "No. No. Don't do this. Please. David Michael. Come back. Don't leave me now." And all the time she didn't even know that the voice was her own.

Stop it, she told herself. This does no good.

She laid the Goldman book on the stand beside the chaise lounge, got up and move to the floor-length window, her sheer champagne negligee and robe flowing gently over one of the heat vents. She looked at her gold, diamond-studded wrist watch. Ten forty-eight. She needed to be getting ready for her eleven- thirty appointment at the beauty salon.

What for? flitted through her head.

Stop it, she again told herself.

She moved to the cavernous walk-in closet and began looking through some of her winter dresses, picking out the bright red on purpose, something loud to dispel the mood that was creeping up on her. Moving to the floor-length mirror in the closet, she held the dress up in front of her.

Yes. This will help.

A ringing phone. Again. Once more. It stopped in the middle of the third ring as Mrs. Knight picked it up in her office.

Anne Madison was already in the red dress and putting on the matching shoes when Mrs. Knight knocked at the bedroom door, almost unheard in the dressing room. Anne Madison walked to the door, opened it.

"Yes?" she asked.

"A Mr. Henderson says he needs to speak to you. About some investments he's looking into in Florida for you."

"Thank you, Mrs. Knight. I'll take it."

She closed the door and went to the phone beside her bed.

"Hello," she said blandly into the phone.

"I think I've found some more investments you might be interested in."

"That's interesting. But why tell me? I told you to go as far as needed. You know what I'm looking for."

"I may have found more than you want -- or need."

"That's not possible. I'm interested in all you can find."

"Some of it is even bigger than you were interested in at first. It may be very expensive."

"Price is no object." What a corny line, she thought. But accurate.

"All right. But I wanted you to know."

"You're an honorable man, Mr. Henderson. I trust your judgment."

"I haven't made any purchases yet, because I keep finding more leads. And each lead is to something better and bigger."

"I trust you, Mr. Henderson. As I said, you're an honorable man."

"Well, I know you must be wondering why you haven't heard anything yet. About your purchases."

"I know you know what you're doing, Mr. Henderson."

"Thank you."

"Deposit another $1.50 please," interrupted an operator.

Mrs. Madison continued after the coins dropped. "I have subscribed to the Tallahassee *Democrat*, the Panama City *News-Herald*, and the Carrabelle *Times*. I'm sure I'll know when you make a move. It's rather interesting -- to come to know a place so well without ever going there. It's like playing detective. I read about a man who was killed on the beach there, suspected of being involved in drugs. And about another young boy--" Pause. Swallow. "-- who died of an apparent overdose. Did you know any of these unfortunate -- miserable -- people?"

"No. I did not. But I was aware of it."

"Of course you wouldn't know them, would you? It's a big area. And you're just visiting there. Traveling through, I think is the phrase."

"Yes, ma'am."

175

"You're a good man, Mr. Henderson. I know you will do right."

"Yes, ma'am."

"I have to leave now. I have an appointment."

"Yes, ma'am. Would you like me to call you if anything comes up?"

"If you like. If it makes *you* feel better. But it isn't necessary on my account."

"All right."

"Thank you."

She hung up and went back to the dressing room.

In the phone booth on the dock in Panama City, Eric Stewart listened to hear the line disconnect. Then he hung up and stepped out into the chilly February wind.

A nice woman, he thought of Mrs. Madison.

A dangerous sociopath, she thought of Mr. Henderson -- Mr. Stewart.

The Sabreliner jet was docked at a pump far to the rear of Panama City Fanin Field Airport. When Brian and Susannah arrived, all preparations for take-off had been completed, and the crew of three was waiting for them. In the late afternoon sun, the Sabreliner reflected the sun's rays making it appear to be made of burnished gold or seasoned copper. They boarded the plane and were introduced to the three-member crew by a pleasant young lady who told them to call her "Sissy." Susannah nudged Brian imperceptibly at the word, "Sissy."

Off over the northern Gulf, across the glow that was St. Petersburg-Tampa and a hundred smaller dots of south Florida towns, sparkling in the night, the Sabreliner started descending toward Miami International an hour and ten minutes later. The eastern coast of Florida was one long narrow string of lights, a mega-city reaching from Homestead to Jacksonville.

At Miami International, the plane made a stop. Brian and Susannah walked around briefly, feeling the balminess of the south Florida winter.

"Feel that breeze," said Susannah, holding out her arms, letting the now-needless jacket fall to her wrists.

"A slice of heaven," agreed Brian.

As the private jet crossed the Bahamas, with Cuba off to the south, fifteen minutes later, Brian sipped a rum and diet Dr. Pepper, Susannah her home-made lemonade. (No alcohol, caffeine or sugar substitutes for junior, there.) All of their likes had been carefully discovered and anticipated.

Suddenly the plane started an evident descent. Sissy came back from the cabin.

"Why are we landing?" asked Brian. "We can't be at Nevis yet, can we?"

"No," smiled Sissy. "We have a short stop to make in the southern Bahamas. One of the Turks. We have another stop in the Caicos."

"Oh?" Brian sounded puzzled.

"The Turks and the Caicos," said Susannah, smiling. "What exotic sounding names. Now we can tell people that we stopped over at the Turks and the Caicos on our way to Nevis -- and what used to be Montserrat. How elegant, don't you think? Why does it sound so familiar? I seem to have heard these names together somewhere."

Brian lightly scratched the right side of his mouth with one finger, the signal they had devised when they first started dating, way back in FSU. It said: "Don't say anything else about that right now. More later."

Susannah saw the index finger scratching the corner of the mouth. She suddenly smiled. "Isn't this lovely? A weekend in the Leewards. Better than the Abacos for doing your neighbors one better.

"Ah, yes," agreed Brian. "I was getting tired of the Abacos."

Sissy went back to the cabin, and Susannah moved over in the seat next to Brian, leaning her head on his shoulder.

"What is it?" she whispered. His broad smile hid the words that came out.

"Say it again," whispered Brian as well as any ventriloquist.

"The Turks, the Caicos, and Nevis."

"And the other one??"

"Monteserrat?"

"Together now."

"The Turks, the Caicos, and Montserrat."

"Again."

"The Turks, the Caicos, and Montserrat."

"I think she's got it. I 'm sure she's got it."

"The Turks, the Caicos, and Montserrat." Susannah's smile faded away briefly before she remembered to keep it for cover. "The Sara Tokars case," she said. There was dread in her voice in spite of the cover-up smile.

"On television a few years back," smiled Brian.

"You don't think --"

"No. Not Tokars. Surely." He interrupted her. "But remember what the islands were mentioned most for? What goes on there?"

Susannah's smile faded again, then came back as she remembered she needed it for cover. "No. Enlighten me."

"Money laundering," he whispered, still smiling.

"Do we have to keep up this smiling when no one's around? It's starting to hurt my face." She turned to face him. Both of their phony smiles dissolved.

They looked at each other with a new seriousness. Then she smiled involuntarily and whispered normally. "What's money laundering, anyway? I've never understood what that's all about."

"Neither have I," he grinned back at her. "All I know is, it can't be good, or it wouldn't be in some many movies."

The plane touched down and Sissy came back into the room.

"Can we get off and walk around a little? asked Susannah.

"We're really not staying," smiled Sissy. "Just long enough to drop off one package, and pick up another."

"Aw, shucks," said Susannah to Brian. "Now I'll never be able to say how much I enjoyed walking around the Turks."

"Fake it," said Brian. "Look out the window, and you'll be able to tell them how much you enjoyed seeing the Turks."

The plane came to a complete stop. Sissy opened the door, and immediately two hands came in to give her two of the now familiar attaché cases. She took the cases and in return gave the two hands two more of the now-familiar attachés. The door was closed, Sissy disappeared up front, and the jet was airborne once more.

Brian leaned over and kissed Susannah on the cheek, then nuzzled his nose in her hair.

"Those attaché cases," he whispered in her ear. "They're identical to the ones I bring back from Panama City all the time."

"Oh, stop that," she said smiling, pushing him away from her. "You're tickling my ear."

Sissy was standing in front of them with two more drinks.

Ten minutes later the plane touched down again, somewhere on the Caicos, and the same scene was repeated.

"If it weren't for all this stopping," smiled Sissy, "we'd be in Nevis by nine o'clock. Now it's going to be ten."

"I thought time wasn't important on the islands," smiled Brian.

"I have a date," said Sissy.

"Time is important," said Brian.

She disappeared again, and Brian and Susannah were left to look out at the night-covered ocean, dotted only now and then by the small groups of island lights. Puerto Rico and Haiti far behind them now on the left. Then off to the south, another string of islands began to light up the sky and ocean.

"What are those?" asked Brian when Sissy returned.

"The Lesser Antilles," smiled Sissy. " the West Indies, the Virgin Islands, Guadeloupe, Saint Martin, and way, way down there, where the large glow is, is Montserrat. The glow is from the volcano Soufriere."

"That's where we're going. Right?"

"Just thirty-five miles from it. Nevis" said Sissy. Her pronunciation of the islands had been flawless.

"Volcano?" said Susannah, looking at Brian. "You didn't tell me anything about a volcano."

"It's such a small volcano -- as volcanoes go. It slipped my mind."

When the plane touched down at Nevis, Brian looked at his watch. Nine forty-two. Sissy might still be able to catch up with her date. He looked out at the landing strip and wondered why it seemed so unpopulated.

"Is this the airport?" he asked Sissy.

"No," she smiled. "This is Mr. Agular's private landing strip. There's his estate over there."

Brian and Susannah looked out at what looked like Disneyworld standing against the night sky which glowed from the belching of the volcano. Spotlighted from every angle in every color stood the Emerald City of the Night --- only mostly pink from all the coral. They walked down the steps, breathing in the warm tropical air, headed toward the limousine waiting for them.

"Does this limo have a trolling deck?" asked Brian as they settled in the back seat, over ten feet behind the driver.

The driver did not respond. Soft music came from speakers hidden around the limo.

"Would you like to dance?" Brian whispered to Susannah. "The ceiling might be a little low, but there's plenty of floor space."

"Nawh," she shrugged. "I'd rather just play shuffleboard 'til we get to the house."

"'House' may be an understatement," he said nodding at the four-story castle in front on them.

"Kind of gives a new meaning to the phrase, 'A man's home is his castle.'"

"In this case maybe it should be, 'A man's castle is his home.'"

The limo stopped at the base of the massive marble steps, lighted on each side from the ground to the top with elegant lighting fixtures. Two men waited to open the car doors and carry the luggage. Brian and Susannah started up the steps when one of the men stopped them.

"The lifts will be easier," he said, pointing to the well-camouflaged chair-lifts on one side of the steps. He spoke with the lilting, clipped accent of a West Indies reggae singer.

He helped Susannah into one of the chairs while Brian got into the one below her. The two men took one seat above and one below them, holding the luggage.

"Everybody in?" asked one of the men.

"Contact," said Susannah.

The lift began moving up the long flight of stairs as they faced back to the receding well-lighted gardens, pool and tennis courts.

"Does this make you think of the cable car at Ghost Town, or what? asked Susannah.

"Actually I was thinking of the ski-lift at Ober Gatlinburg -- or the cable car in San Francisco."

"The one you fell off of?"

"No. The one I managed to stay on, thank you."

"But you were the one who ---"

The lift stopped at a level section at the top of the two-story flight of stairs. They were now on a wide third-floor promenade that extended around the whole building, encased in a gracefully carved handrail that looked to be made of alabaster.

"Oh, look at this," Susannah said, swirling, holding her arms up and out in eager acceptance. "Surrounded by alabaster. Can you imagine anything so exquisite?"

"'Alabaster and lapis lazuli,'" said Brian, making reference to one of their favorite movies, *Making Love*.

"Framed by the music of Gilbert and Sullivan -- with poems by Rupert Brook," said Susannah. "God. It doesn't get any better than this."

"I'm glad you like it," said Agular from the arched door. "I rather like it also. I'm Tony Agular. You must be Susannah."

"Yes, Mr. Agular," she smiled. "And this is Brian"

"Call me 'Tony,' please."

"All right, Tony Please," said Susannah. "I love your place."

"So homey and inviting," said Brian.

"Come in, please. Let me offer you a drink."

All of the unscreened doors and windows had their sheer curtains blowing gracefully in the tropical breeze. On tables, counter tops and shelves there actually were vases, ash trays, statues and figurines of lapis lazuli, catching and reflecting the light in golden-blue rays that dotted the room and flowing curtains.

"My God. The place really is built of alabaster and lapis lazuli," said Susannah. "It's gorgeous. I didn't know the combination would be so beautiful."

"Thank you," said Agular. "The combination is good only if the lapis lazuli comes from Africa. I do appreciate beauty. And others who appreciate it also."

"I'll give you two hundred for the whole place," said Brian. "That's my final offer."

"Well, maybe if I can get you drunk, I might be able to get another ten or twelve million out of you."

"No more than two-twenty-five," said Susannah. "We've got to pay the kennel when we get back home."

"Edward is an excellent bartender." He nodded toward the man beside the bar.

Agular played the model host for the next three days, wining and dining the Withers as they never had been. He excused himself frequently. as much as three hours at a time, but always making sure that Brian and Susannah had everything they needed in his absence.

They swam in the pool, in the Atlantic, they water-skied, they biked around the island, they shopped at quaint stores where they could not pay for anything; Agular had seemingly instructed the entire island to charge him with any of their purchases. Brian sipped rum and diet Dr. Pepper -- Zannah just lemonade -- at attractive little bars looking out over the water. They watched first-run movies in their suite, films that had not even gotten on video yet. They played tennis, and had probably the finest three days they ever had together. Servants stood by to open doors, mix drinks, return tennis balls, drive the boat while they skied, drive them from store to store. Even when they were biking on palm-lined roads, someone would be not far behind in a car. The ostensible reason was to meet any of their needs, but Brian wondered if they were not being watched more than catered to. Their laughter and humor was something Agular enjoyed but never seemed to enter. Sometimes their untethered conversations caused him to only sit and smile, not really knowing how to enter when the *non sequiturs* and *double entendres* flew around the room like errant flies.

On the morning of the last day, Agular asked to speak with Brian alone.

"I am not naive enough to think that what I say will not be relayed to you," he told Susannah. "But at least I must make a pretense at delicacy. So often, what we say in confidence we know will be passed on. And indeed, we sometimes expect it -- what Washington calls a 'leak,' I believe -- but still decorum insists."

"Don't worry about it," Susannah said. "We expected this sometime during the stay. We're not naive enough to believe we were invited here for pleasure only."

When Brian and Agular were alone in the tower of the wafting curtains -- even the constant attendants were gone -- Agular offered a drink, was not surprised when it was refused. He pointed to a comfortable chair, sitting at the same time Brian sat.

"I really can't be led to believe that you do what you do for us without some knowledge of what you are doing." A slight smile.

"We need money," smiled Brian. "I try not to think about it."

"You try not to think about it, but you do. It can't be helped. Right?"

"I suppose."

A few seconds of silence.

"You're very good," said Agular. "You're smart. You do exactly what you're told."

"It's not hard to follow simple orders. Carry something from one place to another. It doesn't take a lot of brains. Besides anyone can do anything for the amount of money I get."

"You're very well educated."

"That takes only a little work. And some money."

"Which you worked very hard for on your own while you were attending college."

"That's right." Brian knew the man would know a lot about him.

"You're not surprised that I know so much about you."

"No." Brian shrugged, smiling. "It's expected."

"Very little seems to surprise you."

"'The best surprise is no surprise at all.'"

"Very good." Agular did not recognize the Holiday Inn slogan.

"It's not mine."

"You're also very modest -- and fair. Others would have taken credit for it."

"It's not hard -- to be modest. Beside, the slogan is kind of trite by now."

"Something you -- and Susannah both -- detest being -- trite. Right?"

"It's right down there next to plagiarism."

"A true Renaissance Man. I think that is what you have been called by people who know you well."

Brian smiled. "I plant the seed first. Most of the time, it's something that would never occur to them."

"But you are anyway. A Renaissance Man, I mean."

"Sometimes I'm afraid it's more an affectation than a reality."

"What better affectation could one aspire to?"

"Unfortunately being a Renaissance man and having money seem to be mutually exclusive."

"Hence --- stooping to us."

"I don't know that I would call it 'stooping.'" Brian indicated the surroundings with a nod of his head.

"Morally, I imply."

"Sometimes the end *has* to justify the means."

Brian and Fordham had talked a great deal about this trip; what to say, how far to go. Brian had not wanted to come because of the obligation that was implied. He really wanted to end the whole thing, but -- as Fordham had pointed out -- it actually <u>was</u> too late now. Brian was now a victim to his own greed.

"You spoke of the money a while ago. There's much more to be had. I'm sure you know that."

"Another thing I try not to think about."

A few seconds of silence again.

"You do know you are working for me. Don't you?"

"It's not hard to figure out."

"I like you very much."

"I don't know how to answer that."

"No answer is necessary."

Silence.

"You could be making more money -- with us."

"I've thought of that."

"It goes against your basic ethic."

"Yes."

"But you're tempted."

"Of course." Brian stood up at this point. "I feel like we're playing a game of cat and mouse here -- and I am definitely not the one with nine lives."

"That's true. I'm baiting you." Agular nodded toward the chair. " Please."

Brian smiled as he sat. "Maybe if I stop answering your questions, this will all go away."

"I don't think you will stop though."

"It's absolutely amazing what money can do to a pragmatic conscience. You know, I wouldn't endure this particular conversation with anyone who didn't have at least a million bucks."

"I'm sure you wouldn't. I'm flattered."

"Don't be. It's more a matter of coincidence rather than achievement."

185

"Aaah. But my achievement brought about the coincidence. My hard work. My brains. They made the money. It didn't just happen."

"All right. I made a mistake. Maybe I should have said 'merit' instead of 'achievement.'"

"Then I would have to concede your correctness. There is little of merit to my achievement -- only greed."

"I'm not trying to be disrespectful. It's just that I really don't know what to say. I anticipated this conversation and had a lot of appropriate remarks -- none of which seems very apropos now."

"Don't worry about it. You're still very charming."

"Not exactly the adjective I've been looking for."

"You job -- profession -- would prove very valuable to us. Your professorship, I mean."

"I had anticipated something like that being said."

"Maybe this conversation would have gone better unspoken. Only anticipated." The remark revealed the first sign of a hidden sense of humor. "We both knew what was to be said. We both knew your reaction and hesitation. I assume we both knew that no answer would be given at this time. 'I need some time to think about it,' I think is your next line."

"I need some time to think about it," said Brian.

"Well, I guess we've finished. All I need to do is wait to hear from you."

"No arm-twisting?"

"Certainly not. How effective would that be on an honest man anyway?"

Later as Agular accompanied them to the plane, he complimented Susannah's beauty once more. Then he repeated something he had said earlier in the day.

"I said I'm sure there really are very few secrets between a husband and a wife. I imagine you knew ahead of time the purpose of this trip."

"I have my suspicions." She smiled.

"I'll bet you do. I imagine the two of you have talked about it."

"It might be better not to answer that," she laughed.

"Well, my dear." He patted her hand. "You could do a lot to push him in the right direction."

"Oh, yeah. Like he listens to me."

"He would be most valuable. In the right positions. And the money. I don't need to tell *you*, do I? Just look around you. It can bring a lot."

"Well, I can't presume that we would be in *this* particular category." She waved her arm to indicate the estate.

"Well, now. We never can tell, can we? We can certainly get a lot closer to this with what I have to offer than you could with just a professorship alone. *N'est-ce pas*? But the professorship needs to be maintained. That's the really valuable asset. To the organization."

"Oh, you glib-tongued charmer, you," smiled Susannah.

"Then I can count on your support? And coercion?" He smiled at Susannah, but nodded toward Brian.

"It's almost an offer that can't be refused," said Susannah.

"That comes next," smiled Agular.

The good-byes at the plane were cordial. Agular's manner made them both feel they might have been coming home for the week-end, he was so warm. A bond had been made. Agular seemed genuinely sorry to see them go.

Brian and Susannah moved from the window of the plane as it taxied away from the lone figure in white on the runway.

"'The rich are very different from you and me,'" said Susannah. "F. Scott."

"'Yes. They have more money,'" answered Brian. "Ernest. Or was it one of his cats?"

"Just think, "smiled Susannah. "We're part of 'the organization.'" She quoted Agular.

Montserrat and its volcano faded into a tiny dark spot in the distance and the Sabreliner headed back to the mainland, over Jamaica, Haiti, and Cuba, with the afternoon sun off to the left, casting golden rays through the windows.

Again Sissy took care of any need Brian and Susannah could think of.

The Panama City Airport was crowded, much busier than two days ago when he had been there. Steve Briggs moved from the parking lot in the mid-afternoon sun to the entrance. He went to the drink machine, got a diet Sprite, and walked, in a business pace, to the telephone booths. Glancing at his watch, he saw that he was ten minutes ahead of schedule. He took a seat near the bank of phones, set his attaché case at his feet, sipped his diet Sprite, and thumbed through a *U.S. News and World Report* he took from his trench coat pocket. Across the concourse from him, well-hidden behind a Panama City *News-Herald* watching Steve's every move was Brian. Brian hadn't known he was going to be trailing Briggs. Fordham had only called and told him to find the man with the attaché at the airport and find out who he gave it to. Fordham also told him to get a ticket to Chicago, just in case he needed it.

Fifty feet down the concourse on Briggs' side, standing in front of a cigarette machine, watching both Briggs and Brian in the reflection from a glass window, was Eric Stewart. He didn't smoke, but he put in three dollars and pushed a button that gave him a pack of Marlboro Lights. If you're not going to smoke, at least you can not smoke something that has less tar and nicotine in it. He placed the pack in his shirt pocket, looked at his watch, ambled casually away from Briggs and Brian, feigned impatience, sat in one of the seats running down the middle of the concourse, and picked up a discarded Atlanta *Constitution*.

Brian reached in the pocket of his overcoat for some gum, pulled out an airline ticket and studied it. Delta flight 436 to Chicago, February 12th, 2000, departing Panama City. He wished now he had told Fordham he had things that couldn't be left undone.

Briggs looked at his watch again. Four minutes. Back to the *U.S. New and World Report*.

Stewart peered around both sides of his second-hand *Constitution*. He saw Brian look at his flight ticket, put the gum in his mouth, and study Briggs momentarily across the concourse. He saw Briggs look at his watch and return to his magazine. He also saw Briggs move the attaché case a little closer to his legs when the man sat down a few seats to his right. Putting the open paper in his lap, Stewart took out his own flight ticket and double-checked. Delta flight 436, departing Panama City for Atlanta, February 12th, 2000. The difference between his reaction and Brian's was that Stewart had no misgivings about his destination. He wanted to go to Atlanta -- home. He had followed the man in the green trench-coat two days ago. He *knew* the green trench coat went to Chicago. He knew where the man went in Chicago. He already knew what Brian was trying to find out.

Briggs looked at his watch again. He put the magazine in his pocket, picked up the attaché, and went to the bank of phones. He placed the attaché close to his feet, and then punched in a number, all the time closely watching the attaché. Across the concourse, Brian watched every move from behind his *News-Herald*. Down the concourse, Stewart watched casually from behind his *Constitution*. He was less concentrated than Fordham since he knew all he needed to know. He glanced over at Brian's intensity. Good man, thought Stewart. Too good to be doing this.

As Steve Briggs faced into the phone booth, he saw the bottom of the dark green trench coat move into the booth next to his. Then the attaché, identical to his, was placed on the floor within four inches of his own. The green trench coat moved only slightly as the man punched in a number and spoke briefly. The hand came down, picked up Steve's attaché, and the coat moved out of the stall. Steve hung up on the recording, "if you would like to place a call, please hang up and dial again. If you would like ----" Click. He picked up the remaining attaché and walked down the concourse toward the min entrance.

Brian watched the exchange carefully. He had seen it two days ago, but had not been prepared to board the plane. By the time he had witnessed the exchange and tried to get a ticket, the plane had already departed. This time he was ready.

From down the concourse, Stewart watched Brian watching Briggs and the man in the green trench coat. The speakers announced the boarding of flight 436 at gate four. He watched Brian make the good move of getting up and going to gate four before the man in the green trench coat. You can't be suspected of following someone if you're in front of him. Stewart himself got up and headed toward gate four, all the time playing his game, watching the green coat, watching Brian watching the green coat. Wheels within wheels within wheels.

When Stewart stepped on board, he was disappointed to find the plane so crowded. He was even more concerned when he discovered that his seat was on the aisle one row in front of and across from Brian, also on the aisle. For a moment he considered taking a later flight, but then, thinking of Audrey and Simon, he decided to stay on board and sleep for the forty minute flight.

He moved to his assigned seat rapidly, his head averted as he passed Brian. Taking the seat he reclined hurriedly, turned his head to the left toward the window, placed his ticket on his chest so the flight-attendant could see it easily, and closed his eyes to pretend sleep. On his way to the seat he noticed that the green trench coat was five seats in front of him, easily observed by both Brian and himself. Before the plane was out of its ascent, Stewart was, in fact, actually asleep.

Brian exchanged his *News-Herald* for a *Time* in the pouch in front of him, and watched the dark green trench coat stand up to remove the coat. The man was now a grey suit. Brian realized he needed to take off his own overcoat. He stood up, removed the coat, and noticed that all the passengers were now clothed for the controlled temperature, except the sleeping man who had entered so hurriedly and gone to sleep immediately -- the man across the aisle and one row in front of him. The man was sleeping a little fitfully, probably too hot.

Brian sat down and alternately glanced between his magazine and the grey suit. Then he turned his attention to an article about the recent middle-east skirmish. He was just moving on to a story concerning the Bosnian conflict when the

190

grey suit got up to go to the rest room. From his peripheral vision, Brian watched the man pass as he lowered his head slightly in an attempt to keep from showing interest.

But just before he lowered his head, for one brief second, he saw the diagonal man in the overcoat turn to look after the grey suit. Brian kept his face down, but saw the diagonal man get up, remove the coat, sit back down and once more appear to sleep.

When the grey suit returned, the diagonal man moved his head slightly. Brian now looked up and took advantage of being behind him. The diagonal man, his head back in a sleeping position, opened his eyes just wide enough to take in every move of the grey suit. The man appeared to be doing something -- to the attaché? -- that Brian could not see. But the diagonal man, from across the aisle had a better line of sight. He definitely was interested in the grey suit's movements, but to everyone except Brian -- the diagonal man appeared to sleep.

The grey suit completed whatever he was doing and settled back in his seat. The diagonal man closed his eyes and returned to either sleep -- or pretended sleep.

Brian returned to his article on Bosnia. His own eyes began to have trouble staying open until a sudden snort aroused him. It was the sudden catching of breath of someone sleeping uneasily. He looked up in time to see the diagonal man turn his face toward the aisle. He had actually fallen asleep again, only now the face was turned so Brian could see it easily.

He studied the face carefully, objectively. As he continued to examine the features, he slowly noticed a familiarity. Yes. He was sure of it. He had seen the face before. There were no distinguishing features, but he knew he had seen it. Up close. He even had the feeling that he and this face had talked somewhere.

The mind races in times of search -- and desperation -- and need. In Tallahassee? At the Radisson there? In Carrabelle? Not too long ago. Sometime since he had been away from home. So certainly not in Jacksonville -- or Pensacola. Some place more intimate maybe. Piano music. His gaze stayed fixed on the sleeping face as he let his mind race like a computer drive, looking for the right slots.

Piano music. Yes. A piano bar in Tallahassee? In Panama City? Talking. Laughing. A bar. Voices. A party. A lunch counter. A blonde. A room all white. A white piano. Susannah. A dock. Like the code-seeking computer in the movie *Wargames*. Six numbers clicked into place in a fraction of a second, followed immediately by seven, eight. Beth's party. <u>And</u> --- the restaurant on the dock in Panama City.

He had to stop himself from slapping his knee and yelling out, "Yes! Yes!" He had definitely seen the man! At that party! The whole party, the whole evening, rushed back to him. And the dockside restaurant. The man in the Greek fishing cap.

If the diagonal man was at Beth's party, and if they spoke briefly, why is he working so hard to avoid eye contact? Why would Brian see him at two places involving the drug/money-laundering ring? Three now. Why not somewhere away from anything connected with the ring? But at the party? The dock? And now in the plane with the grey suit? And also the diagonal man had been extremely interested in the actions of the grey suit. A counter agent? From another department? Drug Enforcement Agency? A hit man? A bodyguard? Just a coincidence?

Then the greater realization hit him. The man was the same one Fordham had wanted him to see that day at the restaurant. He was Stewart, or Henderson, or whatever.

The plane began its descent. The attendant asked for fastened seat belts. Atlanta was four minutes to touchdown. People began to put away books, gather clothing. Brian watched the grey suit sit motionless. He did not reach for his green trench coat. He continued reading his New Orleans *Picayune*.

Damn!! He's not getting off; he's going on to Chicago, thought Brian.

With the sudden realization of a small, unexpected bonus, Brian saw the diagonal man preparing to get off. As Brian watched out of the corner of his eye, the diagonal man collected his magazine and paper, his tan overcoat, all the time spending great effort to keep his face away from Brian. So much effort was spent avoiding Brian, that the man did not see his ticket stub fall to the carpet beneath his seat. But Brian did.

Only six people left the plane at Hartsfield. Knowing he had to get off anyway, Brian took his time. He tried to look like someone staying on board as the diagonal man passed him. He waited until all the others were close to the door before he stood up, picked up his trench coat, and in doing so, dropped his copy of the Panama City *News-Herald*. He grimaced at his own clumsiness, reached down to pick up the paper. When he turned to leave, the ticket stub was no longer beneath the seat that had been occupied by the diagonal man.

Moving hurriedly to the door and the boarding ramp, Brian kept his eye on the diagonal man, who was in the process of becoming the tan overcoat. When life hands you lemons, you make lemon sorbet, thought Brian. Miss the 10:30 streetcar, take the 10:45. Can't make it to Chicago, do something worthwhile in Atlanta.

The tan overcoat watched Brian in the windows of shops facing the escalator. Brian knew it; he was doing the same thing. He could see the face of the man in the rippled reflections from the windows as the man began to walk down the moving steps. Brian began to walk also. The tan coat took two steps at a time. So did Brian. On the main floor, the overcoat broke into a slight jog. Brian followed his lead. Then the man began running. Brian kept up with him. Easy for a beach jogger.

Out the front entrance, amid thousands of frequent flyers, the man jumped into one of the waiting cabs which immediately sped off. Brian took the cab right behind the one racing away.

"Follow that cab," he said. It was a corny line, but somebody has to use it. He got a little bit of a rush now that he got the chance to say it.

Out of Hartsfield Boulevard, up the ten-lane access road to I-85, then north toward the towering silhouettes that were Atlanta. At one time Brian's driver got almost on the bumper of the fleeing cab.

"I don't want to get in the cab with him. I just want to follow him."

The driver backed off slightly.

"But don't lose him," Brian emphasized.

Into the towers that made the city, past one exit after another until a quick turn-off at the International Boulevard Exit. West to Peachtree, then south to Decatur, back to Peachtree.

Brian's cab almost missed the exit, because it was two lanes in toward the median. But quick darting into other lanes let the driver make it just in time. On Peachtree both cabs had to move much slower, darting in and out of available spaces as they opened up in other lanes. Sometimes the two cabs were three lanes apart as they moved back and forth. Then suddenly the leading cab stopped, and the tan overcoat jumped out of the left door, onto the median and began a quarterback's running dodge through the on-coming traffic at the intersection of Peachtree and Decatur, in the shadow of the Oliver Building.

Brian threw a fifty on the driver's seat. The cab stopped, and Brian himself began the same run, in and out of oncoming cars, the first lane coming from behind him, the next four coming from the front. He held up has hand with authority made even more imposing by the College ID that he gripped tightly as if it were a badge of some sort.

Both men went over the hoods of cars, over trunks. At one point Brian jumped from the hood of one car to the roof on another in the next lane.

On the crowded five-o'clock sidewalk of Peachtree Street, the tan overcoat turned south, Brian pursuing. The Georgia Federal Atlanta Tower across the street blocked off the late afternoon sun as the two men ran through the darkening canyon. At the Wall Street intersection, again they had to run interference through the slow-moving traffic, once more hurdling over hoods and trunks. The tan overcoat was always just a mere hundred feet from Brian. Past Wall Street, on down Peachtree, past Plaza Park, up the overpass over the MARTA tracks to the intersection of Peachtree and Alabama. Here the tan overcoat turned west on the north side of Alabama Street, in the shadow of the new Federal Buildings. Then at the corner of Broad Street and Alabama, the east corner of the Federal

Building, suddenly the tan overcoat disappeared down the entrance to Underground Atlanta and the Five Points Station of MARTA. As Brian swung into the MARTA entrance, he could see the tan overcoat at the bottom of the steps, closer now than he had been anytime during the chase. Yes!! Yes!! Take the train! Take MARTA. On the train, there are only so many places you can go. It's a one dimensional plane. Please take MARTA.

On the platform, beside the track, the overcoat ran to the intersection, the heart of the Metropolitan Atlanta Rapid Transit Authority. Trains were moving away, picking up speed, some slowing down, some boarding, some unloading, a few still and silent. At the heart of MARTA, the very center, with arteries spanning out to reach the far points of Atlanta, the tan overcoat turned west, running down the side of the tracks to an archway in the distance. Brian swing left to follow, racing past moving trains, still trains, passengers, thousands of five-o'clock people, hurrying to get home, getting out of the way of the two running men. The overcoat turned out across the tracks, in front of slowing trains, accelerating trains. Brian followed, once having to jump onto the front of one of the moving trains. The tan overcoat fought his way back onto the concourse once more. Brian followed. They both ran haltingly, around people, into people, at people, stopping, sidestepping, running, stopping. And in the race Brian was ever getting closer; a two-foot gain, a four-foot gain, eight feet. Slowly, amid the hectic race, the gap was closing.

At the west end of the underground Five Points Station, again, suddenly the overcoat disappeared, this time through the arch that read UNDERGROUND ATLANTA.

Brian sped through the entrance and for a moment thought he had lost the man, but then saw him running along the mall of stores on the other side. Brian took off again, now having lost all of the ground he had gained, maybe even more. With his college ID still in his hand, he raced along the row of shops and eating places, now beginning to fill with the five-o'clock people.

Suddenly the tan overcoat made a quick turn and was out of sight. Brian raced to the turning place and saw that he had entered a fine clothing store, selling men's and women's clothing. As soon as he entered the open-front shop, he saw that the man had disappeared somewhere behind the racks, maybe into one of the dressing rooms, some secret place in the large shop.

No. You won't get me to fall for that trap, thought Brian. Right now I know where you are. You're in this store somewhere. There are no other ways out. I know the Underground that well. You're here to stay -- as long as I don't come in. Once I come in, and we play ring-around-the-rosy -- moving around these racks of clothes --at some point -- when I'm farther in the store than you are -- and you're out this way, behind a rack close to the entrance -- you slip out. And then, while I continue to play the game, you walk on down the mall, leaving me behind looking for a phantom. I won't give it to you that easy. Right here I'll stay. You have to come out sometime.

Brian stepped back, across the mall where he could see the comings and goings of people in and out of the clothing store. He was glad to have the rest. He sat on one of the benches facing the clothing store, got out a piece of gum, and enjoyed being able to catch his breath. His job was easier now: all he had to do was wait for the tan overcoat to come out. Then he suddenly realized that the overcoat was not coming out, not as long as Brian sat here in plain sight, easily seen. Why should he come out to a man he had spent the last ten minutes running from, through downtown Atlanta in the heart of five-o'clock traffic?

Brian stepped back into a record and tape store next to the bench. He positioned himself behind a small wall that jutted out from the side of the store, the wall that held the side of the sliding fence that came out of the ceiling when the store was closed. Not quite hidden enough, he reached out and, with some effort, pulled one of the CD racks over in front of him.

A clerk came over. "Can we help you, sir?" A little officious.

Brian, still watching the clothing store, held out his College ID briefly. In large letters across the face, it read GCCC. Who knew? Some official Georgia law enforcement agency?

"I may be here a while," he said.

It was when he waved the man away with his other hand, the one with the gun Fordham had lent him, that the man left hurriedly.

Brian kept his eyes on the clothing store for twenty minutes, watching people wonder in and out. Most came out with more packages than when they went in. After twenty minutes, Brian realized he had made a mistake, a BIG mistake. The man could easily have gone in and bought some new clothes, at least a new coat, and carried his old one out in a shopping bag. Brian had been watching for the tan overcoat or the medium blue sport jacket. The man could have come out ten minutes ago in something completely new.

He left the music store, went over to the clothing store, and stood at the entrance until he caught the eye of one of the saleswomen. He asked if she could get the manager to come to the front, and hurry, please. He held out his GCCC card in order to make things go faster. The manager came quickly.

"Yes, sir. What is it?"

"I'm going to have to ask you to close the store for a few minutes. Let the gate down so I can look through the place without someone getting out. There's a man in here somewhere I need to find."

"Came in wearing a tan overcoat? Blue sports jacket?" asked the manager.

"That's him. Where is he?"

"Left about five minutes ago. Said you might be here looking for him. Described you well. But the badge would have been enough."

"Damn! He bought new clothes, right?"

"Yes. sir."

"What did he get? What's he wearing?" Brian was ready to take off, looking for him again.

"A dark blue dress with matching flats. Oh, and a pale blue broad-brimmed hat with matching gloves. Quite stunning, really."

Brian stared at the manager, his mouth slightly agape.

"He said he'd meet you at your usual place," said the manager. "And to let you know how he was dressed -- so you could spot him."

Brian started slowly down the walkway of Underground Atlanta, dejected, duped really grandly, -- twice in one day.

"Have a nice evening," said the manager from behind him.

"Yeah. Right," said Brian.

Snow was still on the ground in places where the sun hadn't reached, even though the last snowfall had been a week ago. As the Mercedes turned into the parking lot at the Mad Bull Construction Company, it slid just slightly on a spot of ice that had formed the night before. Anne Madison parked the Mercedes in the sun to keep the car warm, came into the reception room dressed as if she might have been going out for dinner at the Top of the Tower.

"Good morning, Mrs. Madison," smiled the attractive grey-haired receptionist. "Haven't seen you here in a long time."

"You know my head for business, Judy," smiled Anne. "The place runs far better without me."

"No. That's not so," said Judy with sincerity. "When you worked here, you were on top of everything. You landed more jobs for Mad Bull than anyone ever has."

"That was fun," Anne reminisced. "I wish I still had that old fight."

She turned to look at the three large photographs hanging on the back wall of the elegantly decorated reception room. The large plaque beneath them told who the three people were: "Arthur Madison, Anne Bullock Madison, William Bullock -- founders of Madison-Bullock Construction Company, 1972. Became Mad Bull Construction Company, 1986. Serving Chicago and the Upper Mid-West with Pride."

Anne stared at the picture of Arthur, her dead husband, then at the picture of Bill, her brother, now dead also. The three of them did have a lot of fun in the beginning. The long days. The lunches in. The tours of job sites. Even when the company had grown to be the largest leaser of heavy equipment in Illinois and four neighboring states, she had loved the traveling, the meetings, the competition. She HAD been good at her job. Tough. But fair. A fighter. She could figure the bidding down to the last dime on a ten-million dollar project and then still cut more to land the job. And still give good merchandise. "The Best Building for the Lowest Cost." That had been their motto back in the seventies -- when they were beginning -- and scratching their way into the field.

"Jack is waiting for you now, Mrs. Madison," the receptionist said, breaking into Anne's reverie.

"Thank you, Judy," Anne showed a slight embarrassment, as if her thoughts might have been apparent.

She turned and headed for the door with the name plate, "Jack Madison, Manager, Mad Bull Construction Company." She paused halfway and looked at the door farther toward the front of the building. The name plate read, "Anne Madison. Chairman of the Board and C.E.O. Mad Bull Construction Company." At one time that had been Arthur's office. What was now Jack's office had belonged to her.

She knocked on the door.

"Come in." She heard the cheerful voice of Arthur's younger brother, always smiling, always agreeable.

Anne entered.

"Anne." The grey-templed, handsome man moved to greet her, hugging her with affection. "It's good to see you. You don't come here nearly enough. You've even stopped coming to the board meetings."

"You're doing fine without me. I even stopped reading the minutes -- months ago." She moved to the maroon leather chair facing his desk and took a seat.

"We need you back here," Jack smiled. "We could use your business acumen."

"No. It's a different time." She smiled at him. "And you're doing a good job." She looked at him seriously for a moment. "It's hard to realize that you've done so well when you think about what a bum you were in your twenties and thirties. God, you were awful." She smiled again to soften the words. "The only reason I can say that so openly is because of what you are now."

"No offense taken," smiled Jack. Even when he had been the scoundrel Anne was referring to, he had the Madison charm. He had always had the Madison charm, even when he was twelve, when Anne and Arthur married.

"If it hadn't been for you and Arthur," he continued, "no telling where I would have wound up. How many times you figure you had to bail be out of jail? Not to mention give me a place to stay once in a while?"

"Hundreds?" she laughed. "No. I'm kidding. No more than ten or twelve. But the people you ran around with. My God, what thrash."

"I was a thirty-seven year-old teenager, wasn't I?"

"You were a throwback to the sixties."

"You and Arthur turned all that around for me."

"It turned out to be a mutual relationship. When you needed us, we were there for you. Later when we needed you, you rose to the occasion. But you were a mess back then. A true pothead."

"Don't remind me. That's all behind me now."

"Where are those papers you needed me to sign?" she asked, looking at her watch. "I've got other things to do."

"Here you are." He pushed a stack of papers toward her, folding them back to the correct pages, pointing at the lines that needed her signature. She began signing as he continued talking. "Most of these have to do with the acquisition of the Johnson Company. A few are concerning the new contracts in--"

"Don't bore me with details, please. You know I leave everything to you now. The past two years you've shown your mettle. Your business sense is unquestionable." She looked up at him and smiled briefly. "It's your social contacts that are questionable."

"You've seen the papers, I'm guessing."

"Jack! The Minotti's!! And a picture in two papers! Can't you find someone a little less explosive to run with?" She kept signing the lines he indicated.

"Annie! It was just a cordial drink. I was at Chez Antoine's. They were there. They asked me over for a drink. It would have been rude not to have <u>one</u>. So a picture happened to be taken of them -- while I was at the table. I went back to my table just a few minutes later."

"The paper says you all left for a private party somewhere else."

"Lies. All lies," he smiled. "Thirty minutes after that picture was taken I was home in bed. Sound asleep."

"Pictures like that could lose us some business."

"Could get us some, even bigger. Minotti's have friends too, you know. Not just enemies."

"We don't want to do business with them -- or their friends."

He smiled broadly. "Their friends have more money than their enemies.."

She laughed. A sincere hearty laugh. "Spoken like a true Mad Bull representative."

"Here. Don't forget this stack. These are --"

"Don't tell me. I don't want to know. The less I know, the less I worry. And besides --- the less I interfere, the better you seem to run things. You're making us more money now than when Art, Bill and I were here."

He handled the compliment with sincere modesty. "Inflation just makes it looks that way. What I'm taking in now wouldn't buy as many loaves of bread as what you three musketeers were netting."

"You may be right. But whatever you're doing, don't stop. It's looking good on paper -- and in the banks. Besides, it's not the loaves of bread that interest me, Jackie. It's the caviar and the Mercedes."

"Annie, my dear, my most pressing drive is to keep you living in the style to which you've become accustomed over the past twenty years."

"There," she said, pushing the pen back across the desk. "I suppose that's not too much for one day's work."

"You need to come back, Annie. We need you here. It would be good for you. Besides, we just plain 'ole miss you around here. When you were here last, I was just an inventory manager. Remember? Now we could be working together. A team."

Anne stood, looking around the office nostalgically again. "It might be something to think about. Maybe. But, Jack, I've gotten bitter. You don't lose as much as I lost in such a short time and not become bitter."

"You could change back, you know. Come on, Annie. Come to the cabaret."

The small back-alley bar, far out to the north of Panama City, was as seedy as the neighborhood around it. Brian sat at a booth by a window which looked out on a view to be envied by any bag-lady. Less than three hundred feet away was one of the city dumps. Not your average place to bring a date. Fordham was supposed to meet him here, and was already ten minutes late.

Brian took another sip of his Pepsi and looked at his watch. The place didn't have diet anything.

One of the three customers scattered through the small room had been keeping the juke-box well supplied. Brian was listening to Clint Black doing "Put Yourself in My Shoes." for the third time. He had sort of liked it when it came out some years before, but he was getting tired of it now -- especially today.

Fordham came in, saw Brian by the window, nodded, and went to the bar.

There he order two Icehouse beers, paid for them and brought them over to the table.

"Sorry I'm late," he said. "Traffic was a bitch."

"Not to worry," smiled Brian. "I've just been sitting here enjoying the atmosphere and the view." He nodded toward the dump.

"Well, I picked this place, 'cause nobody's likely to see us together here."

"Not anybody we'd have to worry about. That's for sure."

"Here," said Fordham, pushing one of the Icehouse beers over toward Brian. "Have a drink and quit complaining. You're making more money than I am right now."

"Hank! It's the middle of the day. I've got another class to teach. I can't be drinking this time of day."

"You don't sit in places like this and sip on cokes. Not unless you want someone to get suspicious."

"I think we look pretty much out of place here already."

"Humor me," smiled Fordham. "I'm a hard-working, under-paid government agent. Drink some of your beer, and put that Pepsi out of sight."

"For you, Hank," smiled Brian, following his orders. The cold beer was good. This might be the beginning of a new trend. "Now. What's up?" asked Brian.

"The boys think maybe Beth can help us," said Fordham.

Brian hated hearing anything about 'the boys.' It was Fordham's way of speaking about his superiors -- wherever they were -- whoever they were. Usually when 'the boys' came up with an idea, it involved something a little more out of the ordinary -- certainly a little more dangerous.

Brian rolled his eyes back. "This can't be anything but bad. Get it out fast so it won't hurt."

"They think Beth might be able to help us. And be willing to. She's in a unique position to find out things that we need to know. From Briggs."

"Well, they're right there. A horizontal position is the best one for doing undercover work."

"Glad you see it that way too. Can you take care of it?"

"Me???" asked Brian, stunned. He had assumed Fordham was going to do that same trick with Beth he had done with him

203

-- getting in touch with her, letting her know who he was. "Why not you? This is your ball park, Hank. You know more about it than I do."

"But you're in a better position. And there's no need to expose me. She'll be working with you, so you'll already be exposed."

"You make it sound like something contagious. Like the flu. I'll already be exposed." Brian smiled and sipped his Icehouse. "You constantly amaze me, Hank. The way you keep pushing me out there in front of you. I thought you were supposed to be protecting me."

"We're behind you all the way," smiled Hank. "Even to the witness protection program if necessary."

Brian's smile left suddenly. "Now that little piece of information has never come up before. At least not while I was awake. Witness protection program? I wouldn't be here one second if I had ever heard that phrase mentioned. I know all about those programs, Fordham. I've read *I Am the Cheese*. Please say that was just a joke, Hank."

Fordham looked at him seriously, as if amazed himself that Brian had never realized that there might be a time when he would have to hide.

"Surely you must have known," said Fordham. "That there might come a time when it would be necessary -- at least for a short while."

"'At least for a short while?'" Brian's face had taken on a different color. "That statement implies that it could even be longer. Like maybe forever."

"No," assured Fordham hurriedly. "Certainly no more than a year or two."

"A year or two?" Brian looked out at the garbage dump, which suddenly looked not completely undesirable -- at least representing freedom compared to the thought of two years in hiding. This was definitely something he would not share with Zannah. It wouldn't really be like lying -- more like just withholding evidence.

He looked back at Fordham, almost pleadingly. "Tell me this is a bad dream, Fordham. Please."

"Well ---. It wouldn't be absolutely necessary. But you don't help catch somebody like Agular without having some -- retribution to fear. Most people in such a position would want to be hidden -- at least for a while."

Brian shook his head, unbelievingly. He took a drink of Icehouse, but the same reality was still there. Then he turned back to Fordham.

"You know, Hank. I have dreams. Sort of nightmares really. There are two in particular. One of them is that I'm caught in a spider-web. Struggling to get free. Pulling against this giant web that's so sticky it's like being held by some strange super glue. And while I'm struggling to get out, there are spiders coming at me from all different sides. One of them looks like Agular. One like Cherokee. Another like Steve Briggs. The Swede. And one of them even looks like you, Hank."

He smiled slightly, not a smile of enjoyment. Can you believe that? I'm even trying to get away from you in that dream."

He paused for a moment and tasted his Icehouse again. "And then there's the other dream. In this one I'm running. Running, running. Always running. Down this long dark alley that never seems to end. I can hear people running behind me, trying to catch me. But I can't see them. But I know who they are. They're Agular, The Swede, Cherokee, Briggs. And you. You're in that dream too, Hank. Even though I can't see you. You're one of the ones I'm running from."

Fordham looked over at him sympathetically. Even a look of compassion settled on his face as he looked into Brian's eyes.

"I used to have that dream," said Fordham. "Both of them. When I first started working with the agency. My wife used to have to wake me up every night. Just so I could get out of it."

"But that's you, Hank. That's your work. You've settled for it. You chose it. I didn't. I can't keep on having these dreams over and over again. It's not the life I chose. Or want."

Fordham reached over and gently patted him on the arm. "It'll be over soon. I promise."

"O.K. So you were right, and I was wrong," said Brian. "Just don't say, "I told you so.' Please." He looked at her with a defeated look, smiling slightly.

"What are you mumbling about?" Susannah looked up from her magazine. smiling back at him.

"It's deeper than I thought it would get. Bigger than I thought it would be."

"I told you so."

"How did I know you were going to say that?"

"I'm predictable -- sometimes."

He leaned closer to her on the couch, resting his head on her shoulder. "I think you ought to leave. Go stay with your parents for a while."

"But I don't want to," she smiled at him. "I can't leave you now. What about all that pre-natal bonding between you and junior? Besides, it's getting too exciting to leave now. How often do I get invited on trips to Montserrat?"

"More often than I would like."

They were quiet for a few moments, staring into the fire, listening to the crackling of the flames mixed with the sound of the cold wind outside.

I really would like for you to get away from here for a while. Not that I'm naive enough to think they couldn't find you if they wanted to."

"'They' who?"

"Agular -- the new unknown guy -- Cherokee -- Fordham -- whoever."

"Fordham? You don't trust him now? You *are* becoming paranoid."

I sort of don't trust anybody anymore."

"Bad sign. First sign of alienation from the family."

"Or maybe the first sign of recognizing the insanity I got myself into."

"Then 'Stop the Insanity,' to quote the bald blonde."

Again they were quiet a few minutes.

"I don't want to go, you know," she said, more into the flames than to him.

"I don't want you to go, you know," he spoke back into the flames. "But it's the safe thing to do. Maybe 'Out of sight, out of mind.'"

"I don't think so. Not with these people." Pause. "When do you think I should leave?"

"Right away. Like tomorrow."

"But my job?"

"You were going to have to leave it in a few weeks anyway. You can always tell them it's something to do with your health. Which will be more true than they will ever know."

Silence.

"Tomorrow? That's less than twelve hours away? You do know that, don't you?"

"I know. More than I like to think about."

He turned and kissed her gently. The soft kiss grew into one more passionate, and soon they were in each other's arms, going through the wonderful motions of a bitter-sweet last night together. For a short while neither one of them thought about the impending separation.

Beth sat at the bar, sipping a Marguerita, savoring the salt with each sip. It was alien to her nature NOT to flirt, and so she had to smile at some of the men looking at her in the mirror behind the bar. One man had already come over to ask if he could buy her a drink, and with mixed emotions, she had to tell him she was waiting for someone. And he was handsome too. She had been tempted to exchange phone numbers so she could meet him some other time.

When Brian arrived, she moved with him to a table in the corner. Many eyes followed her in her all-white dress and matching accessories as she walked gracefully across the room.

"Have you been waiting long?" asked Brian after ordering his usual rum and diet Dr. Pepper.

"About ten minutes."

"I'm not late, am I?" he questioned, looking at his watch.

"I'm early," she smiled. "You know I can't resist a lounge with lots of good-looking men. Besides, time is relative anyway. Who's to say what's late?"

"Einstein, for one. And what do you care about handsome men? You've got Steve, the ultimate Adonis."

"Variety is the spice of life."

"Ah, yes. And you do like to mix your oregano with your nutmeg. Along with a dash of rosemary and thyme."

"Rosemary I can do without, but I do want lots of Thyme."

"You're a piece of work, Beth."

"That's what I've been told." She winked at him playfully. "What's this 'business' you wanted to see me about?" She made quotations marks with her hands.

He took a sip of his drink, paused to formulate the words correctly in his mind, hoping they would come out right.

"I think you're a girl who could be counted on to go for something unusual."

"Even kinky," she smiled.

"How about dangerous?"

"Borders on orgasmic."

"Secretive?"

"I'm always discrete. At least until the next affair comes along."

"No," he smiled. "We've got to be more serious than that."

"You mean, like, this is *really* serious, huh?"

"*Really, really* serious."

"I've been known to hold my tongue when it's necessary."

"I need your help."

"If it will help make points with you, I'm available."

He smiled. "We've danced around that tree enough to make a well-worn path."

"Does that mean 'no dice?'"

"It's not you, you beautiful blonde. It's my puritan upbringing."

"There goes that Plymouth Rock excuse again. Falling all over me." She smiled a little broader, the consummate flirt, hating to give up. "Why me?" she asked. "Why do you need _my_ help in particular?"

"Because you're in a particularly unique position. Right where we -- I -- need you to be."

"I caught that," she smiled. "There was a 'we' in there. You're piquing my curiosity."

"Slip of the lip. Not Freudian, I assure you."

"You've taught psychology. I've taken psychology. We'll leave it at that."

"You're too quick," he smiled. "There's no getting around you."

"Only through me. Now. Explain."

Brian paused. So much was at stake here. His life. Zannah's. His future. He could see himself selling Tupperware somewhere in Wyoming. He was also keenly aware of the danger in which he was placing Beth. Was it fair to her?

"I'm hesitant to do this. Not only am I revealing a lot about myself, I may be putting you in danger."

"I've been there before."

"No. I mean _real_ danger. Not just some guy who's after your body."

"How dangerous?" Her smile was starting to fade.

"Maybe -- your life."

"Ooooh." She smiled broadly again. "This is too melodramatic. You're putting me on. This may be the best line I ever came across."

He could think of nothing to do but take the plunge. He walked out on the end of the diving board, and started the dive.

"I'm tied up with the FBI. It's got to do with drugs coming in along the coast here -- and money going out -- to be laundered. I've been working with them for over five weeks now. Steve -- your Steve -- is involved. We want you to go to work in his office. You've told me he's asked you to. We want

you to find out as much as you can. How much comes through .
Where it comes from. Are there more sources besides Agular,
the guy who seems to be the head of it -- down in Montserrat.
Or Nevis. Where it goes. Who else is involved."

"There." He let out a long breath he'd been holding. "Now
you know almost everything. You're in. Whether you want to
be or not."

"Wow," she said. No smile this time. "That's a lot to
absorb in such a short time. You know, Withers, you need to
learn to let go. Get things off your chest."

"Yeah. Maybe you're right. I'm too withdrawn, aren't I?"

"And you want me to do all that?"

"You're ideal for it. If you do it. I said you were in a
unique position."

"You're right. I've never been in this position before."

"I don't want you to answer now. I want you to think about
it. There's too much at stake here for you to answer too
quickly."

"Don't worry, handsome. This one will take some thought."

"I hope I haven't misjudged you in your ability to keep this
quiet. A lot depends on it. Like maybe my life."

She became her playful, teasing self again. "Oh, baby.
You're too important to me for me to jeopardize your life." She
patted him on the hand.

Brian suddenly realized something new. Now Beth had
more control over him than he had ever expected. She was in a
position to make some demands herself now. He had just put
himself in a very vulnerable position, one he had not thought
about ahead of time, had not anticipated. Now she could call the
shots, if she wanted to -- if she came to realize the power he had
just given her.

"I'll do it," she said, looking into his thoughts.

"I just told you. I wanted you to take some time. Think it
over. This is not like accepting a date for the Senior Prom."

"I'll do it anyway."

"Good," he said. It was not a time to be unselfish. He
needed her just as involved as he was now.

"I'll tell Steve tonight. That I want to start helping him at his office. He's asked me too many times. He thought it would never happen."

"Good. Try to get as much information as possible. Especially find out any companies he's doing business with in the Bahamas, the Caicos, the Turks, the Lesser Antilles, anywhere in the West Indies. Nevis in particular. Any banks there. Who he contacts in Chicago. Or any other northern cities. Find out if he has any other connections here besides Captain Andy."

"Who's Captain Andy?" she asked.

"Not important right now," he answered.

He took a breath and then continued. "This stuff we're after isn't going to be lying out in the open. It's going to be well-concealed. Files somewhere else besides his main office. A back room. An office somewhere else."

"Maybe his condo at the beach," interrupted Beth. "And I certainly get to go there a lot." She smiled wickedly again.

"Anything you can find. As fast as you can."

"Why are they in such a hurry?"

"It's not them that's in the hurry. It's me. I want to get out of this thing as soon as possible. I don't know what my life is going to be like when it's all over. But I'm ready to get on with it and find out. Anything to get out."

She patted his hand again. "Poor baby." Her mock sympathy was appreciated. Any sympathy was appreciated right now.

"Anything you can do," he smiled back at her.

"I do have some ideas for immediate relief." Her wicked, leering smile again.

The pressure was on. She was going to get the most out of this. He could tell.

"I have to be getting back." He fumbled, slightly awkwardly. "Zannah's planning on my taking her out to dinner tonight."

He told the lie with the greatest of ease. Susannah had left three days before to stay with her parents in North Carolina.

211

The snows were melted in many places on the estate. The remaining patches lay where the sun had not yet reached, the shady, northern sides of bushes, fences and buildings. In the last two weeks the temperature had climbed a little higher each day, inching its way into the low fifties on this day. The feeling of an early spring was in the air, the smells of March letting the Windy City get a false sense of winter's departure. Sometimes the heaviest snows and the coldest weather move in from the prairies and the lake in March.

Anne Madison stood at the huge window looking out toward the barren garden and lawn, across the water to the towering city. She had paused in the middle of getting ready for a lunch date, the first social engagement she had made in over a year. Off in some far corner of the house a phone ring twice. Mrs. Knight took care of it.

She turned back to her dresser, putting on the gold and diamond ear-rings. The phone in her room buzzed a polite, cricket sound.

"Yes," she said, still looking at herself in the mirror.

"Some man, Mrs. Madison." Mrs. Knight sounded distraught. "Says he has to talk to you. Won't give his name. Said to tell you it was about your friend in Florida. Also -- and this is puzzling -- he's on the unlisted line."

Anne Madison smiled, letting her smile sound in her voice to ease Mrs. Knight's distress. "I know who it is, Mrs. Knight. I'll take it. Thank you."

Anne Madison pushed button number three on the bottom row , the unlisted line. Only four people had access to that number.

"Yes?" asked Anne.

"Can you talk?"

"Briefly."

"This will take only briefly."

"Go ahead."

"There are more."

212

"How many more?" asked Anne.

"Five, six. Maybe more."

"Good." Anne Madison's voice sounded pleased, as if someone had found more of some treasured antiques for her. "I'll take them all."

"Some appear to be very big. Maybe very powerful."

"'The bigger they are ---.' You know the rest."

"The bigger ones will have to be more expensive. Naturally. They're harder to get to."

"That's fine. There's enough money to pay for them. All you can find."

"I think there are even more than I have right now. Maybe much bigger."

"I'll take all you can find. I want them all."

"No matter how big? How high?"

"No matter." A vague smile in her voice. "I want them all."

"This is a big commitment. Very big."

"All," said Anne Madison.

Agular looked out across the waters of the Atlantic, his back to Brian.

"I want you to have more prestige, more importance." he said. Then he turned to face Brian. "It's demeaning for a person of your stature to have to take orders from someone like Cherokee. Not to discredit him. He does fine work. But to recognize you -- your intelligence."

"He doesn't make them seem like orders," said Brian, smiling across the room to Agular -- or Hernandez -- or whatever his name really was. "Besides. Remember? I told you I don't have an ego problem. That's not important to me."

"But it is to me," smiled Agular. "Pre-eminently so. My ego must identify with yours apparently."

"It may upset Cherokee. I'd just as soon leave things the way they are."

"I have a problem with that." Agular's smile was patronizing, but insistent.

213

Brian had flown down alone. He explained that Susannah had gone to visit with her parents for a while. Also she was having a bout with morning sickness.

Brian spent two days on Nevis, swimming, water-skiing, playing tennis with Agular's resident pro, drinking at the quaint little bars, walking on the beach, and most of all, desperately missing Susannah. He knew all along that Agular would wait until the last minute to talk business, a few hours before the flight back.

The waters of the Atlantic sparkled in the early afternoon sun, reflecting the dancing lights through the wafting sheer curtains. The curtains on the Atlantic side of the room were blowing into the room; on the Caribbean side they drifted and waved outside of the doors and windows. The sun on the water made the day look hot and humid, but the cool breeze in the tower made the afternoon pleasant.

"Yes. I have a problem with that," Agular repeated.

Brian smiled calmly. "Don't let it be a problem, Tony. Do whatever you want. I can live with anything."

"I like that about you. You're so adaptable, so flexible."

"I adjust."

"You do everything well."

"I'm not so sure of that."

"I am," insisted Agular. "I know."

"Thank you."

"I'll make the changes. Now. How to tell Cherokee."

"I can tell him," said Brian. "He's not unapproachable."

"See?" smiled Agular. "You handle things. You take problems into your own hands. You make problems go away."

"I'm just going to talk to him. Explain what you want. We're friends -- of a sort. Talking isn't that difficult between friends."

"He's going to resent it."

"He's going to understand it. Accept it."

"What a positive-thinking person you are."

"I'll settle for pragmatic -- practical."

Agular looked out over the water. "I'll be calling you from time to time. At home."

"That's expected."

"There are some other channels you don't know of."

"I'm sure."

"And you'll need to learn the routes, where they go after leaving Carrabelle and Panama City. The connections."

"O.K."

"You're very agreeable."

"I have no reason not to be. You pay me handsomely." Brian had to work to keep from looking awe-stricken in an earlier conversation, when Agular had decided that Brian was worth three thousand a week. Brian was not sure anyone was worth three thousand a week -- for anything.

"Then I guess we're concluded. Wouldn't you say?" said Agular.

"You handled your agenda well," smiled Brian.

"No. You handle responsibility well."

"Thank you," smiled Brian. No one could ever tell that inside he was as uncertain, unsure of himself as he had ever been. The driving force that gave him the responsibility which Agular admired was the desire to have the whole thing over and done, to "make it go away," to use Agular's phrase. He wanted out. Badly. And the only way to get out was to go right through the middle like a down-field drive, bolting right through all the blocks, evading the tackles, driving, driving.

"Until the next time then," said Agular, reaching out to shake hands.

"I look forward to it," smiled Brian.

After arriving at Tallahassee in the early evening, Brian waited until the Sabreliner had taken off. He studied the people in the airport carefully, looking especially for Fordham or someone who might be Stewart, even though he had no idea what Stewart looked like. When he was satisfied that neither was around, he hurriedly bought a ticket to Asheville, North Carolina and made it to the boarding ramp just in time. Landing in Asheville at 8:40, he rented a car. By 9:00 he was in Biltmore

Forest; by 9:20 in bed with Zannah, being held by the only arms that could comfort him and ease the uncertainty he had been living with the past week.

He would leave Asheville at eight the next morning, rent a car in Tallahassee, and still be able to make his two-o'clock class by taking I-10. The whole indulgence was an exercise in extravagance. But why not? He was a man making five thousand a week; one from the college, one from the FBI, and now three from Agular.

Susannah and Dempsey were both pleased to be with him. The week apart had taken its toll on all three of them.

Brian and Cherokee walked along the dock huddled against the side of the river. When they came to the end, a slanted board led down to the river bank where water slapped against rocks along the edge. A wide, well-trod path, not quite a foot above the water, followed the river to its mouth where the path opened onto a long rocky spit stretching out along the east side of the channel. Here the river emptied into the Apalachicola Bay and the spit protected the river mouth for almost a quarter of a mile out into the bay, a long, narrow, high pile of rocks to keep the tides and currents out of the east from filling the channel with sand.

Halfway out the spit the two men stopped, standing close to one another. One pointed to something out toward Dog Island, and the other searched the horizon for whatever they were talking about. Far out across the bay, at least two miles, three Hobie-cats moved in three different directions over the water, one of them dangerously close to turning over.

Brian watched the one Hobie-cat fight the wind. Cherokee found it now and was watching it with him. Just as Cherokee spotted the troubled Cat, the sail boat leaned back up against the sky, righting itself for a brief moment. Then, caught by a strong wind, the sail came down fast, slapping the water. The Cat had capsized.

Brian had been in many such capsizes. He explained to Cherokee that it was part of the game, and not difficult to get the Cat upright again. Cherokee, the solid pragmatist, couldn't quite appreciate the idea that one of the objectives might be to turn the boat over in the water.

"What about all your gear? Coolers? Food? Clothes?" He asked, shaking his head in disbelief.

"Everything's tied down. And the food and clothes are in water-proof bags, tied to the tension ropes that run around the hammock."

"Seems more like work that fun. To me anyway," said Cherokee.

"Well, you've got to remember. Those are probably college kids. The closest they've ever gotten to physical labor in the last five months is carrying books from their room to their classes. Not that those books ever get opened, mind you. Just carried around a lot. So turning over a Hobie-cat, and then getting it upright again is not only exercise for them, it's a challenge."

Just then the sail from the floundered Hobie-cat started its slow, unsteady climb back into the air. Then it was upright again, sailing toward the west end of Dog Island.

"It's still a dumb way to have fun," said Cherokee. "I'd rather sit in a bar and drink, myself."

"To each his own," answered Brian.

"What did you want to talk to me about?" asked Cherokee.

Brian had stalled as long as he could. He sat down on one of the large rocks that formed the jetty. Cherokee sat down next to him. Brian began telling him the outcome of the last meeting with Agular, what Agular wanted, that he, Brian, and Agular would be talking together more, probably direct on the phone, once or twice a week. Brian carefully studied Cherokee's face while he talked, looking for any body-language that would indicate Cherokee's hidden displeasure of this change in the chain of command. There seemed to be none. Brian had been right; Cherokee didn't have an ego problem either. It wasn't going to affect the working relationship between them.

"How do *you* feel about all this?" asked Brian.

"Makes no difference to me. As long as the money keeps coming in."

"It's just easier for Agular to get in touch with me. I have a phone and an answering machine."

"Makes sense to me. Besides," said Cherokee, skipping stones across the water, "it makes things a little easier on me. I'm always worried about the deliveries being made on time. Things like that. Now it's all your problem." He turned and smiled to Brian.

"Well. I guess that's true." Brian studied Cherokee's face carefully. "I don't know that there's an awful lot to worry about, though. Is there?" He was a little confused by Cherokee's statement.

Cherokee laughed. "I was just trying to put you at ease. You're so concerned about how all this will affect me. Hell, man. It doesn't bother me a bit."

"You sure?"

"Sure." Cherokee extended his hand in friendship.

Brian shook his hand warmly, clasping it with his other hand also.

"Let's go have a beer," said Brian.

"Only if you're buying," smiled Cherokee.

"I'm buying," said Brian.

They walked back along the jetty to the mouth of the river, then to the dock, then across the street to the bar.

"Two drafts," said Cherokee to the bartender. "On my friend here."

"Wait a minute," said Brian. "I think I'll have my usual."

"Rum and diet Dr. Pepper coming up," said the bartender

"O.K." said Cherokee in response to Brian's look at him. "Let me try that too. Let's see just what this guy's drinking."

"Two rum and Dr. P's. coming up," said the bartender.

"Diet," said Brian.

"Of course," answered the bartender.

Cherokee's eyes rested on Brian's as he smiled." I guess if it's too much of a sissy drink, I can always make it a double."

"I don't think you'll find it a sissy drink," said Brian.

"We'll see," answered Cherokee, his eyes tightening in on Brian.

What's going on here all of a sudden? wondered Brian. That look. That smile. Almost sinister. He is upset about the change. Damn! I told Agular to let it alone.

"Here you are, gents," said the bartender, placing the drinks in front of them.

"Thanks," said Brian, his eyes never leaving Cherokee's whose eyes and smile stayed fixed on Brian.

Both men reached for their drinks together, touched glasses, and drank, their eyes never moving from the other, the smile still unmoving, slightly insincere.

"To us," said Brian." "And the future."

"As you wish," said Cherokee.

"You're pissed," said Brian.

"No, I'm not." The smile broadened just slightly.

"You're not you."

"Are we being existential here? I learned that word from you."

"We're being observant. Factual," said Brian.

"Good drink."

"Glad you like it."

"You can hardly taste the rum."

"The two flavors 'marry well,' as my Australian buddy would say."

"A drink to get drunk on," said Cherokee.

"All right!" Brian turned and put his glass on the bar. "Let's get it out in the open. You know I don't care one way or the other. I'll call Agular and say, 'Put it back like it was.'"

Cherokee still kept the fixed eyes and smile, even though Brian had turned away, facing the mirror behind the bar. "I don't understand you today, Brian. You're reading too much into nothing. You're over-reacting to something non-existent in the first place."

"Like when was the last time you called me 'Brian?' There's something going on here." He turned back to face Cherokee,

219

and smiled slightly again. "That smile of yours -- has to be one of the wickedest smiles I've ever seen."

Cherokee looked away. "Damn! That is one of the best drinks I've ever had." He finished it all in one gulp and placed his glass loudly on the bar. "Barkeep. Another one of these things. That's pretty good. And another one for my friend here. Oh, and I *did* say he was paying, didn't I?"

"Don't go too fast with them," said Brian. "They're stronger than they taste. That's the beauty of them."

"Oh, I can handle my rum -- boss. That I can."

There's trouble stirring here, thought Brian. It's going to take some fixing.

Spring happens fast in North Florida; one day is cold with a freezing night; the next day is much warmer, and then the following day people are walking on the beaches, lying in the sun in bathing suits. Only the water in the Gulf holds on to winter for a while longer. The air will be in the eighties, warm and massaging to the bare skin, but the Gulf will stay in the fifties for most of March, refusing to let go of the winter that is trying to die. Buds will begin to show on the trees; some flowers will leap ahead of the season, and some people work extremely hard to get ahead of everyone else with the tanning process. Still the waters of the northern Gulf refuse to let go of the winter. Only the bravest, the stupidest, or the drunkest dare to cross the fine line between the sand and the sea.

Beth sat in a chair-lounge on the balcony, her white two-piece bathing suit already setting off the tan she had started in the tanning beds three weeks ago. The sun wrapped her in a warmth that was just right; the March sun can do that, never too hot, always just warm enough, like sensuous fingers massaging the skin. Her dark glasses were not flashy but carried the 'Revo' emblem on the sides, signifying many bucks. Occasionally she would reach for her gin and tonic off in the shade to keep the ice from melting.

Today she was in a classical mood. Through the earphones on her Walkman, she was listening to Ravel's *Bolero*, letting her body move slightly in time to the erotic rhythm. As the music rose in passion, she closed her eyes, blocking out the beach-combers twelve floors below. She became a part of the rhythm and the sun.

The loud crashing, orgasmic finale was one of her favorite sections. She felt it, absorbed it, bathed in it, lived it, every clang of the cymbals, every explosion of the kettle-drums, the wild rising of the violins and violas, the blaring announcements of the French horns, trombones, and trumpets. On the last atomic note of the *Bolero*, she clicked off the Walkman and lay statuesque in the sun, her eyes still closed, and the eroticism of the music fading slowly. It was the kind of music she had to cool down from, like an exercise cool-down. Something you just can't stop too fast.

After a few minutes, she opened her eyes, looked up at some white clouds, which she thought were in the shape of David Letterman's profile, and took a sip of her gin and tonic. She stood up, leaned against the wall and looked at the strollers on the white sand below. Not really high enough for them to look like the usual ants, only like tiny, deformed people, all too short to be taken seriously. But then Beth never really took anything very seriously, even her men, which everyone thought were the most important things in her life.

Somewhere along the line, she had become that friend she envied so much. That one who talked to people about four levels below where her mind really was. She was now an expert at being a Goldie Hawn screen character to everyone around her while her mind was racing at Cokie Roberts speed. She stayed ahead of all her friends, and still didn't threaten to them. They never had any idea she was so perceptive, so innovative, so inventive. To them she was just 'good Ole Beth,' and a lot of fun to have around.

Far down the beach to the east, she could see where the crowd was thicker in front of the Breakers. But the crowd was nothing now compared to what it would be in another week when most of the colleges starting having Spring Break. While she looked down at the students strolling the beach, she had the impression that about every ten minutes or so, the population on the beach increased about twenty-five percent. God! It's an organism, alive and growing, right before my eyes.

She took a sip of gin and tonic, turned over the tape in the Walkman and began listening to the delicate intricacies of Rachmaninoff's *Rhapsody on a Theme by Paganini*. Back in the lounge, she was involved in the lushness of Rockmaninoff, getting to the "Twelfth Variation," when Steve picked up one of the earphones.

"Is anyone in there?"

"Oh, hi, darling," she smiled, taking the earphones off. "I didn't expect you out here today. I thought you had a meeting in Atlanta or Chicago, or some other equally exotic place."

"Did," he answered, taking off his coat and tie. "But it was canceled at the last minute. I was just leaving the office when the call came through. So I treated myself to a good massage, and then thought of the same thing you're doing. Nothing like a little sun-bathing after a good massage."

"Well, I'm glad you did," she said. "I was getting bored here by myself, and was getting ready to leave. You know me. If there's one person I can't stand to spend any time with, it's me."

"Can't understand that. That's the one person I'd rather be with more than anyone else." By now he was down to his lime-colored thong underwear, and getting ready to stretch out on the other chaise-lounge which he had already positioned toward the afternoon sun. "Uuummm," he said, his eyes closed in erotic pleasure. "This feels like a slice of heaven."

"I'm having a gin and tonic. Would you like one?"

"Love it. But I'll get it later. Don't bother."

"No bother. I need to hit mine again anyway." She was up and headed for the kitchen.

"Not too strong, please," he called after her. "I had two before leaving the office. You know me. I have to brace myself for that lighter-than-air stuff."

"O.K. Coming up. One Terri Garr. That's half-way between a Shirley Temple and an Elizabeth Taylor."

When she returned with the drinks and handed his to him, some drops of condensation fell into the forest of hair across his chest.

"Oh-ho," he hollered. "That let's you know it's not really summer yet. That would feel good in July. But now I know it's still March."

"In like a lion, out like a lamb. Here's to you -- us."

"Us." He toasted her, took a sip of the drink and reclined again to soak up the warm March sun. "What are you listening to?" he asked.

"Some Rachmaninoff."

"Put it on the speaker."

"You don't like classical music."

"If it's that 'Eighteenth Composition' thing, I do."

"'Eighteenth Variation,'" she said, smiling at his relaxed body.

"Whatever," he said. Then later, "What's that mean, anyway? The 'Eighteenth Variation?'"

"You really want to know?"

"Sure. Anything with a name like that, and that melodic, has got to have a pretty good story behind it."

She put the tape on the player inside the door, and the music began coming out through concealed speakers in the rooms and on the balcony.

"Well, there was this guy named Paganini, see?"

"Keeping up with you so far." He still faced the sun, his eyes closed.

"And he wrote this incredibly exciting short piece of music-- way back there in the early 1800's. It had a simple progression of chords. Is this making sense, so far?"

"So far, so good."

"Let me know if you want me to go slower. There <u>will</u> be a quiz later."

"I'll be ready."

"Anyway, this one piece of music was so interesting that later on two other composers, Brahms and Rachmaninoff, both wrote long compositions based on it, writing many different ways it could be interpreted."

"And we like Rocky's best, right?"

"Right you are, babe. And each different interpretation of that theme by Paganini is called a variation."

"Even though they all sound different?"

"Correct, doll. But each one uses the same chord progression and the same pattern that Paganini did, almost a hundred of years before them."

"Sort of like, say, a jazz rendition of a classic standard? Like Charlie Parker playing something by, say, Cole Porter, which really doesn't sound like the original at all. Huh?"

"Very good. You *were* paying attention, weren't you?"

"You speak, and I listen."

She lay back on the lounge and enjoyed the sun on her body. For a long time they were silent, listening to the 'Eighteenth Variation.'

"Does the offer still stand?" she asked

"Whatever offer you're talking about, I'm sure if I made it in the first place, it still stands."

"Good. Then I accept."

"That's good. I'm pleased to hear that."

Silence as they lay with their eyes closed, soaking up ultraviolet A and B.

"Which offer?" he finally asked.

"The one where I come to work in your office."

"Oh, that one. That'll be great." Eyes still closed, facing the sun.

"I do have a few conditions though," she said.

"Name them."

"No special hours. Just whenever I can get there."

"Sounds reasonable."

"Some days I won't be in at all. Days before tests and things like that."

"Of course."

"At least sixty per-cent of my phone calls can be personal."

"Par for the course."

"Once or twice a week, I'll have to have a two hour lunch. Paid of course."

"Killer!!"

"And I want the keys to everything you own. And I mean everything. Even your house. And you wife's car."

"I would expect it."

"But I won't put on make-up in the office."

"Good girl."

"And I won't chew gum in front of customers."

"Tacky."

"So? Are the trade-offs acceptable?"

"We have a deal. See you tomorrow -- or whenever."

"No. Not tomorrow. I'm playing tennis tomorrow."

"Whenever's convenient for you."

"How about Monday?"

"Works for me. Now I won't have to try and find you for lunch. You'll already be there."

"You sure? I mean about my working"

"Couldn't be more pleased. Dynamite arrangement."

They both returned to sun-soaking and Rocky's arrangements of Paggy.

Brian held the phone to his ear with his shoulder. The sound of the ringing went on and on. He lost count somewhere around twenty-two rings, and reason told him that no one was home, but emotion kept him holding the phone to his ear, waiting, willing an answer.

She *must* be there. It's so important that she be there, that she answers, that I talk to her. Come on, Zannah. Come on. Pick it up. Come home. I'm having one of my SAD attacks.

She's driving up the driveway now, he visualized. Getting out of the car. Coming around the house. She hears the phone. She's unlocking the front door. Running down the hall. After this ring. O.K. After this one. I want my Susannah.

He placed the phone back in its cradle. He could visualize her ride along I-40 from Black Mountain back to Asheville. There was no one for her to visit but her friend Rita in Black Mountain. Now she was on her way back to her folks' house in Biltmore Forest.

If the Renaissance man had done nothing else right, he had married well. Not only was Zannah beautiful and intelligent, she had the good sense to be an only child of extremely wealthy parents. You don't live in Biltmore Forest if you have to worry about payments on the Bentley or the yacht.

But that brought him to something else to worry about. If Zannah wasn't there, and her parents weren't there, where were the servants? The housekeeper, the cook, the maid? The chauffeur? Somebody had to be there. Unless someone -- like Agular -- had started something moving. Or -- the guy -- the one who had been hired by the Chicago woman. The hit man. Hired to extract revenge.

I'm getting paranoid. At no time in my life have I ever used the phrase 'hit man.' Not in relationship to myself or anyone related to me. Why am I involved with a 'hit man?' Or with Cherokee, for that matter? Or with the FBI?

I don't belong where I am on this small planet -- far off to one side of the galaxy, even farther off to one side of the universe -- within an even larger universe. All time and space are too big and vast for me to have to be in this particular place and time. I don't belong in this peculiar arrangement. I'm a teacher. A good teacher. Hit men do not belong in the life of a professor of Western Civilization.

Why is there no answer? At least one of the people working in that house should be there, should answer. I misdialed. That has to be it.

He picked up the phone again and dialed the complete number. He had been using the 'redial' button, but now he was sure he had dialed the wrong number.

The phone began its succession of rings. Ten. Fourteen. Seventeen. No. I already said that. I've lost track again.

He picked up his cup of luke-warm coffee and took a sip, still listening to the ringing. He knew there was no point in holding on, listening to unanswered rings. But he did.

Zannah! Come on home!! Where are you?

He hung up, walked over to his desk and looked down at his legal pad of notes and the text book opened to the chapter on the Inquisition, the section on the pope's concern with the Albigensons of south France.

"A good 13th century mind," he saw written in his own hand-writing, next to his Dell paperback, *The Columbia-Viking Desk Encyclopedia*, which his father had given to him twenty years before, and it was old even then. "$1.95" was still visible on the spine binding.

"The Inquisition, begun @ 1233 ... continued into the 19th century in the Papal States." The 19th century? That was just back there. Like next door.

"Not to be confused with the Spanish Inquisition begun in 1478 (the 15th century) by Ferdinand and Isabella, buddies of our old friend Columbus. The Spanish Inquisition was noted for its torture and deaths in an effort to get the Jews and Moors out of Spain. Don't get the two mixed up. They're two completely different things. The Inquisition of the 13th century was ..."

I'll try again. She has to be home now. It's after 10:00. It's been a good five minutes since I called last.

He pushed the 'redial' button, and ATC did its thing. One ring ... Five ... Nine ... Seventeen ...

"Hello."

"Zannah?"

She breathed heavily. "Hi, Bri ... Let me go to my room for this. O.K.?"

"Are you all right?"

"Sure. Why wouldn't I be?"

"Well, you sound so ... desperate."

"That's not desperate, hon. That's winded."

"Winded from what?"

"Winded from running to get the phone."

"Why were you running?"

"Because the phone was ringing. Is this an Abbott and Costello thing here?"

"You're sure? You're all right?"

"Let me go to my room where I can sit down. As soon as I get these knives out of my chest, and these chains off my legs, I'll be fine."

"You want me to call you back?"

"That would be considerate."

"I love you."

"Me too. I'll love you better when I can sit down with a cup of tea. O.K.?"

"Three minutes," he said.

"Five."

"Four."

"Three-and-a-half."

Click.

He went to the kitchen, poured another cup of coffee which he couldn't remember was decaf or not. He would know by 11:30 if he wound up tossing instead of sleeping.

He put on Michael Jackson's "Will You Be There?" and listened to the modulations which reminded him of Puccini's "Entrance of Madame Butterfly." When it was finished, he pushed a button on the CD remote and played John Bayless doing "Return to Sorrento." Surely it was three-and-a-half minutes long. She had to be ready by now. She had the cup or tea and was sitting in her room. Waiting. Bayless swept up and down the piano keys.

"That wasn't three minutes."

"It was fifteen."

"It was not enough time for me to get to the bathroom."

"Carry the phone with you."

"I will *not*. I'll call you back in a few minutes."

"I need to talk."

"I need to do something that only I can do."

"Hurry."

"Yeah. Right."

Click.

She didn't call back for seven minutes.

"Where have you been?" he asked when he picked up the receiver --- like before the ring could finish.

"I told you. In the bathroom. Can't a girl have any privacy?"

"I don't mean now. I mean earlier. When you weren't home."

"Bri! Do you have any idea how hyper you sound? Maybe you ought to do more decaf."

"I'm in a paranoid phrase right now. Humor me. And I'm worried about you."

"I'm all right."

"Were you followed?"

"I don't know if I was followed or not. I was followed all the way from Carrabelle to Cataloochee and didn't know it. Remember?"

"You've got to start paying attention."

"If Fordham is busy following you, how could he follow me?"

"That new guy. Stewart. I'm worried about him. You."

"You're not completing your sentences."

"You can fill in the blanks. I'm worried."

"If he's as good as Fordham says he is, then he knows the score. He knows you're one of the good guys."

"Maybe the score doesn't mean anything to him."

There was a short silence.

"He probably has a tap on our phone," said Brian.

"Then he knows a lot more than just the score. He's heard some pretty lurid conversations. Right?"

"I think our phone has a bug convention in it." said Brian. "probably one from Stewart, the FBI, Agular, Cherokee."

"I don't think a phone would hold that many bugs without a fight breaking out. Who cares about us, Bri?"

"The Drug Enforcement Agency, the FBI, Stewart, Agular. All of the above."

"Have you got a fever, hon?"

"I want you to leave."

229

"And go where?"

"Where we went on the third night of our honeymoon." He was careful not to say the name.

"Will you meet me there?"

"Not yet. Later."

"I'll leave first thing in the morning."

"No. Tonight."

"Are you serious?"

"As a heart attack. And don't call me from there. If you have to call here, drive over to the city where we ate that great Greek meal. Remember?"

"Yes. I remember. But now you're worrying me."

"And when I call you, I'll go to another phone. I'm sure they can tell what number you're calling from."

"You really think we're tapped?"

"Like a beer keg at a fraternity party."

"Well ... I don't know what to say now. I think I have stage-fright. I'm not good at speaking in front of large groups."

"I think there are large groups."

"Won't this conversation let them know that we know?"

"It will let them know that we're really sorry we got involved."

"Do we get points for that? Being sorry, I mean?"

"Probably not. But it's worth a try."

"Do you really want me to leave tonight?"

"I really, really do. I'm worried about you."

"Has something come up? Something I don't know about?"

"Not yet. But I expect it too. Any time now."

"Can you talk about it?"

"No."

"O.K. I'll be out of here within thirty minutes."

"O.K. When you get there ... just to be on the safe side... register under the name of that girl in the movie we saw on The Movie Channel last week. Remember?"

"Her real name, or her name in the film?"

"The name in the picture."

"Gotcha."

230

"I love you."

"Me too," she said. Then she was gone.

The meeting was important. Cherokee had arranged it. Brian needed to learn about the pick-up from Zorro, which Brian was fully convinced was not the man's real name. He found out later that Zorro was a job, or position, rather than a man; over the past two years there had been seven different Zorro's.

The connection one Brian, needed to know in order to work with all of the arms of the Agular organization --- or at least the ones in this area. Brian knew there were other entries, but it never occurred to him that he would have anything to do with them. He assumed that each one worked independently of the others.

He had been able to piece together some aspects of the organization by listening and watching, sometimes to things that were not meant for him to hear or see. There was the Cherokee connection, Brian's branch, where the *Miss Betty*, Cherokee's boat -- or rather Travis' boat which Cherokee used for his own benefit, meeting with other ships on the middle ground. Sometimes it was a sea-plane. Drugs were sent in, money sent out. The goods went through Brian who in turn passed them both ways through Captain Andy, then on to Steve Briggs, then to some unknown at the Panama City Airport.

The second connection, which hadn't concerned Brian until now, was one in which a boat from Mexico sent a man in a small dinghy to a pier off the coast of Carrabelle, always late at night, to rendezvous with a man fishing on the pier. This chain had different connections, but still converged with the Cherokee connection through the unknown man at the airport.

Then there was the Zorro connection. Here the goods came in at the little Carrabelle airport. The plane from the Turks, via the Bahamas, via Daytona, was on the ground long enough only for the courier to carry the goods to a bayou hidden in the woods next to the airport. The man in the bateau there exchanged goods, rowed to a back road where he had a truck parked. From there he would drive to Panama City where he would converge with the Cherokee connection through Captain Andy. From there to Briggs, to the man at the airport. In case anything went wrong with the connection at the airport, two separate back-ups were on stand-by, each unknown to the other.

In Carrabelle alone Agular had three separate routes independent of one another. This way if anything interfered with one of the connections, the other two kept on working and picked up the slack from the one out-of-commission. There were still even other connections through other ports of entry, going to different destinations other than Chicago, but that was of no concern to Brian -- not at this time anyway. Never, he hoped.

As Cherokee and Brian got out of the car at the small airport, the March afternoon sun felt vaguely warm against the slight chill of the March wind. The airport was deserted, as it was most of the time, consisting only of a half-mile strip of tar-mac; no buildings, no hangers, nothing to break the dismal surroundings of saw-grass and savannas on one side and one end, swamp and cypress-lined bayous on the other two. Brian had lived in Carrabelle for over three years, and he had never seen the landing strip.

He drove back to the spot Cherokee indicated, parked in a space well-covered with trees, concealed from the air -- even from the strip once the plane landed. At Cherokee's indication, they got out of the car, walked back to the strip, across it to the woods on the other side. A path led into the swampy jungle, opening out onto a small bayou, itself hidden from the air by an overgrowth of pine and cypress.

"What are we doing this for?" asked Brian, holding his jacket tighter against his chest. Out of the sun now, the March chill had become much colder.

"You need to know about other parts of the operation," said Cherokee. "Especially since you're moving up."

There it was again, thought Brian. There is discontent there. "Agular didn't mention anything about this to me," said Brian.

"But he will later on. I know. I had to learn."

"What do you .."

"Ssshhh," said Cherokee, and they stopped abruptly. At the mouth of the bayou, a small bateau rested on the bank. A man sat in the boat, not moving.

"That's Corky," said Cherokee.

"Do you'al know each other?" asked Brian.

"Yeah." Cherokee nodded. "Two -- three years."

"Then why are we being so secretive?"

"Don't want to startle him," said Cherokee. "Here. Get down behind this log." He pointed toward a gigantic fallen cypress lying on the ground long enough to have many parts dead and rotting.

Both of them stooped behind the giant tree, and Brian peered over the top, looking toward the bateau.

"Corky!!" Cherokee called out to the man.

Instantly a shotgun appeared from out of nowhere. Corky looked toward the sound, his gun ready.

"Who is it?" he called.

"Cherokee," he answered. "You all right?"

"Show yourself," yelled Corky. "And no fast moves."

Cherokee whispered to Brian. "Stay down 'til I tell you."

"Don't worry," said Brian. "Can I stay down even after you tell me?"

Cherokee stood up slowly. "How you been, Corky? Haven't seen you in a long time."

"That's true. But you know where I drink. This is a strange place to come looking for me."

"I want you to meet somebody."

A short pause. Suspicion.

"I don't need to meet nobody."

"A friend of Agular's"

"I still don't want to meet him.

Brian could see the man and his shotgun through the space between two trees.

"You got to meet him. He's going to be working with you soon."

Brian hadn't known of this fact. It was as new to him as it was to Corky.

"Nobody told me about it," yelled Corky.

"I'm telling you now," said Cherokee.

"How come this is happening? I don't like change. You'al know I don't like change."

Brian suddenly felt closer to Corky. Corky was expressing Brian's own sentiments.

"That's the way the world is," said Cherokee. "It changes. Things get better."

"Change makes things worse."

Brian was beginning to love Corky.

"The telephone, TV, Penicillin," said Cherokee.

"Crime in the streets, drugs, the L.A. riots, Aids, Bubonic plague," said Corky.

Bubonic plague? thought Brian. The guy's good. Inaccurate, but good.

"Come on, Corky. Let us come out. I got work to do. Places to be."

"All right. But no funny stuff. I'll blow your damn heads off. You know how goofy I am. Nam Crazy. Nervous. Don't do anything funny now. No fast movements."

God, thought Brian. What a lot of directions to follow. He felt as if he should have taken notes. Nam Crazy? That's scary.

"Everything's going to be fine," said Cherokee. "Just relax." He reached down and tugged at Brian's shirt collar.

"You sure this is all right?" whispered Brian. "The guy himself says he's crazy. Nam crazy. And that shotgun doesn't look very welcoming."

"It's all right," whispered Cherokee. "he's all talk."

"What's going on over there?" yelled Corky. "Why ain't you guys come out yet? What you doing behind that tree?"

"Well, to tell you the truth, Corky," said Cherokee, "you've gone and scared him now. He's afraid to come out and meet you now. You've gone and scared your new boss, Corky." Cherokee was obviously enjoying all of this. "That's not the way to make a good impression on your boss, Corky. Tell him you don't mean it"

234

"Mean every word of it. If you don't believe me, make a fast move, and then say 'good-by' to your head."

Brian suddenly had this picture of Walter Houston in *The Treasure of Sierra Madre*, jumping up and down and laughing when he found all the gold. He could see Corky in the same ritual of glee, dancing and laughing around Cherokee's and Brian's severed heads. Nam Crazy.

"We're coming out now, Corky," yelled Cherokee. He pulled more tightly at Brian's collar. Brian's collar resisted, but Cherokee was persistent.

The two men moved slowly from behind the fallen tree and began a slow trek toward the menacing-looking man with the ready shotgun sixty feet down the bayou. Brian could hear the chilling sound-track from *Antarctica*, cold, tense, on edge.

"You behave, now, Corky," said Cherokee as they walked slowly along the bank. "This here's Brian, Corky. He's one of the good guys. He's on our side."

Brian had a forced smile on his face. He couldn't remember ever feeling less like smiling in his entire life.

"I don't like change," said Corky.

"How you doing, Corky?" said Brian. "I'm glad to meet you."

They were within twenty feet of the bateau now.

"I was doing fine, thank you," said Corky. "'Til you'al showed up. You know I don't like change, Cherokee. How come you'al always changing things on me?

"Corky, there hasn't been anything different in the past sixteen months. Since you started to work here. It's always been the same. You get a call. You come out here -- to this same bayou -- and wait for Paul to land the plane. He brings you a package. You give him one. You go back to your truck and take the package to Floyd over in St. Joe. You come back home and wait to do it all over again. No change, Corky. Always the same." Cherokee had the calm manner of someone trying to sooth a frightened child.

Brian could look into the man's eyes now. Definitely a weak link in the chain. Corky's eyes were wild, moving rapidly to hundreds of different places, places where there was nothing in particular to be watched. Crazy eyes. Insane eyes. The man had a lot of private demons. His eyes saw them all at once. No one else could see them, but they were there for Corky.

"Sometimes it rains," said Corky. "Sometimes it's cold. Other times it's hot. Like today. It's nice today."

"That's the way the world is, Corky. It's called living. Sometimes you wake up, it's a good day. Sometimes, you wake up, it's bad. I don't do it, Corky. Nobody does it. It happens. It just is. The world's an imperfect place."

"They shouldn't change the rules in the middle of the game. They should at least wait until one game's over ... before changing the rules." He even began to look sad to Brian now.

"Don't you hate it when they do that?" said Cherokee. "I hate it when that happens. But it's part of the game, Corky. The rules change ... sometimes without us even knowing it ..."

Cherokee laughed slightly. "This morning I got up, it was cold. Now it's a lot warmer. Still cold, but a lot warmer. The sun did that, you know. The sun changed the day from icy cold-- to just sort of cold." He chuckled again.

Corky, for no other reason than that Cherokee was laughing, began to smile slowly, then grin, then chuckle.

God, thought Brian. A real loony-toons here. Why would they keep this guy in the chain? Brian let his own smile become a little broader.

"Say 'Hi' to Brian for me, O.K.?" Cherokee pointed.

"Hi, Brian." Suddenly Corky was a pussy cat. A soft, cuddly, but very big, pussy cat.

"Hi, Corky," said Brian. "Nice to meet you" Yeah. Like dancing with a leper!!

"What time's Paul coming?" asked Cherokee.

"Any minute now," said Corky, looking at his watch.

Just at that moment, they heard the distant drone of the plane engine.

"There he is now," said Corky.

They looked off through the cypress trees toward the sound. No plane in sight yet. But the sound grew.

236

"He's coming," said Corky.

"I can hear him," said Cherokee.

"Me too," said Brian. He had no idea why he felt compelled to enter the game of mentioning the obvious, other than the fact that he thought maybe it might make Corky feel more comfortable.

Just above the trees, still only a moving dot in the sky, miles away, the plane broke into view. But only for people with good eyes.

"I see him," said Corky, pointing. It was the first time he didn't have both hands on the gun.

"Yep. There he comes," said Cherokee.

Brian refrained from saying "me too," again. It was just a little more than corny. Becoming a cliche.

The dot grew bigger, the sound louder. The three men watched it grow in size until it took form and became a plane with wings, a tail, and a nose.

"You guys need to get out of sight," said Corky. The man seemed to become a normal, rational, thinking human being for a few minutes. "Paul won't land if he sees you guys here. Then I'll have to go back home and wait for a call again."

"Right," said Cherokee. "We'll split." He motioned Brian into the trees, out of sight from the plane.

From the trees and bushes, through small breaks in the foliage, they could see the plane circle the strip, reconnoitering the terrain below, and then begin its slow, cautious descent. The sound changed suddenly as the plane touched down, and they could hear it taxiing along the runway, coming up to the spot closest to the bayou. Then the engine raced as the plane came to a stop on the other side of the row of woods and jungle separating the runway from the bayou. A quick silence.

Cherokee stepped back into the open, on the bank beside Corky and his little bateau. He motioned for Brian to come on out with him. Brian came out slowly, hesitantly. He wished Cherokee had seen fit to be a little more enlightening about this meeting. He was certain now that Cherokee was enjoying Brian's amazement and awe --- and slight panic.

Then came the sounds of someone walking carelessly, without concern, through the trees at the end of the bayou, breaking twigs and tree limbs as he moved through a woods and a world in which he felt at home, felt comfortable, unlike the tremulous but giant Corky.

Then the man came out of the woods into sight. He saw the bateau and Corky, Cherokee, and a man he did not know. But his reaction was very different from Corky's.

"Cherokee," he called across the water. "How you been, buddy? Long time, no see. What brings you on this side of the fence?"

"New man I want you to meet," called Cherokee, indicating Brian. "The present apple of Agular's eye."

"Always good to have new blood in the cell block. Too much in-breeding is bad for the species." By now the smiling pilot, carrying one of the ever-present identically cloned attaché cases, was in front of Cherokee and Brian. Corky still sat in the boat, taking in everything that was going on before him.

"Paul Langston," smiled the pilot, reaching out to shake Brian's hand. "Pleased to meet you." He had a friendly, happy face, another one of the people Brian was supposed to dislike but who was turning out to be a likable guy.

The world is simpler when the bad guys are mean and ugly.

"Brian Withers," said Brian, shaking Langston's hand. "Nice to meet you."

"Brian is on his way up the corporate ladder," said Cherokee. "Agular has taken a liking to him. He may be the heir to the throne."

"I think Cherokee is embellishing things a little," smiled Brian.

"He's prone to do that," said Langston. "Especially when he's jealous. And that's what it sounds like. But don't worry. Cherokee gets jealous over dogs getting a bone."

"Ah, is that what it is?" asked Brian. "And all the time I thought he was mad 'cause I forgot his birthday."

Langston turned to the skiff. "How you doing, Corky? Been hunting any lately?"

"No," said Corky. "Just squirrels."

"Get any?"

"Enough for supper. Eight. Maybe nine."

"Good man," smiled Langston. "Here. Take this, will you?" He reached out to hand off the attaché to Corky.

Just as Corky placed the case on the seat and was getting ready to hand one back, the next six seconds exploded into a wild frenzy that Brian saw in slow-motion, going on endlessly, like the shooting scene from *Bonnie and Clyde*. So much action and horror were packed in such a small atom of eternity that the only way his mind could register it all was in a delayed-action sort of replay. The six seconds would remain indelible in Brian's mind for the rest of his life.

From across the bayou, in the woods twenty-five, thirty feet from the four men, other voices suddenly broke into their own whispering.

"Here it is." "I told you it would be here." "There's a lot of it." "Nobody else knows." "We can get 'em, I know."

As the four men turned to the voices, three men broke through the underbrush onto the opposite bank of the bayou, all carrying guns. The air exploded in gunfire; Corky's shotgun discharged five times in quick succession, was loaded again as if by magic, began discharging again. Cherokee produced a Biretta from somewhere in his pocket, fired four, five, six times. Reloaded. Began firing again. Blakey suddenly had a Smith and Wesson in his hand, firing into the intruders. All three of the men were low to the ground, Corky down deep in his boat.

Brian watched the three armed men across the bayou twist, squirm, and writhe in pain and agony, falling to the ground in a slow-motion choreography that seemed to take them hours to complete. Slowly, eerily, the forms of the three armed men began to change before his eyes. A metamorphosis took place and the three men grew younger and younger, less menacing, more youthful, until, when finally coming to rest on the ground, they changed into the teenagers they actually were; the guns they had carried went through a similar metamorphosis, ending up as b-b guns lying on and around the twisted bodies of the kids.

"My God," was all that came from Brian's mouth, softly.

"It's a bunch of kids," said Langston.

"I thought it was cops." said Cherokee.

"What the hell they doing here?" came from Corky.

"Get out of here." Langston pushed the boat out into the water with a swift shove of his leg. The little motor started quickly, and the boat was gone, disappearing around a curve in the river.

Langston and Cherokee started running back toward the run-way.

"Come on, man," yelled Cherokee to Brian who was frozen in space.

He broke loose from the images that had turned him into an immovable paralytic, and ran off following Langston and Cherokee from a distance.

Through the woods to the run-way, Langston headed for the plane. Cherokee and Brian ran across the tar-mac to the car. From behind him, as he ran, Brian heard the plane start, rev up, turn and head down the run-way into the wind from the Gulf.

By the time Brian reached the car, Cherokee was already behind the wheel, waiting, anxious.

"Give me the keys, man. The keys."

Brian fumbled in his pocket, found them, handed them to Cherokee who yanked them from his hands. He started the car instantly. The car pulled back onto the oyster-covered road, turned and headed toward U.S. 98.

When they pulled up to the stop at 98, Cherokee stopped, confused, unable to decide which way to turn, to Carrabelle across the bridge or to Apalachicola, twenty-six miles to the west. He finally turned left and headed toward Carrabelle. Soaring over the spanning bridge, he headed toward the sky, high above the harbor and the little village that hugged the shore. Off to the right, against the distant afternoon coral clouds, Brian could see the plane growing smaller, heading for Ceder Key, Perry, Ocala, Daytona. He suddenly had a strong desire to be on it, heading away, far away, anywhere but here, anytime but now. And what made it even worse was that Susannah would not be home to comfort him, ease his pain.

The car moved down the other side of the spanning bridge, and came to a stop at the Jr. Food Store at the foot of the bridge. Cherokee was talking, but Brian wasn't hearing him.

"Snap out of it." Cherokee shook Brian by the shoulder. "Did you hear me?"

"What?" asked Brian. "What did you say?"

"Get us a six-pack. Busch Lite." He was handing Brian a bill, a twenty.

When Brian got back in the car, Cherokee took one of the beers, popped it and drank half of it in one swift gulp before starting the car. Then he headed back across the soaring, spanning bridge toward the beach.

He pulled off by the motel that faced the old beach, drove almost to the edge of the water and stopped the car, looking out across the Gulf. He took another long drink of beer, emptied the can, tossed it in the back seat and took another from the six-pack that was still in Brian's lap.

"Have one," said Cherokee. "It'll help."

Brian began opening one of the beers, almost like a robot, absently, without feeling. He was staring out at the Gulf and the pink afternoon clouds on the horizon, not really seeing anything --- except the three lifeless bodies lying contorted on the mud bank.

He took a drink of the beer. It tasted more bitter than he remembered beer tasting, bitter and biting. But it did help. The motion of something cold moving down his throat seemed to bring life back into the statuesque body. He could feel the cold going down, down, and with that sensation, reality and the present began to come back over him.

"They were just kids," he said finally, the first thing he had said since leaving the Jr. Food Store. "Just kids with b-b guns."

"Yeah," said Cherokee.

"God! Just kids!"

Cherokee said nothing.

"I've never seen anyone killed before," said Brian.

"It happens," said Cherokee.

Silence again.

"God!" said Brian again. "Just kids. Out playing in the woods. Having a good time."

"Yeah." Cherokee's voice became a little less patient. "Well, they shouldn't have been there in the first place."

The only good thing out of this while bloody, agonizing, violent six seconds was that now --- just now with that statement-- Brian could suddenly let himself dislike Cherokee -- very much.

Anne Madison read about the "Bayou Massacre" in all of the papers she was getting. Susannah Withers read about it in the Carrabelle *Times* she that was mailed to her at Biltmore Forest, and then forwarded by her parents to the hideout in Balsam, North Carolina. Steve Briggs and Beth read about it in the Panama City *News-Herald*. Agular heard about it, with great displeasure, from his information sources which existed unknown even to Cherokee, Brian, the Swede, or Briggs. Henry Fordham knew about it within hours through Brian who wanted desperately to get out of his pact with the devil. But even *he* could see that *now* the only way out of it was through it. He was now so deep in the forest that it was easier to go on out than to try and go back. Now the other side was closer than the starting point.

Eric Stewart read about the "Bayou Massacre" in the Tallahassee *Democrat*, which he bought everyday at Hartsfield International. But when he read it, it was old news to him. He had seen it when it happened. He had been there.

The *Miss Betty* was busy with activity, being readied for a trip to the middle grounds, another fishing trip. The Swede neatly stored canned goods, dry goods, frozen foods, milk, bait, all the things which Cherokee kept shopping for and bringing on board. Blackie was storing the ice which had been dumped on deck by the large tube that had fed it down from the fish house. It was supposed to have been dumped directly into the ice hole below deck, but someone -- Blackie really, but no one said anything -- had not been watching the tube carefully when the ice was released. Blackie also tried to keep up with the water hose and the level of water in the storage container, check all of the fishing lines and tie-lines, splice some of the new rope to the older, shorter lines, making completely new lines out of monofilament, tie on hooks, and cut bait.

The radio in the cabin was blaring out Chicago's "If you see me walking by --- Look away. Baby look away," and whenever Cherokee or the Swede yelled a bit of important information to each other or to Blackie, the radio had to be turned down and the information had to be yelled again. Then they would turn the radio back up, and the whole procedure would be repeated the next time something was said. Not the greatest method of communication, but they seemed to work better under these conditions. The rhythm of the music kept them working at a steady pace -- like chain-gang songs -- only much faster.

The weather was good for fishing. March had come in, and the Gulf waters were warming up -- almost a degree every five days, already way up from the low-fifties of late January. This meant the fish would be coming farther north; the boats would not have to go out as far, and since less time was spent in traveling, more time could be spent in fishing -- unless they were going for more than fish.

The sun warmed the deck of the boat and the dock so that they were more comfortable than the shaded concrete under the eaves of the fish-house. This was the kind of day in late winter when lazy dogs and sleepy cats looked for places in the sun for sleeping. The fish-house cat was curled up on the roof of the cabin, half sleeping, opening his eyes once in a while to watch the activity around him.

Travis came out of his office with a piece of paper in his hand, headed for the deck of the *Miss Betty*.

"What's up, boss?" asked Cherokee, coming down the gang-plank to get another load of groceries from the dock.

"Got a message for Blackie," said Travis. "Somebody from his family is coming down from Atlanta to pick him up. Tomorrow night."

"Damn!" said Cherokee. "We could really use him on this trip too. The fish are going to be moving in."

"Want me to get you somebody new?" asked Travis. "There's some fresh meat in town."

"Nah," said Cherokee. "The Swede and I can do better alone than trying to break in somebody new."

"You sure?"

"Very sure," smiled Cherokee. "A good run of fish and new hands on board at the same time? Spare me."

"Will you tell Blackie?" asked Travis, "About tomorrow night?"

"Something must be wrong," said Cherokee. "They don't usually come for him 'til May or June. You sure you got it right?"

"That's what the guy said. Tomorrow night. But you're right. It is earlier than usual. Maybe they just want to talk to him about something."

"I hope so," said Cherokee. "He's too good to lose. And easy to work with too."

"You'll tell him?" repeated Travis.

"Yeah. I'll do it now."

Cherokee picked up four bags of groceries from the dock and headed back up the gang-plank, handing the bags off to the Swede, talking with him a few minutes. The Swede shook his head in disappointment. Cherokee moved across the deck, carrying the piece of paper which Blackie was not going to be able to read.

"Somebody's coming, Blackie," said Cherokee. "To get you."

Blackie looked at him with his trusting steel blue eyes. "O.K." he said. "When?"

"Tomorrow night."

"I won't be able to go on the trip?"

"'Fraid not. But there'll be others."

"Where? What time?"

Cherokee looked at the paper. "Says here at the fish house. Eight o'clock tomorrow night."

"Is it right, Cherokee?" Blackie asked. "It's too early for me to go back. It's still cold. It'll be colder in Atlanta, won't it?"

"Yeah, I guess so," said Cherokee. "Maybe they just want you for a few days. I don't know. But it's about three months earlier than they usually come for you."

"It's going to be too cold up there. I don't want to go."

"You got to, Blackie. They'll keep you warm."

Blackie looked at him pleadingly, saying nothing.

"You want to sleep on the boat tonight? Or in the bunkroom on the dock? We'll be pulling out at four. That's pretty early to get up if you don't have to."

"I guess I'll sleep in the bunk-room."

Cherokee smiled at him. "Don't forget to shower now. And wash your hair, O.K.?" He tousled Blackie's hair.

"O.K." Blackie sounded like a kid about to cry.

"And take your dirty clothes over to the laundromat. And wash them with lots of soap. You know how hill folks can always smell fish when we can't."

He waited for an answer. None came.

"O.K.?" asked Cherokee.

"O.K.," said Blackie. "You want me to keep on working now? Or go shower?"

"Keep on working, Blackie." Cherokee tousled his hair again. "You wouldn't know what to do with yourself if you weren't working. Besides, we need your help -- as long as we can get it. We'll all go out and have a few beers tonight. O.K.?"

"Yeah. That would be good."

"We'll make the Swede pay," smiled Cherokee. "What about that?"

"That's good. Beer on the Swede." He looked like he wanted to say something else.

"What?" asked Cherokee.

"Can we ask Brian to come too? For beer?"

"Sure," smiled Cherokee, "if we can find him -- and if he doesn't have a class. That's just more beer for the Swede to buy."

"Yeah," answered Blackie, laughing. That thought pleased him.

About an hour later, Travis' wife Betty was working in the office while Travis had gone to Panama City for a propeller for another boat. She came out to the boat with a message about Blackie meeting someone tomorrow night. The message was essentially the same except this one said eight-thirty instead of eight o'clock.

"We already got that message," said Cherokee.

"How could you?" asked Travis' wife. "I just took it. Just now. Like two minutes ago."

"Oh, well," smiled Cherokee. "I guess some things need to be said twice."

When the *Miss Betty* left the dock in the four-thirty cold of dark morning, Blackie stood on the dock and waved them off. Even though he slept in the bunk room on the dock, he woke up when he heard the preparations for cast off. He watched until the running lights disappeared around the last bend in the river. Then he went back into the bunk-room where there were four other empty bunks. He lay down on his already disorderly bunk, and tried to get involved in the comic book the Swede had bought for him. He could still hear the chug-chug of the *Miss Betty*'s engines heading out the mouth of the river. Sometimes, on a quiet night when the wind was just right, a boat's engine could be heard when it was three or four miles off-shore. This night was one of those nights.

Blackie got up and went out to the Pepsi machine. He started to get a Pepsi, but changed his mind at the last second and got a diet Dr. Pepper instead. He had seen Brian drinking it all the time. It was good. The cherry taste pleased him.

Back in his bunk he turned the pages of his comic book, sipping the Dr. Pepper, still able to hear the pumping of the *Miss Betty* across the bay.

After about five minutes, he put the comic book on the floor with the Dr. Pepper, slipped off his shirt and trousers, went to the door and turned off the overhead light. Then he felt his way in the darkness back to his bunk.

He lay down, pulled up the woolen blanket, and tried to sleep, but he spent more time tossing and turning than sleeping. He twisted inside the blanket like a restless child in the dark. Finally his mind began to fall into that floating drifting mode that is a preamble to sleep. Wafting back and forth, drifting down and down, slowly falling into a ---

WILD EXPLOSION!!!! Earth-shaking pounding in his ears, like a thousand sonic booms.

Blackie was at the window in a moment.

Flames and arrows of fire lit up the night like fireworks he had never seen before, reflecting across the waters of the bay and the river. Even wilder than he had seen at Disneyworld. One explosion set off another and another as the dark sky turned into a violent panorama of massive destruction. Parts of the boat flew through the orange and red violence, and the flames kept rising one after another, hundreds of feet into the air, as the sound continued to roar like a thousand airplanes.

Blackie stood transfixed, staring at the video show before him, live and amplified by the waters of the bay, the river and the Gulf. His awe turned into sudden dismay when he realized that the burning mass out across the water was all that was left of what had been the *Miss Betty*.

The next night Blackie waited as he had been told -- for someone to come and get him. At eight-o'clock he sat in front of the fish house with all his belongings crammed -- clean and fresh-smelling -- into one bulging suitcase.

At eight-thirty he looked at his digital watch again. He turned off his Walkman and the country music station. He walked out on the dock and stared at the dark water. Back on the street, he looked toward the village for some sign of the limousine that always carried him wherever his family wanted him to go. It wouldn't come. And after last night, he really wanted to get away, away from this dock, away from this town, away from this place, away from here and the memories of Cherokee and the Swede, away from any place with violence.

By nine-o'clock he was beginning to get nervous. Things weren't like they were supposed to be, and no one was there to tell him what to do. He chewed on his shirt collar agitatedly, and a few tears began to form in his eyes. He didn't know what to do, where to go. Maybe he was supposed to go back in the bunk room and wait. But maybe not.

He was breathing fast when Brian came by at nine-twenty and told him to get into the car. He suddenly felt much better. Someone had told him what to do.

"We'll go back to my house where it's warmer," said Brian. "And we'll call your folks from there. O.K.?"

"But I don't know how," said Blackie. "And what if the car comes? What if Joseph comes in the limo and can't find me? He'll go off and leave me again."

"He'll wait. I promise," said Brian soothingly.

Back in the warmth of the house, Brian got Blackie calmed with milk and cookies. Blackie could also laugh at Adam on *Northern Exposure*. Brian looked through Blackie's wallet for a home phone in Atlanta.

There was so little in the wallet, that it took less than a minute to find the note: "If Robert Paul Franklin (Blackie) gets into any trouble, or needs help, please call collect, Atlanta (404) 555-1276. Thank you. Albert and Belinda Franklin, father and mother."

Brian dialed the number straight through -- Blackie was special enough to him that he didn't deserve a collect call -- and asked for Mr. Franklin. When the man was on the phone, Brian explained the reason for the call, and Blackie's predicament. Mr. Franklin thanked Brian profusely, and said they would have a car in Carrabelle by noon of the next day. He expressed the family's gratefulness that Blackie had not been on the *Miss Betty* when it had blown up. He added to Brian's confusion with his own confusion about the calls the day before. The family had been planning a trip to Europe within the next few days. No one had called to say that Blackie was to be picked up. They had planned on letting him stay on the boat until May. Everything was supposed to have been the same as usual for Blackie.

"Thank God for the mix-up," said Blackie's father.

Eric Stewart had been on the Old Beach when the *Miss Betty* blew, lighting up the Gulf for miles. He had known the day before that it was going to happen, but was surprised that it was not his doing that caused it. He knew that because he knew he was infallible, and he had set the explosion for six-ten. There was no doubt in his mind. He did not make mistakes. The only answer was that it had to be done by someone else in the organization, probably someone displeased with the "Bayou Massacre," someone up higher in the chain of command -- maybe even Agular.

He was glad he had thought to send the message to get Blackie off the boat.

"How did it work?" asked Agular, looking out at the reflecting waters of the temperate Atlantic, not turning to face Jensen.

"It went well," said Jensen. "Just as planned. No problems."

"That radio transmitter thing. It worked as it was supposed to?"

"Just as it was supposed to. When the boat got out of the transmitter range -- four miles -- the bomb was detonated. Everything, everybody completely destroyed."

"That's nice," said Agular, still staring at the Atlantic. "So well thought-out. A lot of work and details go into something that sophisticated. If the boat had waited three hours or two days to go out, it would all have worked out as planned. Modern technology. It's amazing."

"Yes. Quite amazing."

"Did the young retarded man, Blackie, get taken care of?"

"Yes. He's with Withers now. Waiting for someone to come pick him up."

"Good. You know, in the Medieval Period, villages used to take care of their retarded. They thought the village idiot was someone sent by God to test them. For time to time the poor soul was supposed to be inhabited by the spirit of God."

"I've heard that," answered Jensen.

"I'm glad things went so well. Modern technology!" Amazing!"

Anne Madison read about the explosion and the deaths in all three of the Florida papers she received. Two of them came on the same day. She read them in her bedroom which that day looked out over a light, early March snow which had been falling for several hours but not remaining on the ground. She had read the two separate accounts carefully, twice, memorizing all of the details. The name 'Cherokee' had an especially pleasing effect on her. She had heard that name before --- from Henderson.

She went to the phone, dialed her bank, asked for the man who handled her personal and confidential matters. She instructed him to transfer $20,000 to a numbered account in a German bank in Georgetown in the Grand Caymans. The man on the other end of the line asked no additional questions other than her social security number, her date of birth, and her mother's maiden name.

When the conversation was finished, Anne Madison sat in front of the three mirrors of her dresser, looked down at the picture of her handsome sixteen-year-old David Michael, kissed her fingers and then pressed them against the beautifully framed photograph of the boy.

"We've finally started, David, darling," she said, smiling at the photograph. "Two down --- and who knows how-many-more to go."

Then she looked at the reflection of the woman in the mirror, and for the first time in many months, a beautiful smile broke across her face. She looked ten years younger than she had just an hour ago.

Steve Briggs' offices looked out over the World's Most Beautiful Beach from the fourth floor of the Thomas Drive Exchange Building, rising up from the white sand and the well-trimmed lawns. His own office was separated from the others by a glass wall so he could have privacy without looking as though he had removed himself from the rest of the office personnel. Beth's desk, for the few hours of the weeks she used it, was the one closest to his glass door and glass wall.

Beth came through the main entrance. To work. Or whatever it was she did there. The men in the office were always pleased when she came in. The women resented her, detested her, but most of all envied her. Beth woke up every morning looking like most women tried to look after four hours in a beauty salon. It was easy for women to hate her.

Steve was on the phone when she went to her desk. He motioned her to come on in to his office.

While he was ending his conversation with what was obviously a plumbing sub-contractor about the new Alabama Towers in Dothan, Beth stood at the floor-to-ceiling windows looking down at the horde of Spring-Breakers. From early March to early April the beach would be packed with thousands and thousands of college students from all over the country and Canada. At any one time in the four-week period there would be over a hundred thousand students strolling the sand in bikinis, wearing as little as they could get away with in order to get as much sun as possible. The temperature was of no importance to them. If the temperature was in the fifties, they wore the same bikinis they wore when it was in the eighties.

Beth watched the undulating mass of students on the beach below her. The milling, moving, weaving throng stretched out as far as she could see east and west. Down by the Spinnaker Club, the crowd was so thick that no movement seemed possible. She could see at least six different patios jutting out from buildings where bands were playing. She could even hear and feel the heavy thumping rhythm of the reggae band out in front of Steve's own Exchange Building.

"It's a sight to behold, isn't it?" he said after hanging up the phone.

"I had to park on Bayside Road. Took a cab from there, but I think I could have made better time walking."

"Well, I came early so I could get my own parking space for the truck. I went down about an hour ago to run out to the Landmark job. No way. There was even part of a band set up in my truck bed."

"I didn't know there were so many people in the world. The *Champs Élysée* in Paris has never been this crowded."

"We need an office out of town during Spring Break."

"Like up in the woods somewhere. Or in Dothan."

"I'd offer you lunch somewhere," he said, "but we can't get anywhere. I guess it'll be the Exchange Commissary for the next four weeks."

"At least it's good food. Even if you can't get a drink, and it's not very elegant." She smiled at him. "But I *do* know the owner. Maybe we can special-order some Maine lobster or Oysters Rockefeller."

"Don't I wish. What are you doing here today?"

"I needed to use the computer," she said. "No noble thoughts about doing good for the company, or anything like that."

"I'd be disappointed if you had." He smiled back at her.

She turned again to look at the mass of college students down on the beach.

Having fun was the name of the game. She thought if the times she and Steve had walked along the beach. She had never done that with Brian. Even though she liked Brian and admired

252

him, she and he had never done any of the things together that she love doing with her men. Steve had been a strong anchor for her, not that she needed anyone strong. Brian had trusted her. But Steve had trusted her too. What's a girl to do when she had a divided heart? What's more important, old friendships or new trusts?

"Brian knows ... Everything," she said into the plate-glass.

"How could he?"

"He's doing undercover. For the FBI .. and probably the DEA. He's been the new connection between Cherokee and Captain Andy for the past four -- five weeks."

Steve laughed slightly. "How sneaky can they get? A college professor. That takes it. How did you find out?" He was not even surprised that she knew --- apparently everything.

"He asked me to come to work for you. And spy. Said I was in a 'unique position.' Wanted me to find out everything I could."

"Well ... You're doing a good job, I hope."

"He's pleased so far."

"What does he know?" Steve asked.

She turned back to him smiling. "Less than he did before I started to give him some answers."

"Good girl."

"He's in a hurry. To get it over with. To get out of it all."

"Well, we'll have to help him then, won't we? Get out of it all, that is."

"It looks that way," she said. "And he's so cute too."

The nurse glanced over the chart at the foot of the bed. "Stephanie Andropolous, age 66." The chart told the nurse that Mrs. Andropolous had developed Alzheimer's two years ago, had developed diabetes three months ago. Last night she had a stroke and was brought in from Oakcrest Nursing Home at 3:12 am. Now there were needles sticking in both arms, a tube up her nose, and the heart monitor was attached to her chest, beeping a regular rhythm as the green light bounced up and down like a broken TV tube.

As the nurse looked at Mrs. Andropolous, she wondered how the older woman could stay so beautiful in spite of all that was happening to her.

Stephanie, even in this loss of physical dignity, still had a beauty and personal dignity that hung over her like grace. It was certainly nothing the poor woman was doing consciously. Still beauty and dignity lay all around her. 'Grace' was the word that came to the mind of the nurse at the foot of Stephanie's bed.

The door behind the nurse opened. A slight creaking. The nurse turned to see the handsome grey-bearded man wearing the captain's hat. He looked at the nurse, smiled just slightly, blinked his eyes quickly a few times to hold back some tears, and then turned to look at the woman in the bed. He was holding a few sprigs of sea-oats which he moved about without being aware of what he was doing with them. He knew when he picked them that he was breaking the law, but this might be the last time Stephanie would get to see sea-oats. And she loved them more than any flowers. The nurse took the sea-oats from him and put them in an empty vase on a cart just behind him. The man nodded a soft 'Thank You' and went to the side of the bed.

He reached down and took her hand in both of his, never taking his eyes from her face. He wanted to talk to her but felt uncomfortable doing it with the nurse in the room. The nurse moved around beside him, sliding a chair up behind him. Seeing his need to be alone, she quickly left the room.

Captain Andy sat down, still holding the lifeless hand, never taking his eyes from the serene face of beauty. He did not hear the beeping of the monitor. The tubes and needles violating her body were not things his mind chose to acknowledge.

"Oh, Stephanie, Stephanie." He rubbed the wrist and hand gently. One of his hands went up to cup the side of her face. He seemed to let himself become one with her, his gentle touch and voice drifting into her soul and body.

"Lord, I've loved you long, Stephanie. My life has been made more precious for having you in it. Darling, darling Stephanie. I hope you're not in pain. You're too lovely -- too kind -- to have to endure pain. People like you, loving, caring, wonderful people, make the world a happier place with your love and care. And your constant love of life, and that wonderful awe and curiosity."

Somewhere he had heard --- or read --- that talking to stroke victims --- in a coma, was thought to be beneficial to them; the voices of friends and relatives filtered through the seemingly impenetrable barricade and gave them the will to hold on --- to cling to life --- and to fight their way back.

But Captain Andy talked to his Stephanie because he wanted to; he had things to say --- last minute things that must be said.

"Oh, my God, Stephanie. It pains me to see you like this -- when you think I never come to see you, not knowing who I am most of the time. Oh, God Stephanie, you'll never know the pain that shoots through my heart when I come into the room and you don't know who I am."

He still rubbed her hand and wrist gently, still caressed her face, never taking his eyes from hers.

"The times on the beach together --- when we were young -- the trips to Greece -- taking the children to the Acropolis, the Parthenon -- the family -- having a picnic lunch, in the shadow of Mount Olympus. The trips to Mexico, and that wonderful cruise to Alaska.

"I have so many memories of you, Stephanie. And then you slice my heart in two when you have none at all. None at all. 'Who are you?' you ask me. 'What are you doing in my room?' Please, please, darling Stephanie. If you do nothing else in the world, before you go, please, remember me. Remember me. Remember me.

"They tell me you've gone and had a stroke. And that you're lungs and heart are weak also. My God, my darling!! You've never in all your wonderful, loving kindness ever done a cruel thing to deserve all this. These things you have wrong with you, you don't deserve them. You deserve peace and comfort -- and happiness -- and love. And the capacity to give that wonderful love of yours."

All the while he kept looking at the unmoving, closed eyes, still rubbing the soft immobile hand, still caressing the gentle face.

He looked away for a moment, toward the window where the morning sun was blocked by the blinds. His eyes watered up, overflowed, and tears rolled down his face.

"Oh, my darling Stephanie," he continued, looking at the window and the blocked sun. "Please remember me." His head dropped, and he looked at the pale lifeless hand. "Remember me."

As he looked at the pale hand, one finger moved, just slightly. A miracle?

He looked to her face, and the heavens sang to him suddenly. Her eyes were open. Her lips were beginning to move, ever so haltingly. He leaned forward, getting his ear as close to her lips as possible.

"Sea .. oats ... lovely ... Of ... course .. I ... remember ... you... Andy.. My .. Andy."

He kissed her on the cheek, and while his face was next to hers, happy, joyous, he never heard the beeping grow slower .. slower, until it had become a constant tone with no rhythm, no beat.

The two deck hands came out of the little cafe that faced the river and walked down the dock to the *Panama Queen*. The morning was an early spring one. Most of the people on the dock were wearing light jackets or sweaters, but the deck-hands were carrying their jackets over their shoulders, braving the early chill in sleeveless T-shirts. The blonde was carrying an electric saw he had borrowed from Captain Andy. The brunette was carrying some plexiglass to put over the top of the charting table.

As they swung over the side of the boat, a bunch of sea gulls fluttered up from the small dividing pier that separated the opposite slips. The brunette went straight to the radio, turned it on, and suddenly Delbert McClinton was sing "I'm with You," to them.

"Put on some coffee while you're down there," called the blonde.

"You want more? After the four cups you had with breakfast?"

"No. I need it to lubricate the saw with. What do you think? Of course I want more, or I wouldn't have asked."

"O.K.," yelled the brunette. "More coffee coming up."

Delbert kept on singing to them.

The brunette cleaned out the coffeepot, poured some grounds into the basket, filled the pot with water and placed it over the flame.

He suddenly noticed that the sink was clean. Captain Andy must have done it, but it was unlike him. He was always saying he wasn't going to clean up the boys' messes. And he never did.

"Didn't we leave some dirty dishes down here last night?" asked the brunette.

"Yeah. When we ate that Pepperidge Farms Devil Food Cake, remember? Why?"

"It's clean. The captain must have washed them." He looked around at the rest of the bunk room. "It's all clean. The whole place."

The blonde looked around the cabin and the steering deck. "It is up here too. What's going on here?"

The brunette came up from below. They looked at one another a moment. Then at the same time they saw the note taped to the steering wheel with some duct tape.

"O.K., boys. I cleaned her up good. One last time.

"She's yours now. Keep her clean. Make a lot of money with her. (Ha.) The title's already signed, dated, and notarized in the top right drawer. If I ever come back, I'll expect to be hired as a deck-hand -- and I'll be a damned sight better one than either of you two. And I'll clean up after myself.

"When the college guy comes around with a package from over in Carrabelle, tell him I'm not with the organization any more. He'll understand.

"I hope you have as much fun with the *Panama Queen* as I did. Good fishing.

Best of Luck,
Captain Andy"

Eric Stewart sat in his office high over the lights on North Atlanta. He turned from the view of the city at night to a journal before him on the desk. He wrote in it two or three times a week. Some days when he had little to report, he would write what came to mind, musings streams on consciousness, philosophical droppings.

As he thumbed through the pages he stopped on an entry from a few months earlier. Long before Anne Madison had contacted him, before he ever heard the name Cherokee. He read with renewed interest what he had written on another day, in another mood.

******Discipline. It takes discipline. To do anything right takes discipline.

I have little respect for people who do not exercise control and discipline. Weak people.

The world is populated with such weak people. Those of us with the power, control and discipline have to endure them in order to achieve the goals. I know how to act around them; placating, peaceful, serene, submissive. They do not understand me when I become myself. I have to keep up a constant act -- or be an outcast from the mass of common, weak, and undisciplined hordes which I must abide in order to reach the goals I must achieve.

I have stood outside on a freezing night in my underwear. All night. Why? To have the control and discipline that's needed. Anyone can do it. I have stuck needles through my arms and legs. All the way through. Just to gain the control and discipline I require. There is no such thing as pain when you learn that it's only a lapse of discipline and control.

A job is not done well if not done completely. Once -- in the army -- in the jungles of Colombia -- I was ordered to do away with a small-time drug-smuggling ring. A nickel-and-dime thing. Not really of much consequence. It was easy.

I was told to use any means required. I did. Control. Discipline. Commitment. I took out the three Colombians responsible for the mechanical portion of the operation. They brought the stuff in, took the money to the one who was the boss.

I was diligent. I found out that their boss, the guy who controlled the traffic, was the same man who had given me the order to do away with the ring. He had issued the order to satisfy his superiors, to gain favor with them. A sham. A man against himself.

He never thought I would follow through enough to find out that he was actually in charge of the ring he wanted destroyed. I'm sure he thought that if I ever did find out, I would stop there. Since he was a superior officer.

But he was also a weak man. He did not recognize his own weakness. But I knew it immediately -- when I discovered it was he who was in charge.

Well -- There you have it. I was committed -- in control. I had the discipline to do what I did not particularly want to do. I even liked him -- weak though he was. We drank together, smoked some weed together. A fairly nice guy.

He couldn't understand why I had to kill him. He begged. He pleaded. Said he thought I would stop -- when -- or if -- I got to him. After all, we were pals, buddies. He said he even had given me the order as a favor. So I would gain the attention of the people who mattered.

I tried to explain to him that some things, when set in motion, cannot, should not, be stopped. Commitment. Control. Discipline. For every action, there is an opposite and equal reaction. Matter can be neither created nor destroyed. Water seeks its own level. An object in motions tends to stay in

259

motion. An object at rest tends to remain at rest. When an irresistible force meets an immovable object --- Control. Discipline. Commitment. Power.

I am an object in motion. Controlled, disciplined, committed motion. He never seemed to understand -- which in itself showed a weakness on his part. But no matter. He didn't have long to not understand.

I tried to explain the Star Chamber to him the medieval group who carried out justice when it slipped through the cracks in the law -- when it escaped the courts. But again he couldn't understand.

I had to do it. He had ordered me to do it. A lesser person would have given in, listened to his countermands, backed off -- in the name of friendship. But if a job is worth your commitment in the beginning, then it's worth your commitment in the end. If not then you have erred in your commitment in the beginning -- and you are weak, for not understanding the job to begin with.

Mix together Kantian metaphysics, Proustian existentialism, minimalism, revisionism, and you have -- the Superman. I *am* the Superman. Zarathustra's Superman. Scopenhauer's, "The only escape is the negation of the will," Spinoza's "Evil exists only in finite minds and dissolves when seen as a part of the whole."

"Nothing is good or bad, but thinking makes it so." Shakespeare.

And God is in the details. Everything depends on precision. A hair-line trigger. The very exact moment to pull the trigger. The very exact spot to place the bullet. Precision. Precision. The exact strength of the bomb. The exact spot where the bomb will go off. Precision. Precision.

The exact altitude at which the plane will explode. The exact power with which the plane will blow into flames -- and then extinction. Precision. Precision. The exact length of time it takes to die. The exact amount of pain to be endured before the dying. Precision. Precision. God is in the details.

I once read -- somewhere -- an old Crow Indian adage, dealing with being one's own self; a plea for individualism: "Act like a crazy dog. Wear scarves and other fine clothes. Carry a rattle and dance along the road singing crazy dog songs after everyone else has gone to bed." ******

He closed the journal and looked back to the many headlights moving along the interstates to the north.

Soon everyone else will have gone to bed, he thought. I will dance along the road with my rattle ---- Singing crazy dog songs.

With the morning sun on the water behind him, Brian breezed along U.S. 98 toward Panama City. He had no deliveries to make this day, nothing to pick up. His life had been quiet for the last three days, since Cherokee and The Swede had been disintegrated along with the *Miss Betty*. Also Captain Andy had disappeared. Brian had stopped at the *Panama Queen* once -- to see if there were any attaché going back to Carrabelle, and the deck hands had relayed Andy's message.

He hoped the message from Captain Andy could be taken at face value. He sincerely hoped that Captain Andy, either with or without Stephanie, was somewhere on the Aegean Coast of Greece, wading through rocky shallows, sipping Uzo in some little coastal bar. He hoped Andy was with Stephanie; he did not know of her death.

The lights in the car behind him blinked three times. Not an accident. Ah, Fordham. In his car *du jour*. A Thunderbird today. Brian found a deserted road off the long deserted strip of 98 between Apalach and St. Joe. On this particular strip of highway, the road was not near the water as it was in most places; here it was bordered on one side by a wide savannah of marsh grass and ponds, on the other by pine forest. The road he chose turned in to the forest. The Thunderbird followed.

"Where you been?" asked Brian when they were standing together under the pine umbrella. "I haven't seen you in a few days. Since the shoot-out at O.K. Bayou."

"I had some lab work to do. Back in Jacksonville."

"That doesn't make me feel very safe, Hank. I've gotten used to your being my bodyguard. Even though you weren't around during the shoot-out."

"Don't call me 'Hank.' And you did well at the shoot-out."

"Yeah. Only went through two pairs of underwear. What kind of lab work?"

"We got some of Cherokee's and The Swede's things from their lockers in the bunk-room at the fish house. Did a lot of analyzing and checking up."

"What'd you find out? Anything we didn't already know?" Brian had, in the last few weeks, in spite of his desire to get out of 'this mess,' come to use the word "we" more than "you" when talking to Fordham.

"We didn't find out anything that would help us. But we did find some interesting things," said Fordham. "Things that answer more questions about the past than about the future. A few things we didn't know."

Ever since the discovery of the odd man -- Stewart -- there had been speculation as to how Cherokee had gotten the shipment of drugs that Stewart had traced. If Cherokee had taken it from a shipment which came through him, then he would be suspect, and jeopardize his own position. Still it had been that particular trail that Stewart had followed back from Chicago -- without even knowing he was tracking a maverick trail, and not the main one which Brian would lead him to later.

There had been a switch-blade knife found in Cherokee's locker, with some traces of blood in the handle. Analysis of the blood -- DNA finger-printing -- indicated that some of the blood was from the old fisherman who had been knifed to death about six weeks earlier, the old man found stabbed in his truck.

The old man belonged to a different arm of Agular's operation, one not connected with Cherokee, but one he knew about. Cherokee, either alone or with The Swede, had killed the old man, taken the drugs, and then set up the high school kid who was later found and implicated in the old man's murder. The kid had been forcibly overdosed, and some of the drugs had

262

been left with the boy's body to throw off any additional search. Fibers from the kid's clothing and from the upholstery in his car had been found on Cherokee's and The Swede's clothes.

"God," said Brian. "You mean they killed that kid just to keep from being tracked?"

"It was murder with the old man. They couldn't afford to get caught."

"They killed that high school kid?"

"You got it."

"Cherokee didn't have any conscience at all, did he?."

"The typical amoral sociopath," said Fordham.

"They're really always charmers, aren't they? Just like the classic text-book definition."

"All the ones I've met," said Fordham. "And I meet a lot in my job."

"And I've just read about them -- until now. And then still didn't recognize one when I came across him."

"There's another one in the picture too."

"Who's that? Agular?"

"No. Stewart."

"What have you found out there?"

Fordham recited the case file. The story of the Colombian drug ring. A man driven by a need for perfection and an obsessive compulsion to complete any job undertaken, even if it meant his death, even if it met turning on the one who gave the orders. A man who could not stop short of total completion. Driven to wipe out evil at all costs -- like the Medieval Star Chamber -- and all the time having no awareness of his own evil, putting himself over and above the law, always letting the ends justify the means -- any means.

"Have you ever met him?" asked Brian.

"A few minutes. At Beth' party."

"Is he a charmer also?"

"I'm sure he is from reading his file. In another case we worked around one another -- much like we're doing here. People I know who have met him -- and lived to talk about it -- say he's the perfect charmer. The perfect gentleman. Someone

263

you'd want your mother to meet. You sister to date. A regular Ted Bundy."

Neither spoke for a few moments. Then Fordham broke the silence.

"His file reads like one you come across every once in a while, that can't really capture the person well. Something so elusive, and still so powerful, so fanatical -- that it can't be captured in words. A person who remains a mystery even after you've written everything there is to know about him. A paradox."

"You're beginning to sound poetic, Fordham."

"Am I? It must be the effect of hanging with a teacher."

"No," smiled Brian. "That doesn't generate poetry. That produces marginal poverty and terminal weariness."

"You know," said Fordham. "I'm going to miss you --- when this is all over."

Brian's face lit up slightly. "Do you know something I don't, Hank? Is this all about to end?"

Fordham shook his head and smiled. "No. I don't know anything. But it's closer to the end now than it was six -- seven weeks ago. Right?"

Brian looked out toward the water. "Don't get my hopes up like that, Hank. I was sure you were looking at the light at the end of the tunnel. But I guess you're right. I'm going to miss you a little too. You can't go through something like this with somebody and not have a lot of memories. You know what?" He turned back to face Fordham. "This all may very well be the high point in my life. Thirty years from now, when I'm old and dottery and the department chairman at some college is trying to find a way to get rid of me, this part of my life will probably be what I look back on --- with the fondest memories. Of course, by then memory will be strongly influenced by ego. I'll be the hero completely then."

"Of course. And I'll be the hero in my memories."

"You want to go get a beer?" asked Brian.

Fordham looked at him with genuine fondness. "That would be good. Yes. Except for two things. First of all, it's still morning. And second -- you and I can't be seen together -- around here at least." He shook his head regretfully. "Yes. I'd love to sit and have a beer with you. But another time. Another place."

A soft breeze from the Atlantic blew across Agular's large bedroom which opened on three sides to views of the water and beach. Here too the curtains drifted out across the room, floating on the ever-constant breeze.

Adam Spencer, Agular's newly-hired valet, packed the bags meticulously. The shirts neatly folded on one side, the underwear and socks in perfect order on the other. He paused to look at his watch. 3:16 ... pm. Two hours and forty-five minutes before Agular's plane left. Plenty of time. But Spencer didn't like any last minute stuff. It was a fetish with him. Last minute stuff really annoyed him. Last minutes were for relaxing, looking forward to the trip, having a refreshing drink, and resting so that others who were not as well-organized could rush around taking care of their last minute stuff --- while you sipped your drink and relaxed.

In the garment bag, he carefully placed one medium-brown suit, three pairs of casual slacks, a green sweater and a light blue sport coat. This was more than the garment bag was meant to hold. Everything would become wrinkled. But the other garment bag he found in the closet had some moth balls in it, and he wasn't going to have any of these clothes smelling of moth balls.

A pair of penny loafers, in a shoe-bag of course, was placed in the suitcase next to the socks. Then a neatly rolled second belt of kangaroo hide. One flower-power tie was secured in the lid of the suitcase.

Then he turned his attention to the toilet kit. It was already stocked with the necessities which stayed there, even when no trip was in progress. It was a grab-me-take-me kit; Coast soap, Arm and Hammer gel toothpaste, Oral B-40 toothbrush, Gillette Plus disposable razors, Barbasol Lime shave cream, a miniature of Calvin Kline's *Obsession*, a miniature of Davidoff's *Cool Waters*, four foil packages of Alka-Seltzer, a pack of Zantac, cinnamon Dental-Floss, a pill bottle with ten five-milligram Valium, one miniature of Absolut vodka, one of Bacardi Rum.

The garment bag, the suitcase, and the toilet kit all belonged to a meticulous man of good taste, precision, exactness, almost a compulsive man.

"Very good job, Adam," said Agular, coming from the shower in a terry-cloth robe.

"Thank you, sir." Adam was pleased with the recognition.

"You're a pleasure to have around," said Agular. "I don't know how I got through so many years without you."

"You've done very well, Mr. Agular."

"In the fours days you've been here, I've come to feel that I've known you for years."

"You're very kind, sir."

"They say you can't make new old friends. But I feel as if that's what you are, Adam."

"You're an easy man to work for, Mr. Agular," smiled Spencer.

"Only because I think we must have so much in common," said Agular. "Tell me that quote again. the one you told me last night."

"The Scopenhauer?"

"I think it was Spinoza."

"Oh. *That* one. 'Evil exists only in finite minds and dissolves when seen as part of the whole.'"

"That's it. Excellent. I like that very much. You must write it down for me."

"My pleasure."

"I see you have everything ready for my little jaunt. And as usual, you've done a superlative job." He was combing his hair in the mirror above the dresser. The way he held his hands made the missing finger on the left hand more prominent.

"I hope I continue to please you," said Spencer.

"You do. You will. You're quite intelligent. I respect that. You had a hard time achieving your education. And then your

266

decision to leave --- an intolerable situation --- an intolerable surrounding. I respect *that*."

"Your research into my background is equally admirable."

"You expected it?"

"I looked forward to it. To see if I would meet your standards."

Agular had almost finished dressing. Spencer had anticipated his needs during the process and conversation, handing him things he had not even asked for yet.

Jensen came in the room with some papers to be signed, and apparently wanted to talk to Agular alone. He politely turned to the new man. "Adam, would you excuse us for a few minutes, please?"

"Of course, sir." Spencer turned to leave the room.

"No," said Agular, looking at himself in one of the many full-length mirrors about the room. "That won't be necessary, Jensen." He looked at Jensen briefly before turning back to the mirror. "I've decided to take Spencer -- Adam, that is -- into my complete confidence, Jensen. I find him a man of modest ambition, and highly trustworthy. Anyone who can quote Spinoza, Schopenhauer, Kant <u>and</u> Hitler in the same paragraph can't be all bad. I suspect Spencer's intelligence has already provided him with enough knowledge about us that secrecy is unnecessary. Besides -- he may prove very helpful to us -- in some other position which is not so ignoble."

Jensen seemed slightly uncertain as to the advisability of this move -- even of that particular statement in front of the new man. But he was used to Agular's immediate approval of some people, his tenancy to take those whom he liked immediately and treat them as proteges. Jensen was noticeably more at ease when Spencer declined the invitation to stay.

"If you don't mind, sir," said Spencer, "I *do* have some things to tend to in the laundry room. Shirts. Trousers. That sort of thing. If I don't get them now, they may become wrinkled."

He had already done what needed being done here. There was nothing he could hear that would be of any interest to him.

The moving body had already been set in motion, and he knew what a moving body tends to do once set in motion.

"Now, Spencer," smiled Agular at himself in the full-length mirror. "I'm sure you would rather stay here and repack that garment bag. There is a new one, much larger, in the bottom right drawer in the dressing room. I forgot to tell you about it. And it doesn't smell like moth balls either."

He was ready to prove to Spencer that he trusted him. Jensen didn't even bother to show his disapproval this time.

"Go ahead, Jensen?" said Agular. "What is it?"

Spencer went into the closet and returned with the larger garment bag. This one would not wrinkle the clothes. He began moving the clothes from one bag to another.

"Go ahead, Jensen," said Agular. "It's all right."

"I've just been talking to Briggs in Panama City," said Jensen. "What he tells me is very disturbing."

"Tell me, Jensen. I can handle disturbing better than you."

"He tells me that Withers, the college professor you like so much, is working with the FBI -- and possibly the Drug Enforcement Agency."

"That *is* disturbing," said Agular, trying on another shirt, never taking his eyes from the mirror. "I'm extremely sorry to hear that. He is such a bright young man. And such a good sense of humor."

"What do you plan to do?"

Agular turned and faced Jensen. He motioned for Jensen to take a seat in the purple chaise-lounge. Agular sat in the light grey lounge not far from Jensen.

"Plan to do? Well, Jensen. There seems to be a limited number of choices here. Like one." Agular turned to Adam Spencer. "What would you do, Spencer? To someone who has worked his way into your confidence, in an effort to betray you? To try and turn you over to your enemies?" He was toying with Spencer. All three of them knew it was a test.

"That all depends on the amount of commitment you have to your goal," said Spencer. "Your commitment, discipline, and control. If you are totally committed, as you should be --

otherwise you should never be involved at all -- then, with that total commitment, you do not have a choice. There is only one course of action. You cannot allow your goal -- or your commitment -- to be jeopardized."

God!!! Had he *ever* passed the test!! He hadn't stopped at an answer. He had given a dissertation.

"That's admirable," said Agular. I don't think I could have expressed it better. Or maybe I should say I couldn't have rationalized it better. Wasn't it eloquent, Jensen."

"Yes. Yes." Jensen was more ready to accept Spencer now. "Quite eloquent. Quite interesting."

"Now I'm more pleased than ever," said Agular. "I was unhappy about having to lose that very interesting fellow Withers. But now I find he may be replaced by someone even more to my liking."

Agular was so pleased with Spencer's answer that he could not stay seated. Again he was in front of the mirror. "Contact someone, Jensen. Have them take care of Withers. Shame. It could have worked out so well."

"All right. I'll get on it right away."

"And I guess -- " He seemed almost sorry to say it. "You know, I'm always sure that husbands tell their wives everything when they're as close as those two obviously are. I guess we need to take care of her too. Pity. So pretty."

"I'll take care of that also," said Jensen.

"Does this meet with your approval, Spencer?" Agular smiled at the man who was busy packing his clothes.

"Commitment requires commitment," said Spencer. "Besides, sir. 'Mine is not to reason why. Mine is but to do and die.'"

"Excellent, Spencer," said Agular. "A quote from Browning always gives a conversation an air of legitimacy."

"Sorry, sir. Kipling," said Spencer.

"I love being surrounded by intelligent people," said Agular, smiling.

Jensen got up and started to leave. Agular stopped him.

"Jensen. I think I'm going to need you on this trip after all. You can be ready by six, can't you?"

"Yes, sir. I'll pack now."

"Only one night. Two at the most."

Adam Spencer looked at the two men from the dressing room where he had almost finished repacking Agular's garment bag. The morning had been an informative one for him: first he had learned that; 1) Withers had been found out, 2) Withers was on the list to be terminated, 3) Withers' wife was on the termination list also, 4) the two terminations had been passed on to Jensen, and 5) Jensen was now scheduled to go on the trip to the mainland. A nice cycle. What goes around comes around. It would all take care of itself. The cycle had completed itself neatly -- right in this room -- all within a matter of no more than fifteen minutes. He hadn't had to do anything to form the completion. He still wouldn't have to. Strangely enough -- it had been completed before it had begun.

The late afternoon sun, almost setting, cast a golden glow across the beaches. Adam Spencer stood on the third floor alabaster promenade, watching Agular and Jensen going down the chair-lift beside the massive steps. Just before getting to the limo, Agular turned to look back at his castle, and in so doing, saw Adam Spencer on the third floor watching them. He waved up to Spencer magnanimously. Spencer waved back, feeling the breeze blow through his loose-fitting island shirt.

It was completed before it was begun. A paradox. But true.

As the plane took off, Spencer leaned back into one of the porch lounges, his bare feet propped up on the alabaster railing, smoking one of Agular's ten-dollar cigars and sipping some of Agular's Myers Rum. Occasionally he deliberately tapped some of the ashes on the porch floor.

He watched the Sabreliner taxi down the private air-strip, head into the prevailing wind coming off the Atlantic. It rose smoothly, and Adam Spencer tried to estimate its altitude as it climbed. A hundred feet. Two hundred. Three. Five ... A thousand. Two thousand.

He had a feeling of exhilaration as he watched the climbing plane. Anticipation. Excitement.

The explosive device in Agular's garment bag was attached to an altimeter set to detonate at five thousand feet. Now he wished he had set it for three, so he could see it better. The sun on the horizon cast a copper color on the rising plane and the coral clouds behind it. A beautiful background for an explosion.

Two thousand-five. Three. Three-five. He really wished he had set it for right -- rriiiiighttt -- *there*. That would have been the best place yet. The best seat in the house. Four thousand. Four thousand-five ---

Ooops! His estimation was off. What he thought was four thousand-five was actually five thousand.

The wild burst of flame which grew out into a gigantic aura, maybe two thousand feet across, lit up the twilight sky with a brightness he had not expected from a daylight detonation. The gigantic burst of extravagant flames pounded his eyes five seconds before the sound of the explosion touched his eardrums. Light travels 186,000 miles per second, sound only about 1/5 mile per second. Slow. He knew that.

Also Spencer noticed a phenomenon that was a little disconcerting to the effect of the explosion as a whole; the wind from the Atlantic carried the sound across the island, blowing the sound waves away from their source. By the time the sound got to Adam Spencer, it sounded as if the explosion came from almost a right angle to the actual explosion.

Spencer watched as the enormous ball of fire slowly settled toward the sea, dissipating as it descended. He took a long drag from the expensive stogie, sipped the Myers Rum and enjoyed the scene. He might even stay overnight, it was so pleasant. A luxury he hardly ever afforded himself. The breeze, the rum, the food, surely the best place to stay on the island, maybe all of the Caimans.

The flames were disappearing now, almost no trace of anything solid -- no trace of the remains of the plane. Extinguished. Dispatched. Annihilated. Terminated.

What goes around comes around.

And it had been completed before it had begun.

He went to the second-floor music-room, sat at the concert grand, flexed his fingers, and began playing, magnificently, "The Eighteenth Variation." He played so brilliantly, one could only wonder why he was not a world-class concert pianist.

The Panama City airport was almost empty when Steve Briggs entered shortly after midnight. No one on the mainland had yet heard of Agular's demise. Looking at his watch, Briggs realized he didn't have to spend time reading a paper he wasn't interested in. He was already ten minutes late.

He went directly to the bank of phones and immediately connected with the voice he listened to four or five times a week. "If you would like to make a call, --- please hang up and ---." On the floor next to his right foot was the attaché case. In less than a minute the other attaché case was set down beside his. The grey herring-bone suit in the adjoining booth was there less than a minute. Then the hand of the grey herring-bone reached down and picked up the attaché case closest to Briggs' leg. Then the grey suit was gone. Steve picked up the remaining attaché and walked down the deserted concourse.

The grey herring-bone boarded the flight for Atlanta and Chicago, able to take a choice of seats. There were no more than ten other passengers on this late flight. He chose a window seat midway in the plane, put the attaché up in the carry-on compartment, then took off the suit coat. It was almost too warm in the plane for Brian. But what can you do? No chance of cracking a window.

Sitting down, Brian turned his attention to the view below him, watching different south Georgia and Alabama towns flow underneath him; Marianna, Chattahoochee, Bainbridge, Dothan, Eufalla, Augusta, Montgomery -- Columbus --. He and

Susannah had been in all of them on what they called their "Growth and Expansion Weekends," those trips when they went to festivals, craft shows, the dinner theatre at Eufalla State Park. There had even been an over-nighter to Caryville, Florida, for the annual Worm Grunting Festival.

This trip to Chicago had been unexpected. He had been in his office that morning, getting ready for a class. The phone rang, and a man who identified himself as John Ammons told Brian that he would have to make the trip to Chicago tonight. The directions would be in an envelope attached to the attaché case that would be left for him later today.

"Where will I get the attaché? I'm just getting ready to ---"

The line went dead. John Smith apparently didn't want to hear any excuses and was going to have things his way.

Fortunately -- or unfortunately, depending on the weather in Chicago --- Brian had dressed more academically than usual today, since he had to make a short presentation at a meeting of the social studies faculty that afternoon. The grey herring-bone had been a present from Susannah's folks, and Susannah had flown to Barney's in New York to pick out "the ultimate Ivy-league attire." It did have the look of something Robert Mitchem might have worn in *Ryan's Daughter*, and he told her that every time he put it on, he had the feeling that his IQ went up ten points. Like the brain given to the scarecrow by the Wizard of Oz.

When Brian came back from his morning class, the attaché case was on his desk, an envelope on top of it, all in spite of the fact that his office was locked. But he had weeks ago given up being surprised at any breach of security.

The envelope had the sparest of directions in it, was paper-clipped to a round-trip ticket to Chicago and five one hundred dollar bills, apparently to travel in style. Eleven-thirty-four p.m. at the phone booths in the airport -- the exchange -- don't make any personal contact with the guy at the airport -- don't even look at him -- the switch -- an address in Chicago -- the time to be there -- the name of the person to make the exchange with. That was all.

After the stop at Hartsfiled International in Atlanta, Brian put aside the <u>Newsweek</u> he had been reading, pulled his neck-tie even looser, and slept until the touchdown at O'Hare.

He took a cab to the Chicago Hilton, stopping at a convenience store to get a diet Dr. Pepper, ordered two shots of rum from room service, mixed a drink, but was asleep before finishing a fourth of it.

After the seven-thirty wake-up call, he showered, ate cereal, dry toast, orange juice and coffee in his underwear --- yesterday's underwear. Uuuggghh! If there were time later. Maybe. It sure would make him feel better to buy some more. Not many things worse than wearing yesterday's underwear, especially after today's shower.

Dressed and downstairs he was in a cab by eight-twenty, headed north on Lakeshore Drive. The ride took almost half an hour. He enjoyed the trip. He had never been in Chicago before. Paris. London. But never Chicago. The temperature made the grey herring-bone suit just right. And he could feel his intelligence rising slowly since he had put it on after breakfast.

The cab turned off Lakeshore Drive and was now in an industrial section far to the north of town. Turning north again, the taxi passed a chain-link fence surrounding many silent bull-doziers, cranes, even combines. On the right, up ahead was a well-designed two-story office building. The cab slowed to a stop in front of the building.

"Here we are," said the driver. "You want me to wait?"

Brian looked at his watch, then at the building. "Yes. I'll just have enough time to get to my flight."

The cab parked in the paved, well-designed area beside the building. Brian got out with the attaché case and started toward the front door. The sign across the top of the building read "Mad Bull Construction Company."

The trim grey-haired receptionist whose name plate said she was Judy Smathers, greeted him with the usual smile and, "May I help you?"

"I'm John Monroe. Here with some papers on the Hernandez project for Mr. Madison to sign."

"Oh, yes." she said. "He's expecting you. Have a seat. I'll let him know you're here."

Brian sat in an expensive, comfortable leather chair and looked at the pictures across the rear wall. Arthur Madison, Anne Bullock Madison, William Bullock. Three handsome people. Anne Madison was an extremely beautiful woman, at least when that picture was taken.

Brian got up and walked over to read the captioning beneath the pictures. He suspected immediately, when he saw the names of its founders, how the company had arrived at its off-the-wall name. Mad Bull Construction Company. An impressive name. Memorable. Makes one wonder what it means --- where it comes from --- until you see the names: Madison and Bullock.

"You can go in now," said the receptionist. "Second door on your right."

A common miscommunication. A conflict between habit on one's person's part, and unfamiliarity on another's. From where he had been sitting, where the receptionist normally addressed most people with this phrase, Jack Madison's office would be the second door on the right. But from where Brian was standing at the moment, when he turned right, away from the photographs, Jack Madison's office was the first on his right; the second on the right was Anne Madison's.

Brian turned, walked toward the door, the second on his right, briefly saw the name 'Madison,' knocked lightly on the door and opened it.

Anne Madison had a picture of David Michael in her hands. Obvious but repressed tears filled both beautiful blue eyes as she turned quickly toward the door.

"Yes?" she asked, softly.

"I'm sorry. I was looking for Jack Madison."

"His office is the next one down." She pointed.

The receptionist was directly behind Brian now, holding his arm. "I'm sorry. This is the wrong room. It's that one." She was steering him away.

"I'm sorry," he said. I must have misunderstood you." He turned back to face Anne Madison. "I'm sorry for the mistake. I hope I didn't disturb you."

"No," answered Anne Madison, on her feet now, holding the picture to her breast. "Don't worry about it."

The receptionist closed the door and was steering Brian toward the next door.

"Is she all right?" asked Brian. "She's crying. She's upset about something."

"I'll see to it," said the receptionist. "Here we are." They were in front of Jack Madison's office.

She opened the door. "Mr. Madison, this is John Monroe. This is Mr. Madison."

She left, closing the door behind her, leaving Brian feeling very clumsy and ineffective.

"Come in," smiled Jack Madison with his usual affable charm, that winning personality which he had turned into a full-time profession. "Have a seat, won't you?" He motioned toward the chair across from his desk.

"Thank you," said Brian. "I feel like I've imposed on the lady in the next office. I'm sorry about that. I went there by mistake, and she was in a very private moment, I'm afraid. She was crying."

"Please," smiled Jack, "don't worry about it. She'll be fine. I assure you." Big smile.

"I hope so. I feel so foolish."

"She's my sister-in-law. My brother's wife. She lost her sixteen-year-old son about half-a-year ago. At times the memories come back over her a bit more than she can bare. We just talked her into coming back to work. So, you see, we're making progress."

"Well, apologize to her for me, please."

"I will. But you don't need to let it bother you. A harmless mistake. Certainly not intentional." Big smile. "You have something for me?"

"Yes." said Brian -- John Monroe. He put the attaché on the desk.

Jack Madison reached in a cabinet behind his desk and took out an identical attaché, handing it to Brian/John.

"Here you are," said Jack Madison. "One for me. One for you. A fair exchange. *N'est-ce pas*?"

"Thank you," said Brian/John. "I'm new at this, as you may know. Is there anything else? Or is that it?"

"That's pretty much it." Jack continued oozing charm and personality. "Like the 'ole Peggy Lee song, huh? 'Is that all there is? If that's all there is, my dear, then let's keep on dancing.' Yes, Mr. Monroe. That's all there is. So I guess we just keep on dancing."

"Well, then," said Withers/Monroe, rising. "I guess I'll be leaving then. I need to get back to O'Hare for my flight to Panama City."

"That's a no-no, John," smiled Jack Madison. "When transporting, we never let anyone know our destination or point of departure."

"I knew that," smiled Brian/John. "That was just a test. I'm actually on my way to Sri Lanka."

"Ah, good. Beautiful country. You'll love it there. For two days."

"Give Mrs. Madison my apologies -- and regards."

"I can make that happen, John. No fear."

"And I guess if I'm going to make my flight happen, I'd better be going. Nice meeting you."

"The pleasure was all mine."

Brian was out the door. In the lobby he paused for a moment to look at the large photo of Anne Bullock Madison. A beautiful woman. Still. Maybe even more beautiful now than in the photograph. Now that she had seen and felt more of life. He was sorry for her pain. But it had added to her beauty. He remembered the eyes he had burst in on, the eyes he had startled and surprised. Those eyes were taking the place of the eyes in the photograph as he stared at it, and they looked back at him with such intensity that he knew he would never be able to forget them. They were now as much a part of him as his own breathing. God!! The most beautiful eyes I've even seen. And maybe the saddest.

He turned, nodded at Judy, the receptionist, went out to the waiting cab and was whisked away in great speed to O'Hare International via the interstate. They were at O'Hare in less time than it would have taken to go back downtown.

On the mezzanine outside the a restaurant at the airport, he had some decaf and an English Muffin with cream cheese, watching the planes arrive and depart. The outside table offered an invigorating temperature. He missed Susannah; he missed Dempsey; he missed his classes and normalcy; but most of all, he missed today's underwear. And he kept seeing those eyes. The most beautiful, saddest eyes he'd ever seen.

When Brian arrived back in Panama City the first thing he heard about was Agular's and Jensen's deaths. Fordham caught him before he got on campus for his night class. They had gone to a little neighborhood bar on the road from the airport, one they expected to be a quiet place, but so many Spring-Breakers jammed the World's Most Beautiful Beaches that the overflow was spilling into bars and lounges all over town, even dumpy little neighborhood bars like this one.

"The web is getting smaller," said Brian, thinking about his nightmares.

"But the end of the alley is in sight," answered Fordham, remembering what Brian had told him about the dreams.

They sat quietly for a few moments, looking out over the people in the room.

"How much money do you think is dropped in this town each night of Spring Break?" speculated Fordham, watching the college kids at the bar, the video games, the improvised dance floor where none was supposed to be.

"Half a million, easy," shrugged Brian. "Maybe more than a million."

"God! That's a lot of partying."

"You sound jealous, Hank."

Fordham smiled. "I am. Extremely."

Fordham told him about the explosion of the Sabreliner the day before, obviously the work of Stewart, whom the agency was sure now was the hit man known throughout the world as Godzilla.

"Godzilla," smiled Brian. "They all have such corny names. Like 'Scylla' in *Marathon Man*."

"I don't think they give themselves the names. I think they come later -- from others."

"Well, he sure is knocking them off at a pretty steady pace," said Brian. "The Swede, Cherokee, Jensen, Agular. Now that he's started, looks like he's going to take them all out. Which is good news for me. I hope he does."

"Only Briggs and Simpson -- Beth -- left that you can identify. Since Andropolous split for Greece. A tap in Briggs office let us know that Briggs knows about you."

Brian was pleased to hear that Captain Andy was in Greece and out of the picture.

"Briggs knows about me?" asked Brian, surprised. "How did that happen?"

"Beth told him."

Silence. Disbelief. A blank expression. The slack jaw.

"Beth told him?"

"That's right. Doesn't say much for you and me, does it? We don't read 'em like we used to."

"I can't believe it," said Brian, stunned. He threw down his drink and motioned for another one. "I can't believe it."

He reminded himself of someone whose car had just been stolen; the way they keep going back to look at the place where it was, like they're in a bad dream and trying to wake up; maybe one time when they go to the place where the car was, it will be back. "It was right there," they say over and over again. "Right there." Then they go away and come back again. Like trying to sneak up on it.

"I can't believe it," said Brian again, shaking his head. "I just can't believe it."

"Well, if it'll make you feel any better," said Fordham, "she wasn't actually involved. She knew about it. But she didn't run with it. Though she didn't run from it either. She never did anything to be in the show -- except to blow the whistle on you."

"God! I can't believe it."

"Believe it. As much as she had the hots for you, she must have liked the future better with him."

"He's married -- with kids."

"Go figure --- but at least she's got *him*. She was never going to get you."

"Or maybe she did," said Brian. "Maybe this was her way of paying me back -- for not giving in -- to her charms. She got me after all."

"'Hell hath no fury like a woman scorned.'"

"Thanks for sharing that with me, Hank. You could have gone all night without saying that."

"Yeah. I could have. But it just fit in -- right there."

"Beth told! I can't believe it."

"You need to believe it enough to face the consequences."

"Tell me that doesn't mean what I think it means."

"Now that Godzilla's domino theory is in motion; now that Briggs knows about you -- even with Agular gone -- the rest of the game reads like this: Will Stewart -- Godzilla --- get to Briggs before Briggs gets to you? And if not --- what to do with you."

The laughing, boisterous college students in the bar could not have been in greater juxtaposition to Brian's thought at that moment. Dread/joy. Fear/pleasure. Panic/glee.

"Well, Hank." Brian looked at him, no trace of a smile this time. "What do I do now? Too late to take up target practice."

Fordham looked at him with respect and hope.

"You want to come in?" asked Fordham. "We can bring you in. Right now."

"Come in?"

"Susannah would have to come in too."

"Come in?" The sound had the same clang as an iron gate closing behind him, the same feeling as a prison sentence. He saw the medieval knight ride into the deserted de' Medici castle, and the portcullis slammed shut behind him. God! He had known he didn't want this, but hadn't known that the choice was coming so soon. He had never thought it would actually come to this as an imperative to save his life. He played the words over again; "Will Stewart -- Godzilla -- get to Briggs before Briggs gets to you?" Again.

"Well?" said Fordham.

Brian looked at him. He felt trapped. Run? Die? Or come in?

"No," he said suddenly, more firmly than he had expected. "No. I don't. It sounds like purgatory to me. No. It's going to be run or die, Hank. But not 'Come in.'"

"Calm down, Withers." Fordham sounded soothing. Suddenly he felt very sorry for his friend Brian.

Brian took a sip of his fresh drink. He gained his composure with a quick shake of his head, and a silent uttering of his long-time mantra, "Dominion." He had forgotten his power word for a long time now. "Dominion," he thought to himself again. "Dominion."

"Nothing so bad is going to happen that we can't handle it," said Fordham.

Brian looked at him as if ESP had developed between them. "Thanks, Hank. I needed that."

On the way to the campus, Brian stopped at K-Mart and bought a package of Britannia briefs. In the men's room on the second floor of the Social Studies Building, he changed underwear. At last today's underwear had replaced yesterday's. Call it the Superman effect; Today's underwear made him feel more sure, more certain. He was regaining control. There had been a problem ever since the morning shower in Chicago. Now the world was getting back on course.

Anne Madison opened the package that had been delivered by Federal Express. Inside was a copy of the Nevis *Daily Journal*. The second lead story -- with pictures -- was about the death of Agular and Jensen, the drug-lord and his top assistant.

She read the story twice. A strange feeling of exhilaration came over her. She looked out of the window and relished the feeling of triumph. The deaths did not depress her. The triumph invigorated her.

She went to the phone, called her bank, again requested another transfer to the numbered account in the German bank in Georgetown. This time the amount was considerably larger than the last time -- a hundred thousand.

Brian turned onto US 98 in the sparse late-night traffic. Out across the bay the running lights of some shrimp boats moved slowly along the back side of Dog Island. Closer in, faster moving lights indicated a few mullet boats seining in the shallower waters. A few flashlights coming on and off just off-shore told where hearty men were wading in the waters, cast-netting for mullet.

He headed down the dark highway toward the small village of Carrabelle. Almost no cars were on the road. He pulled off the road in front of Daphne's Gun and Beauty Shoppe, stopping in the dark parking lot, near the phone booth.

He left the motor running as he got out and went into the booth. The light inside the booth had been broken, and the only light he had came from a distant small neon in the window of Daphne's.

He dialed 1-800-COLLECT, then the number in North Carolina, and when the recording asked for his name he answered, "E.Z."

When the recording came back saying the call had been refused, he hung up and returned to the car. It was what he had expected.

He drove down the highway toward the E-Z Serv Store about a mile closer to town, and pulled in to the lot next to the phone booth there.

The store had been closed over an hour. He wished he had planned the call better so he could get something to nibble on while he waited for Zannah to get to one of the pay phones nearby up in Balsam.

The plan called for him never to talk on the phone from the house, and for her never to talk on the phone from the cabin. He would call collect from a pay phone and give the name of whatever phone he would go to for her to call back; E.Z. for the E-Z Serv Store, Don for the one in front of Daphne's Gun and Beauty Shop, Ike for the one at the IGA, Sam for the one at Suwannee Swifty.

Zannah had the numbers of all four phones. After refusing the collect call, she would drive down to one of the pay phones either at the ole deserted grocery store or the rest-area out on the highway. Invariably at night she would go to the rest area where the light was better and an occasional deputy's car would drive by. Then she would place a call, putting it on a new ATC card they had issued for Mountain Enterprises -- with a billing address at a post-office box in a small village about fifty miles north of Asheville.

Brian sat in the car waiting for the phone call. He was glad when the call came through in a few minutes. He was getting cold -- and hungry. The late-night munchies had pounced on him just after David Letterman's Top Ten List, but he realized then he had waited later than he meant to.

"I Love you, and miss you something awful," he said as he picked up the ringing phone.

"I'm sorry. I must have the wrong number," said a strange voice.

"Zannah? That's you. Isn't it?"

Pause.

"Zannah?"

"Yes. It's me, Goofy. Who else would be calling a pay phone in North Florida at this time of night?"

283

"The way my life's going, I can think of quite a few people. Fordham.

Hendersun. Briggs. Or maybe someone new interjecting himself into my life. Take you pick."

"Well, you just be more careful how you answer phones from now on. I don't want you to wind up committed to one them after you profess such undying love."

"Well, I do. Love you and miss you something awful."

"Me too. At least I have Dempsey. You don't have anybody."

"All alone."

"Poor baby," she sympathized

"You want to have phone sex?"

"Not out here in public."

"Agular's dead," he said.

"That was a great lead-in. You'll have to remember that more often."

"Nothing like a good *non sequitur*. Especially when it's good news."

"Is this good news?"

"I'm not sure. But I think so. Maybe it's all close to being over."

"God! I hope so. I want to come home."

"There are still a few loose ends out there. Like Briggs. Beth. And that guy Henderson -- or Stewart -- or whatever his name is."

"Let me come home now. Please. Pretty please."

"Sorry. I love you too much to have you back here right now."

"If I didn't know how to take that, I wouldn't know how to take that."

"It's always good to talk with someone with a quick mind."

"It's not my best asset, you know."

"It's up there close to the top though."

"I may decide to be insulted by that. I wanna come home. Do you hear that, all you people out there listening in on this call? I wanna come home. Hurry up and leave my husband alone so I can come home."

"I have the feeling you want to come home."

"Just try me. I dare you. Tell me about Agular."

He told her about the plane. At least what Fordham had told him.

"Well," said Susannah. "I'm sorry. He knew how to throw a good weekend."

Anne Madison made her way through the sidewalk traffic of State Street, at ten-thirty on a morning when the sidewalk crowd was only slightly less jammed than at noon or five o'clock. Her appearance was so altered that even her brother-in-law -- even Brian Withers of the sudden infatuation with her -- would have trouble finding her in the person she had turned herself into. Gone were any traces of the elegance and dramatic stylings that were part of her. Her hair was loose, uncombed, even dirty looking, covered partly with a wide-brimmed man's straw hat for the beach. There were holes and tears in the old hat. The man's white shirt was tied around her waist, above old, baggy, torn blue jeans, rolled up at the bottom. The charcoal grey cardigan sweater was also filled with many moth holes. She looked like a bag-lady without the cart. No make-up, a few smudges of soot on the face and the shirt. She had accomplished what she wanted. No one would ever suspect this bag-lady of carrying ten thousand dollars in cash in her pocket.

She went first to an office on the sixth floor of the old World Mart Building, "Stanley Ruben, Private Detective."

Ruben's secretary was not well-trained in office decorum; she chewed gum as if she were getting paid for it, popping it frequently. She had no problem letting anyone who came in know that they were interfering in her life and duties, which consisted mostly of chewing the gum and talking on the phone -- personal calls, of course. She was the perfect "before" in before-and-after pictures advertising some secretarial school.

No smile ever crossed her face, and her voice was shrill and bitchy enough to freeze water.

"What do you want?" she asked Anne Madison. Get right to the point, girl.

"I'm here to see Mr. Ruben."

"He know you're comin'?" A quick look at Anne's clothes brought a look of unconcealed disgust.

"He told me to be here at eleven o'clock."

The secretary looked at her watch. "You're two minutes early." Could this beast possibly be interested in accuracy? "What's your name?"

"Alice Barks." She started to take a seat.

"Don't sit in that upholstered chair in those clothes. Sit in that leather one there." Absolutely charming. Wham. Right in the kisser. That was every client's desire. And leather? That chair could give even vinyl a bad name.

Anne/Alice sat in the chair allocated for dirty people, and waited two minutes until her appointment time. Then --

"You can go in now."

The bitch. There hadn't even been anyone in with him. She just wanted a tight schedule -- as long as she controlled it.

Anne opened the shaded-glass door, closed it behind her and walked over to Ruben's desk.

"You got it?" she asked.

"You got the money."

"You get the addresses?"

"Yes. It was hard. A lot of work. So many aliases. You know you're dealing here with one of the toughest in the world? And one of the most dangerous. Have to be careful gathering info on this man. If it ever gets back. Too bad. I had to get the help of two other P.I.'s."

She had suspected it would be hard, considering the person involved in the assignment. She knew when she hired Henderson/Stewart she was getting the best -- and the most neurotic. Now the man in front of her was giving her the 'ole shake-down.' She had expected that too. She had worked with the same guy fifteen years before in some dealings for Mad Bull.

He didn't recognize her. But she remembered. He was good. But he pulled a shake-down then too. They had agreed on three; she was ready to pay five, but would try for four. The guy had been extremely accurate and thorough the first time.

"We agreed on three," she said.

"I can't do it. The other two P.I.'s were expensive. I had to spend more than I thought. It's got to be six."

Anne turned and started for the door.

"All right, five. But that's the bottom."

"I've got three-five. Take it or leave it."

"Four." The vague sound of a question mark.

She started to accept realized she would be caught in her own lie. "Haven't got it. Sorry." She turned toward the door again.

"All right. Three-five. But you're killing me." Yeah. Right.

She pulled out a pre-counted wad, handed it to him. He gave her a large manilla envelope.

"What am I getting here?"

"Home address. Office address. Sister's address. Phone numbers all around. All aliases we could find. Present most-often recurring name. First job we could find. Last three. Plus income from each of the last three. Numbered accounts in Switzerland, Georgetown, Australia." More than she had bargained for. More than she needed.

"Good," she said, then left.

In the really seedy gun-shop two blocks away, she asked for Antony Falconi, gave the lady her name, Alice Barks again, and was led to the same back room she had been in two weeks before.

Antony had magnifying glasses on the top of his head, could have been handsome if he cared.

"You said today," she said.

"It's ready," he replied.

"Two thousand, right?"

287

"Right." He reached to a shelf behind him, brought out a neatly wrapped package in brown paper, sealed well, about the size of three cartons of cigarettes.

"Ready for shipping?" she said.

"No extra charge," he smiled.

"Thanks." She gave him the two thousand and left.

In her room at the Radisson, she showered, changed clothes, stuffed the bag-lady clothes into an old beat-up suitcase. At the writing desk across from the bed, she opened the manilla envelope, glanced through it quickly for the information she wanted. She was impressed with the good work Ruben had done, and how neatly it was presented. Certainly never touched by the hands of his secretary. But Ruben could have saved himself a lot of money. All she really wanted was his real name, present working address, and the name and address of a family member living somewhere else.

She placed the brown package on the desk, addressed it, put the name and address of his sister in Des Moines, in the upper left hand corner. She then wrote "FRAGILE" in two places on the package. Leaving the room, she dropped the old suitcase in the laundry drop, took the elevator down, caught a cab in front of the Radisson, and went to the Chicago First National Bank Building to her lawyers' offices.

He saw her immediately and listened to her instructions. If anything of a violent nature should happen to her, he was to mail the package as soon as possible. Simple enough. What violence would possibly come to a woman of her social position and integrity? Well, one never could tell. She got up to leave, stopped at the door and looked back at the lawyer.

"Be careful with it," she said. "It's breakable. I've had it packed and wrapped professionally, but don't drop it if you can help it."

Ten o'clock in the morning. In his office at the college. Getting ready for his eleven o'clock class, closing in on the Renaissance. The *Quatrocento*, di Vinci, Michelangelo,

Raphael, the de' Medici's, Columbus, Botticelli and *The Birth of Venus* ("Woman on the Half-Shell" to every college student in the world), Richardson, Defoe, Cervantes, Spinoza.

Only about half the class would be there. The magnet of the northern Spring-Breakers out on the World's Most Beautiful Beaches would draw the others from class to the shores to meet and play with their northern counterparts -- even though final exams were only two weeks away.

Brian was dressed much more casually today than on the last two days when he had to wear the grey herring-bone suit -- two days in a row. Today it was a pair of Dockers and a Union Bay soccer shirt, brown boat shoes by Jordache (no socks), and a *L'Autre Mode* jacket, his cheap copy of *Members Only*, which he had found in Montgomery Ward. A splash of *Curve* drew it all together handsomely; he easily belonged in a copy of *GQ* or *Details*.

He looked at the wall calendar. Let's see here now. Six more one-hour meetings with the M-W-F classes; four more meetings with the one-and-a-half-hour classes on T-H; two more meetings with the three-hour, once-a-week classes. God bless Mrs. Simpson. I hopes she gets an 'A.' It would kill her not to.

Beth!! I can't believe it! I wonder why I have such a hard time accepting that. Is it a blow to my ego? My own masculinity? That she would so cleanly -- so violently -- cut the cord. Or is it a blow to my intelligence? -- that I made such an error in judgment? God! I'll never believe it. But I have to, don't I?

It happened. It is.

But that still doesn't mean I have to accept it, does it? Maybe -- to get right down to the root of the whole thing -- maybe I just have a really hard time admitting that something can happen that I just plain don't *understand*!! I'm supposed to be too intelligent not to understand anything, and so I rationalize by kicking into the I-can't-believe-it mode. It's probably a little bit of both.

289

There isn't much time left in this semester -- to get back on the track. Thank God for text-book Test Banks -- even though I hate them. I have to use them anyway to save time this semester.

The phone!! How long had it been ringing?

"Hello."

"Get out of there. Right away." Beth.

"Why? What are you talking about?"

"Steve's on his way. He's going to kill you."

Pause. The answer to Fordham's question: "Will Stewart get to Briggs before Briggs gets to you?" He started to ask 'why,' but he really already knew.

"I've got a class in twenty minutes."

"Can you teach it dead?"

Pause. His mind racing.

"Get in the game, Withers," she fairly hollered through the phone. "Get off the bench. Get out of there, now. You hear me?"

"Why are you telling me this? You were the one who told him, about me. Remember?"

"Call it temporary insanity."

"Then or now?"

"Take your pick. But be quick. You know where The Alabama is? Student bar close to the Miracle Mile Amusement Park?"

"Yeah."

"Meet me there as soon as possible. I have a plan."

The far door at the end of the hall slammed against the wall ominously. Brian knew who it was.

"Thanks." He hung up and ran to the door of the office. The phone missed the cradle and fell to the side of the desk, swinging like a pendulum. A hundred feet down the hall Steve was walking with strided determination.

Brian turned left and started through the maze of students, headed toward the opposite doors and the stairs to the parking lot. He was walking fast instead of running, hoping not to attract Briggs' attention. Briggs was headed for Brian's office, not really watching what was going on in the hall.

Brian reached the stairs, knew he was out of Briggs' line of sight, took the steps two, three at a time, reached the bottom and went out the large glass doors to the faculty parking lot.

Briggs rounded the open door to the empty office. Gone. A pair of reading glasses on an open book. The phone swinging back and forth beside the desk. He picked up the phone.

"Hello." He could hear Whitney Houston singing "The Greatest Love of All" in the background. Beth's favorite song. Her signature.

"Beth."

No answer.

"I believe that everybody --- has somebody," Whitney sang.

On the other end Beth listened without moving. She couldn't hang up. That would be a dead give-away. She breathed just barely, moving the mouthpiece slowly

away from her face. She started to cover the mouthpiece but realized that would be an equal give-away, blocking out the music so suddenly.

"I know that's you, Beth." His voice grew louder.

Brian had reached his car, finally found the keys, got in to start it.

Briggs dropped the phone. It began swinging again. He left the office, ran through the students milling in the hall, reached a classroom two doors down and across the hall. He opened the door abruptly.

Dr. Walker and his entire class turned to see the wild looking man standing at the door.

Briggs left the door and ran to the opposite end of the hall through the thickening crowd of students. He looked out of the plate-glass windows to the parking lot below. Brian's car was pulling out of the parking space.

Beth left the phone off the hook in case Steve came back. She quickly changed the CD player to one of Led Zeppelin's old albums, one she hated, and left the apartment.

Briggs took the steps two at a time.

From the office where the phone still swung back and forth, Stewart stood at the door and watched Briggs terrorize the classroom, then run to the window to watch Brian leave the parking lot.

From the far end of the hall, Fordham watched Godzilla watching Steve Briggs looking down on the parking lot watching Brian Withers. When the two he could see had left the hall, he ran into Brian's office. He hung the phone up, picked it up quickly and dialed a number.

"Where?" he said into the mouthpiece as soon as the other end was answered.

"The Alabama. A bar. Out on the beach. By the amusement park."

He hung up the phone and started down the hall.

Beth's car was racing down the bay road from her apartment, traveling west. She would stay off the three beach roads as long as possible.

Brian drove to the college entrance on U.S. 98. The highway was jammed with college students from all over the country, all in bathing suits. Good thing he was going to turn right. But stupid to be going to the middle of the beach in the middle of a hundred thousand partying Spring Breakers.

He pulled onto 98 and started toward Hathaway Bridge, headed into the World's Most Beautiful Beach Party

Briggs reached his truck, "Briggs Construction," and saw Brian headed past him on the other side of the wall. Briggs pulled in front of cars twice to get onto 98 and start toward the bridge.

Stewart came down the front steps of the Social Studies Building, ran to his rented Dodge Dynasty at the far end of the lot, started it, saw the crowd trying to get out the entrance, and chose to drive right through the low concrete block wall to get into the flow of traffic on 98.

Fordham raced down the same steps, twenty seconds behind Stewart -- Godzilla -- and ran to his rented Lincoln Town Car, parked only one lane farther away form where Stewart had been. He saw Stewart make the new exit from the parking lot. Once in his car, Fordham took advantage of Stewart's new exit, entering the traffic on 98 trough the gaping hole in the college wall.

Beth came to a quick stop on the Back Bay Road and the corner of Tenth Street. She turned left and headed toward the high rises in the distance.

Brian reached the top of Hathaway Bridge, saw the construction truck just moving onto the bottom of the bridge behind him.

Stewart, two hundred feet behind Briggs' Construction truck, never let the truck out of his sight. He was fast approaching the base of the bridge, weaving in and out of the spring partyers as he went.

Fordham, two hundred feet behind Stewart's Dynasty, moved along the causeway to the bridge. He knew where he was headed, which gave him an advantage over Briggs and Stewart. The Town Car swerved merrily in and out of the partyers, all headed for the beaches, all holding cans of beer or paper cups with Tom Collins, Margueritas, Bloody Mary's, and various other mixed drinks.

There were songs from every university and fraternity in the east; Georgia Tech, Sigma Chi, Auburn, Cornell, FSU, Kappa Alpha, Montana, Oklahoma, Notre Dame, WCU, Ohio.

The journey was a trip through the United States by college songs from New England to Arizona and Texas.

"Hey, man! You want a beer?"

"Have you got a light over there?"

"Want a drink?"

"Hi, cutie."

"Hey, man! Come on out to Little Birmingham."

"Would you have any Grey Poupon?"

Down the other side of the bridge, Brian looked carefully at the separation at Four Points; Thomas Drive along the beaches, the amusement park and the high rises, crowded; the Back Road, even more crowded with cars trying to avoid the traffic on Thomas Drive; the Back-Back Road, also jammed. Thomas Drive along the beach actually looked to be less crowded. Probably so many Spring-Breakers walking in the street that cars can't get through.

293

He chose Thomas Drive and headed toward the high-rises and the roller coaster, the parachute jump, and the water slides. *Bad move*, Brian.

By the time he reached the roller coaster, he was moving two miles an hour. The only consolation was that Briggs couldn't go any faster either.

Briggs, higher up in his truck cab could keep an eye on Brian's car.

Stewart had moved up a little closer on the bridge and could easily keep track of Briggs' truck because of the high cab.

Fordham, back on the bridge, had closed the space between his Town Car and Stewart's Dynasty. It was also easier for him to keep his eye on the high cab of Briggs' truck, and he knew that Stewart was somewhere in between himself and the truck, even if he couldn't see him.

Two miles an hour for all of them. Then down to one. Then -- beside the roller coaster and the amusement park, everything stopped completely. All four cars in absolute grid-lock in the middle of the World's Most Beautiful Beach Party. Horns blowing -- not in anger but in merriment. Students singing school songs. Everybody drinking and working for the perfect tan. The ever-present smell of warm Coppertone. Laughing. Car tape- players and CD players, UB-40, Chicago, Sting, Genesis, Beck, Elliot Smith, Smashing Pumpkins, Raging Slab. Nine Inch Nails.

The roller coaster flying through space right above the street. The Ferris Wheel churning. The Parachute Jumpers, and from somewhere a calliope grinding away with memories of childhood. Out over the water, ski-fliers soaring ten stories above the water, sail boats, jet-skiers, water-skiers, and above it all, the Goodyear Blimp being passed by a by-plane towing a sky-sign hawking MTV, another one pushing *CKone*. There has never been a circus, carnival or Mardi Gras with as much exposed flesh, bodies unable to take in all that was vying for their attention.

The bikini-clad students all over the sidewalks and in the streets, covering every available bit of space, drifted by -- were pushed by -- the cars and trucks in the gridlock on Thomas Drive, U.S. 98. Brian looked at the people moving all around his car. Moshing was rampant. A beautiful tan girl, held aloft by many hands, slithered through his passenger window, over his lap, and out the drive-side window. "Come join us," she smiled, passing through his lap. "I can't get out of the door," he answered. "Come out the window," she smiled, "like me. But take your clothes off first." As she moved out of the window, her body was hoisted by waiting arms and hands and moved away over the heads of the thickening crowd. "Bye," she smiled at Brian. "Follow me." Her neon yellow bikini was wafted away by hundreds of hands. He was tempted.

Another girl jumped into the air and never touched the ground again. Her body was immediately hand-propelled overhead like a cloud in an unchoreographed ballet. Then a man's body became the object of the undulating hands, and suddenly a swarm of airborne bodies was being passed along over the crowd, all to the accompaniment of the childhood memories of the music from the calliope hidden somewhere in the amusement park. Other sounds filtered in and out; Boyz 2 Men, Alanis, The Rolling Stones, Mariah Carey, Hootie and the Blowfish, the sounds of the by-planes, rebel yells, and Texas A & M cattle calls.

The four cars locked in immobility in the midst of thousands of cars locked in a sea of humanity could not have been in a more unlikely chase scene. Yet they were still following one another, watching one another, chasing one another in this new form of pursuit.

Brian looked back to the cab of Steve's truck, as he had done all the way from the college and over the Hathaway. Steve had not lost sight of Brian at any moment of the chase, either while it was moving, or now that it was frozen in the horde of tan, writhing bodies. Stewart could easily see every move of Briggs' high cab. Fordham could not see Stewart's Dynasty, hidden in the maze of cars, but he could see Briggs almost as well as Stewart could, and he knew that Stewart was still somewhere in between. Fordham had also been able to determine that all three of the runners ahead of him were not aware that he was there.

Then suddenly one movement began a domino effect that would involve all four men. A very beautiful, bikini-clad girl was lifted onto the roof of Briggs' cab where she started dancing. Steve ignored that, although it *had* to be ruining the roof of the cab. What he couldn't ignore was the 220-pound football player in briefs who jumped onto the roof and started dancing with her.

Steve could not open the door enough to get out to stop it, so he started out the window.

Ding! (Brian) Ding! (Stewart) Ding! (Fordham) All three began coming out the windows in order to stay in pursuit.

Brian was convinced that Steve was coming out in order to come through the mass to get him. So thought Stewart and Fordham. As soon as Briggs saw Brian coming out of his window, he was certain Brian had decided to run for it -- through the crowd. Stewart and Fordham had come to the same conclusion.

Brian started pushing his way through the crowd, running whenever he could, which was never more than three feet. Briggs chased Brian with the same obstacles, but because of his wide football-player shoulders, he didn't go as fast as Brian -- at first. Within seconds he realized he could use his wideness to his advantage, using his shoulders as blocking pads, pushing people aside with them. Behind him Stewart -- Godzilla -- moved through the crown with the gracefulness of a ballet dancer in a well-choreographed script. He had done this before. He turned sideways, back and forth, almost slithering, ducking now and then to avoid impediments. He was actually gaining on Briggs --- which was not his game plan. He didn't want to get in touch with him; he only wanted a clear line of fire at him, which would never happen in this crowd. So he chose to continue to follow, but at a slower pace. Fordham had watched Godzilla and quickly learned the ballet method of getting through the partying crowd. He also realized he didn't want to catch up with anyone, only to keep all three in sight. If there turned out to be a choice of who to take out, he knew it would have to be Briggs. In this particular game of cops and robbers, Fordham and Godzilla happened to be on the same side -- for two entirely different reasons, but still on the same side.

A passage-way of about ten feet suddenly opened up in front on Brian. He took it. Obliquely it led to a patio where the reggae band was playing. Darting up the opening, he wound up running through the middle of the band.

"Go, man." "Go for it." "Just do it."

Past the reggae was a three-foot wall separating the patio from a ten-foot wide plot of lawn. The treasured, emerald-green lawn, rare so close to salt water and salt air, led between two hotels to the beach. Only a few of the sun-worshippers had made their way over the wall to the path of lawn.

Brian jumped up on the wall and disappeared on the other side, running toward the beach. Briggs came through the band, over the wall and onto the lawn, followed quickly by Godzilla and then Fordham. For a few seconds only, all four of the men were on the long, narrow lawn. Just before Brian jumped over the rear wall into the sea of tanning flesh on the sand, a shot rang out loudly, and some plaster twelve feet up on the corner of the building broke loose and fell onto some of the partyers. Briggs was not so good a shot that he could claim accuracy while running. Godzilla and Fordham both watched the falling plaster and wondered why Briggs had tried something so impossible.

Most of the partyers who had heard the shot above the booming bands and combos thought it was someone setting off firecrackers. Brian saw the plaster shatter just ahead of him and knew what it was. He started running west in the sand. Here the crown was just slightly less dense, allowing more space for running. Godzilla followed him in a generally westerly direction, but the crowd had a tendency to force him a little differently than he intended to go. Brian was forced closer to the water; Briggs was being driven toward the high-rises on his right. Godzilla and Fordham followed at a gaining pace but were experiencing the same separation, Godzilla being pushed toward the hotels, Fordham to the water's edge.

Brian and Godzilla, a hundred feet apart, could hear gasps and calls of people around them as they ran through the crowd of college students, most staring up at something above them. Brian and Fordham, farther out from the hotels, did not hear the calls and gasps, but out of the corners of their eyes could see the cause; students on the upper floors of the buildings, like Indian cliff-dwellers, climbed from one balcony to another, either edging along the indentations in the buildings, leaping, using ropes or reaching out to other students to pull them over. Some of the braver -- or more foolish -- were even going from building to building, either across bouncing boards or on swinging ropes. Brian and Fordham did not have time to take in the bizarre scene, but got only a general impression of what was going on.

Briggs began to make a special effort to work toward the water and Brian. Godzilla followed him through the crowds of laughing revelers. Brian, watched Briggs in particular and worked his way toward Briggs' general direction, consciously moving diagonally toward the hotels. The buildings slowly passed by all four of the runners, more buildings, and more. Godzilla was slowly gaining on Briggs and followed him toward the water.

When Briggs reached the water, he temporarily lost Brian, but quickly found him again back across the crowed beach, now beneath the towering hotels. Godzilla watched Briggs with caution; Fordham watched them both. As Godzilla and Fordham watched the wild chase in front of them, they saw Brian move to the edge of one of
the hotels filled with balcony climbers. Simultaneously they both knew what was about to happen.

Brian grabbed one of the hanging ropes and started a calisthenics maneuver of hand-over-hand climbing, pulling himself slowly up to a second-floor balcony. Briggs made the mistake of inexperience; he fought his way across the beach, pursuing Brian. But Godzilla did what experience would do. He stopped completely, standing still at the edge of the water, looking back to the hotel walls, a Crow Indian scouting the other side of the canyon for the mountain goat. You can't kill the goat on your own side on the canyon. It's the goat on the other side that's easy to get a sight on.

Brian moved over to his second balcony by the time Briggs started up the rope. On the second balcony, Brian found two more vertical ropes coming from balconies somewhere above him. The third floor? The seventh? The fourteenth? He started up one of the ropes.

Briggs, now on the first balcony, paused, took aim, fired, shattered more plaster. Some of the Spring-Breakers were now aware of what was going on. They instinctively went to the side of the underdog -- the unarmed Brian.

"Go man." "You can make it." "Go for it."

Briggs' second shot nicked the rope about three feet above Brian's head. The rope began to pull and unravel with each over-hand grab of Brian's hand. Climb. Fibers breaking. Up. Snapping sounds. One more. The unravelling going faster now.

Brian swung his hand over and above the break just as the bottom of the rope came loose and fell to the concrete patio four floors below. The next hand up brought him within two feet of the top of the next balcony. But now the rope began to swing from his motions. He could tell from the wide arc the rope made that it was tied far up, perhaps even ten floors higher.

Briggs, now on the balcony below Brian, looked up at the climbing, swinging man. The gun in his hand had already scared the people off the balcony. It was his balcony now. He leaned far out over the side, holding the second rope, looking up at Brian above him, Taking careful aim from his almost horizontal position as he held the rope.

The shot was louder than the first one. People along the water's edge screamed. People beneath Brian and Briggs screamed. Another much louder shot.

Godzilla, from his side of the canyon, had waited for the mountain goat on the other side to come into clear view. And had bagged him.

Students moved away from Stewart at the water's edge. Stewart stood motionless, still aiming at the building with his Ruger Mark II, semiautomatic.

Briggs shot again, but it was an involuntary reaction of his finger on the trigger. The bullet went out over the Gulf. He held onto the rope a few seconds longer, his leg now hanging over the inside of the balcony. Then his hand let go of the rope, and he fell downward over the edge of the balcony, falling to the concrete patio. A chorus of horrified screams came from around his body.

Fordham turned to see Godzilla again. But he was gone. No sign of anyone running through the crowd. Just gone. Out in the clear water behind where he had stood was the distinct form of the Ruger Mark II, pointing off toward infinity through the white sand and sparkling water.

No one in the crowd saw Beth, on the water's edge, with the small hand pistol still pointed in the direction where Briggs had been.

Stewart moved through the crowd back toward Thomas Drive. He was the only one involved who knew it wasn't over.

There were still two more to go. Maybe three, depending.

"You got off easy," smiled Fordham, looking at Brian and Susannah from across the table. "All that work, and now you don't even have testify."

"You almost sound disappointed." smiled Susannah, "that we don't have to give up everything and go into that horrible witness protection program."

"On the contrary," said Fordham, holding his gin and tonic almost directly between them. "I couldn't be happier. But your man Brian, there. He's very good, you know."

"Tell me about it," she said.

"I hate to give him up. He's so good. It's fun to watch him work."

"Tell me something I don't know," she said.

From where they sat in Mary Jo's Restaurant, they could look out over a small bayou to the harbor, the bay, and the Gulf beyond. Traveling lights on some distant shrimp boats moved out through the mouth of the river. Some more moved back and forth farther out across the bay.

"It's not over yet, you know," said Brian, sipping his rum and diet Dr. Pepper. "Not if what I read in Godzilla's file holds true."

"Well, at least your part is done," said Fordham. "You came all the way through the forest."

"And a damn long forest it was," said Brian.

"You know," said Fordham, over the candlelight, "I didn't know it was going to be so involved -- so big. Or I wouldn't have gotten you into it. None of us knew how big it was. You uncovered that for us."

"Blind luck," said Brian.

"What's going to happen to Beth?" asked Susannah.

"Susannah would like to have her locked away somewhere," laughed Brian, teasing Susannah.

"I would not," said Susannah, swatting him on the arm. "You think I can't handle the competition? I want to be able to say I hung on to you by beating her at her own game."

"Actually nothing will happen to her," said Fordham. "She never was that involved in anything. Only aware of it. The most incriminating thing she did was to rat on you." He nodded at Brian.

"Which led to probably the most memorable afternoon of my life," said Brian. "About which I have one regret."

"What is that?" asked Susannah. "I hope it doesn't have anything to do with Beth."

"No, but I really would have liked being moved over the crowds, the way they were doing some people on the streets. You know. Passed along up there, over everybody's head. What do they call that? Moshing?"

"You're perverted," said Susannah. "All those strange hands touching you. Ugh!." She shuddered with disgust.

"That's the part I think I'd like," he said, smiling at her.

301

She swatted him on the arm again.

"We finally got a lead on the woman who hired Godzilla. The wealthy woman out of Chicago, Anne Madison."

Brian said nothing, but gears were clicking in his mind. He wasn't quite sure he knew what he knew.

"What will happen to her?" asked Susannah. "Not that she hasn't been through a hell of her own already."

"I personally would leave her alone," smiled Fordham. "The boys in Chicago might just do that. Technically, she should be charged -- with murder. But it's hard to go after someone who's done so much of your work for you."

"Yeah," said Susannah. "Look at the scum she did away with."

"'Mine is not to reason why,'" said Fordham. "Etc. Etc. Etc."

"What about the Chicago connection -- of the drug ring?" asked Brian.

"He'll get picked up. We've had him pegged for a long time now. We just didn't know he was connected with this same organization here in Florida. But he's ours easy. If Godzilla doesn't get to him first."

When Susannah and Brian walked in the front door at ten-fifteen, Dempsey came to welcome them. Susannah went to the couch, took off her coat and flopped in front of the still, quiet fireplace.

"Light me, Bri," she said. "Let's have some atmosphere on our first night back home." She closed her eyes peacefully, listening to Brian move around the room behind her. "That was nice of Fordham -- the agency -- to take us out to dinner, wasn't it? Especially when we probably made more money out of it all than he did. But it was a nice gesture. A good piece of closure."

"Un-huh," Brian muttered behind her.

"What are you doing back there? In and out of the bedroom, and all that moving around?"

"I've got to leave, Zanna. It's important."

302

She was up, looking at him. "It's over. It's finished. What have you got to do? Where?"

"Chicago. I've got to. I'll tell you about it when I get back. Maybe tomorrow. The day after for sure."

He was out the door. Susannah sat on the couch alone -- but with Dempsey at her feet, both staring into the unlit fireplace.

On the plane from Tallahassee, staring out the window into the darkness, Brian saw The Most Beautiful, Saddest Eyes he had ever seen, the beautiful, blue, tearful eyes of Mrs. Anne Bullock Madison. He put it all together in the car on the way home from the restaurant. When he remembered Jack Madison in the office of Mad Bull Construction Company.

"She's my sister-in-law. My brother's wife. She lost her sixteen-year-old son about half a year ago. At times the memories come back to her a bit more than she can bare."

Jack Madison. Then the gap -- where there should have been a bridge -- leading over to Anne Madison, whose son had died from an overdose of drugs -- and the ring that she had hired Godzilla to do away with -- led right back to -- Jack Madison -- her brother-in-law. With Godzilla's fanaticism -- his unswerving dedication to carrying a job all the way through to completion -- so he would not have to admit that he may have been wrong in accepting the job -- his twisted thinking that made him believe it was better to complete a wrong task rather than to admit that he was wrong to begin with -- his inability to know when a job was finished ---. Put it all together, and the tearful woman with The World's Most Beautiful and Saddest Eyes --- may have just hired the one hit man on Earth who just might, out of duty to her request, kill her in his perception of carrying out her orders. After all, Jack Madison did work for her.

Brian could see the face, those eyes, the tears from the eyes of Anne Bullock Madison. He could still see them, superimposed over the photograph in the waiting room, when he fell asleep somewhere over Tennessee.

It was after three in the morning when Brian got off the plane at O'Hare International. Chicago two times in four days now. For someone who had never been there before, he was doing a good job of catching up. Since he had been at the Hilton before, he went there again.

At seven the next morning, he showered and, thanks to forethought, put on clean underwear, today's underwear. He ate his dry toast, orange juice, half an apple, and coffee. Not having spent much time in the north, he was surprised to see the light snow falling outside in mid-March. He hadn't really brought the right clothes for this kind of weather, but he wouldn't be out in it more than a few minutes at a time.

At the Mad Bull Building, he let the cab go and then went in, being stopped by the ever-efficient Judy.

Smile. "May I help you?"

"I've got to see Mrs. Anne Madison. Right Away. It's urgent."

"Do you have an appointment?"

"No. I don't. But this is terribly important. Maybe even a matter of life and death." He grimaced. "That sounds corny, but it's true." There, he thought. He'd finally gotten the chance to use that line, at least once in his lifetime.

"Your name, please?"

"Brian Withers."

Couldn't put anything over on this woman. She had a better memory than that, and she remembered something different from a few days before. The smile left completely now. She couldn't remember what the name was, but she knew it wasn't 'Brian Withers.' The faintest signs of a nervous smile came back to her lips.

"No," said Brian quickly. "John Monroe." He smiled at himself. He was amused at his own ineptitude in playing this very strange game he had never played before.

"And you don't have an appointment? Mr. -- Monroe."

"No. But it's terribly important. To her. Not me. She may --"

He stopped talking and headed for Anne Madison's door.

"Stop. Stop. You can't go in there." The receptionist was already around her desk and doing the double tasks of trying to stop him and at the same time, not get too close to him. "You can't go in there. Stop. I'll call security."

Brian was already at the door, opened it, and looking again at The World's Most Beautiful and Saddest Eyes.

"Mrs. Madison. I *have* to talk to you. It's about Stewart -- Henderson. It's a matter of life and death." Got that line in again.

In the small tea-room six blocks away where they went to be alone, they looked out over the lake and watched the light snow falling on the water, disappearing, dissolving. The snow did not stay on the streets, sidewalks or buildings, but it was beginning to accumulate on the ground and shrubs.

"You're a very determined man, Mr. Monroe." She was the only woman he had ever met who could be distant and compassionate at the same time. There were many contradictions in her.

"I think you have reasons to worry about your safety, Mrs. Madison."

"Why do you think such a thing?"

"I know about your connection with Stewart, Henderson, Donaldson, or whatever you call him."

"How do you come to know so much about something I have no knowledge of, Mr. Monroe?"

"My name is Withers. Brian Withers."

"You called yourself John Monroe when you were here a few days ago. Which is it? And why should I believe you?" A vague trace of a smile.

"I'm really Brian Withers. I used the name John Monroe, because I was instructed to when I delivered a package to your brother-in-law. I'm a college professor. But I've been working with the FBI to help break up a drug ring. The one that supplied the drugs which killed your son."

She winced slightly, almost unnoticed. She smiled again, watching him intently. "Are you making this up as you go along? Or did you have to memorize it ahead of time?"

"Mrs. Madison." He was on the edge of frustration. He had flown over 1100 miles to save this woman's life, and now she was playing with him. She wasn't admitting anything, and she believed even less.

"I've come here to warn you. Your life may be in danger. I've flown over 1100 miles to do what I think might help save your life. I can't show you any badges or official papers. But what I'm telling you is true."

"You're so convincing, Mr. Monroe. -- Withers, but --"

"Brian. Call me Brian."

"All right. If you'll call me Anne."

Ah, thought Brian. We're getting ready to bond now. Maybe she's starting to believe me.

"Stewart -- or Henderson -- or whatever you know him as -- is a strange man, Mrs. --- Anne. He has a bizarre turn of mind."

"An interesting phrase. I've never heard it before. 'Turn of mind.' Why do I have the feeling that you're treating me with kid gloves?"

"All right then. Let's say he has very strong psychopathic tendencies."

"That sounds better. More basic. But I've known that all along." She had suddenly opened her whole hand. No more stalling, hiding behind pretended innocence. "He wouldn't be in that line of work if he weren't. I wanted the best. I got the best. There are trade-offs. You sometimes have to take the bad with the good."

"But I mean really, *really* psychopathic. Not just a trade-off. More like a lethal gamble."

"Brian -- I've been in business for years. I know the business world. I know the business of business. You don't ever hire a private detective without at least two reports on him from two other private detectives. It takes a lot of work to find-- and hire -- the best hit man around. But you have to find out

306

who's the best from other hit men. I did my homework on this one."

"Have you read any files on him?"

"Three."

"Do you know about the Colombian drug ring he wiped out?"

"It was in two of the reports. I'll never use the other one again."

"You know how it ended?"

"He did away with the officer who hired him. I know. So?"

"Do you know about Agular?"

"I do."

"Do you have any idea where most of the drugs from Agular's ring wind up?"

"I didn't. Until about a week ago."

"And?"

"I always had a feeling that Jack Madison would be my downfall. I didn't really ever think he could stay straight. Yes. I know. I came back to work because I suspected."

"Suspected what?"

"Don't we both know where this is going?" She smiled. "Yes. I know that the drugs come through Jack Madison. My brother-in-law. The head of Mad Bull."

"Of which you are chairman -- and CEO It's really your firm. You run it. You control Jack Madison. You've come full circle, Anne. And you've hired the one man in the world who is so compulsive that he has to go full circle. Stewart's job won't be over until he's gotten you. too."

Anne Madison looked at him intently, but still smiling slightly. The eyes were still The Most Beautiful an Saddest Eyes in the World. Hypnotic. He couldn't get free from the grasp they had on him.

"I've known that, too," she said. "When I found out the ring came back to Jack -- I knew -- in Henderson's mind -- that meant that it came back to me, also."

"You've got to leave. Right away."

She smiled broader. "There's no way to run from that man. You should know that better than I by now."

"Then go into hiding. Something. Until the FBI can get him.!"

Again the smile. "There's no place to hide from him either. And as far as the FBI getting him -- we both know better than that. -- He's one of the most valuable tools the FBI has. Far more valuable to them where he is than any five men they've got. -- If he fell asleep on a bench in Central Park with six FBI men watching him, they'd all deny they ever saw him. He saves the FBI millions a year. The FBI will never bother that man. He's respected on both side of the law."

Brian had come to save her life. He expected to see her shocked, stunned, frightened. Not stoic and -- yes -- even prepared to die. He never suspected that FBI would consider turning its back to Stewart. But her case was indisputable. Stewart *was* valuable to them. And they had the power -- *to do nothing about him* -- *to endorse him* -- *even to sponsor him*.

Brian was the one in awe. He had no answers. He couldn't even think of a good question.

Anne smiled again. "I almost hired a hit man -- to take out this hit man -- but I have too much respect for him, too."

"You're just going to stay here? And take it?"

"No. I didn't say that."

"What then?"

"I have plans. Already set in motion. You know physics, I'm sure. 'A body in motion ---,' 'For every action ---,' etcetera. This too is one of those paradoxes of physics. It was over before it was begun."

"What are you going to do?"

She reached over and touched his face lightly. "You're married, aren't you?"

He nodded.

"And you both love each other very much."

He nodded again.

"My David Michael would have turned out much like you. You remind me of him. You're both -- Renaissance Men of sorts. He wouldn't have been a teacher though. He was going into business administration. You would have liked each other."

"I sure I would have. Any son of yours would be an immanently likable person."

"What a charming thing to say. It would sound so idle and patronizing, from anyone else. But from you, there's a sincerity -- and charm. I wish you could have known him."

"I wish so, too."

The silence now between them was a bonding silence. Their eyes never left one another. She still had her hand against her face as if caressing the face of David Michael. He wanted so much to do something, say something that would change her mind.

She would not run. She would not hide.

The Rolls-Royce pulled into the parking lot. Jack Madison drove this car even more carefully than his '68 Corvette. He had a tape playing Elton John's "A Step Too Far", followed by Dave Grusin doing "On Golden Pond." He had patched the two together on a tape of his favorites. Leaving the car, he walked no more than ten feet toward the building when the thundering spray of machine-gun fire rang out over the silence of the light snowfall.

The sound echoed and reverberated into the dark, snowy alleys, across the yard of silent, empty cranes and bulldozers, a sound of the quick, agonizing end of life, the sound of the repetition of death. The body seemed to defy gravity, not falling directly, but bouncing, twisting, jumping in space, writhing tormentedly as fast as the sound of the machine-gun, keeping time with it, until finally gravity won out, and the body fell in the snow, which now was almost solid red with blood flowing from the shaking body.

Then silence. The greatest silence in the world. Only the sound of snow, snow, snow. Silent snow, secret snow. The rented Thunderbird in the back of the parking lot started up -- a soft, clean engine sound. On its slow and methodical way out of the parking lot, it moved just inches from the still and red body. At its closest point, it splashed some of the blood-soaked snow up and back onto the head of what used to be Jack Madison. Some splashed onto the side of the car.

Then silence again. And the sound of silent snow.

Anne Madison walked out of the side door of her house, headed for her Mercedes in the garage. The March air was fresh. The day was warmer than it should have been for a Chicago March. A light breeze blew across the barren lawn, but the smell of spring came from somewhere beyond the wall that was supposed to keep her world safe from the world out there. It was supposed to --- but it hadn't. It didn't. It wouldn't.

She stopped for a moment at the garage door and smelled the air again. Spring was definitely somewhere close-by --- hiding behind the garage, beyond the greenhouse, maybe in the woods that separated her house from the other houses unseen and unheard off in the distance.

She turned and walked along the sidewalk through what soon would be a lawn bordered by flowers, with bright colored flowers dividing the sidewalk from the lawn. She suddenly slowed her pace and became an admirer of the world around her, a tourist visiting her own back yard for the first time in almost a year.

Life becomes so much sweeter when the time grows shorter. No child ever appreciates a sunset as dearly as the grandmother. No teenager ever sees as much beauty and glory in a sunrise as preciously as his grandfather. No young man with small children of his own ever knows the fine majesty of the sound of the surf on a shore half so well as his own father. Each wave lapping up on the beach is one more gigantic 'tick' in the great world clock that counts the seconds, minutes, hours, days and years.

No child looking out over the meadow to the setting sun is ever going to die. No teenager, laughing with his buddies as they walk in the light of sunrise is ever going to die. No one is going to die --- until the end of the moving conveyer is in sight, and all the power and the glory of thirty thousand sunrises and thirty thousand sunsets have gone unnoticed, unenjoyed, unseen --- and wasted.

"Ubi sunt qui ante nos venerunt?" "Where are those who have gone before us?" The moving conveyer goes on and on and never stops, only wraps around the last roller to make its empty up-side-down journey back to where it moves up around the first roller and becomes a conveyer again. And we all ride along the conveyer belt, pawns moving toward the last roller.

"Success is counted sweetest by those who ne'er succeed," and life is counted dearest by those whose days are few. Whose hours are few. Minutes. Seconds.

Oh, what a lovely day it was to Anne Madison, probably the most wonderful day of her life. She put her arms out to embrace the day and turned around and around like a waltzing doll. The smells, the sounds, the feel of the approaching spring along her arms and on her face, the blue of the March sky dotted with white clouds of ambling sheep; the day was too glorious and mighty to be overlooked. The feel of the March sun on her body, through her dress -- was like the warmth of the fingers of God massaging her out of the cold of winter. It was a day to be enjoyed, tasted, felt, wallowed in.

I hope the end is fast.

Ah, such a wonderful breeze.

I don't want to suffer.

The sky was never so blue.

Please don't let it drag on and on causing a loss of dignity.

Why have I never noticed that heavenly smell of freshness before today?

A bolt of lightening would be the best. Fast. Instantaneous. Immediate. You're there. Walking along the street, happy in the beauty of the day --- then -- zap -- like a fly being swatted by an expert swatter --- you're gone -- not even a fourth of a second. No time for pain. No time for regrets, recriminations. Alive -- happy -- ZAP -- gone -- not unhappy -- not anything.

I've hired the best swatter there is. Surely it will be fast.

311

She came back to the day with all its power and glory. She would ride along the lake and enjoy the sun over the water. She would listen to the sounds of the breeze, the birds, the traffic -- even the sounds of the traffic and the people arguing on the sidewalk had suddenly become sounds to be enjoyed.

She went to the garage, opened the door, opened the door to her car, turned the keys and heard the perfectly tuned motor whir. She pressed her foot on the accelerator, enjoying the feeling of muscles bringing inanimate things into submission. It was all there to please her. She had already passed a handful of obstacles that could have brought on the lightening -- opening the garage -- the door to the car -- turning the key -- pressing on the accelerator. He was good.

At the florist's, she got the new arrangement, visited with the clerks in the shop, enjoyed the interplay with other people. Then she went back to her car. Again, each movement of her body against plastic and metal, leather and wood, made her appreciate the day more, admire him more.

In the cemetery, she brought the new arrangement up the small incline to David Michael's grave. She sat it down on the long horizontal slab so she could brush aside the leaves that cluttered the monolith. A spider had begun to build a web behind the headstone. She started to brush it away, but was suddenly caught by the beauty of the morning dew in the perfectly formed symmetrical web, the fine droplets of dew reflecting a thousand rays of sun. She was pleased with the relationship between herself and the spider.

She came back to the front of the headstone, and reached down to pick up the old arrangement.

ZAP

The swatter struck with instant precision. She never knew it. The lightening came and went instantly.

Fordham sat in Brian's office, telling him of the death of Anne Madison.

"You don't seem surprised," said Fordham.

"I'm not," said Brian. "She knew it was going to happen. She never really told me, but I knew what she was talking about."

"I guess that ends it all. Neat and tidy. Huh?"

"No. Not yet."

"You know something I don't know?" asked Fordham.

"Yes. I do."

"What?"

"Let me keep that as a surprise for you," said Brian, teasing Fordham. "You enjoyed keeping me in suspense so much. Let me have this one as pay-back on you."

"Aw, come on," pleaded Fordham.

"I'm just a kid," smiled Brian. "Humor me."

Stewart came into his office after an absence of almost three weeks. His trip to Nevis, followed by his trip to Chicago, then meeting Audrey and Simon in Bermuda for a week, had kept him away so long that he actually enjoyed the feeling of coming back to work. He learned a long time ago that he was project-oriented rather than process-oriented. Now one project had been brought to its conclusion. It was time to move on to the next one, with other people, other places.

He had four projects waiting for his time and attention. Two of them had come to the surface, suddenly more important. One of his first tasks would be to weigh the factors of each, to decide how to prioritize them, and maybe see if it would be possible to work on more than one at a time. On the project he had just completed, he had been able to leave it now and then to take care of two smaller jobs.

The stack of mail under his mail chute was almost scary.

He put on some coffee, turned the heat on to cut through the March chill that had been left in his office while the world outside had moved into April. He took off his L.L. Bean jacket and put on his Mr. Rogers cardigan. Waiting for the coffee to finish, he went through the mail hurriedly, dumping the junk mail into the trash basket. Then he reviewed what was left, separating what looked like bills from what looked like letters. When the coffee was made, and he stopped to pour a cup.

Gooood coffee!! Sometimes there's nothing like your own home-made coffee.

Back at his desk, he sipped coffee and continued to work with the mountain of mail. He carefully glanced through all the back issues of the many newspapers he got, to make sure he wasn't putting aside any first class mail caught up inside the papers. He retrieved six letters this way, knowing he would probably not get back to any of the old newspapers, especially the Tallahassee *Democrat*, the Panama City *News-Herald*, and the Carrabelle *Times*.

After getting all the mail divided and sub-divided, he turned his attention to the packages, One package contained new checks. He could tell what that one was. One was from WaldenBooks for two hard-to-get books he had ordered. Obvious. Another from a lock company in St. Louis, which he had no recollection of ordering. One package from his sister in Des Moines. Not so obvious. The packages from his sister and the lock company went immediately to the bathtub where they would stay underwater at least half an hour. While they were soaking, he began opening the letters, reading them and sorting them.

Two cups of coffee and an hour later he began to open the two soaked packages from the tub. He stayed in the bathroom to open them since they were dripping.

The package from the St. Louis lock firm revealed a mass of wires, chips, buttons, and soggy, foul-smelling explosive; it was put together fairly well, but had become invalid in the water. He smiled. He *was* good.

The package from his sister would not have bothered him so much if it hadn't been for the handwriting which he didn't recognize, Tearing off the brown paper, he found a soaked, almost dissolved cardboard box inside. Under the lid of the cardboard box was a mass of styro-foam peanuts protecting another cardboard box. Inside that box was a lot of stuffed, soggy paper protecting another box which had been beautifully

314

gift-wrapped in expensive-looking metallic grey foil, taped well, with a crushed wet bow on top.

He peeled off the handsome foil wrapping, saw the box from Tiffany's, and carefully, almost pleased, opened the lid. He had wanted a new gold necklace and had let her know it. The lid came up begrudgingly, swollen from the water.

ZAP

The well-aimed swatter landed quickly. He had been there. Now he was gone.

Brian looked out to the water which he could see in the distance past the traffic moving along 98, two blocks away, the town's only artery. The May afternoon was a typically comfortable north Florida spring day. Warm but not too warm, a cool breeze off the Gulf, but not too cool. Old Mr. Weston was mowing his yard across the street, in his usual over-alls, hiding from the sun under a wide-brimmed straw hat. Years ago Brian had asked the old man why he mowed the lawn in the middle of the day when the sun was bearing down, why didn't he wait until later in the evening when the sun was low and the heat not so bad.

"Brian," the old man had said, smiling. "Stand still and tell me what you feel. Right now. Here. In this front yard."

Brian obeyed, stood still and noticed the strong breeze coming from the Gulf.

"That breeze," said Brian.

"Exactly," Old Mr. Weston said. "Now you come out here around six, seven, o'clock and see if you can feel it. That Gulf breeze dies down about five, six every night. I'd rather be in that breeze in the sun than in that shade in a calm."

Brian had walked out at six that night and found Old Mr. Weston was right. The Gulf breeze died down late every afternoon. Another good thing for a Renaissance man to know.

The bay was dotted with the multi-colored sails of Hobie-cats, darting across each other's paths. Brian would have liked to be out sailing with Susannah laughing and pointing out things

315

he would be too busy to see. But he had to begin work on the Summer A mid-term -- as soon as he finished waxing the car. He had planned the afternoon well -- but tight.

He had finished jogging on the beach, washed Dempsey, and in another twenty minutes he would be through with the car. Then a shower. Then his computer to finish the mid-term which had to be turned in to the department secretary by twelve o'clock tomorrow in order to get copied, collated and stapled in time for the exams next week.

He was tired just thinking about it.

He put the waxing materials away on the side of the carport. Susannah came out, trim and attractive in shorts.

"Lemonade? Beer? Cocktail?" she asked from the front door.

Allen, in diapers, came up behind her, grabbing at the side of the door -- and the hem of her shorts. He laughed out at Brian, holding up a plastic Big Bird for daddy to see, and then fell down heavily on his rump.

"You know," said Brian, shaking his head, smiling. "That <u>has</u> to hurt. You'd think they would give up trying to walk, getting their eyes jarred out like that. I think I would."

"You never do," said Susannah. "You don't give up on anything, no matter how hard it hits you."

She came out into the yard carrying Allen, and went to the play pool under the shade of the tall sycamore tree. Stepping over the edge of the plastic pool, she sat down in the cool water and placed Allen gently in the water beside her. He laughed and thrashed the water.

"I'd ask you into the pool. only you have to wait until I get out."

"I think we both could fit," he said.

"Not so well that we'd want the neighbors to see.

"We'll try it after dark sometime."

"Like tonight?" she smiled.

"Sounds good to me."

The phone began to ring.

"Could you get that for me, please?" he asked. "I' busy putting away some car wax here."

She threw a wet ball at him accurately. "No. I don't mind at all. If you'll mop up the floor after me."

He started for the front door. "Be careful while I'm gone. You'al don't have on life jackets."

"Eight inches of water does not a danger make."

He disappeared inside to catch the phone. Susannah bounced Allen on her knee, played with him and the tiny Big Bird. Once she waved to Old Mr. Weston across the street, still cutting his grass in the afternoon sun and the Gulf breeze. He waved back, yelled something she could not hear over the roar of his power mower.

She looked out at the bay beyond U.S. 98 and watched the purple/lime/orange/blue sails of the Hobie-cats darting around on the bay. Some were beached on the back side of Dog Island.

Brian came back out, came over to the edge of the pool, stepped over the rim and sat down, fully clothed, in the water with Susannah and Allen. Water started flowing over the top of the plastic sides. Allen thought it was the highlight of his day -- or what he could remember of it. Susannah started laughing.

"Who was that on the phone, Moby Dick?"

He waited a second. Smiled. Holding back something deliciously amusing. "It was Fordham," he said.

"Fordham? We haven't heard from him in over a year now. What did he want?"

"He wanted to know if I could help him again. On another case."

"I hope you told him to put *that* idea where the sun doesn't shine."

"Well, actually. I didn't."

"Is this going to be something I want to hear? Especially when I'm surrounded by water so close to you?"

"You know what I told him?"

"Tell me. Fast."

"I said I had to see what Zannah had to say about it."

"You couldn't go ahead and take a wild guess?"

"Well --- I had an idea -- but I thought I'd check first. He sends his regards, by the way."

The space around him was suddenly filled with splashing water. He was drenched. His shirt sagged under the weight. And more water kept coming.

"I give up," he yelled. "I give up."

Peace and smooth waters were restored.

He looked at her and together they smiled.

"But it's right close by -- just up the road in Tallahassee," he said.

Another barrage of water covered him as he smiled and held up his hands in surrender.

The End

ABOUT THE AUTHOR

Mack Mangham has lived in virtually every section of the country. Born in Macon GA, he went through the Miami school system, attended FSU for an AB in psychology, got an MA in psychology and creative writing at Goddard College in Plainfield VT. Then he did additional work at U. of NE, U, of OK, U. of MO, U. of AR, UCLA, U. of OR, U. of FL and FAMU. He uses the excuse that college life was easier and more fun than working.

In a greater attempt to keep from going to work, he played in piano bars in Daytona Beach, St. Petersburg, Atlanta, Chicago, New Orleans, St. Louis, D.C., Dallas, San Francisco and New York. When reality finally caught up with him, he went to work at Gulf Coast Community College In Panama City, teaching Western Civ., psychology, sociology, Eng. Lit. and creative writing for 14 years. Then he moved to the mountains of NC where he spends his time doing corporate and international research and writing action-intrigue novels like *The Accidental Agent*.

He goes to the gym from 5:30 – 7:30 each morning, plays racquet ball, mountain climbs, skis (sorta), but says his two favorite exercises are catching every movie that comes out and driving 85 MPH on Interstates, listening to tapes of classical, 70's and "elevator" music. He attends most of the cultural and artistic events at WCU and does a lot of his writing on campus benches in an attempt to remain the "perpetual college student." He also likes to write on overlooks on the Blue Ridge Parkway, on the porches of houses with beautiful views where the owners have gone back to Florida for the winter, in pastures off deserted mountain roads and, in general, just about any place where he shouldn't be.

He's been claiming to be 56 for a few years now, and says he still doesn't know what he wants to be when he grows up. "I'll be a kid all my life – just an old kid."